CHRISTINE RELEASED

By Ea Burke

Edited by Cecile Sarruf

Published in North America and Europe by Running Wild Press. Visit Running Wild Press at www.runningwildpress.com Educators, librarians, book clubs (as well as the eternally curious), go to www.runningwildpress.com for teaching tools.

ISBN (pbk) 978-1-947041-27-1

ISBN (ebook) 978-1-947041-42-4

Printed in the United States of America.

In memory of Marissa, who wept and believed in the healing message of this novel.

Dedicated to all who strive against the violence in their lives.

Acknowledgements

Enormous thanks to all those who supported and guided me through the process of bringing Christine to the world. I want to thank especially Susanne Davis and Mara Berkley for their insights during Christine's early formation; Suzanne Kingsbury for all manner of brilliant counsel on creating and promoting a well told story; Michael Fleming and Cecille Sarruf for their fine editing; Tim Weed, dear and caring listener; my friends and family who, like all of the above, believe Christine's story is important and needs to be told, but particularly my son, Dan, who deeply inspired me to persist to this moment.

SECTION 1

CHAPTER 1

She opened her eyes and looked to the heavy February dawn. *Shit.* Christine Bancroft unfurled from the broken stuffed chair where she had slept under her wool coat. Her feet landed on the cold wood floor. She slumped forward feeling for her handbag, then for the cigarettes inside. *Man, it's freezing in here.* She could see her breath. She focused on lighting her cigarette: the scratch of the match, the sudden flame. She looked for an ashtray, but found only empty beer cans and debris in the gloom and stench. The chair she had slept in, reeked of old sweat, food grease, stale beer, and smoke; the nasty, braided rug by her feet reeked too; the chewed-up couch a few feet away reeked. The guy on the couch who slept under a filthy blanket, breathed through his open mouth, and gave off his own stink.

She grabbed a beer can to ash, drew in more of the hot smoke. She tried to remember the guy's name, maybe it was Stu. He worked at the Georgia-Pacific mill. She forgot what he had said he did there.

***

He was part of last night's freaking mess. It had begun when her friend Megan begged her to go with her to meet up with this guy, Jamie, when he got off his shift at midnight. She hadn't gone out with him yet and she wanted Christine to come along, in case things got weird. Christine had figured, sure, help her friend out, maybe have some fun. She remembered Jamie: last year when she was a sophomore and he was a senior, kind of a redneck, but not really scary. Besides, she figured, maybe he had a friend who was cool. They planned to meet Jamie at The Arcade, the only place open at midnight that wasn't a bar. Christine had slipped out of her house, after her mother had gone to work and Frank and the kids were asleep—like she'd done plenty of times before—and met Megan down at the 7-Eleven.

The Arcade was a hole. A bunch of loser kids hung out there looking to get loaded or laid, or looking for a place to crash. Even bigger losers were the old guys picking up kids, getting them loaded. By midnight it was different. Most of the kids were gone, but a few remained who might need a place to crash for the night, or the girls who might want to hook up with a guy getting off work.

After midnight, the mill workers poured in, from Georgia-Pacific and the Culbertson paper mills, just off their shifts, not yet twenty-one years old, with pints of schnapps in their coat pockets. Then the place lit up, or lit up as much as it was going to. It was still a hole, with a worn-out linoleum floor, scarred paneling, and fluorescent lights spazzing from the crumbly ceiling. A couple video games, a couple pinball machines, two vending machines, and a jukebox were in the front room. In the back room were two ratty pool tables and benches along two walls. On any given weekend in 1987, The Arcade was one of the liveliest places in Branford, Vermont between midnight and 2:00 a.m. closing.

By the time the two girls blew into The Arcade, it was nearly empty. The police had just been by and the kids were gone, scattered into the night or taken away to their homes or the homeless shelter. A couple of dirtbags played pool in the back. The owner sat on a tall stool in the front room, paging through a tattered *Car and Driver* magazine. He nodded at the two who passed him to get a couple Cokes from the machine—Megan with her brushed-out hair, no hat, eyeliner, fashion jeans, heavy cologne, Christine wore an oversized wool coat that went past her knees, Lee jeans and

Sorel boots, a handmade wool knit cap with tufts of her walnut-brown hair feathered by her temples and out the back.

A few minutes later, Jamie and a dozen other mill workers streamed in, and soon the two girls were chatting with a few of them. Christine watched Megan kick the flirtation into high gear with stupid little laughs, while touching her hair, touching him, resting her hand on his arm. And Jamie responded; his eyes roamed all over Megan. Christine knew that if she looked down at his crotch, she'd see a big old hard-on pressing against those Levi's. *Whatever.* Jamie steered Megan to the Asteroids machine for a game. Christine didn't feel like following the two around, watching them paw at each other. Two of Jamie's friends talked away at Christine with boring work stories meant to impress her.

She broke in, "Hey, wanna play some pinball?" She'd kill some time, let these guys win most of the games, let them pay. Nothing intense, just waiting for Megan. It wasn't so bad except one of the guys was pretty drunk and was making an obnoxious play for Christine. She ignored him, although she was getting tired of his bloodshot bullshit.

Coming up behind Christine, Megan whispered loudly, "Chris, I gotta use the john, c'mon." As soon as the plywood door of the tiny bathroom shut behind them, she blurted, "So Jamie like wants us to go back to his place, do a little partying, whaddaya think?" She couldn't wait for an answer, and began pleading, "C'mon, do me this favor, okay? You know I'd feel a lot better if you came. But if you don't want to I can go alone, drop you off at home."

Christine shrugged, "All right, sure, but we're not staying long." Megan was out the door. "Sure, no problem."

While they drove to Jamie's, the sleet began falling hard, the roads freezing over. Salt trucks wouldn't be out past midnight, while the storm was still blowing. No salt had hit the road the girls were on, the road along the railroad tracks that ran past the mills, lit against the lousy night. No cars were on the road either, except Jamie's ahead of them, its red tail lights just visible through the glazing windshield. The drunk at the pinball machine was in the car with Jamie.

This sucks. Christine asked, "So, you know where we're going?"

Leaning over the steering wheel, staring hard through the weather, Megan answered, "He said they lived just past the mills, along the river."

She was talking about Dogpatch—the rundown loggers' cabins at the end of town, miles from Christine's home.

"You have snow tires on this thing?" Christine asked.

Megan ignored the question, followed the taillights that had turned off of the paved road onto a narrow dirt road, which crossed the railroad tracks to a flat of land. Several dim shapes and squat unlit buildings appeared. The car ahead of them pulled up to one and stopped.

"We won't stay long, promise."

Yeah, right.

***

The place was tight, dark, cold, and it gave off a wicked stench. Christine felt grime on the wall when she entered. She wasn't taking her coat off.

Just inside the doorway, Jamie directed, "Hey Stu, show the ladies the living room while I grab us some beers." Jamie went one way down the dim, narrow hallway, Stu went the opposite way. The girls followed Stu to the living room.

Trash was everywhere—empty cans, fast-food wrappers and stray French fries, magazines, socks, greasy rags, cigarette butts. Christine took it all in. *This so sucks.* A mammoth stuffed chair, a broken-down couch, and a coffee table all faced a twenty-four-inch-screen television on an aluminum stand. Megan fell into the huge chair.

Stu asked, "Wanna smoke some pot?"

Without waiting for their answer he flopped down on the couch and pulled a crumpled baggie and a small wooden pipe out of his jeans. Christine pushed a stained *Maxim* aside and sat on the couch, away from Stu. She listened to the sleet pounding hard against the windows and the tin roof, while wrapped in her coat and saying nothing.

Jamie came into the room with a six-pack of Budweiser, and Megan had him squeeze in with her on the chair. The pot sucked: harsh, weak leaf. The beer sucked: Christine hated Budweiser. Jamie and Megan were all over each other in the chair. And Stu looked at Christine like she was his.

She jumped up. "Hey, you guys mind if I see what's on?"

Flipping through the channels, she passed some talk show with that North guy yammering about freedom fighters, and settled on a *Baywatch* rerun. She returned to the couch without asking if the others agreed. She didn't care if they did.

Pulling his face back from Megan's neck, Jamie made his move, "Hey, there's something I gotta show you, back in my room. Wanna see it?"

"Sure."

The two scrambled out of the chair and disappeared down the hall.

Christine called after them, "Hey, Meg, don't forget we have exams tomorrow."

A few minutes later *Baywatch* ended. Christine listened for sounds from down the hallway. She heard nothing over the storm outside. "Hey, Stu, you drive?"

Stu snorted through his scraggly moustache. "No way. Got my third DUI, an' the cops are watching out for me. Besides, I'm kinda wasted." The creep turned on his "wasted" grin, then said, "Let's get high."

She didn't answer, slumped deeper into her coat. *Whatever.* They smoked the pot without saying anything. The last embers in the pipe died as Christine drew in the final smoke. She leaned to the coffee table to tap the ashes out on a pizza box. Stu slid closer to her as she leaned back from the table. He threw one arm around her shoulders, tried to kiss her face and reach for her thigh in one clumsy lunge.

Christ! She got both of her hands on his shoulders and pushed some space between them, insisting, "Whoa, whoa, whoa."

He came back at Christine, slower, reaching for her thigh. She had to keep him off her, she had to make him stop. He pressed forward. *He won't!* She had to take control.

"Hold it." With one hand on his shoulder Christine reached for his belt. He stopped. She firmly pushed him back as she unfastened the belt. He leaned into the sofa, away from her.

Christine worked his penis out of his pants. She stroked it, but only felt the weather slashing at the world outside. She released him when he was spent. "I'm gonna go wash up," she muttered. His eyes were still shut as she got up.

Christine felt her way down the corridor, looking for Megan. She heard her, them, screwing behind a closed door. She continued to the bathroom, where she stood at the sink, scrubbed her hands raw with icy water, stared, but didn't see herself in the mirror. She stopped scrubbing. After a long silence she made her way back through the cabin, past the closed door, to the living room. The asshole was sprawled on the couch, pants still open, head thrown back, mouth gaping open, snoring. Christine turned the TV off, turned the lights off. She slipped out of her boots, tucked herself into her great wool coat and into the huge chair, where she sank into the darkness and the storm.

***

The dawn light pushed into the cabin. Christine dropped the lit cigarette butt into the beer can, heard it hiss. It was time to go. *Get out before Stu the creep wakes up. And screw Megan.*

She pulled on her boots, wrapped herself in the weight of her coat and walked out the door without looking back. The damp cold, clean and evergreen sweet, gripped Christine.

Mucking through ankle-deep slush, Christine decided that she was through with Megan, who'd be all into lowlife Jamie and his lowlife friends, wasting Christine's time with shitty beer, lousy pot, and constant hard-ons. Besides, Megan had screwed her over, leaving her alone with a scumbag. As Christine's boots sliced through the wet slop, the intensity of her anger slowly lost itself in the distance she covered. After a couple miles she decided against a huge split with Megan; after all, Megan had a car and usually had pretty good pot. Besides, Christine didn't need the drama. She decided to just chill, let Megan do her Jamie thing, and check out what else was happening.

Who was she kidding? There wasn't anything else happening. Everything was so boring and predictable, she couldn't stand it. School sucked, period. Her friends and the stoner crowd, were morons. New friends? The preps and the jocks made her gag; the Christians and the geeks were pathetic. Branford sucked. The so-called big town in the valley was a joke: not even ten thousand people lived there. People always said something big was going to happen, someday. *Bunch of losers.* And home sucked the most—extremely crappy, especially since loser Frank moved in. The guy was a total jerk, he didn't even try to be nice. Well, maybe nice to Matt and Charlotte, but they were only kids. He hated her, she knew that. Which was fine because she hated him right back.

Christine reached the plateau above the river valley. The road home was level from there, about two miles to go. If she could, she would keep walking straight out of town. On the wider road, the sky opened up above her. Christine kept striding, watching the day arrive on lead-gray wings.

A couple blocks from her street, her nerves tightened. Was it seven yet, was her mother home from work? She wasn't in the mood for a big scene. And if Frank was there, it would be a lot worse, the way he blew up at every little thing. She ground her teeth, her jaw working hard as she turned the corner to her street. Three houses down the block stood her home, a modest Cape. It sat quietly in the neighborhood of Capes. And there was her mother's beat-up Corolla and Frank's dumb-ass pickup truck in the driveway. *Shit.*

***

Lynne Bancroft sat at the kitchen table by the window with the lights off. Bone tired. She held on to a cup of cold, black coffee, and looked out at the snow cover anchored by the dense shapes of bare trees, parked cars, and silent houses. She had just gotten home from work as an LNA at the local hospital. It had been a tough shift; she had busted her hump helping bring a set of premature twins, with complications, into this world. Kept them alive until the medevac helicopter carried them off to the regional hospital up north. She stared out at the vague dawn, thinking about the mother who had been left behind worried sick about her babies.

The sound of Frank shuffling down the hall to the bathroom upstairs brought Lynne back to her kitchen and cold coffee. The sound reminded her that she hated the mess he made in the bathroom; crumpled towels, spilled toothpaste, piss splash. She heard the toilet seat bang against the toilet tank—and she couldn't stand the way he yelled at the kids, and fought with Christine. Constant fighting. She hated it. But it was her fault, she knew that: she had let him move in just after Christmas. Lynne heard him pissing and thought what pained her most was that she couldn't get by without him, couldn't get by without the money he gave her for the bills. The toilet flushed and the water passed down the pipe running through the kitchen wall behind Lynne. She lit a cigarette.

A movement in the gloom outside. Lynne watched as a figure neared the house. Closer, the shape became distinct; she saw a face. *Christine?* She thought her daughter was upstairs, asleep. Panic smothered Lynne's confusion when she finally recognized the girl silently approaching. Why was she out there? Was she all right? Then a small fury fired up—*she's been out all night!* Before Lynne could get up to turn on the light, Christine came through the door.

Lynne hissed, "Where have you been?" Her eyes raked her daughter for evidence of harm as Christine faced her: red-cheeked, bleary, smelling of cigarette smoke and the wet morning. No sign of injury. Christine threw the light on and caught her mother sitting at the table, looking worn out. She glanced towards the hallway, past Lynne; her eyes flashed fierce seeing Frank standing at the threshold. She stepped up to the table, picked up the pack of her mother's cigarettes.

"Mom, not now." She shook a cigarette out. She knew her smoking drove Frank nuts. He started, "Listen, you owe your mother an explanation—"

Reaching for the lighter on the table and without looking at him, Christine cut him off, "Screw you, Frank." Evenly, clearly.

She lit the cigarette, inhaled deeply, and blew the smoke out of the side of her mouth. He pounded the doorjamb with the side of his fist, sputtering. Christine looked at him, daring him to lose it. She walked toward him. Frank's face and neck burned deep red as she closed the few feet between them. Before she reached the doorway, he exploded past her, nearly plowing into her. At the kitchen door, he grabbed his coat off the hook, then hauled off and punched the wall, his fist smashed through the drywall into a stud. Howling, he threw open the door, kicked open the storm door, and hurled himself through the slop to his truck.

Christine turned to her mother, crushed the butt into the ashtray, "I'm going to bed," and went upstairs.

Screaming inside, Lynne buried her face in her hands. He could have smashed Christine in the face; he could have broken every bone in her face; he could have lost control and beaten her to within an inch of her life! She had seen his eyes. He was that close, with Christine daring him, pushing him. Lynne's stomach spun vomit. She heard Matt and Charlotte coming down the stairs. She wiped her tears away with the back of her hand—they'd be needing breakfast. She breathed in, she had to steady herself. Her last thought before the other children arrived: Christine couldn't be alone with him. Ever.

***

After Matt and Charlotte left for school, Lynne went to Christine's bedroom. Standing at the doorway, she demanded, "Just what the hell do you think you're doing?"

Christine mumbled from underneath the covers, "Trying to get some sleep." "You're not going to school?"

"I can't. Can't you just call me in sick? I've really got to get some sleep." Christine pulled the blanket down from her head. "Please."

"Because you were out all night? Are you kidding me? Where were you?"

Christine leveled her gaze at her mother, "My friend Megan was having a problem with her boyfriend, she wanted to talk, she was really upset. We drove around. The weather was bad and we ended up at her place. The roads got too dangerous for driving."

Lynne wasn't buying it. "You weren't out with some boy?"

"No!"

It doesn't matter. Instead, Lynne said, "I want you to stop the fighting with Frank." Angry, Christine replied, "Yeah, well, I want Frank out of our house."

"That's not . . . he can't . . . look, he's here, so that's the way it is. If you can't stop fighting, then I want you to stay away from him, don't say anything to him."

Christine heard the concern, shot back, "Sure. Fine. I'll stay as far away from him as possible. Never say another word to him. Act like he isn't even here. But you know what would be a whole lot easier? If he wasn't here at all!"

The accusation stung, it silenced Lynne. She left the room.

CHAPTER 2

Lynne sat down after shaking the counselor's hand, the family counselor her shift supervisor had told her about. Lynne was there to help end the fighting at home. She had been reluctant to make the appointment, thinking she would have to tell a complete stranger all about her life, her problems. But the fighting had to stop. The man introduced himself as Tom Hansson. He had a firm handshake, a nice smile. He might have been close to her age, mid-thirties.

Lynne shifted in the chair, feeling the institutional-strength fabric of the cushion rasp against her thigh. She looked at the photos on the wall. People who would be her age, taken a few years ago. Hansson and friends at a ski lodge, in kayaks on white water, in some dense forest. A fit young woman, her blonde hair pulled back, was in all of the photos. No kids. *What am I doing here?* This guy had no idea what she was dealing with. People like him could sit back in their little clinics and judge the losers who showed up at their door as they pulled down a paycheck, waiting to go on their next adventure. Lynne stopped looking at the photos on the wall. She was worn out. The hell with it, she didn't need anyone's pity.

Hansson watched her a moment before he asked, "How are you, Lynne?"

Walls inside her trembled. "Not so good." She then let loose non-stop about how her kids were such a mess since Frank had moved in a couple months ago; how Matt was getting in trouble in eighth grade, and Charlotte, in fifth grade, was more withdrawn than ever; how Christine and Frank were constantly at each other's throats. She told Hansson about last Friday, when Frank had gone ballistic, punching the wall. She murmured, "It could have been Christine." She shook her head slightly, staring at a spot on Hansson's desk. "I can't make it stop, the fighting. I hate it." She looked up, "I don't know what to do."

Hansson leaned forward, "Why don't you ask him to leave?"

He made it sound easy. It wasn't. She had been so lonely and Frank had been nice to her at first—funny, generous. She had needed that after all those lousy years with her ex-husband, Mark. She and Frank didn't laugh anymore, they weren't happy. But she couldn't make ends meet without his money: a couple hundred towards the mortgage, a couple hundred toward food and heat each month. She answered in a low voice, "He helps with the bills."

"The children's father, is he paying enough child support?" Her heart raced. She didn't want to talk about Mark.

Hansson broke into her silence, "Lynne?"

She couldn't stop herself. "No. He doesn't pay what he's supposed to." "How much does he owe?"

"He should be paying four-fifty a month. He doesn't always pay the full amount. He's behind more than a thousand."

She realized, if she had that money, she wouldn't need Frank's help, wouldn't need to put up with his crap anymore. Lynne caught herself, she was dreaming; she'd never get that money out of Mark. He would give her what he wanted to, and that was that.

Hansson said. "Have you tried to collect what he owes?" "No." Lynne couldn't look at the counselor.

"Does he know he's behind with the child support?" Lynne squirmed. "I don't know. Probably."

"You know the court can order him to pay, if he's behind."

Ashamed at her weakness, she muttered, "I suppose so."

"Do you want me to show you how to get back support? Help you with the court forms?" Lynne saw a crack of hope and shrugged. "Sure."

Hansson smiled slightly, "All right." He then explained to Lynne the information she needed to gather in order to explain what was owed, and how the matter would be reviewed by a judge. At the end of the session, Hansson promised Lynne he'd have the court forms the next time they met. Lynne smiled, feeling she just might make something happen right.

***

Frank's weight ground against Lynne as he pushed inside her, his face lowering to press kisses on her face. She smelled the steak they'd had for dinner on his breath, felt the grease smear from his lips to her cheek. Matt and Charlotte were in bed asleep. Christine had left before dinner, knowing Frank would be home. She had told Lynne she was catching a movie with some friends and not to wait up. Lynne had to talk to Frank about the fighting; he had to know things needed to change. Maybe counseling could help him figure out how to get along better with the kids, maybe some kind of anger management. She'd have to ask Hansson what he thought.

Uncomfortable under Frank's thrusting, his pelvis banging against hers, Lynne shifted slightly and let her soft belly take some of the impact. She rocked her hips with his, gave him some play. A smile started up on his face. She remembered it was already the second, the mortgage had been due yesterday. She didn't have the money for it. She'd have to make sure she got it from him in the morning and get a check out in tomorrow's mail.

He was going at it. Lynne licked her lips and tasted him. It was time to wrap it up. Clenching her vagina around his prick, she brought him crashing home. No more than three minutes later he was snoring, mouth wide open. Lynne lay there wide awake—it was just past ten o'clock. She ran through her mind the bills that were due and overdue and what she could pay.

***

Lynne watched Frank across the table littered with the late morning's breakfast dishes, watched him chew the last of his yolk-sopped toast. They were alone. Matt and Christine were already off with friends. Charlotte was up in her room. She reached out, "I'm late with the mortgage, and..."

He cut her off, telling her he had the money upstairs.

Her chest tightened. It had to be now. "There's something else." He shifted in his seat, his eyes narrowed at what might be coming.

"It's about the blowup you and Chris had last week, it really upset me. I thought we should talk." She saw him redden, his eyes glow hot, but he didn't say anything. She continued, "We've got to figure out how we can get along here..."

Agitated, he shot back, "Wait a second, have you talked to her about her behavior that morning?"

"No, I thought we should talk first, being the adults."

Frank shoved his chair back, leaned forward, his fists on his knees, "I don't know, Lynne, I don't know as I've got an answer." He fixed his eyes on her.

"I'm not asking you for the answer. I'm asking you to work with me."

"I'm not so sure." He stood.

She couldn't believe it. "Not so sure? About what?"

"I don't know. This whole deal. I mean...things have been happening awful fast, maybe too fast. Maybe I'm in over my head with this situation, the kids and all. Maybe I'm not equipped to deal with a teenager, you know."

The words hit Lynne like icy rain. *He's saying it's over.* She wanted him out of her face. "Yeah? So you're leaving, is that what you're trying to say?"

He avoided her glare.

"So leave.

He looked at her with questioning eyes.

She was sick of the sight of him. "Now. Pack your stuff and get out."

He started about "the good times," and how he still had "real feelings" for her. It was a load of crap. She cut him off.

Twenty minutes later he was at the kitchen door with his suitcase and duffel bag. He counted out four fifty-dollar bills and handed them to her, saying, "Like I promised." He peeled off another fifty. "To help out."

Numb, Lynne didn't refuse the money. It was as if she was watching a movie, like it was happening to someone else. On the rear porch, Frank offered to let Lynne know where she could reach him, once he found a place and settled in.

"Don't bother." She shut the door before he could turn his back on her, stood there as if the world had fallen away. She braced herself against the doorframe.

***

Saturday afternoon, with bright sunshine pouring through the open bedroom window with the cool March air and Depeche Mode drifting out the window, four girls huddled on the bedroom floor, a quarter pound of marijuana dumped on a spread-out newspaper, a triple-beam scale close by, sticky green buds, resin glistened on the compressed leaves, smelling like pine pitch. The girls had smoked a joint and Christine was seriously high.

She nudged Megan. "Where'd you get this shit?"

"My brother, he brought it down from Burlington."

"Yeah? He do that a lot?"

"Nah, not too much."

"Where are your folks?"

"Skiing. Up at Stowe for the weekend." One of the other girls slurred, "All right."

The voice sounded to Christine like it was spoken through a tube. She watched Megan hunch over the scale to weigh out the pot—she was in for a half ounce. She kicked back, listened to the faint sounds of the neighborhood coming through the window, watched the clouds cruise across the blue sky, felt the sunshine on her face.

A male voice surprised the girls. Christine turned from the window to see a man in the bedroom doorway looking right at her. A sheet of lightning ripped through her. He was focused on her with gorgeous, dark blue, piercing, fucking eyes. Her crotch tingled. *Whoa!* Christine checked out the rest of him: long legs, muscular shoulders under a gray T-shirt, rope-muscled arms, a fine face, black hair combed straight back. She returned to those gorgeous eyes; he was still looking at her!

Megan spoke. "Jim, this is my friend Christine, I don't think you've met before." He smiled at Christine. "No, I don't think so."

She echoed "No, I don't think so."

The other girls cracked up. Megan asked him if he wanted to smoke a joint. Christine knew if she had any more, she'd be too stupid to talk but she didn't care, she wanted him to stay.

"Nah, thanks, I'm running late. So, pretty kick-ass, huh?" The girls chorused, "Yeah."

As he turned to leave, he said to Megan, "Mom and Dad don't need to know I've been around, okay?" Then he was gone.

Megan went back to measuring, the chatter resumed, one of the girls filled a bowl with a bud and lit it. Christine got higher and couldn't stop thinking about his eyes on her.

***

Lying in bed, Christine slowly woke up with a smile while remembering yesterday—roaming Megan's neighborhood in the afternoon; cruising downtown and getting some guys to buy beer for them; trying to make dinner at Megan's and burning the shit out of the Ragu sauce, boiling the spaghetti to death; watching stupid television; laughing a lot, stoned the entire time. It was the best time Christine had had in a long time. She and Megan were cool, and yeah Jamie had already dumped her after two weeks.

She hadn't asked Megan about her brother, although she wanted to, like did he have a girlfriend? But she found out he went to the University of Vermont. Maybe she'd find out more about him today. They'd planned to drive out to the lake and scramble around.

"Christine, breakfast." Her mother called from the bottom stair. It was time for the Sunday routine: pancakes with the family, with Frank the asshole sitting at the table glowering at her. But Christine knew it meant a lot to her mom, having all of them together for Sunday breakfast, so she'd put up with Frank and his attitude. Christine squinted and shuffled into the kitchen.

Lynne turned from the range. "When did you get in last night?"

"Good morning to you too. Not late. Before midnight." She put her hand over her heart. "Swear to god." She looked to Matt and Charlotte at the table. They weren't scowling at her like usual, but seemed kind of scared or shaken up. She asked, "Hey squirts, what's up?" *No Frank.* To her mother, "Where's the big guy?"

Lynne answered, while fixing up a plate of pancakes. "Oh, you missed it." "Missed what?"

Handing the plate to Christine, "Frank and I had a talk yesterday. We decided it was best we split up."

"No! Yesterday? Just like that? And he moved out?" Christine set her dish on the table and took a seat.

Lynne nodded, yes. Christine studied her mother's face, saw that her eyes were sad while the rest of her face worked at appearing cheerful. He was an asshole, but it still had to suck for her mother.

Trying to keep it lighthearted, she saluted with her glass of orange juice, "Good riddance I say. What do you think twerps?"

Matt and Charlotte looked at their sister like she was insane to joke about something so important.

Christine caught herself. *Show some respect.* "You alright Mom?" "I'm okay." Lynne knew she wasn't fooling anyone.

With a lighter tone, Christine responded, "Well then let's eat, because I'm starving."

The family dug into the food, no one wanting to talk anymore about Frank.

CHAPTER 3

Hansson smiled. "I'm impressed." Lynne had just told him how she had split up with Frank five days earlier. She heard his admiration, but didn't think much of it. The breakup wasn't that impressive, it just felt like something that happened to her, like bad weather passing by. She shrugged.

He asked Lynne if she was relieved Frank was gone. She couldn't say. Yes, she was relieved he wasn't around. She didn't have to worry about him smacking Christine. And yes, she was relieved the kids were much better behaved these past few days—almost like they were being especially good for her. But no, the extra money he'd given her was already gone and she wouldn't have enough to pay the bills coming due. So it was hard to say she was "relieved." He was just gone.

She answered, "Yes, kind of."

"Good. Last week you were concerned you needed Frank's financial help. Is that taken care of? Are you set financially?"

"No."

"You're still owed the back support?" Lynne nodded, trying not to look away.

"Are you still interested in getting a court order for the support?"

It was stupid to try. "It won't matter, he won't pay."

"Even if a judge ordered him to?"

Why bother explaining. "Mark will figure a way out of paying if he doesn't want to pay."

"If you can back up your claim with some records there's no reason why a judge wouldn't order payment."

She could say to the penny how much he was behind.

"Child support actions are designed so a person doesn't need a lawyer." Hansson showed Lynne the forms. He was right—they were simple, easy to fill out.

But it wouldn't be simple or easy, not with Mark. She asked, "So I get a court order, who's going to make him pay?"

Hansson started to explain about contempt of court, liens, and garnished wages. It sounded to Lynne like she'd end up having to get a lawyer anyway because Mark would make her drag it out of him, just for spite. "I don't know, it sounds awfully complicated."

"You might not have to get into all that. Maybe he just lost track. You might want to ask him first, about what he owes, see what he says."

Mark hadn't made any mistake. Lynne knew if she asked him, he'd be furious. It didn't matter: she needed the money. Dry mouthed, she answered, "I'll do that, give him a call. I'll let you know how it turns out." She added, "why don't you give me those court forms so I can look at them."

***

Christine absently watched the dazed fly buzz in the corner of the plate glass window beside her. The fly was depressing. Its drone was depressing. The dirty plate glass window was depressing. The afternoon sun beating through the window was monotonous. She didn't even want to think about how depressing the rest of the scene was: the dishwater coffee sucked; the place smelled like lukewarm grease; the linoleum floors would never be clean; the plastic booth would always be sticky; the same tired "Fuk" would always be carved black in the tabletop. The regular fat asses sat at the counter, shooting the shit and eyeing the schoolgirls from under a bank of cigarette smoke. Friday afternoon at the Downtown Coffee Shoppe was the most depressing suckhole in the universe.

The two girls sitting in the booth with Christine whined about being out of pot and not knowing where they could get some. She stopped listening. It was too annoying for words. Instead, she added another creamer and packet of sugar to her coffee and squashed the fly with a wadded up paper napkin. She faced away from the girls, to the sun's heat, her eyes closed, deciding she'd head home in a few minutes. She had a Spanish oral the next day she had to ace to get her average up to a C. She took a gulp of the lukewarm coffee.

The restaurant door banged open, jangling the bells that were tied to the handle.

Christine didn't have to open her eyes to know it was Megan. The girl slid into the booth, pumping enthusiasm. Christine didn't turn away from the sun; the upcoming euphoria over scoring some pot would be too pathetic. She was right—Megan reported some hash might be available and the two other girls were thrilled. They were morons. Suddenly compelled, Christine opened her eyes. There was Megan's brother, Jim, driving a late model Saab convertible directly outside the window, going maybe 15 miles per hour, looking right at her, his head turned as he passed so their gaze didn't break for a long moment. *Whoa!* It was perfect, *fucking perfect.* The other girls missed it, busy figuring out how much hash they could afford.

Christine interrupted, "Hey Megan, when did your brother get into town?" "I dunno, I didn't know he was."

"Yeah, I just saw him drive by. Any idea where he might be heading?" Megan shrugged off the question. "No idea. So you going in on this Chris?"

"Nah, I'm broke. Listen I've gotta take off." She was too wired to sit and deal with any more of this crap.

Christine dashed out onto the sidewalk, squinting in the late afternoon sun, then headed in the direction the Saab had taken. A few steps and she saw him, parked a half block away. She pulled it together and managed a very cool walk toward the car. She could see he was watching her in the mirror. She fixed her gaze on his, and kept walking.

When she got to the car, he turned to her, "Want a ride?" "Yeah."

She drank in his spiced smell, the leather seats' warmth pressed through her jeans. As Jim accelerated the Saab out of town, the air rushed, wicked, through her hair, over her face. She stole looks at him as he drove. She watched his forearm tensing, releasing when he shifted gears, his nasty blue eyes when he turned to speak to her, his lips. She let her eyes drift down to his thighs.

He asked her a few questions. Was she a friend of his sister, what school did she go to, what grade was she in? She told him the truth. Answering her questions, he told Christine he was a junior at UVM and that he came down to Branford a lot, but not every weekend. They were driving through a neighborhood, set in the hills, overlooking the river valley, where the houses below weren't visible from the tree lined street.

Suddenly he said, "I gotta do something, wanna come?" "Sure."

A block later Jim eased the Saab up a long gravel driveway to a new ranch style house. He asked Christine if she wanted to go in with him.

"Yeah, o.k." *Why not*?

A stocky, dark whiskered man in his thirties answered the door and greeted Jim with a handshake, pulled Jim close and slapped his back while looking at Christine. There was no doubt he was checking her out, but not sexually. Released, Jim introduced Christine to the man, JT.

JT nodded at Christine, then smiled broadly, his light brown eyes flashed from stone cold to warm. "Pleased to meet you."

Christine nodded, sent a small smile back at him.

Jim spoke. “Me and JT need to talk. Wait here, alright? We’ll just be a few.” “Sure.”

JT showed Christine to the living room off the hallway. She sat on a spotless white sofa and flipped through a People magazine she found on the coffee table. She knew what was happening; Jim was scoring. She didn’t care. A few minutes later the two men returned, both sniffling, eyes bugging. *Coke!*

Jim asked, “You ready?”

Christine stood without a word. At the door JT embraced Jim, then Christine. She felt his power, she smelled it. Releasing her JT said, “Again, pleased to meet you.”

He was telling her they connected, and she agreed. “Yes.”

The sun had gone down. It was getting cool, the weak heat gone. Before he started the Saab, Jim asked, “You gotta be somewhere?”

It must be dinnertime but that didn’t matter. Christine answered, no.

He smiled. “Wanna do some lines?”

Yeah! “Sure.”

Jim drove to a quiet street a few blocks from JT’s, parked, pulled out a small vial and a short silver straw. After laying out two lines of white powder on his wallet, he handed it to Christine with the straw. She looked into his gorgeous eyes, mouthed “thank you,” then bent over and snorted the coke. *Yeah.* Feeling it as she lifted her head slowly, her hair drifting back from her face, her sparkling brown eyes rose to meet Jim’s eyes. She knew she had seduced him, completely, in that instant. He stroked out two more lines, smiled at Christine then bent over the wallet, his black hair falling forward. When he straightened up, his eyes shone at her.

She wasn’t going to go for it, not tonight. She didn’t want any back seat, clumsy grab-ass. No, when they did it, they were going to do it right. Jim looked like he was about to make a move. His eyes glowed on her. She decided they'd better get going before things got weird.

A little coy, "That was nice. Thanks."

They looked at each other. She leaned over and put her lips on his. Full lips, playful touching, briefly. When she pulled back, she whispered, "Bye." Christine got out of the car and stood by the door before Jim could respond. "Find me next time you're in town." She turned and walked away, into the night—her mind sparked, her lips sparkled, her crotch hummed. Loved it.

***

Lynne circled the number written on the back of a bill's envelope. One thousand two hundred, that's what Mark owed. She had checked her records three times and had come up with the same number each time. She hadn't been able to think of anything else since she'd gotten home from the counseling session that afternoon. She had to do this. She paced to the phone, backed off. She had to do this now. It was the second week in March, and he hadn't sent the March payment yet. On top of the twelve hundred. *He should be home by now.* She'd leave a message for him to call if he wasn't home. She had to start getting dinner ready, so it had to be now. She stubbed out her cigarette, left it burning in the ashtray, reached for the phone on the wall.

Mark picked up.

Lynne wasn't ready. Her throat squeezed tight, "Mark, I haven't gotten this month's check yet."

He responded, both contrite and accusingly, "Oh Christ Lynne, you sure you didn't get a check right around the first?"

"No, I'm sure."

"Well I'll take a look at my check register just in case, and get something out to you as soon as I can, if I messed up."

'Something.' 'As soon as he could,' 'If he messed up.' Lynne heard him telling her he couldn't be bothered. She couldn't let him do it; call all the shots, like he always did. She sat down, weak.

"Lynne, are you there? Lynne?" "Yes."

He demanded, "Is there anything else you want?"

She had to, "Yes. There's back support you owe, too. We need to talk about that." The words passed through Lynne's mouth like wet ash.

Silence, then measured, "What are you talking about?"

Dread seized Lynne. It was the tone Mark used when his rage was building, regardless she continued, "We need you to pay what you're behind."

He spat, "You've got to be kidding. You're kidding me right?"

"No." Lynne squeezed the receiver. She couldn't let him beat her down. "Not saying I owe you a dime, but how much are you after?"

She had to. "Twelve hundred dollars. On top of the March payment." Lashing, "Twelve hundred dollars! You're crazy Lynne, you know that." She hung in, "No, I've been keeping track. It's twelve hundred, Mark." "Well forget it."

Hanging in, "But the kids..."

"Don't start whining about the kids. They do alright and I know it."

He'd crossed the line. Lynne shot back, "Mark, you don't know how the kids are doing, goddammit. You haven't seen them since Christmas. Don't go telling me the kids are alright—"

Mark lowered his tone, slower, "Hey listen Lynne, don't start accusing me. You know it's not all my fault if I can't see the children as much as I'd like. You haven't exactly been co-operative..."

Lynne was speechless, furious.

He attacked, "Besides, I am not very comfortable coming to the house with what's-his-name lounging around. And you want to know something, I am very uncomfortable with him living with the children. I mean what kind of message does that send to the kids?"

Losing her grip, "Frank's gone, he doesn't live here anymore."

"No? Oh, I get it now. This guy leaves you and suddenly it's like you're short on cash, so you come after me, thinking you can shake me down. You can forget it Lynne because I sure as hell don't owe you any god damned twelve hundred bucks. I'll send you a check for March, but you can forget the rest."

He was shouting at the end, then there was silence, then the dial tone. Reeling, Lynne hung up. She lit a cigarette, hands shaking, drew the smoke deep into her lungs. She blankly stared out the window long after she finished the cigarette. The house was quiet.

The front door slammed open. It would be one of the kids. Before she pulled herself up to get going on whatever she had to do, Lynne swore he wasn't going to get away with it this time, the bastard. She'd take him to court, have a judge tell him to pay up. She'd file those papers, first thing Monday.

CHAPTER 4

Mark Bancroft received a notice of the child support hearing a week after Lynne had called him with her absurd demands. He called an acquaintance from his old engineering firm in Vermont, who he knew had been through a difficult divorce. They had stayed in touch since Mark had relocated to Albany. He asked for the names of the toughest divorce lawyers in the Branford area, and anywhere else in Vermont, if necessary. The answer: "Max Blum. This guy'll rip your ex a new asshole. Best there is. Do whatever he tells you to do and you'll kick ass."

Mark was in Blum's office the following week.

Blum scanned the court papers as Mark sat across the massive black oak desk. The attorney's large, heavy lidded eyes looked either bored or contemptuous. Mark figured he could appear malevolent, very easily.

Blum looked up. "The mother wants some back child support? Why not give it to her?" He didn't give Mark a chance to answer. "Because you want to screw her. Am I right? You know my retainer is twenty five hundred dollars? Of course you do, my girl told you that and you paid it, otherwise you wouldn't be sitting here." The lawyer leaned forward. "The retainer is more than twice what she claims you owe, and I will take all of it. I'll probably take more. Do you understand?" He leaned back, "With that said, do you want to continue?"

Mark didn't hesitate, "Yes."

"Alright, let's begin then. You don't dispute what the divorce decree says regarding your child support obligation, do you?"

"No, I—"

Blum cut Mark off, "No, you don't. And she says you paid her this sum, here in the filings. Of course you paid her more than that.

Didn't you? In fact you paid her more than she was due under the terms of the support order, didn't you?"

Mark understood what the lawyer was doing. "Yes, I did." "You paid her cash sometimes. Didn't you?"

"Yes."

"Of course you kept track of all that you paid her. Didn't you?" "Yes, I did."

"In writing." "Yes."

"And you still have that written record." "Yes."

"Send it to me. This record shows that you have paid the mother more than what you owed her, correct?"

Mark agreed.

"Of course you made record of the payments at, or near, the time the payments were made?"

Mark smiled, "Correct."

"Because making up the record now could cause the judge to question whether you have accurately recalled what you have paid. We don't want the judge to doubt your word." Blum paused. "The mother must be lying or confused. Tell me about the mother."

Mark wasn't sure what, exactly, the lawyer wanted. Nevertheless, he began, "Lynne? Umm. She lies like crazy, always has. She's jealous of my new family. Just broke up with her boyfriend, she told me he recently moved out. She works as a LNA, works the graveyard shift, so she's making pretty good money. I don't know what she's trying to pull—maybe she's gone crazy because of the breakup with the boyfriend.

Maybe she's trying to make me look bad to the kids. She's always doing that, you know? Always has. I can't imagine the lies she tells them." Mark saw Blum make a couple quick notes as he spoke.

When Mark finished, Blum ordered, "Get me that payment record immediately, the hearing is only three weeks away. Make an appointment with my girl for the day before the hearing so we can go over your testimony." He didn't ask if Mark had any questions. The meeting was over.

***

Lynne hadn't been back to see Hansson since he'd given her the court papers, three weeks ago -—even with a sliding scale fee, she didn't feel like she could afford the twenty five dollar sessions. But when she got a copy of Blum's *Notice of Appearance* in the mail, two days ago, she called for an appointment to meet with the counselor.

She handed the court papers to Hansson. "The hearing date's in there, Friday, April 17, two weeks from now." She watched him go through the documents. He congratulated Lynne. The way he said it made her think he didn't believe she would follow through. It didn't make a difference. What mattered was that Mark had a lawyer, and he was going to screw her. She had tried for the past two days to get a lawyer, but couldn't afford one. Legal Aid no longer handled child support cases, since its funding had been eliminated.

"Mark has someone named Blum representing him. Do you know anything about him?" She asked.

Lynne saw Hansson's smile deaden as he answered. "He's been around, does divorces. But that's okay, the judge will probably give you some leeway if you're appearing on your own."

She tightened up in her chair. "Yeah, but I have no idea what these hearings are like. I have no idea what I'm supposed to say or do."

Hansson explained she would do fine if she kept it simple and showed the judge her record of Mark's payments.

Lynne relaxed, "I can do that. It's all in my check register, I always deposited his checks."

"Did he ever pay cash?" "Never."

"Or pay for things he might have thought was part of his support?"

Lynne thought a moment, "No, not unless he's counting Christmas presents, which is something he'd do. Other than that, no."

"When did he start falling behind in his payments?" "About six months ago, about when his baby was born."

"Why didn't you bring up the overdue support before now?"

Because she was overwhelmed with everything else going on in her life at the time; because she was terrified of confronting Mark, of making him angry; because she was getting by and sometimes that's more than good enough. She answered, "I don't know." She shifted in her chair.

Hansson softened, "The judge might want to know that."

"Can I just say I had hoped he would get caught up, but he never did?" She didn't want to get into what a manipulative jerk Mark was.

"That could work. Do you think he didn't pay the full amount because Frank was living with you?"

Lynne blushed deep red. "They're going to bring that up?"

"It's possible. Did Mark say anything about Frank living with you?

She hesitated. "When I told him about the back support ... he brought Frank up." She stared hard at a spot on the throw rug.

"If he brings that up, you just say he should have gotten the court's permission before he started cutting back." Hansson suggested.

"Okay." She'd remember, he should have gotten the court's permission. *He's going to get nasty, bring Frank into this.* She asked Hansson if he could go to the hearing with her. He pulled out his appointment book. He couldn't. He was involved in meetings upstate that day. He apologized, told her she would do fine. Lynne didn't believe him, her stomach turned.

***

Friday afternoon, school’s over, hanging out—Christine leaned against the car, parked in Megan’s driveway. She waited for her friend to drop off her books and grab a jacket, buzzed from the joint they had smoked on the way. She watched the clouds drift above the budding trees. From out of nowhere, she heard the moan of a car engine downshift, then tires grab the driveway asphalt. Christine spun her head to the sound and there was the black Saab with Jim at the wheel. A bolt tore through her.

She tried acting casual with a broad, sweet “hello.” He was sweet back at her, “Hi.”

She’d been thinking about him constantly the past three weeks, since that time when they went to the coke dealer’s place. She had wondered if she was going to see him again, trying not to care.

She didn’t speak until he was out of the car and walking towards her. “What’re you doing in town?”

He stopped three feet away from her. “Heading to JT’s, what’re you up to?’ “Hanging out with Megan, we’re gonna pick up a couple other girls, ride around, get high. You know.”

“Wanna get together?”

She wanted to reach out and touch his chest. “Yeah, sure.”

“I’ll pick you up at McDonalds in about half an hour, after I’m done.” He smiled.

Forty minutes later, Christine jumped into the Saab as it idled. In the meantime, she had decided she was definitely going for it. She had had Megan drop her off downtown, explaining she had to pick some stuff up for her mother. Then she had stopped by the Rexall to pick up a pack of condoms.

The stiff March wind blew road salt residue hard against the Saab as she raced to it. Landing in the passenger seat, she quickly kissed Jim. “Hey.” She was ready to go. “Let’s get out of here.”

He didn't move and instead asked, "Wanna do some coke?"

Here? "No. Your folks don't get home from work for a while, right?" "Yeah. Friday nights they usually go out for drinks after work."

Christine threw him a huge smile. "Let's go to your place."

On the way to his parents', Christine had rubbed Jim's thigh, had gotten him so worked up, he almost sideswiped a couple of parked cars. She was nearly in his lap by the time they reached the house, her hands everywhere, loving it. They burst into the silent house. She grabbed his hand and they charged, giggling and stumbling to the basement den. Behind the closed door, their last line of defense against surprise, they devoured each other across the room, on the couch. Flying hands grabbed, stroked, unfastened; hips and thighs shifted, pressed, locked. Then it was done. She pulled herself out from under him, still breathing hard, and put her clothes back on. She watched him get it together.

He grinned up at her. She liked that. He asked, "Wanna do some lines?" Suddenly she didn't want to be there, the house empty, feeling strange. "Okay."

Her body hummed as they rode through a brilliant afternoon, going nowhere in particular, tunes blared from the radio, when Jim said he had to get back up to Burlington. He was late. He had customers waiting. "Where do you want me to drop you off?"

There was nowhere Christine wanted to be, she wanted to go with him. Someday she would, she knew. "Just leave me off downtown."

When Jim pulled the car into a gas station, at the north end of town, to fuel up, Christine found a pen and a scrap of paper in his glove compartment. She wrote down her number and handed it to him saying, "Call me." She searched his eyes, saw what she was looking for; he would. She leaned over. They kissed deeply before she finally left.

***

Lynne turned around from the sink, surprised to hear Christine come through the door. She called out, “Hi honey, what are you doing home? I thought you were out with Megan.”

Christine breezed into the kitchen, “She ended up having other plans.” She smelled pasta. “Any left?”

Lynne pointed to the refrigerator. “We just finished. You may want to heat it up.”

Christine ladled spaghetti and meat sauce into a pan, turned the heat on low and stirred it. When the food was ready, she served herself a bowl and sat at the kitchen table. That’s when she spotted some official looking papers folded between the salt shaker and the napkin holder. “Hey mom, what’s this?” She spread the papers out.

Lynne wasn’t sure what she wanted to tell her daughter. “That? Well, your father’s behind on his child support payments and he wasn’t being very co-operative, so I’m taking him to court.”

Wow, go mom! “Like how much is he behind?” Reddening, “That’s none of your business.”

“Like a lot?”

Lynne didn’t respond.

Christine kept reading the *motion* and found out for herself. She read Blum’s Notice of Appearance and asked, “Dad’s got a lawyer, who’s your lawyer?”

As she dried her hands, Lynne answered she didn’t have one, but added she had a counselor who was helping her prepare.

Surprised, Christine blurted, “How long have you been seeing a counselor?” “Since—not long, after...” Lynne’s memory triggered her sense of loss. She calmly continued. “After that morning. When Frank punched the wall.”

Christine saw the tears, she put the papers down. She went to her mother, held her.”

Lynne rallied a weak smile, "Well things are a lot better now than they were, eh?"

That weak smile shook Christine. Her father was going to kick her mother's ass in court. No doubt. She could do nothing to stop it from happening. She wolfed down her food and didn't say another word about the back support or the hearing. She couldn't stop her father from hurting her mother, even if she wanted to. She never could.

***

This was how Mark liked it. Quiet enough to hear the clock tick on the den's mantelpiece, with Nancy upstairs reading, the baby asleep. Friday evening, end of the week, with a tall tumbler of scotch, he settled in his easy chair. The room was dim beyond the light cast by one floor lamp. A thought drifted in, persisted, and annoyed him. That support thing was coming up, a couple weeks away, and Blum wanted payment records. He reached for his drink, took a long sip; it was time to make some records.

He turned on the overhead lights, sat at his desk, researched all of the checks he had written to Lynne since they had separated, and figured out most of the dates he had visits with the kids and would have been in contact with Lynne. He could plausibly spread out the supposed twelve hundred dollars over the visit dates, and add a few hundred extra, like Blum suggested. He drew up a list of cash and check payments, with amounts and dates. He used two different pens and a pencil on sheets of paper from an old notepad he found in his desk drawer. He crumpled the paper slightly and added a couple random jottings in the margins. He was done in less than an hour.

CHAPTER 5

The morning of her hearing arrived. After she got off her shift, Lynne couldn't eat breakfast, she was so nervous. She smoked a couple cigarettes, which did nothing to calm her. She drank coffee until she started to shake. She got the children off to school. Matt and Charlotte didn't know about the hearing—Lynne figured there was no sense putting them through an emotional ringer. Before she left for school, Christine hugged her mother, whispered, "Good luck."

"Thanks, sweetie."

An hour until the hearing; nauseous as she dressed, Lynne repeated to herself that she had to do this for the kids.

Blum and Mark sat at a table at the front of the courtroom. They turned and stared at Lynne as she entered the vast room, stared at her as she walked the length of the room to the table where the bailiff had told her to sit, dared her to look at them. She did, and saw the glowering lawyer, saw spiteful Mark. He looked sharp, crisply dressed in a navy blue suit, and she was crumpled in a shapeless spring dress that no longer fit her well. She should have put on some makeup. She felt haggard. The lawyer and Mark looked away from Lynne at the same time and nodded to each other.

Twenty minutes after the hearing was supposed to start, the judge, a wiry old man with piercing black eyes, took his place at the bench. Without apologies, he started right in, briskly telling Lynne to take the witness stand. When she arrived at the stand, he told her to swear under oath to the matters she was about to testify to. Lynne didn't know what she was supposed to do; she swore to tell the truth.

The judge immediately ordered, "You may proceed."

What's that mean? "I'm sorry..."

He stared at her like she was a child wasting his time. "Tell the court why you have brought this claim."

Lynne took a breath, smoothed her dress down against her thighs. "My husband...my ex-husband is supposed to be paying four hundred fifty dollars a month in child support. Sometimes he pays it and other times he doesn't, or pays part of it. I've kept track and I figure he's behind twelve hundred dollars. I've asked Mark to pay what he owes, but he won't. So I'm asking for a court order telling him to pay."

"Anything else?"

What am I supposed to say? "No."

The judge looked to the table where Mark and his lawyer sat. "Your witness Mr.

Blum."

Blum slowly walked across the space between his table and the witness stand and stopped a few feet away, which felt very close to Lynne. He then asked, "Are you under the influence of alcohol or any controlled substances at this time, Mrs. Bancroft?"

What? "No! No I'm... I'm just tired. I don't feel so well..." Solicitously, "Have you been to see a doctor?"

"No, I..."

"Mrs. Bancroft, you have no records of the amounts the children's father paid you for their support, do you?"

"No, well yes, my checkbook register. That's how I kept track. When I deposited his checks."

"How did you keep track of the cash he paid you?" Lynne didn't understand, "He never paid any ..." "Are you certain of that?"

She shot back, "Yes."

"You're under oath, Mrs. Bancroft. Don't you think you should think before answering?"

Hating the way he spoke to her, Lynne snapped, "I don't need to think, he didn't pay me any cash."

"That you can remember. You asked him for the money you are claiming only once, correct?"

"Yes, but..."

"You had been living with a man, to whom you weren't married, just before you asked the children's father for more money. Isn't that correct?"

What's happening? "Yes, but it's not like..."

Blum pressed on. "How long had this man been out of the house before you went to the children's father for more money?"

"Well, maybe...I'm not so sure..."

"How long? What was the date he left? The month, the year?"

"I... the beginning of March, I think." "Of this year?"

What's happening? "Yes." Lynne felt the judge's eyes on her, felt his contempt. Blum walked back towards his table, then turned to face Lynne. "It's only April,

Mrs. Bancroft. You certainly didn't waste any time, did you? You work as a licensed nursing assistant, an LNA at Branford Memorial Hospital, correct?"

Lynne admitted she did. Blum asked her how much she made as a nurse

She answered, "Ten dollars and fifty cents an hour."

The lawyer snapped at her, "You testified that you need this money."No, I said Mark owed..."

He moved towards Lynne and asked, "Since your separation from my client, have you used any controlled substances?"

"No! Well..." She faltered. "I mean marijuana, a couple times, I guess.""And did the man who was living with you provide you with drugs?"

"No." Lynne thought about Frank bringing pot home a few times, maybe Dexedrine. Sweating, she added, "Well yes, I guess so."

"Have you stolen pharmaceuticals from the hospital?" "No, never!"

Blum stepped back. "Are you under the influence of any medications or controlled substances at this time?"

Angrily, "You already asked that."

"So I did. I have no further questions of this witness, your Honor."

The judge told Lynne she could step down. She heard his disgust. Head down, she walked the long distance from the witness stand to her table. She sat alone, beaten down.

When asked whether he had any evidence he wanted to present, Blum indicated Mark would take the stand. Still upset, Lynne barely heard Mark's testimony, but she knew it was all lies. She heard the perfect pitch to his voice, effectively transmitting his integrity and a little bit of hurt. Nothing over the top, all so believable.

Mark testified that he, in fact, had paid Lynne more than he owed and he had the ledger, carefully kept, to prove it. The ledger was entered into evidence. He testified that Lynne sometimes seemed out of it when he came to see his children; that he thought at first it was because she was tired from the shift she worked, but then it seemed like something else. He testified that he was concerned about how well the children were being cared for, especially with the boyfriend living there but, fortunately, he had moved out before Mark had the chance to file paperwork with the court. He didn't want to upset his children's lives by seeking a change of custody, taking them away from their friends and school, and he hoped Lynne would better care for their children now that the boyfriend was out of the house. Mark added that he hoped the money he was giving Lynne for the children wasn't being used for drugs.

Lynne heard Mark's last comments about the boyfriend and the child support being used for drugs. *You son of a bitch!* She burned hard at his lies, bit her tongue. Blum thanked Mark, the judge thanked Mark, and he was invited to return to his table. Lynne wiped tears away and sat up. She watched the judge write some notes.

The judge looked up. "Anything more, Mr. Blum?"

"No, your Honor, except in the way of argument."

"You have the right to present argument, but I'll tell you, it isn't necessary. I've heard enough."

Blum confidently waived final argument. Lynne didn't know what she was doing, but she felt she had to say something. She stood, looked directly at the judge, "Your Honor, I want to present an argument." He said nothing, glaring at Lynne as she continued, "My ex-husband's lawyer made me look bad, but I have to tell you that Mark never gave me any cash. Ever. I'm certain of it. He owes what I said. Please order him to pay what he owes." Lynne quickly sat down, breathless.

Blum started to stand, but the judge raised his hand slightly and spoke directly at Lynne. "I'm not going to do that, Mrs. Bancroft. I am very concerned about what I have heard in this courtroom today. You have, in effect, admitted to the use of illegal drugs. You have failed in your obligation to your children to raise them in a wholesome setting. And then you have called the children's father a liar for failing to give you more money than he is obligated to. In light of the compelling evidence presented by the father, I regard your testimony as perjured and I am inclined to levy a sanction against you." Lynne felt she was drowning in an unreal sea of insanity.

"But I won't. I am going to show leniency this one time. I don't know where this misguided idea to blackmail the father came from, but I recommend that you straighten up, focus on your children's needs and get on with your life. You better hope I never see you in this courtroom concerning the welfare of your children, because I will not be so lenient again, I can assure you. The order of the court is that petitioner's request is denied."

Blum stood up. "Thank you, your Honor." The judge left the bench without looking back.

Lynne buried her face in her hands. *What the hell just happened?*

"Ma'am there's another hearing that needs to get started."

Lynne looked up at the bailiff and the strangers staring down at her. Mark and his lawyer were gone.

From the courthouse into the full powered mid-morning sunlight, Lynne drifted through town in her own fog, her mind bitter with scenes from the hearing. After a couple blocks, she turned into the Downtown Coffee Shoppe for no other reason other than to stop somewhere, anywhere. She sat in a window booth where someone had carved "Fuk" in the tabletop, ordered a cup of coffee. The coffee was god awful, but the sun's warmth reached her and it felt good. Her confusion and anger wore down the longer she sat. She had no idea what to do next, what was next, how she'd get by, she and the kids, no idea, blank. She just wanted something nice -- a good cup of coffee, some laughs, a friend. Something. The sun lost its heat. She was so alone.

***

Christine dug deep into her closet, rummaging for something to wear. Jim had called last night, asked if she wanted to go out for dinner with him and JT, and she wanted to wear something other than jeans and a T-shirt. She found what she wanted; a mid-calf length skirt with oversized tropical flowers in jade, ivory and fuchsia against black. Deeper into the closet, she found the raw cotton blouse that went with the skirt. She gathered the sandals that were meant for this outfit. She found pretty bracelets as a finishing touch. She knew she would look great.

Lynne smelled her Rive Gauche over the boiling potatoes and the warming meatloaf, turned to see her stunning daughter in the kitchen doorway. She asked Christine where she was going.

Swaying her skirt slightly, Christine replied, "Out with Jim, for dinner, not sure where."

Lynne didn't remember any mention of Jim before, but he must have been special, judging by Christine's appearance. A wispy memory rose in Lynne—warm spring nights, youth, feeling delicious and desired. She almost told her to 'be careful', instead she said, "Have fun."

Christine remembered before she turned to leave. "You had that court thing today, how'd it go?"

Lynne's smile collapsed.

Christine knew; her mother had been beaten up. "I'm sorry."

Lynne looked away from her daughter, sought distraction in the boiling pot. A car horn sounded.

"I've gotta go." Christine flew out of the house.

She landed in the Saab, planted a quick kiss on Jim's lips. She wanted to get as far away from her parents' shit as possible. "Where we going?"

He told her about a Chinese restaurant in Brownsville, a couple exits up the interstate. It was JT's idea. Christine asked why.

He didn't know. "Maybe it has something to do with how much I'm getting." He grinned at Christine, "half a key."

Half a kilo! Holy shit! "And you're doing the deal at the restaurant?" "Yep." Jim accelerated.

The Hunan Garden was a single level, plate glass and concrete paneled eatery, set in a solitary strip mall just off of the Brownsville interstate exit. A rusted out K-car, a Buick LeSabre and a Yamaha motorcycle were parked in front of the restaurant. Christine looked for police. No other vehicles were in sight.

Once inside, they were greeted by a broadly smiling Chinese man, hugging menus to his chest. Christine scanned the dining room, as he led them to their seats: An elderly couple at a small table along the far wall: *the LeSabre*, a scroungy family of five in a booth to their right: *the K-car*, at the bar off the dining room, a dark skinned guy in a bitching black and red leather jacket, with a coke in front of him and his eyes on the TV: *the Yamaha*. He could be a narc. Did Jim see the guy? The way he was ambling along, oblivious, she figured he hadn't noticed. *Nope, no way.*

Jim told the waiter someone would be joining them. They were seated at a table for four near the older couple. The guy in the leather jacket threw down his drink and left. Christine tried to relax. She wondered where the guy was going, wondered how much money Jim carried. If things went wrong, they would be going wrong big-time. She couldn't worry about it, just had to chill, the only thing she could do.

They ordered drinks: a Budweiser for him, a Coke for her. They fell into small talk about what they were doing that summer. Christine said she'd be going back to her sucky job as a lifeguard at the town pool. Jim said he'd stay in Burlington, sell cocaine, at least until his lease ran out. "Yeah, I flunked out. Haven't told the folks yet, so yeah hang out for the summer, maybe get a job. And you can, you know, come visit, hang out."

"Yeah, sounds great." *Yes!*

JT noiselessly arrived. "Hello Jim. Christine, right?" He touched her on the shoulder, hot fingers through the thin cotton as he said, "Nice to see you again." She smiled up at him.

He took a seat, ordered a Dewars on the rocks. When the waiter left, he began, "I appreciate you coming up. Hope it wasn't too much bother."

Jim answered no, then blurted, "Are you still at the house?" JT's face hardened at the indiscreet question. "Not so much."

Christine nodded, she understood; the place was too dangerous. The dealer changed the conversation; asked Jim how things were going at UVM.

"I'm outta there. I stopped taking courses this semester." JT turned his attention to Christine, "And your plans?"

She could tell Jim felt the snub. She answered, "I'm looking for work, thinking of moving to Burlington." She saw JT catch Jim's surprised reaction.

"There's a lot happening in Burlington, much more than Branford. I think you'll like it. I think you could do well there." JT looked Christine in the eyes.

She looked back then broke the gaze. Turning his attention to Jim, JT asked if he had the amount they had discussed. Jim said he did.

JT finished his drink. "I need to leave." He lowered his voice, "There's a baggie taped inside the toilet's water tank in the men's room. Put the money in the baggie and leave it in the tank. Do it now."

Jim nodded, left the table. The restaurant was filling up. Two couples were seated nearby.

JT asked Christine, "You're moving up to Burlington, with Jim?" "Maybe."

"I'd suggest you don't waste your time with frat boys. You're better than that." He reached into his jacket pocket, took out a pen and slip of paper, "This is my number. Jim doesn't have this and you're not to give it to him. Or anyone. Understand?"

She nodded yes.

"You can contact me if there's something you need, or want."

Christine weighed what was happening. Was he coming on to her? Offering to set her up, adding her to his talent? If there was a narc in the restaurant, he saw what just happened - - was he using her as bait? Any of it—all of it? She couldn't say, it didn't matter; she didn't flinch, she responded, "I appreciate this." She folded the paper before slipping it into her handbag.

Jim returned. JT leaned forward. "I'm going to leave now. Finish your meal. Don't take the interstate back, take Route 5. When a motorcycle comes up behind you and flashes its lights, pull over." JT peeled off a hundred dollar bill from a wad of cash, placed it on the table. "For dinner. Nice to see you again Christine." He got up and went to the men's room.

Was he ripping Jim off? They could do nothing about it. How much money was in that toilet? Christine watched Jim go white, knew he was thinking the same thing. Jim started to get up, she put her hand on his forearm. "You have to do what he says."

He looked at her, worked up.

"You don't have a choice." She thought on JT's stone cold eyes, the frat boy comment—he'd fuck Jim over without a second thought.

Jim kept looking to the exit. "Yeah, you're right." They had wonton soup and egg rolls, then left.

A single headlight appeared behind them a few miles south of Brownsville.

"Good." Jim murmured, breaking the silence that had stifled them since they left the restaurant. Christine looked around; they were nowhere. Nothing but forest, not a house in sight. The car skidded onto the broad shoulder, gravel crunched violently beneath the tires before coming to a stop. A moment later, the motorcycle pulled up alongside Jim's window. She saw the red and black leather jacket a few feet away, *the guy at the restaurant*. The hand-off, no words, and the motorcycle let out a fierce whine, taking off down the road like a bat out of hell.

Jim coughed. "Well that was pretty intense." "No shit."

He pulled at the duct tape that bound the package, "Maybe I should check out the merchandise."

You've got to be kidding! Some state trooper cruising along would definitely investigate a car stopped in the middle of nowhere. She said, "Not here, okay?"

Jim lit up. "Hey, let's go to Burlington."

A few minutes later they flew up the interstate, ripped on some cocaine Jim had brought with him. With the roof down, the airstream and the speed, the night swallowed them. The nearly full moon hung like a god, lighting distant peaks, broad fields, scattered villages, silver rivers. It was brilliant.

The magic was spent by the time they pulled off of the highway an hour later, into the starkly lit plastic strip mall mess on the outskirts of Burlington. It dragged Christine down. Jim didn't seem to mind, weaving through the traffic. "Let's check this stuff out first, then we'll go catch some music."

That sounded good to her. When Jim pulled into a modest apartment complex of two story brick rectangles and parked in front of one of the nondescript buildings, Christine was surprised—it was so straight. "This is where you live?"

"Yeah, what did you expect?"

Inside, she checked the apartment out: wall to wall beige carpeting, slightly used earth tone furniture, clean linoleum kitchen and bathroom floors, fluorescent lights in the kitchen and bathroom, hollow plywood doors, medium grade fixtures and cabinetry.

No clothes on the floor, a couple dishes in the sink, no toothpaste or soap scum on the bathroom sink, no gross smells. It wasn't a guy place.

"Nice pad."

"Thanks." Jim pulled a triple beam scale from a cabinet over the refrigerator.

The package of cocaine, bundled in brown wrapping paper, had been placed on the spotless round kitchen table with the salt and pepper shakers and a napkin holder. Christine noticed a small uncurtained window over the sink. She wondered who could see into the room. At least they were on the second floor. Seated at the small table, Jim unwrapped the outer layers of packaging, revealing four plastic bags of white powder. He then silently set each bag, one at a time, on the scale.

Pleased, he looked to Christine after weighing the last bag. "Weighs out."

She smiled back.

"Now let's see what we've got." Jim took out a pocket knife, slit an inch along the seam of one of the bags, dipped the knife blade in and extracted a tiny mound on the blade's tip. He studied it closely for a second before the powder disappeared up his nose. He wiped the residue off the blade with his wet forefinger before licking the finger. His eyes shined at Christine. "Primo!" Peering into the bag's slit, "Hardly been cut. Check it out."

Christine had never seen so much cocaine in her life. Fistfuls of glistening powder. JT hadn't screwed him after all. Four thick lines later and she was off, the drug grabbed Christine like a riptide. Jim leered at her. Jumping out of her skin, Christine threw herself at him, plastering furious kisses on his face, his neck. She heard him laugh, "Let's do it."

They tumbled to the bedroom. The lights were out. They tore into each other, a fierce blur in Christine's mind. Rocketing on the coke, she was too high. Jim's body radiated white, the synthetic bedspread scraped her skin, sheets tangled and the bed groaned. He was on her, then in her, he pounded at her manically. Pounded her into the ugly bed. Christine surrendered to him, felt removed as she watched them fuck from a distance - - pale figures in the dark - -until it was over. Her body echoed the assault in ragged waves. After Jim rolled off her, he lay rigid beside her.

She couldn't lie there jangling, she was way too high. She bolted for the bathroom. She stared at her huge eyed face in the cabinet mirror, her heart racing, she clutched the sink. She soaked a washcloth in warm water; wiped her face, her neck, her chest, her stomach, her vagina. She found no relief. She was out of control, she had to get out of that tiny room.

When she came back to the bedroom, Jim asked her with a tight smile, "Hey, you alright?"

She came and stood at the end of the bed. "Pretty high." "No shit." Jim sprang up in one motion. "Let's go out." Some kind of relief. "Yeah, that sounds good."

He left for the kitchen. "I'm gonna weigh out a few grams, be just a minute." "Yeah, sure." She breathed herself down as she got dressed.

***

Five hours later, the Saab tore up the ramp to the southbound lane of the interstate, to Branford. Christine relived the night through a wired haze: rocking out in a packed R&B bar, hardcore punk in some huge hall, a couple of dives with jukeboxes, lots of vodkas and orange juice, and weed, and lines of coke all night long; guys coming up to Jim and disappearing with him; she and Jim making out everywhere. So goddamned high. Jim had fronted her an ounce to sell back home, the cocaine tucked in the waistband of her skirt. How great was that? She looked over at him, streaking through the night, stared down the highway. She could eat him up. And fucking best of all, at one of the dives, alone in a booth, all over each other, he said it would be very cool if she came and stayed with him for the summer. She said yeah.

The moon was sunk into the western mountain ridges, the darkness in the east was lifting. They'd be home about six, with everyone still asleep. It was excellent.

CHAPTER 6

A few weeks later, eleven o'clock on a Saturday morning, Lynne wasn't ready to start the day. She'd finished her coffee, thought of lighting another cigarette. She decided against it. She had to get the kids up. Matt had his game at one and had to be at the field by twelve - thirty. They had to eat and shower. She didn't know if Charlotte had any plans. Probably not. So, she could go to the game. Christine would be gone soon after she woke up, if today was like any other Saturday. That could be a problem, because Mark had called last night and insisted on seeing the kids this weekend, including Christine. He had been drinking. He had started off by yelling at her about how much his lawyer cost him for the child support hearing, and how he was through being nice, and how she couldn't keep him from seeing his children. She knew he had been drinking because it was about seven o'clock on a Friday night and she'd bet he would be into his second tumbler of scotch.

Lynne had tried to tell him there wasn't enough time to plan a visit, but that set him off, calling her a bitch and demanding to know each child's schedule for the weekend. When she told him Matt had a baseball game Saturday afternoon, he said fine. He'd see them all there. Then she tried to explain that Christine, most likely, had plans already, and he went off on her again. He warned Lynne she'd better make sure Christine was at the game. She answered she'd tell Christine what he had said, which seemed to satisfy him. Lynne put the cigarette back in the pack. She didn't have much time if she was going to try to convince Christine to see her father that afternoon. She groaned as she got up from the kitchen table.

Christine ducked her head under the covers to escape the light filling the room, despite the drawn curtains. Sleeping late on Saturday was the sweetest. She was pretty wiped out—it was after three in the morning when she had gotten in. She'd drunk a lot the night before, did a lot of coke. There probably wasn't much of JT's cocaine left, maybe a couple grams. Over the past few weeks she'd sold most of it, made a ton of cash, and had a ton of fun with what she didn't sell. She needed to get Jim to hook her up with some more. She'd ask him when she saw him tonight. His parents were out of town, Megan was throwing a party, and he said he'd be down.

She missed him. It had been three weeks since she had last seen him, that night up in Burlington. They'd talked on the phone a few times. He'd call after her mother went to work. Christine liked the way he said he missed her, couldn't wait to see her, and couldn't wait until she was up there in Burlington with him. Yeah, she'd said, she couldn't wait either.

She still hadn't figured out how Burlington was going to happen. Just take off?

Leave a note to her mother, like: don't worry? That was too weird; she couldn't see doing that, knowing how it would tear her mother up if she ran off like that. She'd figure it out.

Lynne knocked, called out, "rise and shine" and was through the bedroom door before Christine had a chance to answer. She crossed the room to the windows, drew back the curtains. Sunlight poured in.

Christine threw the blanket away from her face: *where's the coke, the cash, my bag?* She didn't see her bag, couldn't let her mother see her looking for something. She protested, "Hey mom, how 'bout some privacy, huh?"

Lynne stood at the foot of the bed, "No, you need to get up. I'm leaving soon for your brother's game. Charlotte's going, your father's going to be there. He'd really like to see you."

"What?"

"You heard me, and besides you've got to get back to June Campbell about the lifeguard position. She's been holding it open for you, but she's got to get your application. Today."

Christine spotted her bag hanging on the back of a chair, zipped shut. She was supposed to deal with the lifeguard job now? It didn't matter because she wasn't going to be around. *Might as well say it,* "I'm not really interested in working at the pool, mom.

I'm thinking of spending the summer up in Burlington with my friend Jim." She winced a little, waiting for the reaction.

What did she just say? "Jim, the boy you've been seeing?"

"Yes."

"You can forget it, because that's not going to happen." A fierce headache struck Lynne. A huge fight was coming.

"Hey, we've got it all figured out. Jim says he can get me a job easy, just for the summer. I'll be back in time for school."

This is not happening. "Does he even know you're sixteen? How old is he? And what does he do in Burlington?"

Christine answered he was twenty and a student at UVM. "Besides, I'll be seventeen this summer, so that shouldn't be a problem."

Shrill, "Shouldn't be a problem! It's not going to be a problem, because you're not going." Shaking with anger, "I've got to get your brother and sister ready for their visit with your father. We'll talk about this when I get back, because we're not done."

As Lynne turned for the door, Christine shot back. "I don't care what you say. I'm going."

Lynne's shoulders tightened, her head throbbed as she walked to the door without saying anything. She knew; Christine was going to do what she wanted.

***

At the ballpark, seated in the bleachers, Lynne couldn't stop thinking about Christine going off with some guy she knew nothing about, some creep. Off to Burlington, where anything could happen. She had to stop her, but she knew: Christine would go.. If she tried to stop her: *she'll run away, she'll disappear.*

Charlotte nudged her mother, pointed out Mark striding back and forth in front of the bleachers searching for them. She waved to her father.

Mark spotted them and called out. "There you are. What are you doing sitting way up there? The seats down here have a much better view."

The jerk was yelling at them in front of all these people. He was waving them down, "C'mon."

Charlotte was already getting up, Lynne had no choice. At the spot chosen by Mark, he tucked Charlotte under the chin. "How ya doin' sprout?" To Lynne, "Where's Christine?"

"Home. Sick. I'm going to get some water, want any?"

Charlotte did, Mark didn't. While returning with the water, Lynne watched them from a distance. Both stared straight ahead, not talking, looking brutally awkward.

After Lynne took her seat in the sun drenched bleachers, Mark stabbed away at small talk. Charlotte sucked on ice cubes, giving her father enough response so he didn't feel slighted. Lynne silently sipped her water, glad Mark wasn't talking at her. The game began and the talk ended. Lynne's thoughts slipped back to Christine. How could she stop her from going? Forbid her? Threaten her? *She'll run away*. Have the police bring her home if she leaves? *She'll disappear, maybe forever*. Lynne's guts tightened. She had to convince her daughter not to go, *because anything could happen.* She knew how things could happen: *pregnant at nineteen and married to Mark*. One thing leads to another, then you're screwed and it's over.

"Hey that was some play!" Mark shouted towards the field. "Way to go Matt!" At Lynne, "Goddamn double play, how about that!"

She looked at Mark. *I've got to stop her.*

Lynne brought her attention to the game, to Charlotte's visit with her father.

Mark, the jerk, was ignoring his daughter, focusing intently on Matt and the play on the field. Charlotte had shrunk into herself; hands clasped between her pressing knees, shoulders bowed beneath a weight, needing her father's attention. *Same as always.*

Lynne slid closer to her youngest, leaned against her a little to remind her she was there. She saw Charlotte's responsive smile, and wished it could be that simple to reach Christine.

"Helluva game!" Mark punched Matt's shoulder, when the boy approached his family in the bleachers at the end of the game. Before his son arrived, Mark had been talking up the team and the game with different people nearby, all excited, ignoring Lynne and Charlotte.

"Hey let's go grab a bite to eat, my treat." Mark announced.

No! Lynne had had enough for one day. She wasn't going to suffer through some agonizing meal, dealing with his non-stop manipulative, passive aggressive, borderline rage crap. She wasn't going to put her kids through that either. And she badly wanted to get home. Christine might still be there. She had to talk to her. They had to talk.

"The kids have plans." Lynne's words hung in the air. "Sorry."

Mark stood silent, darkened. The children became uneasy. Families pressed past them.

"The kids had fun, I'm sure they'd love to do something again soon." Matt broke away from his mother to hug his father. "Bye dad, thanks."

Charlotte followed her brother. "Yeah thanks, dad." Mark held them both, glaring at Lynne over the children's heads. She flinched. He made her feel like dirt. Again.

***

The phone rang. Lynne listened to hear if anyone was going to pick it up, until she recalled that Matt was already out with his friends. Charlotte didn't usually pick up.

Christine wasn't home. She put the bowl of leftover salad down on the counter, picked up the receiver. She heard Mark hiss, "Don't you ever do that to me again!"

Shaken, "Do what, Mark?"

"Keep the kids from having a good time with me, that's what." Steeling herself, "And how did I do that?"

"The kids wanted to go with me after the game, and you know it. Don't think I don't know you've been poisoning their minds about me. I can see it clear as day."

Lynne snapped back. "Listen Mark, you're blowing this up into something it's not. The children just had other plans. That's all."

"Other plans!" He yelled into the phone "When I want to see them, they don't make other plans!"

She tried to get through, "Mark, you have to understand. They want to see you, but they have other things going on that mean a lot to them."

"What kind of crap is that? You read that in some magazine for whiny women?" She didn't answer. There was no answer when he was this toxic.

Using his rational tone, "Listen, I want to see Christine. Next weekend. I'd like to have her come over here. I'll pick her up Friday night, drop her off Sunday afternoon."

There's no stopping him. "I hardly see Christine on the weekends. She's really busy with her friends and all."

"What are you telling me, that you're not going to let me see my own daughter? What's your sickness, Lynne? Is this all too threatening to you?"

Trying to hold up, she tried to reason with him. "Mark, it's just about having realistic expectations..."

"Realistic ex-pec-ta-tions! Fuck you, Lynne. You can't keep her from me..." She couldn't take anymore, she was wasted. She hung up. The phone rang—two, three, four rings. Lynne didn't pick it up. She just stood by the phone, shaking.

"Aren't you going to get that?" Christine was at the doorway, heading for the phone. The ringing stopped. "Why didn't you answer it?"

"It was your father."

Christine observed her beaten mother. "What did he want?"

"Nothing."

"The visit didn't go so good?"

"It went fine. Matt's team won." The words floated weakly from Lynne's mouth, then her tone hardened. "Your father wants to see you."

That's what this was all about, *screw that.* "Yeah, well I don't want to see him." Lynne nodded. "What are you doing home?"

"Getting ready to go out."

"Where are you going?"

Christine just wanted to be gone. "Megan's."

Lynne had yet to meet the girl, although she knew she'd heard the name before.

She started, not knowing what she would say, "This idea of yours, going to Burlington with some man, it's a bad idea. A really bad idea. You're too young. Things happen. Things you don't expect. Believe me. What's he doing asking someone your age to live with him? I can't let you go, that's all there is to it. You can't go."

Christine glared at her mother. “Jim’s a good guy, he’s not that much older than me, and I’m really sick and tired of this sucky town. So I’m getting out. And I don’t care what you say.” She saw the fear in her mother’s eyes. She softened, “I’ll let you know where I am. I’ll give you his phone number. I’ll call every day, well almost every day. I promise.” Christine reached out to take her mother’s hand and smiled. “It’s just for the summer.”

She’s going. “He could treat you badly.”

Christine shook her head, *he won’t*, “Nothing will happen. I’ll be okay.”

She’s going. “Why don’t you go someplace with your girlfriends, your friend Megan, if you want to get out of town. Get a job together at some resort.”

No, Christine had this worked out.

She’s going. Her daughter held her hand. Lynne heard, “I’ll stay in touch. I promise.”

She promises? Lynne had to believe. If they lost touch, if Christine disappeared, *what could be worse?* She couldn’t think of what could happen if she lost Christine. If they stayed in contact, then maybe no harm would come to her. The phone’s ring shattered her thoughts.

Christine let go of her mother’s hand. “I’ll get it. He’ll only keep calling. It’s me he wants to talk to.” *I won’t let him hurt her.*

“Hey Chris, it’s me, Jim.” Shouting over music slamming in the background.

Christine wondered if her mother heard the noise through the receiver. She cut it short. “I’ll see you soon. I’m on my way.” To her mother, “That was Megan.”

A hard pit set deep in Lynne’s gut. She was certain; she would lose Christine if she tried to stop her. *I can’t lose her*.

Christine came up behind her mother, wrapped her arms around her. “You okay?” Lynne blinked. “I’m fine.”

"Listen, I've got to get going."

Lynne nodded. And she was gone.

***

Christine entered the May evening. Sweet scents came from newly mowed lawns and blooming gardens on her maple shaded street. She passed set back Capes, passed the kids hanging out on their bikes. She didn't notice any of it. Her head was full of her father. *What the hell does he think he's doing;* demanding to see her, screwing with her mother? Why didn't he stay away—*he has his new family.*—why did he come back and ruin their lives? She walked hard through the neighborhood. He wanted to see her. That wasn't going to happen, she would be in Burlington. He wouldn't be able to find her. Her thoughts flipped. If he found out about Burlington, he'd stop it. *He can't know.* Striding downhill, towards the river, a quick panic struck Christine; her mother would tell him. He'd get it out of her somehow. She had to make sure her mother said nothing to him about Jim or Burlington.

She marched past old tenements that loomed over her—three stories high. They were once crammed, she had heard, with large mill worker families: French Canadian, Irish. Not anymore. All the mills were closed: the furniture factory, the lumber mills, and grist mills before them, all strung along Chapman Brook tumbling to the Connecticut River. The tenements had slid into ruin and disrepair. Their sagging porches stood just a few feet back from the sidewalk and the street's traffic. Paint chips and broken glass dusted the bare ground and cement. The window casements and clapboards were weather beaten. The sick smell of damp rot seeped from the structure's depths. The buildings still held tenants: old people and the disabled, some junkies, and newcomers from Massachusetts, Connecticut—young women with babies and toddlers and guys hanging out on the porches. Who were they? Black, Hispanic, white, a few of their kids had started going to her school, tough kids with their own thing going on. How bad did their lives have to suck to end up in Branford?

A couple blocks downhill and the tenements gave way to empty lots, with vacant mills back by the brook. Dusk fell on the broken down buildings. Christine had to look at them, she always did. The ruin gave her something; solid proof of the desperation that surrounded her. The empty lots became parking lots, fronting a couple renovated mills.

These mammoth brick and glass blocks had been put to new uses: a plumbing supply warehouse and showroom, a woodworking shop and some other businesses. She didn't buy it, all the hype about "Branford's revival." The place was a toilet and anybody who said different was a moron.

At the bridge that crossed Chapman Brook, Christine stood over a narrow rock gorge, where the water rushed and tumbled through, not far below her. She watched the torrent and felt the same power that had been around forever, felt it through the iron girders and in her gut. She received the vibrations with a deep satisfaction, listened to the steady roar of the waterfall. She always stopped on the bridge to witness the power, or to imagine the place before Branford existed.

Beyond the bridge, there once had been a mill pond long gone before she was born. She had seen the pictures. It had been drained and paved over for more retail space, which now held a hair stylist, a pet store and a Rexall. Christine stiffened as she approached the Friday night scene: the parking lot filling up with loaded cars of teenagers gathering to cruise the downtown: jocks, greasers, hangers on, *whatever* —a couple dozen kids wired on the night's promise; beer, ass, grass, *whatever*; wired for disappointment. Christine walked faster, looked straight ahead and avoided cars peeling out of the parking lot. *Losers. Freaks.*

Four story high block-long buildings, dating back to the last century, rose before her filled with apartments, offices, shops and the Downtown Coffee Shoppe. At the corner of the first building, a bunch of kids, between twelve and fifteen years old, spilled into the sidewalk outside the arcade, hanging out. Christine checked out a few punks huddled by the arcade's doorway. They passed a quart bottle of beer in a paper bag between them. No one she recognized.

One of them, shirtless and glazed on glue, veered at her, "Hey, wha's happnin'?"

She didn't answer, brushed past him on the sidewalk.

He got in her face, "Hey, wanna do a bowl?" She didn't break stride, didn't answer.

"Bitch." The others laughed, yelled at her back, "Slut."

She flipped them off without looking back. *Losers. Freaks.*

The cruising cars streamed the four block long downtown in both directions, lines of cars passed, slowly. Juiced teenagers hung out of their cars and pickup trucks calling out, flirting, showing off, seeing and being seen. The kids who weren't old enough to drive, cruised the sidewalk. Christine cut her path through them. Halfway through downtown a new, silver BMW convertible slowed down alongside Christine. She didn't notice.

"Hey Bancroft, got any blow?"

She turned around to see Billy Hawthorne, Randall Binghamton and Lily and Wendy Collins looking up at her—the girls giggled at Hawthorne's bold move.

Hawthorne looked pleased with himself.

Furious at being called out like that, with cops everywhere, Christine wanted to claw his smug prep face. "Fuck off clown."

The BMW revved and lurched away, Hawthorne shouting over his shoulder. "Bitch!" The others laughed.

Hate, hate, hate this place! "That wasn't very nice."

What now? Christine whipped around to the direction of the voice to see an open faced boy peering at her from the cab of his pickup.

"You need a ride somewhere?"

Christine sized up the driver: his honest smile, another boy in the driver seat half in shadow, also smiling and the hard worked Ford truck. *Farm boys.* She was only half way to Megan's, three quarters of a mile to go, "Yeah, sure." Climbing into the truck bed, she found a tow chain, a couple cinder blocks, a scattering of hay and a couple empty Budweiser cans. *Yep, farm boys.* In town for the Friday night excitement. They offered her a seat in the cab.

"No thanks, just as soon ride back here." They offered her a beer. "No, thanks. I'm not going far. Just up to my boyfriend's. He's home, sick." They didn't know where Megan's street was. She told them she'd give them directions as they went.

Coming to the end of the downtown district, just past the rise with the courthouse, Christine directed the boys to take a left. They turned from the Main Street glare into the sudden darkness of an old residential neighborhood of massive three story homes, with maples arching over the houses and the street. Once the homes of large, wealthier families, they now were cut up into apartments: three or four to a building, filled with restaurant workers, office workers, construction workers and some young families. She knew a few people who lived in the neighborhood: older brothers and sisters of some of her friends. There were some hippie types too, who drove beat up Volvos with New York and New Jersey plates. They hung Indian bed sheets over their windows. How long would it take for them to figure out what a loser place this was?

She directed the boys. "Okay, take a left here."

The pickup climbed a steep hill, rising above the crowded river flatlands to a plateau that was once a dairy farm, but now was spread with split level ranch houses on quarter acre lots. Built back in the sixties, they were homes for insurance agents, bank officers, school teachers and store owners. The streets were wider, the trees fewer. Wide lawns stretched back from the roadway to houses without porches. Black asphalt driveways led to two car garages. A lot of kids from her school lived up there. Christine hated this part of town most of all, so perfectly ugly.

"Here it is." She pointed to a split level just up the road, a couple blocks away from Megan's so the boys wouldn't catch on about the party. She hopped out of the truck before it came to a full stop. "Thanks guys. You know how to get out of here? Just turn around and keep going downhill back the way we came."

Just through the front door, Megan rushed at her, "Chris, Chrissy! God, I'm glad you're here!"

Man she's wired. "Hey."

Christine looked past the girl to see who else was at the party. She couldn't see anyone from the entryway.

Megan lowered her voice, "Remember my brother Jim?"

Christine nodded, she almost forgot she hadn't told Megan, or anyone, that she was involved with him.

"Well he's down from Burlington and he's got some amazing coke. I mean really amazing. You've gotta check it out."

"Definitely." Christine wondered where he got it. If he had gotten it from JT, why hadn't he brought her along? She wondered how much he had scored, how much he'd be willing to let her have. "Where is he?"

In the den, the Clash pounded out of speakers, about a dozen high school kids stood around drinking beer; nobody Christine cared about. She saw Jim with a beer in one hand, on the couch between two girls she didn't know. He was talked to the blonde on his left. *Really?* He noticed Christine in the doorway and shot her a smile.

The blonde followed his gaze. Christine looked her down, sent a smile back at him. The music was too loud, the whole thing was too much. She backed out of the room. He could come to her.

"My brother was in there," Megan protested. "Yeah I saw him. It's just... I've got a headache."

Over Megan's shoulder, Christine spotted two guys in the kitchen she didn't recognize. They looked back at her, kind of shady, the sort of creeps who'd rip a place off during a party. She lowered her voice and asked, "Who are the assholes in the kitchen?"

Megan turned to see who Christine was talking about. "I dunno, some friends of Jim's from Burlington."

One of the guys leered at the girls, ran his tongue over his lips. Christine stared back, hard.

Jim spoke, from just behind Christine, "Hey."

The two turned away from the creeps, with Christine answering, "Hey. You know your friends are scuzzy, don't you? They're gonna rip off your parents' stuff if you don't keep an eye on 'em."

"You think so?"

Get a clue. "Yeah. What are you gonna do about it?" He didn't have an answer.

"I need a beer," Christine said.

He offered to get her a Molson. She said sure and he headed for the kitchen. Megan asked, "God Chris, you are really intense tonight, what's up?"

Before she could answer, she heard Jim shout, "What the fuck are you guys doing?"

The two girls hurried to the kitchen where they saw the creeps at an open cupboard, cereal dumped on the floor. One of them held a box of donuts, both of them had white powder around their mouths. The three men were laughing like 'fuck you' to each other and the world. One of the assholes, the one with the tongue, caught

Christine's eye, looked her over again. She shot a look back at him that said *fuck you too.* She got her own beer from the refrigerator, left the kitchen. Megan went to find some pot.

Christine went to sit alone on the stairs leading up to the second floor -—she had to get away from the noise. She felt the cool beer bottle on her cheek, eyes shut: *something's really crazy tonight.*

She heard Jim's voice. "Hey, there you are." He was right in front of her. "I was wondering where you went."

Now you know. "Your friends are jerks."

"Ah, they're not so bad. Eddie can be too much sometimes, but hey who isn't."

She ignored the sorry-assed answer. "Megan tells me you scored some awesome coke, you been down to see JT?"

"Nah, I haven't seen him since that time with you. He's like, disappeared. He wasn't answering his phone. Maybe his phone's disconnected, nobody's seen him."

Jim continued, "...who knows, probably laying low down in the islands, something like that. No, I got it from this guy in Burlington selling ridiculous shit. I mean the shit's right off the plane. You gotta check it out."

Before she could answer, he handed Christine a silver straw and held out a small canister. She looked at the front door, a few feet away; anyone could come through that door, like the cops. *What the hell.* One hit off the meager mound he piled on the joint of his thumb, another—flash and twinkle. *Nothing wrong with that!*

Jim did his hits, leaned into Christine, eyes wide, "What did I tell you."

Yeah. She was racing.

He grinned. "You think you're high now, you oughta try shooting this shit up." He leaned closer, his face inches away from hers."We're doin' it, later, you wanna check it out."

No! Christine flashed on needles, tied off veins. She'd been there, too close, but had never done it, never wanted to – it reeked of death, the needles and the veins.

Jim continued, "...like you wouldn't believe. Whaddaya say?"

His face so close, he was all she could see, his eyes searchingly hers. His dilated pupils were huge, black, deep. She could fall into those eyes, slip in with him, he wanted that. She felt it. He wanted her to do it. "Whaddaya say?"

She tasted death coming off him like dry rot. "No." He shifted. She continued. "Not tonight."

He leaned back, his eyes darted away. "Sure. Well we were thinking of kicking it off soon. In case you change your mind."

Christine watched him, said nothing.

"Listen I gotta go check out Eddie and Murph."

She didn't want him to leave her; she didn't want to be alone now. She needed something that she didn't understand.

He bent over a little. "Give me a kiss."

She craned her neck up to him for his quick kiss. *Don't leave.*

He was gone and in the next moment, Megan appeared with a lit joint. A couple skinheads cruised through the doorway, glassy eyed. *This is bad.*

Megan giggled through the pot smoke. "Get this, Jimmy says he's gonna bang some of that coke of his, said we can get in on it if we want. Excellent, huh?"

Cold reply. "He said that?"

"Yeah he did." Megan handed the joint back to Christine. "I'll go let him know we're in." And she left. The noise amped up. Something wild was happening. *I'm outta here.*

Christine, high, stumbled into the darkness, to the street, under a broad sky.

Walking, her mind careened. *He's cool, right? The coke and all. Right? Partying with his friends, no big deal. Guys can be assholes.*

So what. She needed him to be different. *It doesn't matter, he's good to me.* Walking. Beyond the streetlights the road turned to a paved lane, then to dirt lanes past highland farms along the hills above Branford. She wanted him. *He's better than anything and anyone around here. He'll treat me right.* The night didn't argue back.

She walked for hours in the hills and vaguely headed home. She ran down all the losers in this town, the boredom, stupidity, and cruelty, day in and day out, week after week. Burlington and Jim would be better than all that. He had to be. He would be. What happened at the party was nothing. Compared to the shit in her life, it was nothing. Shit like her father showing up and screwing everything and everybody up. That's what she had to get away from.

She arrived home long after midnight; spent. In bed, in her final conscious moments, she remembered Jim's eyes searching hers; she tasted the dry rot. An icy finger touched her breastbone. She shuddered. *What?* But she was exhausted; with no more thought, she fell asleep and plowed her fear under.

CHAPTER 7

The morning after the party, Jim called from Burlington. Christine was in the kitchen when the phone rang. She picked it up and he asked, "Where'd you go last night? I was looking for you."

"Sorry. I wasn't feeling so good." When he asked her, she said she was feeling better. He told her he missed her. She liked that. "I wish you were here with me now."

She liked that even more. "Hang on, only five weeks until school's done." He said he couldn't wait that long.

She laughed. "When are you coming down again?" He said he didn't know.

"I'll miss you. Soon, okay?" "Yeah, soon."

Christine hung up, saw her mother standing in the kitchen doorway. Lynne tried to be calm. "Was that him?"

"Yes." Christine didn't want to deal with her mother again. Lynne had been all over her that morning about going to Burlington. She didn't want to hear any more about it. She got the message; it was dangerous, foolish, all that. It didn't matter, she was going. She pushed past her mother, left the house, into the stupidly sunny Sunday afternoon. She had nowhere to go.

The next week Lynne barely saw Christine. When she saw her daughter, they fought. Christine refused to back down. Lynne refused to give her permission to go to Burlington. Christine disappeared for the entire weekend.

Shortly before dinner on Sunday, as Lynne took a pot roast out of the oven, Christine entered the kitchen and sat at the table, "Hey."

Lynne slapped the meat onto a platter. "Where have you been?"
"I told you, Megan's."

"All weekend?" "Yeah, more or less."

Fuming, "How was I supposed to know you were going to be there all weekend? You didn't call, you didn't leave a number. Is this the way it's going to be when you're in Burlington, no way of contacting you, no way of knowing where you are?"

Matt and Charlotte looked at each other; waiting for the next fight.

Christine glared back, then realized her mother's point, dropped her eyes. "No, you're right. I'm sorry." Looking up, "I'm sick of fighting about it. I hate it."

"Me, too." Lynne placed the platter on the table. "How about we don't mention Burlington at mealtime. A truce?"

"Sure. Truce."

The phone rang, Christine got up from the table, answered it, and heard her father's voice. "Chris! Great, I caught you. You're so hard to get a hold of. I figured I might have a chance now. The reason I'm calling is to set up a visit. Sometime next weekend, or the weekend after that, if next weekend doesn't work. It doesn't have to be anything fancy, just get together for a meal, anything really."

"I'm not sure dad, there's a lot of stuff going on and I don't know what Matt and Charlotte are up to."

Chirping, "Well, it could just be the two of us..."

No! "No, I think they'd really like to come, too. Maybe dinner, Friendly's. They'd like that. Not this coming Saturday, but the one after should be good."

Less chipper, "Okay. That sounds good. It's a date. I'll pick you guys up around six. So, that's squared away, how have you been? I haven't spoken to you in ages."

She told her father she was fine, that school was going well. She could tell he wasn't listening—he had gotten what he wanted. *Like always.*

"Well that's great sweetie, I'm glad to hear that. Listen, I should get going. Really look forward to seeing you." He hung up.

Christine told her brother and sister at the table, "We're having dinner with dad two Saturdays from now." She told them they didn't have a choice.

She caught her mother watching her, that same stupid fear in her eyes. She didn't feel like giving her mother the little 'don't worry' smile. She didn't feel like giving anybody anything. She went to her room without saying a word.

***

They glided in Mark's car through the spring warmth and late afternoon sunlight. The windows were rolled up and the air conditioning blew high and frigid. Christine was too cold, freezing in her light T-shirt. From where she sat pressed against the passenger door, she could smell her father with that same scent of scrubbed skin and musky aftershave. She stared out while he threw questions at Matt and Charlotte about stupid shit. She stopped listening. She knew he kept glancing over at her, barely turning his head.

He finally asked her a couple questions about how she was doing in school, then "You seeing anyone?" He asked like it wasn't a question, that it was her turn to say 'not really', and he would joke that a pretty girl like her should be seeing someone, and that would kill a couple minutes.

She left the script. "Yeah, I'm seeing this guy, Jimmy."

Her father looked at her as if she was suddenly real.

Christine knew she had to bring up Jim sometime that night; at some point she'd tell her father she had to go because she had a date. Jimmy was in town and she was getting together with him as soon as she could. She had almost cancelled the dinner, but knew it would create a huge mess. She was prepared; she had warned her brother and sister she was going to tell their father about Jim, and they had better go along with whatever she said. It would be best if they kept their mouths shut, but if he asked them they could say

Jimmy went to their high school, ran track, drove a Saab, and they liked him. Obviously they were to say nothing about Burlington. She had told them she was going to tell their father she was working at a camp for the summer. That's what she and mom had agreed to tell him. And if they blew it, she would make their lives miserable forever.

Mark grinned tightly. "Hey, great. What grade's he in?" "Senior."

"What's his name?" "Jimmy."

"Does he have a last name?"

She decided to make something up. "Hauptman." Her father looked at her funny.

She didn't flinch. She added, "We have a date tonight, right after dinner." Her father snapped his head back to the road

The meal was an ugly disaster, all because of Christine and her boyfriend and their date. Mark brought Charlotte to tears with nasty comments about her being weak and plain. He built Matt up with his success at sports and his friends, only to stomp him down by saying it was meaningless and juvenile. He told Christine the food she ordered would make her fat, the soda she was drinking would rot her teeth, all the food served was crap and that it was a terrible idea to even eat there. Then he complained they hadn't been to visit him—they didn't even know where he lived—they had never seen his new baby. He complained he missed them and loved them, that they were getting older without him. He touched Christine on her wrist and elbow, he touched her hair. She squeezed her body tight. She figured he might be right: the food was crap, and Charlotte was weak, and Matt was just a boy. Thankfully, he didn't ask any more about Jim. Mark dropped them off at home. Christine stared at her father's car as it drove away.

Matt and Charlotte ran into the house, but she stayed to make sure he wasn't coming back, hoping she'd never see him again, that he'd leave them alone. Maybe he would. What mattered was she had made it clear to him she was going to be working at a summer camp all summer and couldn't be reached. She noticed his eyes darken after she spoke. *Good.* Now she had to make sure her mother got the camp story down cold.

***

Christine slid into a chair at the breakfast table. Matt and Charlotte weren't down yet. The last day of school, half day: clean out lockers, pick up report cards. Year-end stuff. She knew her mother would be asleep when she got out of school.

Lynne was sitting at the table, the smoke from her last cigarette hung over her, as she held a half filled cup of coffee.

"Mom, Jim and I were thinking there wasn't any reason to wait until the weekend. So, I might as well head up to Burlington today."

That wasn't the plan. They had made a plan, last weekend when Lynne had met Jim—he seemed nice, a good student working on a degree in Business Administration—here in their kitchen, over dinner. She liked him. He didn't seem that much older than Christine. They had agreed Lynne would drive Christine up to Burlington, so she could see where her daughter would be, that it was safe. This was important. And it was good he had given her his address and phone number. That was the plan.

Christine said, "I just want to go. Jim will be here when I get out of school.

I've already packed. I'll call when I get there."

As if set in stone, she was leaving. It felt like death. It was that certain. Lynne felt lost. "Do that."

Christine went to Lynne, bent over and wrapped her arms around her mother's neck, held her, whispered, "I'll be alright mom, don't worry." She was that certain.

Lynne held Christine's arms, and felt the restless shifting, the straining—there was no stopping this. "You have to call. Promise."

Christine gently pulled away. "Promise."

***

Jim and Christine ripped up the interstate, top down on the Saab. The wind stripped the reek of Branford off Christine. Cocaine scoured her mind free. The sudden decompression off the highway hit her hard, as did the traffic and traffic lights, humid heat, asphalt and car exhaust. They arrived at Jim's seriously ugly apartment complex.

Jim carried her bags. They passed a bank of mailboxes, perhaps a dozen, set into the wall just inside the entrance to Jim's building. Christine realized she might never know who these people were, and that was okay. They wouldn't know her either. She passed their odors and their sounds in the stairwell, in the hallway. She didn't ask Jim about the neighbors, she didn't care.

The door open, they stood just inside the threshold of his apartment. A vast space surrounded Christine; *this is it.* Jim brought her bags to the bedroom, she followed. He dropped them on the bed. The space between them expanded. She felt nothing sexual.

She knew he felt the same, it was weird. She asked where she should put her things. He showed her a couple empty drawers in his dresser, empty hangers in the closet. He asked if she was hungry, if she wanted to go get something to eat.

"Sure, let me unpack first."

He went to the living room to see what was on ESPN. The sound of the television from the other room filled the void.

***

He took her to his favorite Italian restaurant, recommended the manicotti and sausages. She ordered them. She'd never had manicotti. Jim chattered away, a lot of one- sided small talk about things to do in Burlington. She half listened, looked around, saw no one and nothing familiar, except him. He was everything she knew here. It was him and then nothing. *What happens next?* She dropped her thinking and resumed listening to him, because that was all that was happening.

He said something about waiting to hear about a job as a salesman at a Saab dealership. She thought he already worked there.

Should be any day, he said, maybe tomorrow he'd hear back. And tomorrow, he continued, they should get her some fake I.D. saying she's twenty one so she could get into clubs and get a job where they served drinks. He knew a guy who could get her a fake license. He would pay for it. She asked if he had spoken to any of his friends about a job for her, like he had said he would.

He shrugged. "Not yet. We'll make the rounds, tomorrow. I'll introduce you to some people I know."

Tomorrow. There was a plan. She squeezed his knee under the table.

***

The light on the answering machine was pulsing when Lynne got home from the hospital the next morning. *It's her.* "Hi, mom. Sorry I didn't catch you before you left for work, but we didn't get in until late, went out late for dinner. Everything's fine, got up here just fine. Love you, talk to you soon." Very relieved, *like she promised!*

CHAPTER 8

Christine laid in the tangle of sheets with Jim asleep beside her in the morning. She had never spent the night in a man's bed before. It felt strange. He snored, and she listened to his sounds in the early light.

After they made love. Jim announced he was starving. "I know this place, best brunch in town." An hour later, they were being seated at a sidewalk table at a Bistro on Pearl Street in the glorious summer sun. Christine wore a loose sundress. She glowed and sensed the glances she was attracting. She felt perfect.

The man who seated them knew Jim and Jim introduced him to Christine. "Chris, Jeff is the manager. Chris is new in town, just got here yesterday."

Jeff smiled at Christine, shook her hand lightly, his eyes slightly roved her body, "Nice to meet you." As he still held her hand he asked, "Are you looking for work? I have a hostess position opening up next week, if you're interested."

Yeah! As he released her hand she answered. "I am."

His eyes roved some more as he told her to show up Monday at 10 a.m.: white blouse, black pants, no jeans. She'd train on Monday, start on Tuesday; she could fill out the application before leaving.

When Jeff left, Christine half whispered, "Can you believe that?" Jim couldn't. He asked if she had ever hostessed before.

She answered yes, even though she never had.

"This place has a really intense lunch rush, business people and all that during the week." He warned her.

She said that wouldn't be a problem.

Throughout her meal, Christine subtly watched the staff at work, particularly the hostess. She seemed to be the gatekeeper, the one who controlled the flow of customers, the table turnover. As she and Jim finished their coffee, the Friday lunch crowd began to arrive. This hostess made it appear effortless, but Christine imagined the job could be a nightmare if it wasn't done right. She took in details, how the woman spread the customers among the wait staff, how she cleared a few tables or brought out silverware when the busboys were swamped, how she dealt with the customers who waited to be seated or served. The woman was always in motion, yet never seemed rushed. She was smooth. *I can do this.* Christine smiled, with the sun on her face.

After brunch, they strolled the lakefront, poked around some stores, tore off some afternoon sex back at the apartment. At five o'clock they drove to the North End and picked up Christine's fake license at the back of a rundown mom and pop grocery. Then they ate great pizza at a little place around the corner. It was Friday night, they'd go clubbing later and try out Christine's new ID.

***

They went out around ten o'clock, stopped by a couple bars, had a couple drinks. At each place, Jim disappeared with someone for a few minutes. Christine knew he was selling coke, figured it was his Friday night routine. That was okay with her. They had done a couple lines, she cranked along just fine, sipping her vodkas and orange juice. Around 11:30, Jim mentioned a club he wanted to check out called The Grind.

When they arrived, they heard heavy metal music blasting into the night. Once inside the cavernous black walled club, they were slammed by a manic version of "Hit Me with Your Rhythm Stick." Hardcore punks and head bangers—tricked out with Mohawks, piercings, shredded clothes—threw their bodies into each other, into walls, or stood defiant in a sound storm.

Christine watched Jim scan the crowd, saw him make eye contact with a man across the hall, not a punk. He took her by the arm, led her across the room, through the thrashing bodies, to the man and a woman who was with him. Jim leaned in close to the man, while they held their handshake, his mouth to the man's ear, the man checked out Christine. Christine checked the woman out: very thin, breastbone showing where her neckline plunged, no tits, sharp cheekbones, dead eyes. The two men left without a word to the women. Christine watched them disappear, as slashing guitars ripped the space apart.

When Jim came back he was lit up, so was the other guy. The man left with the woman. Jimmy scanned the crowd again. It was too loud, too messed up, Christine wanted out. A man, dressed in black, leaned into Jim from behind, mouth to Jim's ear.

She thought; *narc?* Then she looked at his eyes—no, he wanted it real bad. Jim turned to her, held up his index finger that he'd be back in a minute. *This sucks way too much.* She signaled back she was going outside.

Christine leaned against the outside wall, by the club's door, ignored by the crowd on the sidewalk. A Ramones' set pulsed into the halogen night. She was seriously pissed he drug her around like this. A couple minutes later, Jim popped out the door, saw her. Wired, he talked before she could speak, rambled about running into a good friend, doing a little business, hope she didn't mind. Shit like that. She could tell—his eyes. *He's been shooting up!*

She walked away. He caught up. Before he could open his stupid mouth, she let him have it, "Not okay. At all."

Face to face, he shuffled. "I was just, you know, hooking up."

"I know what you were doing, and I'm not gonna be dragged around like this.

Not happening. Got it?"

He looked away, it was shitty. "Yeah."

She had a killer headache, told him she wanted to go back to the apartment. It sucked. Too high to sleep, Jim watched television late—old movies. Christine watched awhile then went to bed.

Her brain rattled from that stupid club, she lay there pissed at his fucked up behavior. Her second night in Burlington.

***

A cold front moved in and brought chilly wet weather for the weekend. Saturday, Christine and Jim settled in: sex, TV, eating in. He did a few lines of coke, but Christine passed. Not in the mood for cranking up, if all they were doing was hanging out. She could really go for a joint, for staring out the window at the steady drizzle. Jim said there wasn't any pot around. Saturday night they ate out, went bar hopping, ran into people Jim knew, did more coke and sold more coke.

Sunday afternoon, still raining, with the television on, Christine wanted to go for a walk, but there was nowhere to go. She was to start her job tomorrow and she looked forward to it. She remembered she had to get some clothes for work, and asked Jim if he'd take her shopping.

He looked up from the TV, some animal show about cougars. "Sure. Gotta shower and shave first." He then tapped out some powder from his silver canister onto the tray he used for chopping coke and said, as much to himself as to Christine, "Getting low, gonna have to hunt some down today." He stroked out four lines. Christine didn't want any, and he inhaled all of the cocaine. Rubbing his nostrils clean, to himself,

"That's the stuff." He flashed Christine a half smile and got up to get ready.

While Jim showered, Christine remembered he hadn't said anything about the job at the Saab dealership. She thought he was supposed to hear about it this weekend. She decided not to ask, just in case he didn't want her to know.

An hour and a half later, Christine was back in the apartment, alone. After she had bought a couple pairs of black slacks and three white blouses at some mall, Jim had told her he wanted to hit some places and see if there was any coke around. She was already annoyed with him—he had paced and rummaged and slouched and grumbled the entire time she tried to find the clothes she needed—and she had no desire whatsoever to roam the bars looking for drugs. Instead she bought a Burlington Free Press and a Dunkin Donuts coffee at the mall and decided to hang out. Alone. Settling into his chair with the paper and the coffee, she decided she'd made the right choice returning to the quiet apartment.

Sometime past seven, Jim returned. The first thing he said to Christine, "Nothing, jack-shit. Everybody's dry or holding onto what they got." He shook his head, stood over her, smelled like gin and tonic.

She had fallen asleep in his chair. Barely awake, she listened to him and could care less about what he said. She asked, "Are we still going to Pearl Street?" She had wanted to go back to the bistro all weekend to check it out some more. Earlier that afternoon, he had promised they would go there for dinner.

Short tempered, "Yeah, you ready to go?"

Does it look like I'm ready to go? She shot back, "Give me a couple minutes."

When she got up he flopped into the chair and pulled out the tray that held the razor blade and straw. She heard him chop the coke before she was out of the room. When she came back, dressed, he was watching another animal show and the tray was put away. He hadn't even asked if she wanted any. Not that she did, *but still.*

She stepped in front of the television. "Let's go."

Christine ordered osso bucca for the first time, and loved it. She had a glass of Rioja with the braised veal shank and stewed vegetables, using her new fake ID for proof of age. She'd have to remember her new birthday when she filled out her application tomorrow. Watching the staff at work, much more relaxed than Friday's lunch shift, she picked up a few important details. Jim held his own with the conversation, but watched every new customer that came in. She figured he was looking for a drug buddy. She decided all of his friends were probably cokeheads. It would have been more annoying if she wasn't enjoying her food and thinking about her new job.

They hit a few bars after dinner, had a drink or two at each. Jim searched, talked people up, and came out with nothing. Christine rolled with it until around midnight when she took Jim's arm—they were sitting in a dive bar, their drinks just finished—and told him, "I've got work tomorrow, let's go."

He looked around the near empty bar, "Yeah, sure." He wasn't happy, she didn't care.

***

Jeff, the manager, scanned Christine's completed application, set it aside. "Claire's the hostess today, you'll be shadowing her. Tomorrow you're on your own. It's going to get really busy, so don't get in her way. It's up to Claire whether she splits her tips with you. Any questions?"

Christine had none.

The hostess and a couple waitresses converged at a table in the dining area, setting up: they filled salt and pepper shakers, folded cloth napkins. A waiter set the tables with silverware. Jeff introduced Christine to Claire and left. The hostess looked bothered when she told Christine she would show her around after she finished her setup. The waitresses introduced themselves as Wanda and Louise. They seemed nice. They smiled.

Christine pulled up a chair and reached for a napkin from the pile. "Need help with those?"

Claire showed Christine around the restaurant, introduced her to the waiter, Claude, and the cooks. She didn't bother with the busboy or the dishwasher, but Christine introduced herself anyway because it seemed rude not to, and because she knew they could make or break her. They looked alright, although the dishwasher smelled like last night's booze and she was pretty sure the busboy was stoned. The hostess briefly went over the waitress station: its silverware drawers, water pitchers, glasses, napkins, coffee cups and saucers, and the built in cooler by the station that held the butter pats, creamers, condiments. Christine was to make sure the wait-staff had what they needed. If they ran low on glasses or silverware, she was to tell the dishwasher. If they needed something brought to the table, they would tell her. She was to set the tables, if the busboy fell behind, and he probably would. If he really fell behind, Christine was to bus the tables as well. In addition, she was to seat customers when Claire took over her shift.

They returned to the wait-staff and finished the setup, Christine restocked sugar and Sweet 'N Low packets. A pair of businesswomen entered the restaurant and Christine watched Claire glide to them, menus in hand. She seated them in Claude's section. Two more business people came in and a tourist couple, then another group of business people. Claire efficiently guided the stream of people. Within fifteen minutes the restaurant was full of noise and motion, the staff focused on their roles.

The waitrons flew past Christine with their orders and food, and snagged her with various requests: water refills, coffee refills, ketchup, butter, clean silverware. The busboy ambled along. Everything was a crazy blur. At one point, there was a line at the door, and several empty tables that hadn't been cleared. Claire shot Christine a look.

She responded, grabbed a washrag from the busboy to finish a table cleanup and told him, "Go get started on table six. I'll be right behind you."

She wiped and set the table, caught up to the busboy, just as he finished, and kept up behind him, until the tables were full again. Christine felt the sweat on the back of her neck as Wanda asked her to take a plate of butter to table nine. All the noise and motion sorted into a pattern, and Christine loved it. An hour later, a second wave was seated and most had placed their orders. Some new customers arrived, but things had begun to slow down.

Claire came up to Christine, handed her some menus, "Here, you take these."

The hostess then disappeared. Christine was on her own. *No problem.* She handled the rest of the shift. Watching the last couple of tables finish up, she was joined by Wanda, who remarked, "Good job."

Christine beamed inside, thanked the woman, and added, "I'm not used to working a lunch rush like that."

The waitress smiled and told her she did fine.

Yes!

At the end of the shift, Christine sat with the waitrons, as they restocked condiments and rehashed the day. She got to know her co-workers as they told their own stories: Claude, in his twenties, gay, kind of anxious, his partner a professor in the UVM biology department: Louise, a local, plain, her father a farmer, her husband drove a bakery delivery truck: Wanda, hard edged, in her thirties, had lived with her boyfriend for the past few years, talked about this great Louise Erdrich book, *Love Medicine:* Claire, chilly, was switching to the dinner shift "to make some real money." Her husband was a grad student studying political science and no, she hadn't liked *Love Medicine*. Christine would read it anyway. The dinner shift started to arrive. The lunch shift was almost finished with their duties. Jeff stopped by their table and told Christine to be there tomorrow.

A thrill surged through her. "Okay. Thanks."

Christine jumped into the Saab – Jim had been waiting for her in the parking lot – she gushed, "God, it was great!"

"That's good." His voice was flat.

Even behind his sunglasses, Christine could see he was high, *whatever.* She continued, described the people she met, especially Wanda. "You'd like her, she's really cool." And the rush, "you wouldn't believe it, it's like you get into this really intense flow, like your body's doing its own thing and it's all working out." And the money, "it's only fifteen bucks, but it was a Monday and besides I had to split the tips with the other hostess." Jim didn't say anything, which sucked. She asked him, "So, what've you been up to?"

"Nothing much, hanging out." "Hear anything about the Saab job?"

He didn't look at her, but she noticed his jaw grind before he answered, "Nah."

That's it? She didn't say anything, they drove in silence. It was sunny, hot.

Christine decided she wanted to go to the beach for a swim.

Jim just said, "Sure."

Christine's body gently hummed from the sun, the swim and the shower she had taken when she got back from the beach. She saw that it was just past five, and figured her mother would be up, starting her day, so she called.

"Hey mom, guess what? I started my new job today. I'm a hostess at this fancy restaurant." She filled Lynne in on the details of her first shift.

Lynne caught the excitement in her daughter's voice. "Sounds wonderful, dear." Christine heard her mother masking pain. "Did dad call?"

Lynne hesitated. She didn't want to ruin things, but answered, "Yes, yesterday. He wanted to talk to you. I told him you had already left. For that summer camp you came up with. He wanted your phone number. I told him I didn't know it offhand, but I'd have you call him. He asked me the name of the camp you're supposedly working at. I didn't know what to say. I made something up like Camp Evergreen. I didn't know what to say."

"Mom, don't worry. I'll call him right after I get off the phone with you. Listen, here's the story...I'll tell him we go off camping a lot, like for days at a time, so I can't really be reached, and can't call either. I'll give him a phone number close to the number of a real place, but I'll tell him they really don't want parents calling. I'll tell him the Camp Evergreen thing is just like a nickname, what everyone calls the program. Alright? I'll let you know the name and number that I give him, alright?"

Lynne's voice was thin. "Call him. Please."

Pissed. Didn't her mother hear what she just said? She kept her annoyance out of her tone. "Sure, mom. I will." *He's got to leave us alone!*

***

Mark removed the geraniums from their plastic trays and transplanted them to the larger pots, working the soil around each of their root balls. Nancy and the baby were off visiting Nancy's sister. He tried to enjoy the quiet, the warm evening light, the soil in his fingers, but he couldn't stop thinking about that damn phone call with Lynne yesterday, with her saying she couldn't remember Chris' number, that he couldn't call it anyway, they could only call out, that she couldn't remember the number for the camp's main office and the camp name: *Camp Evergreen*. After the call, he searched and found nothing in the telephone directory that was anything close to that ridiculous name. Obviously, she was hiding something.

He had called Blum's office as soon as he arrived at work. Blum's assistant called him back with the name of a private investigator. Mark hadn't called the referral, in case he was overreacting. He knew himself well enough to know he could get worked up pretty easily, although he was better than he used to be. But no, this was all too weird—he decided he'd call the PI in the morning. He wiped the dirt off his hands and went inside to freshen up his vodka and tonic and take a piss. As he cut a wedge of lime for his drink, the phone rang.

When he hung up the phone, Mark was satisfied. Chris sounded great. She said she loved working at the camp. She said she'd call him when she could, but that they were often in the woods for days at a time. She told him they would definitely get together when she got back to Branford at the end of the summer. She said she loved him. He stood by the phone and realized he was smiling. She always made him feel good. He wouldn't need the PI after all.

CHAPTER 9

Friday afternoon: Lynne sat in a therapist's waiting room, but she wanted to leave. She had called for the appointment because she was terrified Mark would find out Christine was in Burlington, however that was no longer a problem since Christine had spoken to her father. She didn't want to stay and talk about her screwed up life with another stranger, but Hansson had told Lynne he knew this woman from the Rape Crisis Center and that she might help her. She stared hard at the woven rag rug in the waiting room.

The door to the office opened and a tall, fifty year old woman stepped across the threshold. The woman extended her hand. "Hello, Lynne? I'm Miranda. Won't you come in?" Lynne took the hand; it was warm, strong. Miranda held her gaze. Lynne felt her calm demeanor.

Seated in Miranda's office, Lynne sensed her surroundings in immediate detail: the shifting light and shadow on the wall, caused by the lace curtains and leaves outside the window, the tempered click of the mantle clock, the ornate figures carved into the aged bookshelf, the nubbed texture of the upholstered chair's arm, where she rested her hand, and the scent of lavender soap on Miranda. The woman seated across from Lynne was upright, but not stiff. She may have once been slender, but was now fuller yet trim. Her hands rested on her lap, comfortably. A wedding band caught the sun's light. Her fingers were interlaced, tan against the light blue of her summer shift. The shift draped to her knee, her legs crossed at the ankles. Lynne looked to Miranda's face. Her mouth was firm, yet soft. Her eyes were lined at the corners, suggesting many smiles over the years.

The woman's forehead was creased by age and concern. Light brown hair, threaded with gray, framed Miranda's tan face and neck and rested at her shoulders. Her eyes were deep brown. She asked Lynne why she was there.

Lynne wasn't ready for the question. "Why did I make this appointment?" She shifted in her seat. "I have a daughter... Christine. She's away from home and she's living with a man. Her father doesn't know. He's been looking for her. He'll be furious when he finds out." Lynne twisted her hands as she spoke.

"Christine is how old?"

"She's sixteen, will be seventeen next month."

"And how old is the man she is living with?"

Lynne answered, "Twenty."

"Are you separated or divorced from her father?" "Yes. Divorced."

"And you don't want the father to know. Christine doesn't want her father to know she's living with this man?"

"No, I mean yes, we don't."

"What will happen if he finds out?"

Panic gripped Lynne. *If he finds out!* "He'd take Christine away."

Miranda, gently. "Do what you need to do to protect your daughter and yourself."

Lynne realized she needed this woman. Miranda then asked how Christine ended up living with this man. Without hesitation, she told about the morning Frank punched the kitchen wall. She described her relationship with Frank, then her relationship with Mark. The years of abuse and neglect. All the crap that pushed

Christine out the door. Lynne paused, shook her head and whispered, "I didn't know. This is hard." Miranda acknowledged how hard it must be for Lynne, yet assured her it would be worth trying.

***

Friday afternoon. Off her last shift of the week with a pile of tip money, Christine slipped into the Saab. 'Hey!" She leaned over to kiss Jim's taut lips. When she leaned back, he told her he got the job at the dealership. He didn't sound very excited.

"That's great!"

He shrugged. She didn't understand.

He told her it pretty much sucked because they gave him lousy shifts: opening every day, Monday through Saturday, nine to five. He started the car, "Who the hell buys a car at nine in the morning. You'd think they could at least give me an evening or two!"

He shifted hard and the black convertible shot out of the parking lot.

Christine wondered. What did he expect? He was, after all, the new guy. "So, tell them you want some evening shifts. Be aggressive, they'll like that from a salesman." He looked at her like he understood, "Yeah."

She twisted in her seat to face him as he wove the Saab through traffic and smiled. "We should celebrate. The end of my first week. Your new job. The fact that it's Friday." Yeah, she was happy. It had been a great week. She had made plenty of money in tips. The work was a kick ass adrenaline high and the women she worked with were a lot of fun—talking about their boyfriends, about Jeff hitting on all the help, about movies, books and music. Wanda had lent Christine a copy of *Love Medicine*, which she had devoured. After their shift Thursday, the waitresses and Christine had hit the downtown shops and a café, where they gossiped over iced teas and iced coffees. It was great.

The evenings were different. She and Jim would go out to eat, have some drinks, but all the while, he looked for cocaine. She didn't like most of the people he chatted up. It was boring. Obviously, he hadn't scored any coke today, otherwise he would have done lines in the parking lot, and he'd be all cheerful and shit. She figured it would be the same routine tonight, which sucked because she really felt like celebrating.

Then it hit her*: Montreal!* Two of the waitresses, the college girls, said Montreal was a blast. The city had clubs that rocked all night long, great food, all kinds of restaurants; everybody speaking French, like it was Europe. It beat moping around Burlington all weekend, scrounging for cocaine.

While stopped at a red light, Christine leaned over, rubbed Jim's thigh and felt him go hard immediately. "Let's go to Montreal tomorrow and stay overnight."

She had him. He murmured, "Yeah, sure."

***

The late morning light shone harsh in the apartment kitchen and on Jim and Christine. It beat against their hungover brains, certainly a rough way to wake up. After some orange juice, coffee and toast, Christine started to feel better. Across the table, Jim didn't look so good. Slumped in the chair, he nursed his coffee.

She asked, "You still want to go to Montreal?"

Squinting against the brightness, he didn't look like he wanted to go anywhere. "Yeah, sure. Just give me some time to wake up."

Good enough. She headed off to shower and pack. As she undressed in the bedroom, she heard him talking on the phone.

He greeted Christine with a broad smile when she came out of the shower. "Excellent news, I got a tip on some blow. We can pick it up on the way out of town."

She said nothing. So, he was happy now. He wouldn't be in a bad mood in Montreal. He wouldn't ruin the trip because, he had his coke. It was pretty fucked up, she decided. A couple of hours later, they swung by a row house in South Burlington, picked up an eighth of an ounce of cocaine, did a few lines and then, flew up the I-89 to Canada. Christine glowed as the convertible swept her along in wind and sun.

The eastern horizon lightened to dawn when they stumbled into the hotel. A techno beat still pounded Christine's entire body as the coke wore off. She was ragged and exhausted, but it had been fantastic. Partying all night long with all kinds of people, Jim had totally been into it. She watched him fumble with the room key, his head bent down.

She snuggled into him. "I had a great time." "Mmmm."

They stumbled into the room and collapsed into bed.

The phone screamed. Christine slapped around until she found it. The front desk called, telling her it was past eleven o'clock and they needed to check out. Her brain was scrambled, her eyes burned harsh.

"Rise and shine, they're kicking us out." She told Jim. He gazed at her through one bloody eyeball.

He stirred, reached for his jacket lying on the floor and croaked, "We need some get up and go." Fumbling around in the pockets, he didn't find what he was looking for. "Man we did a lot of blow last night." He lurched out of bed, lumbered naked over to his overnight bag, found what was left of the cocaine. "Not much, maybe we should bang it." He pulled a syringe from the bag.

Christine rasped, "No!"

He looked back at her, stopped.

"I don't want to. I don't want you to." She couldn't explain to him the grip in her guts.

He kept looking at her, motionless. "OK." He put the syringe back in the bag.

Is he kidding? "We can't bring that. We're crossing the freaking U.S. border!" Jim looked annoyed. She didn't care. "We're busted for sure if that's in the car." He didn't say anything, just looked at her like she made no sense.

"Leave it here. I'm serious."

He took the syringe out of his bag.

After brunch, they hurtled to Vermont with Jim flying on the last of the cocaine. Christine hadn't done any. She had wanted to relax, take their time at an outdoor café, lounge over coffee in the sweet midday sunlight, suck on the last of the hashish they had picked up the night before. Instead, Jim was too wired to eat. He stared at her as she ate her omelet. His leg shook the entire time. They left as soon as she finished her meal, a sliver of hash tucked into her cheek.

The American border guards tore the car apart. They found nothing. Jim didn't say anything about it when they got back on the road. Christine didn't bring it up either. He seemed kind of pissy. *So what* They would have been really screwed if the cops found his works. She looked over at him driving, one hand on the wheel, the wind blowing his black hair back, and realized, he could be really fucking stupid. He should be thanking her for saving their asses.

She started to think about him shooting up, but she broke that thought of. She turned back to face the long highway ahead, the sun and the wind.

CHAPTER 10

Thursday night. Christine looked up from her book, *Tar Baby*, and noticed the time: just past six - thirty. She was deep into the book and surprised it had gotten that late. *Where is he?* Since he had started the job Monday, Jim would come home around six every night. He got off work at five, but would tell Christine he'd been with some of the guys from the dealership before coming home. Last night she had said fine, just call and let her know when he'd be home. He hadn't called.

Whatever, she liked the book she was reading. Wanda had lent it to her. She liked the quiet, having the time to herself, before Jim would blow in and grab her for dinner and drinks. She picked up a half smoked joint from the ashtray. Lit it. Took a couple hits. She liked having some pot. Wanda had sold her a quarter ounce the day before, and it was nice.

Jim had been kind of weird about it when she rolled up a joint last night, asking where she got it. He hadn't smoked any before they went out. He said he didn't want to get stupid. She explained it wasn't that strong, but he still didn't want any. Instead, he chopped a few lines. He said he liked his edge. Then he told Christine he could make a ton of money selling coke at work. The salesmen were dying for it. He said he was thinking about it. Remembering their conversation, she took another hit, *what is he, a fucking idiot?* If word got out to the wrong people, he'd be screwed. She should have said something last night, should have told him to get real. But she hadn't. *Like it would matter*. She picked the book up and returned to her reading.

That's when she heard banging out in the hallway and wondered what was happening. Something bashed around outside the door, muffled voices. The door flew open.

Jim, followed by a couple men, careened through the doorway.

Loud, "Hey Chris, look who I ran into after work! Remember Eddie and Murph?

At the party, back in Branford?" The other two came up next to him in the living room. They reeked of beer, their eyes bugged.

Of course she remembered the two creeps. "Sure." Eddie gave her a "Hey, how ya doin'?"

She didn't answer.

Jim didn't seem to notice. "We figured we'd come back here and do a little partying."

Flat, "Sure." What was she supposed to say? Two of the biggest lowlifes she had ever met were standing in her living room, loaded. *This sucks!*

Jim kept it going, "Grab a seat guys while I put these beers in the fridge?" The two men looked at Christine as she stared back at them.

Murph called out to Jim heading down the hall. "Hey Jimmy, what'cha got to eat?" With that the two quickly followed Jim to the kitchen.

Christine went to the bedroom, shut the door, and threw herself on the bed with blind anger. *Does he have any idea how incredibly rude it is to show up loaded with a couple loaded creeps with like no warning? Is he seriously that clueless?* The music in the living room cranked up, and the morons were practically yelling at each other. She didn't have to put up with this bullshit.

"I'm going out." She announced as she entered the living room.

Wanda was on her way to pick her up—thank god she was home. In the living room, she froze. There was Jim, tying off one of the buttheads, while the other was cooking up coke at the kitchen table. She grabbed her bag and jean jacket, bolted for the door.

Jim kept his eyes on Murph's vein. "Yeah?" He responded, clearly distracted, like she shouldn't interrupt him.

As the door slammed behind her, Christine heard one of the assholes say, "So, what's with her, man?"

And Jim answer, "Hell if I know."

Fuck you!

Christine climbed into the battered Subaru as soon as it came to a stop at the curb, "Get me out of here."

As the car pulled away, Wanda asked her what was up.

Christine shot off that she was pissed at Jim for coming home late, wasted, with a couple assholes.

"Yeah, that's no good."

"No, it's not." She asked her friend if she had dragged her away from anything.

"Nah, me and Ron were just hanging out, watching the tube. Wanna go someplace and bitch?"

Christine said, yeah.

Wanda handed her a stone pipe packed with a marijuana bud. "Here you go." It was good to be with this woman.

A few minutes later, the two made their way into a dive in North Burlington: a bar, a few stools, a few tables, the Red Sox on the television, a noisy air conditioner pushing around stale air. A mixed age crowd talked or watched the game, and some just drank Budweiser on tap. Wanda ordered a couple drafts and they grabbed a table.

Christine continued the conversation they had begun in the car. "So, it's like all the time with the coke: he wants it, he's looking for it, he's doing it, he's looking for it again. And when he runs out, he's like, miserable. When he's got it, then fine, everything's good, but even that can kinda sucks with some of the people we end up hanging out with. Bunch of cokeheads."

She stopped before she got into Jim shooting up or selling. She didn't want to get into it. Fucked up shit like that gets around and she could be out of luck. Wanda was probably cool, *but you never know*. She took a sip of the flat beer.

Wanda nodded, “Gawd, a coked up car salesman. I feel for you.”

They laughed, but it was serious. Christine had to know. “I mean what the hell Wanda, what’s it gonna be? Am I supposed to put up with this crap, and what if I don’t? What if he can’t knock it off? here’s that leave me?”

The other woman straightened up, looked into her glass as she spoke. “From what you’re telling me, sounds like Jim might have a real problem with the coke. Maybe he’s gonna have a hard time dealing with it.” Her voice was hushed. She looked up at Christine. “I know. I can’t go near the stuff. Grabs me and won’t let go. When I’m doin’ coke, I don’t want nothing else. You hear what I’m saying?” She cleared her throat, “You’ve got to let him know where you stand and he’s got to decide, is the way it sounds to me.”

Christine heard experience talking. She just wanted things to be good.

Wanda nodded, “Sure you do. And they will be, just maybe not the way you originally planned.” Dead serious. “Chris, you’ve gotta take care of yourself.”

“I will.”

“You get in a jam, you let me know. Need anything, you let me know. Some bucks, a place to crash, a night out. Anything, understand?” She reached across the table and placed her hand on Christine’s. “You hear me?”

Christine smiled, “Yeah. Thanks.”

***

Christine watched him sleep. Sunday morning was quiet. They had to talk.

Thursday night was too much; she had let him know that. He said he got it. Maybe he did, he didn't bring anyone home Friday. They had gone out and it was the same thing: drinking, doing lines, catching some music. Saturday though, they had gone to a Fourth of July barbecue at the home of one of the other Saab salesmen. There were a few other couples. Jim disappeared with some of them, did coke for sure and came back lit up. Everyone had been intense, drinking hard.

What did they think of her? She was so much younger than the other women. None of them had talked to her. She saw the way they had looked at him—he was the man with the cocaine. And at her—she was his piece of ass. Some of them had disappeared without Jim, so he must have been selling. He was going to get busted. *I know it. And why should I care? He can do what he wants.*

It wasn't that simple. She watched him breathing. She wanted to be with him. She didn't want him hurt. She remembered Thursday night, when she was leaving: the smell of the chemicals, the sight of him tying off that guy. She didn't want him shooting up.

She didn't want him dead. Her heart ached deep. When he woke up, she'd have him promise he wouldn't shoot up anymore, ever. He had to do that for her. Otherwise she couldn't stay with him.

He saw her watching him when he first opened his eyes. "Hey."

"Hey."

"What's up?"

"Nothing. Just thinking."

He didn't say anything.

She had to say, "I'm scared, the shooting up. You could..." She looked away, her heart ached. "You have to stop."

He smiled some charm at her. "Hey, don't worry, nothing bad's gonna happen." She didn't smile. "Promise me you'll stop."

He looked at her on the pillow across from him, her eyes wet with tears. "I don't know if I can do that. I'll promise you today. That's the best I can do."

What kind of lame crap is that!? She didn't call him on it. If she did it would all be over, and she wasn't ready for that. She needed to believe things could work out. Maybe he was right, the day-at-a-time thing; maybe that's the best anyone can do. When he brushed a tear from the corner of her eye, she wanted him to be right.

"Alright, promise me today."

CHAPTER 11

Monday, July 11, 1987

Christine woke suddenly. *What?* Jim lay next to her, asleep, and he smelled stale from last night. He'd gone out—he hadn't said where he was going and she didn't care, so long as he didn't bring any clowns home in the middle of the night. She remembered him sliding into bed a few hours before, around three o'clock. She hadn't roused. He lay motionless beneath the sheet. Something wasn't right. The new dawn silence weighed heavy, like the stillness before a thunderclap.

A fist smashed against the front door, shattering the morning. Christine screamed.

"Police! Open up!"

In the next instant, the door flew off its hinges with a spray of splintering panelboard. Eight Burlington police officers and Vermont State troopers swarmed through the doorway, handguns drawn. They charged through the small apartment, a riot of slamming bodies. Two troopers burst into the bedroom. Revolvers pointed at Christine, who sat bolt upright clutching her T-shirt's neckline and at Jim, who leaned on an elbow.

Shouting, "Up! Hands up goddammit!" Christine stared at the gun aimed at her face.

Two more officers charged into the room. The first two approached the bed. "Hands up goddammit!"

She threw her hands in the air. She didn't see what Jim did. She couldn't take her eyes off the revolver pointed at her. She felt him being yanked up by one of the officers.

"Hands behind your head!"

They were still yelling—these guys were crazy wired. They'd waste her in a heartbeat if she messed up. Christine froze, her terror locked down her every muscle.

A cop at the door. "They're in here!" More cops, more guns. *Fuck!*

The closest trooper yanked Christine out of the bed by her bicep. He lifted her with one jerk and slammed her against the wall next to the headboard. Her arm twisted high behind her back, her face pressed sideways against the wall. She screamed in pain, heard something smash in another room. *Fucking Jimmy. Fucking moron.* She had no idea what Jimmy was holding, or where he kept it. Maybe nothing would turn up – god, she hoped so. Pain ripped up her arm, her shoulder, her neck, clawed at her skull. This cop pissed her off, jacking her up like this.

A calmer voice through the confusion. "No one else here, chief."

Someone in charge spoke from bedroom doorway. "Alright fellas, let's ease up.

This one's gotta stick, so keep it clean, you hear me? You read 'em their rights yet?

"No chief, not yet."

"They say anything?" "Nope."

Someone murmured. "Break it down guys. It's all gotta be good." From the living room. "Bingo!"

"Falcone, what's it look like?"

The voice from the living room. "Coke. About an ounce." Christine died inside. *That's it, all over.*

From the other side of the bedroom came a muted voice. "You really fucked up, asshole. Ray Dugan's kid is dead and it looks like you done it."

Christine winced, her face pressed against the wall. She heard Jim moan. The trooper lowered her bent arm, cuffed it—yanked her left arm behind her, cuffed it and began, "You have the right to remain silent....". She heard the voice across the room, recite the Miranda warning to Jim a beat behind. She heard Jim bleat. "I want to talk to a lawyer."

The trooper, next to her ear, "You got something you wanna say?"

She didn't answer. She didn't want to say anything to anyone. *Fuck you.* "She say anything about wanting a lawyer?" Another cop, behind Christine. "Nah."

The new cop, to Christine, "You can sit down if you want."

She turned from the wall to face the bastard who had roughed her up, and the other cop, and all the craziness beyond them—cops everywhere. She caught sight of Jimmy being led out of the bedroom in handcuffs, a trooper held him by the bicep. Just her and these cops now. The bastard checked out Christine, who wore only a T-shirt and panties. He kept looking until he was finished. If she sat down, he'd be looking at her crotch. A drip of fear began down her clenched throat.

"Okay, stand if you want." The new cop spoke. "There's something I want you to know before they haul you off. You and your friend are in deep shit. There's a kid dead. Not any kid, Ray Dugan's kid. Dugan's the State's Attorney, the guy in charge of prosecuting scum like you. He's ripshit right now. Swears he's gonna fry your ass.

Maybe if you help us with the case..." He pulled a picture out of his shirt pocket, held it up in front of Christine's face: a dead man on a table. "You know him?"

She saw a dead man. She didn't say anything.

"No? How about this? Anyone you know?" He put another picture in front of her, a yearbook picture.

Jesus Christ! Christine couldn't breathe, the blood drained from her through the floor; it was Jim's skuzzy friend, *Eddie*! She flashed on him eyeing her at Megan's party, donut powder around his mouth. She couldn't speak, her head spun wild.

"The kid died from an overdose. Cocaine. We got it on good information that he got it from your boyfriend. We want to know where your boyfriend got it."

Stunned, she stared at the cop, his words came at her through a long pipe. "Christine. Your name's Christine right? According to this driver's license we found. You have a chance to save your butt, understand? We just need you to answer some questions back at the station, alright?"

I don't know anything. She remained mute.

The other cop, the bastard, impatiently broke in. "I think you want to tell us what you know, like where's the rest of the coke, like who was your boyfriend with last night, like when was the last time you saw Eddie Dugan alive or dead." The bastard was leaning in on Christine, his face inches from hers. Hissing at her, "And if you don't, Dugan's gonna slap you with obstruction of justice charges, and then you can kiss your life goodbye 'cause they're gonna throw your ass in jail for a long, long time."

The cop's face swam in front of Christine. She smelled a sick meaty odor coming out of his pores. She couldn't breathe, but managed to say to his face, "I want a lawyer."

The trooper straightened up. "Fine. Just remember this, you and your lawyer better help us out with this case. Because otherwise you're screwed."

The other cop turned to an officer with brass insignia on his lapel. Christine realized the man had watched the entire time. "Chief, we got nothing. She's asked to speak to a lawyer."

The chief called into the living room. "Anderson!"

A female officer appeared beside him. He nodded at Christine. "Take the suspect into custody. Full cavity search before you leave the premises."

The woman nodded, looked at Christine. Christine saw hate in the woman's eyes. "Yes, sir."

***

Christine arrived at the Burlington Police station lockup a little after seven that morning. As soon as she got there, she called a phone number an officer had given her. "Hello, is this a lawyer? I've been arrested, and I'm being held, and I don't know what's going to happen to me." Her voice cracked as she finished. It wasn't until then that Christine felt like she could cry. She held back.

A calm voice told her his name and that he was a public defender. He asked Christine her name and she told him.

"Where are you, Christine?"

"The Burlington Police station, I think." She looked around the waiting room for a clue. From the doorway, officer Anderson nodded yes.

"Alright Christine, it sounds like you're being held in custody. A prosecutor is probably going to talk to the officers who arrested you and decide whether you should be charged with a crime. If he decides you shouldn't be charged, you should be released sometime this morning. If he decides you should be charged, and the judge agrees, you'll be arraigned, meaning charges will be brought against you in court. Arraignments will start around one this afternoon. If the charges are serious, if there's a felony, you have the right to have a lawyer defend you. If you can't afford a lawyer, the court will appoint one for you, a public defender."

"It's serious." She wasn't going to cry. "Someone needs to tell my mother what's happening."

The man said he would. Christine gave him her home phone number. The clock on the wall read 7:25. Her mother would be getting home from work. "Tell her I'm okay." That was all she could say. The lawyer promised he would. She didn't understand what was going to happen to her except that it sounded like things would be decided soon.

"What's your name?"

"My name's Sam Dreyfus."

"Thank you, Mr. Dreyfus." She hung up.

Officer Anderson led Christine back to her cell in the basement of the police station. A stench of piss, booze and grime rose to meet her at the top of the stairs.. As she passed those men, nearly twenty of them among three cells taunted her. "Hey fuck me, baby." "C'mon suck my dick, baby". "Right here, baby." She stared straight ahead, feeling like they had their filthy hands all over her.

Her cell, the last in the row, held one other prisoner, an emaciated female, sprawled face down on a cot, unconscious and smeared in her own vomit. *Junkie.*

Christine sat on the edge of the other cot in the cell. Her anus, swollen from Officer Anderson's rough search, throbbed against the cot's metal frame, her vagina throbbed. She hurt deep from the probing fingers, deeper than she knew. The stench surrounded her, gagged her. Eyes shut, she had a vision of her mother receiving the news of her arrest; her mother breaking down. She could see Wanda and the others starting work, wondering about her. Tears burned down Christine's cheeks.

***

The Corolla hit the interstate ramp going fifty. Lynne had to reach Christine, had to see that she was safe. She had her checkbook, showing a balance of two hundred thirty dollars, and directions to the courthouse. She floored it when she hit the interstate. The man on the phone, a public defender, had told her Christine sounded alright. He had said she would be arraigned that afternoon, and she might need a lawyer. He had told her he didn't know anything else. The old Toyota rattled and shook as it approached eighty five. Lynne didn't notice. She wiped her tears away and kept her eyes on the road. She had to see her baby safe.

She found the courthouse, she found the court clerk—the person she needed to see, according to the security guard at the building's entrance. The clerk, an untidy woman in her late fifties and busy with a huge looming man, ignored Lynne at the counter. The clerk and the man were going back and forth, making no sense to Lynne. The man seemed angry, frustrated, then silenced. The clerk was firm. She had unflinchingly prevailed. He moved on.

As soon as he turned away from the counter, Lynne threw out. "My daughter is Christine Bancroft. I got a call that she's in jail, and she is going to be in court this afternoon."

The woman across the counter didn't look at Lynne until she had finished returning the huge man's papers in a file. "And what can I do for you?" She asked as if she had asked that same question a dozen times that day, thousands of times in her life.

Lynne nearly burst out of her skin; wasn't it obvious what she wanted? "I need to see my daughter. Christine Bancroft."

"She's not in the holding cell. Have you tried the lockup at the police station?"

Lynne, confused and agitated, responded. "No, I haven't. I was told she would be here."

"If she's being arraigned, that's not till this afternoon. That's when she'll be here."

Lynne noted the clock against the back wall read just past ten.

The woman offered, "Listen, you might want to try the police station, it's just down the street. She might be there. If not, come back around twelve thirty and I'll see if I've got any paperwork on your daughter. What did you say her name was?"

Lynne watched, grateful, as the woman wrote Christine's name on a yellow legal pad.

"I'm sorry ma'am. No visitors.," said the chunky officer.

"But the woman at court said Christine might be here. I need to see her, I'm her mother."

"Like I said, no visitors, ma'am."

"Can you tell me if she's here?" He said he couldn't.

"But the lawyer said—" Lynne stopped. "Can you tell me where the public defender's office is?"

The officer gave her that information. Thank god it was nearby.

Once she arrived, Lynne pulled the crumpled piece of paper from her pants pocket, read the name she had taken down that morning. "Sam Dreyfus?"

The young woman at the battered government surplus desk asked if Lynne had an appointment. Before she could answer, a short, raven haired man with a deeply creased face stepped into the reception area. "I'm Sam Dreyfus, and you are?"

Relieved, "You called me this morning, told me my daughter's in jail. Her name's Christine Bancroft. My name's Lynne."

Dreyfus invited Lynne into his office: a cubby-hole half buried beneath stacks of manila file folders and loose papers on every flat surface. "Please." He cleared some files from a chair with a broken arm and indicated Lynne should sit. He asked what he could do for her.

"I can't find my daughter, Mr. Dreyfus. She's not at court. And they won't tell me whether she's at the police station. I thought maybe you might know." Lynne heard her desperation. She pressed her palms into her thighs.

"Mrs. Bancroft...Lynne, you might not be able to see your daughter until she's brought to court for the arraignment. They don't let friends or family visit prisoners in the lockup. Otherwise, the place would be a madhouse."

Fear ripped through Lynne. She blurted, "But she's only sixteen! I'm her mother!"

Dreyfus' brow furrowed. "She's sixteen? If that's the case, she should be in a juvenile facility, not the lockup. There must be some mistake." The lawyer was up and leading Lynne from his office. "Let's get this straightened out."

The officer at the desk was not pleased to see Lynne back, and not pleased to see Dreyfus with her. Ignoring Lynne, she asked, "Sam, what are you doing here?"

"I received a call from a juvenile, Christine Bancroft, this morning. Her mother is here to see her."

The cop blinked, swallowed hard. There weren't supposed to be any juveniles downstairs.

"Is Christine Bancroft in custody here?" Dreyfus inquired. The cop tried to stay gruff. "Yes she is, but—"

Pressing, "In that case her mother would like to see her. Now."

Descending the dank cinder block stairwell behind the officer, and with Dreyfus beside her, Lynne held her breath against the stench and dread that thickened with each step. . At the foot of the stairs, she saw Christine at the barred door of the cell furthest from her. Christine grasped the bars. She looked to her mother as if she had been waiting. *Christine!* Lynne rushed past the policeman.

"No contact!" The cop barked.

She stopped a foot away from Christine. All of the noise and stench dissolved, there was nothing except her daughter in front of her. She furiously searched Christine's face for signs of harm. Her daughter appeared small and shaken, but otherwise undamaged.

Christine's heart flew. Filled with relief, she couldn't stop herself from crying. "I'm so sorry, Mom."

Lynne ached fiercely as tears welled up. To herself as much as to Christine, she whispered. "It's alright. It will be alright."

Dreyfus took Lynne by the elbow. "Maybe we should go now. You'll see Christine in a couple hours."

Lynne wasn't sure what was happening as they she and Dreyfus walked the hard pavement under a pounding mid-morning sun.

What was she supposed to do now? Lynne realized she didn't know why Christine was in jail. She asked.

Dreyfus hesitated. "I haven't seen the charges, but my office has information your daughter was in an apartment that was the subject of a search warrant this morning, where a felony quantity of cocaine was found." Dreyfus didn't mention the Dugan kid's death – he didn't want to speculate.

Lynne stopped listening. The sun bleached her vision white. Her head spun around the edges of a blanched emptiness. Her knees buckled. She felt a hand take hold of her arm to steady her. She heard a voice from away, "Are you alright?" "I'm fine." She managed. Her surroundings and Dreyfus' concerned face returned to her. "I think I need to sit down, maybe some water."

***

That morning, shortly after eleven - thirty, Assistant Attorney General Walter Matson, who was handling the Connell prosecution, called Chittenden County State Attorney Ray Dugan, father of the deceased Eddie Dugan, as soon as he left the meeting in Judge Armand DiSipio's chambers. "Ray? Walt here. DiSipio's not going to sign the *Information* against the Bancroft girl. Turns out she's sixteen and he says we don't have enough on her to bring adult charges relating to the homicide, not even enough to tie her to the drugs on the premises. He wants her tried as a juvenile."

Dugan roared, "Fuck that! Who says she's sixteen. Where'd that come from?" "Turns out she had a fake I.D. Her mother's up from Branford, it checks out." Dugan wanted to slam the phone, but he didn't. He quickly sized up the situation.

Walt Matson was the best prosecutor in Vermont. He knew what the judge wanted. Besides, Dugan had known DiSipio since law school, knew he wouldn't throw the girl to a jury. He'd want her tried in the juvenile system, and that was completely unacceptable. The kid would get released to her mother, pending the outcome, get slapped with some wimpy juvenile probation and somewhere along the line, she'd disappear on him. A kid like that wasn't sticking around. He wasn't going to let that happen. The little bitch most likely had information about Eddie's death, information that could convict her scumbag boyfriend, convict the bastards who supplied the shit that killed his son. Maybe she was directly involved. He was taking this case to the wall, nail every bastard out there who had anything to do with his son's death, including this kid. He would make sure of that.

He knew what to do. The kid was definitely out of the control of her parents—he'd get SRS, Department of Social and Rehabilitation Services, to bring a delinquency action alleging she was in need of supervision, then get an immediate Emergency Detention Order and take the kid into state custody. The kid wouldn't surface in court for a couple of days until the hearing on the EDO. That would give him enough time to get to her. And if he couldn't get anything out of her then, he knew SRS could drag a case like this out for a year, keep the kid in state's custody until the parents proved they were suitable to get her back. With the coke and the overdose, she wasn't going home anytime soon. Meanwhile he'd make sure she told him everything she knew.

He had to act fast and get the EDO, before the kid got released from the lockup and disappeared. To Matson, "Walt, don't drop the charges yet. You've got to stall for time. When's her arraignment?"

"The end of the day, with Connell, after the other arraignments."

Dugan looked at the desk clock: almost noon. He had four hours, tops. "Okay Walt, put her last. Don't pull the *Information* until I tell you to, even if it pisses DiSipio off."

He'd fax the officers' affidavits down to the Branford SRS office right away. He'd call the district office director, let her know this kid's going to be sprung in a few hours, released to the mother. He'd tell her they had to get the EDO up to Burlington before then, so the sheriffs could take the kid directly into SRS custody from the holding cell.

Twenty minutes later Dugan hung up from his call with the Branford SRS district director. She'd have the Bancroft kid in SRS custody in time. The sheriffs would pick her up at the Burlington Police Department lockup no later than 3:00 pm.

***

Christine sat alone in her cell. The other prisoner had been taken away. *Why am I still here?* Exhausted and nauseous from her McDonald's lunch, she stopped thinking.

She lay on the cot, rested her aching body and aching mind in the dim quiet. She'd find out what was happening when it was time. She shut her eyes, but the morning replayed behind her eyelids in cruel detail. She forced her eyes open, waited.

***

Lynne sank into a wooden bench in the corridor which lead to the court clerk's counter. She had filled herself with diner food: a hot turkey sandwich with mashed potatoes and gravy, along with a couple cups of coffee. Drained, she'd been awake since yesterday afternoon. Her head pounded with a dull pain behind her eyes, which quivered from the coffee's bitter jolt. The lawyer, Dreyfus, had told her to wait here, that arraignments would start at 1 o'clock, that he'd be back shortly before then, but he'd be busy with other clients. He had told Lynne to be there, in case something happened. The clerk had told her Christine wasn't in the holding cell. She looked at her watch: twenty minutes to one. Her exhaustion pressed down.

Within a few minutes, the empty hallway began to fill with people shuffling through the doorway singly or in small groups. All sorts of people: unwashed, in grungy jeans and T-shirts, others scrubbed, in ill-fitting dress clothes, businessmen and tradesmen with booze reddened faces, stylish men and women clearly from out of state, probably DUI's up at the mountain resorts. They all seemed to know to go to the counter to pick up their paperwork. They intently read their charges. Some snorted, others murmured. Most said nothing, waiting for the next step in the process. The defense attorneys arrived. Men and women in tailored suits gathered up the better dressed defendants. Men and women in shabby tweeds and corduroys, the public defenders, waded into the knots of the rougher looking characters, sorting out who the defendants were from the bystanders. Lynne's head swam in the currents and eddies of bodies in motion. A swirl of mangled odors surrounded her: fried food, soiled diapers, laundry detergents, cheap and expensive colognes, machine grease, and patchouli. In the commotion, she noticed Dreyfus as he talked to a woman, while reading the woman's paperwork. Then he moved on to his next client.

Her eyes burned as she watched him. She shut them and saved herself from the nauseating whirl around her. She felt the mass of bodies thin out, heard a door repeatedly squeak open and shut. A man's deep voice announced that the judge would be seated in five minutes.

She heard a voice beside her. Dreyfus, "Lynne, there's no paperwork for Christine yet. Kind of strange, don't know what to make of it. Probably nothing. Stay here and I'll keep you posted. Gotta go." With that he was gone, through the door where the others had gone.

Lynne melded into the bench, alone in the hallway. She dragged down into a fitful half sleep, her head wretchedly dipped and whipsawed. People passed by her in broken focus as the afternoon wore on and the courtroom steadily emptied. She fought off her stupor and decided to go out for a cigarette. She needed the nicotine boost. She wouldn't be long. She wouldn't miss anything. She returned to the stale corridor. There was Dreyfus coming at her, talking as he approached. "Lynne, great news! They've dropped the charges against Christine! Seems like they didn't have much to go on, the judge said forget it."

Lynne broke wide open, *Thank god!*

***

She must have fallen asleep, she must have been dreaming. Christine sat up, unsure. Images of Eddie were still fresh in her mind: leering at her in Megan's kitchen, hovering over lines of cocaine on Jim's coffee table, shooting up in her living room, staring from some undefined empty place. She shook her head to lose him, but she couldn't—he was dead. She felt no sadness, no regret or shame for his death. He was a creep; that's all she knew or felt about him. Her thoughts vanished when she heard the sound that had awakened her. "Mom!"

Lynne rushed into the space that separated them. Christine flew to the cell bars. An old cop wheezed behind Lynne, warning her away from the bars before she could get close enough to touch her daughter.

It didn't matter. "Honey, they've dropped the charges against you. They're going to let you go!"

"We don't have any paperwork saying she's free to go." They both looked as the officer spoke. "Until I hear from the State's Attorney, or the judge, telling me to release her she stays put."

"I'll go get Dreyfus to sort this out." Lynne assured her daughter. She spun around and raced to the stairs, not wanting to waste another minute.

I'm outta here! Christine couldn't contain herself. She paced the ten by eight cell like a big cat in a cage. Soon, she heard people at the top of the stairs, heard them coming down. No hint of her mother in the mix of voices. Serious footsteps. She knew they were coming for her. Something wasn't right. Dead still, standing in the center of her cell, she waited for them to appear. Two women and two men came around the cinder block stairwell. A fat cop led a stern faced woman. She wore plain black slacks, an ordinary pale blouse and short cropped hair. A uniformed man and woman appeared last—sheriffs. The old cop reached the cell. Christine hadn't moved from its center. No one had spoken yet. The cop began to unlock the door.

Through an overwhelming confusion, Christine forced, "What's going on?"

The door open. "Come with us miss," the male sheriff said.

Something's wrong. "Why, where are you taking me?" No response.

"They dropped the charges against me. I'm being released, right?"

The male sheriff answered. "We don't know anything about that, miss." The plain clothes woman spoke up. "I'm from the Department of Social and Rehabilitation Services. I have a court order that says I'm to take you into custody on behalf of the department commissioner." The woman raised her hand, holding a document.

Christine panicked. "No! I'm supposed to be released. My mother went to get the lawyer."

The two sheriffs stepped into the cell.

The female sheriff spoke. "Miss, we have a transport order."

"Where's my lawyer? I want my lawyer."

"You don't have a lawyer." The caseworker said.

Christine stiffened. Harshly, "Yes I do, and I want to see my mother. She's around here somewhere. I'm not going anywhere until..."

"Come with us now, miss." A male sheriff interrupted her.

The two sheriffs stepped forward on either side of Christine, each grasped an arm.

"What the hell do you think you're doing?" She snarled.

"Hands behind your back." Fury blind, "Fuck you!"

The male sheriff yanked Christine's arms behind her, twisted her wrist so that a sharp pain shot up her arms to her skull and exploded. The female sheriff slapped on the handcuffs. Berserk with raw fear, Christine bolted for the cell opening three feet away—she had to get to her mother. With her hands bound behind her back she slammed into the doorframe, her head smashed into the door's iron hinge. She fell hard. Sprawled on the floor beyond the cell, cheek on cold cement, blood already streamed into her eyes from the cut on her forehead. She heard a woman mumble, "Shit, this is just great." Christine tried to get up, unseeing, her hands cuffed behind her, confused. Two pairs of hands grabbed her, lifted her by her armpits, and rushed her up the stairs.

"No more trouble, miss." The male sheriff commanded, as they left the station through the back door.

Christine tried to get her feet under her, but couldn't. "Where are you taking me?" She howled.

"You're going to a place where you'll be safe." The caseworker behind her spoke.

Safe from what? Out of her mind, she shrieked, "Get my mother! She's here somewhere!"

***

The desk sergeant's words stunned Lynne. "Say that again." Dreyfus demanded.

"She's not here. A couple sheriffs and an SRS caseworker from Windham County showed up with an EDO. They took her away."

Lynne turned to the lawyer. "What happened? Where's Christine?"

Although he didn't know specifically what happened, Dreyfus explained what he could. "The Department of Social and Rehabilitation Services took her into their custody. They used a court order called an emergency detention order. They're used to taking children out of dangerous situations."

Lynne stared at him. She didn't understand. "But I'm here to take her home." She teared up. "There's no danger now."

"Lynne, someone's probably being overprotective. It will get straightened out, don't worry. She'll be back with you in no time, and for now I'm sure she's somewhere safe."

"Where?"

"I don't know. A foster home, maybe a group home." He told her Christine might not be returned home that night because the child protection people would be trying to sort out if she was "at risk". He explained, however, that she would be home within 48 hours because the law required that a child couldn't be held in custody any longer than that, without a judge's review and approval. "I'm sure the SRS people will be in touch with you before then." Dreyfus assured her.

Lynne shook her head, she wanted to know, "Who can tell me where Christine is, when she'll be home?"

Dreyfus looked at his watch. "It's after four thirty, there's no one you can call. The SRS office is closed for the day. You should get home, maybe someone is trying to reach you there. If not, call the SRS office in Branford first thing tomorrow."

Tears streamed down Lynne's cheeks to her silent, pressed lips.

"Don't worry, I'm sure it will all work out tomorrow."

Lynne held on to the lawyer's ragged promise through her long drive home.

***

Stonebridge slid into Christine's view. It rose from the deep green dusk hung with summer haze. She tried to make the campus buildings out more clearly, but the Demerol shaded and blurred the stone wall edges, the ivy smothered facades and the black windows. She knew she was messed up. She knew they had doped her up when they gave her the needle "for the pain" before they stitched her up at some hospital near the police station. She knew they had fucked her up because she had been a pain in the ass. Thickly, she remembered shouting about her mother, throwing her body around in the back seat of the sheriff's car. This place smelled dark. *I'm here*. She'd see her mother when someone decided she could. That's all she knew. Then she smiled at a stupid joke; maybe Wanda could get her out of this.

The detention center's admissions staff watched Christine arrive; hair wild, eyes glazed, a purple bruise swelled from the fresh gash and black stitches down the center of her forehead. At the placement facility, "Christine Bancroft, DOB - 8/8/70," matched the information contained in the intake report that accompanied her: "extremely violent", "possibly under the influence of controlled substance(s) or suffering from withdrawal from substance(s)", "suspect in a drug related (cocaine) homicide". By the end of Christine's slurred "interview." the intake person had also added "possible suicidal tendencies" to the report.

She was taken away to a six by eight foot room, no windows, with a naked fluorescent bulb high above, a solid iron door with a barred slat that could be slid open and shut from the outside, and an iron framed cot welded to the floor. Her room. The harsh lighting was brutal. Christine realized, through the Demerol sludge, that this was where she would spend the night, which seriously sucked. Her head pounded, distantly. It was going to hurt a lot worse, she knew. The guard released her from her restraints. He had a baloney sandwich and a tin cup of water for her. She sat on the edge of the cot and ate, even though she was nauseous. The guard left, the slat on the door was slid open. She saw him look in at her. Her head pounded from the light, her body ached an enormous weariness.

"I'm really tired, can you turn off the light?"

"Can't do that." And he was gone. The slat stayed open.

She lay down, pulled the thin blanket over her head against the relentless brightness and begged for sleep. Long hours later, she slipped into a jagged, ugly deep.

***

Lynne lay fully awake, unable to shake her fear that Christine was hurt somewhere. She knew she was not safe, as the lawyer had promised. Coming on midnight, Lynne wished she had someone she could call, who could tell her Christine was alright, who could take a message to her telling her everything would be okay. Instead she lay there in the dark; powerless until tomorrow. Images from that long, horrible day ground like glass behind her closed eyelids. Long past midnight, exhaustion sucked her into a fitful sleep.

CHAPTER 12

Tuesday, July 12, 1987

No windows, no clock, the constant fluorescent light far overhead. Christine did not know what time it was when she woke up did not know how long she lay awake before the panel slid open on the door.

She saw the eyes, she yelled at them. "Hey, wait a second." The panel slid shut. She remembered, maybe, that the panel had opened and shut throughout the night. Her stomach ached, knotted. She sat up, shouted, "Hey, you hear me out there? I'm hungry!"

She had sat up too quickly, throwing her Demerol tinged equilibrium off, pounding blood into her badly bruised forehead. *Oh god!* The pain throbbed behind her eyes. When she put her hands up to her face, against the pain, she felt the blood crusted in her eyebrows, felt the rough stitches and the tender, swollen skin. She saw the blood on her T-shirt, her jeans stained with crude brown specks of blood. She walked to the iron door, pounded it, shouting, "I'm dying in here, anybody out there?"

The door slat slid open, eyes appeared. "Step back from the door."

Metal scraped the lock's works. She stepped back. A hefty female guard pushed the door open, but did not enter the room. Christine saw another guard, male, a few feet further back.

"Turn around and put your hands behind your back."

She did and was quickly put into handcuffs. Neither guard said anything as they led Christine down a long hall; cinder block walls and acoustic panel ceiling, fluorescent lights and no windows, plywood doors with name plates. She didn't ask where she was being taken. It didn't matter. She was going where they took her. The hallway led to a common area with picture glass windows. The sudden light and space overwhelmed her. She saw outside - a gray day

- before they headed down the next corridor; wider, windowless, sturdier doors. They passed a couple girls, about fourteen years old, tough. The girls watched Christine like she was a passing animal, looked her up and down, their focus on her forehead. She knew she must look really messed up.

They stopped at a double door. A woman in regular clothes met them in the hallway and asked, "Christine?"

She nodded.

"I'm Julie Mellon. I've been assigned to you."

Julie Mellon was in her twenties. She wore pink lip gloss and a little eyeliner, her light brown hair was pulled back in a short ponytail. Christine figured people probably described her as "cute". *God my head hurts.*

"I thought you might want to freshen up." Mellon held out soap, a towel, a washcloth, toothpaste and a toothbrush.

The guard released Christine's handcuffs. She took the items.

"The bathroom's through there. Mavis will show you. When you're done I'll see you in my office." With that Mellon was gone.

Down another corridor before they stopped, the female guard pointed for Christine to go through a door. On the other side, was a large bathroom with a half dozen stalls, a half dozen sinks and one long polished metal mirror above the sinks. Christine noticed her reflection, saw the damage. *Jesus Christ!* Black eyes were nearly swollen shut; her forehead a purple mass pinched in the middle by bloody black stitches: her hair a shocked tangle. Flecks of blood crusted her hair, her brow, her temples. She touched her face gently, watched her reflection, and matched her pain to the location of her fingers. She soaped the cloth with lukewarm water and carefully washed her face, the water sweet against her skin. She lathered the washcloth with hot water, and scrubbed her neck, her hairline, her ears—it was good. She scrubbed her arms. She took off her T-shirt and bra and scrubbed her armpits, her shoulders, her breasts and breastbone, her belly. She reached down into her unzipped jeans and scrubbed her pubic hair. She scrubbed at the long night's grime.

The guard, Mavis, interrupted. "That's enough, miss."

Christine didn't need to be told twice. She didn't want to lose what she might be able to get. She put the washcloth down, took the towel, dried off. She scrubbed her mouth with toothpaste, combed her hair in line with long, careful strokes. She still hurt, bad, but she felt better than she had for as long as she could remember.

In Mellon's office, the woman told Christine. "Tomorrow is your detention hearing. I see that it's scheduled for 10 o'clock. The sheriff will be here to transport you about 8:00."

Christine saw the desk clock: it was nine thirty. She was starving.

"I don't know if you will be returning here after the hearing, so we won't move you in with the general population."

"What are you talking about? I'm going home tomorrow. We straighten things out and you send me home, right?" The crazed feeling that had grabbed Christine at the police station tore through her again.

Mellon blinked. "I don't know. I can't say what's going to happen. It's possible you'll be returned to your mother."

Christine's head pounded like a freaking drum. She tried to be calm. "So, tomorrow I'll know."

"Yes. Meanwhile you'll remain in the room you slept in last night."

No! "I've got a question. Is it possible to turn off the light at night? I'd sleep a whole lot better."

Mellon remembered the "suicide watch" notation in the intake. "We can't do that."

"That really sucks, y'know. Why not? Why can't you turn out the fucking lights when I'm fucking trying to sleep?"

Mellon eased back in her chair; created more distance from the inmate, looked for her exit strategy. She called to the guard in the hall. "Mavis, would you come here please." To Christine, firmly, "It's policy. It's for your safety. There's nothing I can do about that."

"You're kidding me, right?" Christine saw the fear in Mellon's face, felt the presence of the large woman approaching behind her. Her head pounded. She had to keep calm. As evenly as she could, "No, you're not kidding. Okay. But if you could do something about the lights, I'd really appreciate it. Can I ask you something else? My head really hurts, is there something you can give me?" She tried to smile at the stupid woman.

Back in her room, the pain slightly ebbed from the Extra Strength Tylenol. Christine seethed under the blanket she had thrown over her head. This mess better get straightened out tomorrow. She emerged when the door opened. Mavis left her a small box of corn flakes, a carton of milk, a plastic bowl and spoon - the first of three meals brought to her room that day.

Later that morning caseworker Mellon wrote up the incident in Christine's charts; "the juvenile's threatening behavior required that she be physically removed from the administrator's office."

***

Lynne sat at the breakfast table with the papers spread before her, the house quiet—the kids gone. She had refused the urge to open the large manila envelope in the driveway, where the sheriff had served her. She read the document headings: Petition for Temporary Custody; Supporting Affidavit; Summons to Appear at the District Court at 10:00 a.m. on July 8, 1987. *Tomorrow*. She started reading the Petition and was quickly confused. It seemed to say that the SRS people were asking the Court to let them keep Christine. It didn't say anything about keeping her for just a couple days, like attorney Dreyfus had told her. She didn't see anything about when Christine would be coming home. Her stomach churned. She looked for some explanation in the supporting affidavit.

The affidavit's words reached Lynne through a sickening blur as she read about Christine's boyfriend selling cocaine; about a young man who was dead from injecting the drug; about the cocaine found in the boyfriend's apartment; about Christine being found in the apartment when the police arrived with a search warrant; about Christine's arrest. She stopped reading after "evidence of the juvenile, C.B.'s cohabitation..." The paper trembled so hard in her hands, she had to put it down.

Lynne rubbed her eyes, went back to the Petition. "C.B. is clearly beyond the control of her parents, and is a child in need of care and supervision, therefore she should remain in the custody of the Commissioner of the Department of Social and Rehabilitation Services." She buried her face in her hands. *Chris isn't coming home!* An enormous hole swallowed Lynne as she felt a vast emptiness.

Sometime later that morning morning, the electric hum of the wall clock brought Lynne back to the room, and at that moment she decided she had to speak to the people who wrote those court papers. She needed to let them know they had it all wrong; that Christine couldn't have been involved with that cocaine business and she needed to come home. Lynne pushed away from the table, tipped her chair over as she got up. She found the phonebook, found the listing for the S.R.S office. She stopped.

Holding the telephone receiver, she realized if she said the wrong thing she might make things much worse. *I better call a lawyer.*

She went to the courthouse that morning and applied for a court appointed lawyer, like Dreyfus had advised her to do. A few hours later, Emmet Fitzgerald called to tell Lynne he had been assigned to represent her. He said he handled cases like Christine's.

They were called CHINS cases, meaning children in need of care and supervision. She told him what the affidavit said and explained Christine wasn't really like that, that she had a good home and that it must have been a mistake. Lynne said she wanted to call these people and tell them Christine should come home now.

The lawyer responded sharply. "Don't speak to anyone from SRS at this time. Do you understand?"

Surprised, she said, "Yes, but it sounds like they aren't letting Christine come home tomorrow. Are they?"

"I can't say without seeing the paperwork, without talking to the caseworker."

Something slipped loose inside Lynne. "You have to tell them nothing like this will ever happen again." *Tell who? Who decides! Who are these people!*

Overwhelmed, she needed to end the phone call. She'd find out tomorrow.

CHAPTER 13

Wednesday, July 8, 1987

Christine breathed in the thick and humid morning air like it was precious. The hazy sun which filtered through the oaks and maples was almost too beautiful. She drank it all in, as she walked towards the sheriff's cruiser in handcuffs. Where she was headed, she had no idea. She knew she had to make a good impression on whomever these people were. Although her hair was washed and carefully combed, and although she wore a clean bandage for her stitches, there was nothing she could do about the high purpled bruise, the swelling, the purple that rimmed her eyes. It would have helped if she had some makeup, but she was grateful that Julie Mellon had gotten her an orderly's smock to wear over her blood stained T-shirt. Under everything, there was the pounding in her head—She had barely slept in her eternally light-blasted room—the Tylenol they had given her didn't help enough.

They drove past the massive stone buildings, still dark despite the morning.

On the road, Christine closed her eyes against the pain and gave herself over to the rhythm of the cruiser as she traveled to her destination.

***

Lynne wondered what the lawyer thought of her letting Christine live with a drug dealer as they walked from attorney Fitzgerald's office to the courthouse. All he had said was that it was regrettable, but they would work it out with the child protection people. He didn't seem to judge her when he had asked her about the family, her work schedule, Christine's school performance. He appeared to be a straightforward guy, a soft spoken family man with a couple young children and a nice looking wife, who smiled from the pictures on his desk. Lynne was comfortable walking with him, telling him about her job and the kids.

"Lynne, your daughter got herself into some very serious trouble. The State may be reluctant to just send her home now. How would you feel if they sent Christine home, but kept the case open so they could monitor your situation for a while or until they were satisfied she would be safe with you?" Fitzgerald asked.

She couldn't think of a reason why not.

"I'll see if the caseworker will go along with that." He paused. "Do you think the father will agree to that arrangement?"

"I don't know." She hadn't thought of Mark being involved in this. *Oh my god.* Had he gotten the same papers she had? The petition and the affidavit? The courthouse loomed before them.

"Why would Mark be involved?"

"As Christine's father, Mark has a right to know she's in custody, and what plans are being made regarding her—so long as she's in custody."

"I don't know what he'll think, whether he would agree to that." *He'll be furious!*

Lynne's knees grew weak.

Once inside the courthouse, Lynne scanned hallway and the few people present: no Mark. A woman in her forties approached them. "Emmett, I heard you were on this case, representing the mother. I've got the daughter."

Fitzgerald introduced Lynne to the woman, Laurie Simmons. She was from the public defender's office, and Christine's attorney. He nodded to two other women in the hall, they nodded back.

He asked Simmons, "LaValley's the caseworker? Have you talked to her about what she's planning on doing?"

"Let's talk." Simmons steered them to a room.

Before the door had shut behind them, Simmons spoke. "They want to hold on to Christine, they say she's a danger to herself. Check this out." She handed Fitzgerald a document.

He spoke as he read it over. "Lynne, this is a supplemental affidavit saying Christine has been threatening people since arriving at Stonebridge. They have concerns about drug withdrawal. They've kept her in isolation, concerned she may be suicidal."

The lawyer swam in a pale light before Lynne's eyes. She forced out, "What's Stonebridge?"

Fitzgerald explained it was a juvenile detention center. He then turned to the other lawyer. "Not good. But I don't see any mental health expert making these assessments, just some administrator, this Julie Mellon."

"Doesn't matter. Overbeck's going to see this and have a bird. He'll do whatever SRS wants."

"Have you had a chance to meet with Christine? Get an idea on how she's doing?" Fitzgerald asked.

"No. She hasn't arrived yet."

Fitzgerald, looking at Lynne. "Her mother would like to have Christine returned home. She's willing to take on SRS supervision. But with this new information, I don't know if LaValley will go for that. Let's run it by her though and see."

Lynne broke in, "What's going on?"

"This report says Christine has been behaving dangerously. The State wants to keep her at Stonebridge. They might not be willing to go along with the supervision idea we were talking about. And maybe she shouldn't go home if she's having some serious problems."

"What problems?" Lynne was astonished.

"I'm not sure. This affidavit isn't very specific." He turned to Simmons. "If we can't get Christine home, we have to get her evaluated immediately. I mean if she really needs help, we need to know and get her out of Stonebridge."

Simmons agreed. "I'll petition the judge to order a psych eval. See if Sol Leventhal's available to get right on this."

"If Christine needs help, will she get it at this Stonebridge place?" Lynne asked. Both lawyers answered no.

Fitzgerald added, "We'll get Christine removed from there if she needs psychiatric care. And if she doesn't, we'll do everything we can to get her home to you." He asked Simmons, "Any idea, where the father stands on all this?"

"No sign of him. I'll check to see if he's here."

Lynne wanted to see Christine right then. She needed to see that she was okay. There was a tap at the door. It opened halfway. A head appeared, round, with a pixie haircut, eyes set close together over candy apple cheeks. "Gotta minute?" The woman asked. The rest of the woman, short and wide in loose clothing, poured through the doorway. She stood before Lynne with her outstretched hand to shake. Almost cheerfully. "Hi, I'm Rose LaValley. I'm Christine's SRS caseworker. You must be Lynne."

Lynne recognized the name from the paperwork. She stared at the hand of the woman who had written all those terrible things about Christine. LaValley dropped her hand.

"How's Christine?" Lynne's voice shook.

LaValley looked down, suggesting regret. "Not so well, I'm afraid. She seems to be having some difficulties at her placement. Here." She handed Lynne and Fitzgerald copies of the supplemental affidavit.

Lynne didn't want the paperwork. She just wanted to hear that Christine was alright. She knew this woman wasn't going to give her that.

Fitzgerald spoke. "We've seen these. Is there any professional follow up going on? An evaluation? Some care or treatment?"

"No, we haven't had a chance." LaValley kept her eyes on Lynne as she answered.

Fitzgerald launched at the caseworker. "This affidavit describes a very serious situation. Christine's receiving no care?"

"She's dangerous." LaValley tensed up. "They've segregated her from the population and kept her under observation. The situation is under control." The hostility crackled in the small room.

Simmons toned it down. "I want to talk with Christine before we jump to any conclusions. Have you met with her?"

"No, not yet."

"How about the father, where's he stand on this?"

LaValley reddened. "We haven't been in touch with him yet either."

Fitzgerald was incredulous. "Has he been served with notice of today's hearing?"

Defensively, "We don't have any contact information for him. No one has been forthcoming."

"You haven't found the father. You haven't met with the child and really have no idea what condition she's in. You've made no contact with her mother and you have no idea what her home circumstances are. This is screwed up Rose." Fitzgerald fumed.

The caseworker stood mute.

The bailiff opened the door. "Judge is on the bench, let's go." Lynne was stricken. *What the hell is going on?*

Judge Overbeck seated at the raised bench. He watched the parties enter. Lynne looked to the front of the courtroom and saw him glare at her—it was the same judge from the child support hearing. He seemed to recognize her. *Of course he remembers me.* And he'd been reading all those things about Christine. Lynne dropped her eyes and walked behind her lawyer to one of the tables at the front of the room. She took a seat beside Fitzgerald and didn't raise her eyes.

Christine shuffled wordlessly between two sheriffs through cement block passageways leading from the carport entrance at the rear of the courthouse. Her ankles and wrists were cuffed. They stopped at a door. *This is it.* She straightened up for whatever was on the other side. The door opened to a large room. She could not see beyond the broad framed sheriff leading her. She followed him into the room. As they walked, a distance between Christine and her escort grew. She was able to make out three tables before her. Each seated with people staring at her. Her mother sat wide eyed and pale at one of the tables, devastated by the sight of her.

Lynne watched her chained daughter enter the courtroom and immediately witnessed Christine's grisly face; the gash, the purple and green bruises, the black eyes – *My God!*

Christine passed in front of the judge. She followed the sheriffs to a table where two women sat. As she crossed the courtroom, she glanced briefly at the black robed, bony old man who scowled down at her like she was garbage. She looked away to her mother, sent her a small smile that said, "I'm alright. Don't worry."

Lynne choked back a cry.

Fitzgerald jumped out of his chair before Christine reached her lawyer's table, "Objection to the juvenile being held in restraints! The mother requests they be immediately removed." Simmons joined in the objection.

The judge lashed back at the two lawyers. "I have affidavits before me that describe a disturbed and violent young woman, so I do not feel the State has abused its authority in transporting her in restraints. Proper precaution I'd say, seeing what we're dealing with. However, I believe this courtroom is adequately secured. So, I will allow them to be removed." The judge addressed Christine. "No funny stuff young lady, do you hear me?"

Christine nodded, politely answered. "Yes sir." *Asshole.*

Lynne was stunned. *"What we're dealing with"? "Disturbed?" Doesn't he see she's been hurt?*

"Are we ready to proceed?" The judge rifled through some papers on his desk, annoyed. "Wait a minute—" He looked up at the table where Christine sat. "Does this girl have a father?"

The state's attorney answered. "We don't know sir. The juvenile has refused to speak, and the mother has not been forthcoming with that information."

Overbeck leaned forward. "Is that correct attorney Fitzgerald? Is your client withholding information from the court?"

"No sir, my client has not withheld anything." "So what is it, does the girl have a father?"

"Yes, sir. He does not live with the mother." Fitzgerald responded.

The judge snapped. "I want the father's address given to the court clerk before the mother leaves the building. Do I make myself clear?"

"Yes, your Honor."

Overbeck addressed all those present. "This, being an emergency detention hearing mandated by statute to commence within forty- eight hours of the juvenile's detention, we must commence. However, I am going to afford the father a full opportunity to be involved in these proceedings, including the emergency detention hearing, as is his right. Therefore, this hearing is deemed to have commenced. It will be continued and resume two days hence. In the meantime, based on the affidavits filed in this court, documents which detail a set of circumstances strongly suggesting the girl is in need of care and supervision, and is, in fact, a grave danger to herself and others, I order that she remain in SRS custody for the time being."

Simmons rose from her seat to speak. "Your Honor, if I may. I am very concerned as well about what has been reported in these affidavits. If these characterizations of my client are in any way accurate, then I am seriously concerned about her safety at Stonebridge, which is not equipped to deal with the issues suggested in the affidavits. I ask that you order an immediate evaluation by a qualified mental health professional to determine Christine's needs, and for SRS to follow any resulting recommendations. Specifically, I ask that Dr. Leventhal be authorized to conduct the evaluation, or his designee, if he is not immediately available."

The judge stood up with file in hand. "I'll do no such thing. The juvenile shall remain in SRS custody for now. They are responsible for her care and wellbeing. They don't need me to tell them how to conduct their business." He then left the courtroom through a door behind his chair.

When the door to the judge's chambers shut, Lynne looked to Christine, who looked back. Again the smile that said, "I'm alright, mom." Lynne tried to return her smile. The two sheriffs came up to Christine.

Simmons called out to the sheriffs. "Wait a second, please. I haven't had a chance to speak to my client. We need a few minutes."

LaValley hemmed. "I don't know. These boys have a long ride ahead of them and probably want to head out."

"Rose, some really serious things have happened. I need a few minutes with Christine." She asked the sheriffs, "You good for a few minutes?"

They appeared annoyed. One said, "Sure, just don't make it too long."

Simmons took Christine by the arm. "Come with me." To the sheriff who started to follow them she said, "We're alright." Fitzgerald attempted to follow too. "Not now, Emmett." Christine and Simmons were joined in the meeting room by the slightly stooped older woman with blue tinted hair, the one who had sat with them at the table in the courtroom.

Simmons began. “Mrs. Gladys Fromme is going to join us. She’s your court appointed guardian ad litem, your advocate. She watches over us lawyers to make sure we treat you fairly.”

The woman smiled. She held out a small boned hand for Christine to shake. “Hello dear. Sorry we didn’t have a chance to properly meet before.”

Christine grabbed the woman’s hand, held the cool skin in the heat of her two hands, and stared into her guardian’s pale blue eyes. “Good, so you’re going to help get me out of that place?”

Fromme looked away from the clutching girl. Simmons spoke. “Why, Christine? What’s going on?”

Christine let go of the frail hand. “The place sucks. They’ve got me in this room all the time, alone, it doesn’t have any windows. The light’s on all night. I can’t sleep.”

“That’s not good. I’ll call up there and find out why, straighten things out.”

“Good. You do that, ‘cause I need some freaking sleep.”

“Christine—Chris, how did you hurt your head?” Simmons asked. “What happened?”

Christine put her hand to her forehead. “You mean this? I kinda lost it when they were taking me out of the jail cell. I hit my head on the doorframe.” Through a twisted smile, “Big mess.”

“No one hit you? Pushed you?”

“I don’t think so, not that I could tell.”

Simmons, quieter, “Did you intentionally hurt yourself?”

“Huh? No! It was an accident. Like I said I kinda freaked and next thing I know, Bam! Hit my head.”

“They’ve got you on a suicide watch. Any idea why?”

What! “Jeez I don’t know. Maybe the cops thought I was trying to hurt myself doing something stupid like trying to run away handcuffed.” She saw the lawyer and the old woman look at each other.

"This woman up at Stonebridge, Julie Mellon said you threatened her, that you had to be physically restrained." Simmons said.

"No way. I haven't threatened anybody. About the only person I've seen is that dipshit Julie who says she's like in charge of me and—oh—she doesn't mean when I was telling her I needed the light turned off so I could sleep? Is that what she's talking about? Sure, I was pretty upset after she said she couldn't. But no, I didn't threaten her. Not at all. I was just pissed off. And nobody restrained me. They just took me away."

"Listen, Chris, I know it's tough up there, but you've got to settle down. They've pegged you as bad news and they can come down pretty hard on you if they want. Don't give them an excuse. Understand?"

Christine nodded. "Yeah, I'm getting that."

"Here's my card. If you think you're being mistreated, you let me know. Right away. Tell them you want to talk to your lawyer. Right, Gladys?"

The small woman nodded, while watching Christine.

Simmons added, "I mean it. It can get pretty rough up there. Your mother's lawyer and I are going to get you out of there as soon as possible."

"And get me home?" "As soon as possible."

"I didn't have anything to do with that death." Christine blurted. "I wasn't there and I didn't know anything about it until the cops arrested me. And I want you to know I didn't have anything to do with Jimmy selling—" Tears burned her eyes. "I wanted him to stop. He said he would." She wiped her sleeve across her nose. "I saw it getting crazy. I was thinking of leaving, you can ask my friend Wanda, we worked together. She works at the Pearl Street Bistro. I told her what was happening. She'll tell you."

Simmons made notes on her legal pad. "Good, Chris. This is good. I will." The sheriff knocked sharply at the door. "Time to go."

Christine looked at her lawyer, panicked.

Simmons answered, "Just a sec." To Christine, "Alright Chris, you've given me some things to work with. Like I said, we'll get you out of there and home as soon as we can. I'll get attorney Fitzgerald to fill me in on your home situation. No problems there?"

"No. My mom is a good mother. This isn't her fault at all."

"Alright. How about your father? Would he be a suitable place for you to live? In case we need a backup plan?"

Cold, "Forget my father. I don't want to live with him. And he won't want me ruining his life either. Find me someplace else if I can't go home."

Simmons nodded. Fromme agreed.

The door swung open to two sheriffs standing just beyond the threshold. Christine stepped into the corridor. She saw her mother and the other lawyer. Lynne raced past the officers, threw her arms around her baby. Christine threw her arms around her mother.

Lynne whispered, "Be careful."

"I will."

"I'll see you soon."

Christine held on. "I'll be home soon."

She felt someone's firm hand on her shoulder. She immediately let go of her mother and separated. Fitzgerald took Lynne by the elbow to guide her away; she shouldn't see her daughter being cuffed. Christine, her arms behind her, her head bowed, shuffled down the corridor between the two officers. Lynne watched her daughter until she disappeared through a door.

***

Branford slid by, unspooling as Christine rode out of town. Thin memories stirred: places, people. Ghost memories. *What's happening to Jimmy?* She floated out of town in the back of a sheriff's cruiser. She was going back to Stonebridge. She gazed out the window. *No one knows what's happening to me.* Christine shut her eyes, exhausted. She just wanted to rest in quiet darkness.

***

Lynne couldn't sleep when she got back from court. She knew she wouldn't be able to. Lying in bed, the day's images ground in her mind: Christine shuffling into the courtroom, her battered face, her brave smile. Her arms handcuffed behind as she was led away. She had to get some sleep. She had to work tonight. The kids would be home for dinner in a few hours.

She couldn't sleep. She got up and went to sit at the kitchen table. She smoked a cigarette and stared blindly out the window. She couldn't imagine what was happening to Christine. She prayed for it to end.

***

When she returned to Stonebridge, Christine was handed over to Julie Mellon, who took her down corridors. At one point a hulking girl stood in a doorway and stared at Christine with hard, dull eyes as she approached.

"Minard, where are you supposed to be?" Julie Mellon didn't wait for an answer. The girl didn't speak. Christine passed her; felt her power. The girl towered over her. Christine stole a glance at Minard's large, misshapen head; breathed in the sick smell of the girl's sweat and tooth rot. She caught Minard's gray eyes lock onto hers like a pit bull on meat. The girl wanted to fuck her up.

Mellon stopped at the doorway of a large room down the corridor. "Alright then, this is the reading room. You're to stay here until supper. Paul is in charge." She nodded to a man seated in the room. "Paul, this is Christine Bancroft., Room 223." She nodded to Christine.

The man checked Christine out as he rose from his desk and approached the two women. Mellon was gone before he could reach them.

"I'm Paul." Buff, smooth skinned, dark, not much taller than Christine, his eyes roved from Christine's eyes to her lips to her breasts, as he extended his hand for her to shake. His charm-drenched smile showed a set of fine white teeth.

He's kidding, right? But she had to take his hand, still extended. She nodded. He squeezed her hand, holding it a moment too long before releasing her. "A pleasure." With a short sweep of his arm, he gestured for Christine to enter the room. "Please join us."

She looked past the creep into the room. Two girls were sprawled on a beat up couch, their eyes shut. Another girl sat immobile in an overstuffed chair, staring straight ahead, *stoned or something*. There was an empty threadbare, overstuffed chair, an old oak conference table with four matching straight-backed chairs, a bookshelf with a few volumes of books and a couple stacks of magazines. Paul didn't move, his smile still worked. Christine had to press by him to get into the room, brush against him. She passed through the chemical reek of his deodorant, aftershave and mouthwash. She knew he watched her ass as she walked to the bookshelf.

Christine looked over the half dozen ragged Harlequin paperback romances, a few really old hardcover books, a dozen or so ratty copies of *Seventeen* and *Glamour*, a few *National Geographic* magazines from the 1970's. Christine grabbed one of the *National Geographics* and dropped into the unoccupied easy chair. The girl in the other chair, slack jawed with bloodshot eyes, sniffled and stared at her.

Christine said, "Hey."

The girl looked down at her legs.

He's watching me. If she looked up from the magazine, he'd make eye contact with her and take it as something special between them, *some shit like that.* She hated him, making her act like she read the stupid magazine. He probably got all hard as he, imagined what she felt like, imagining what she looked like naked, what she looked like when she fucked. If she wanted to, she could get him crazy horny; part her lips a little, stretch her neck, spread her legs, rub them. *No way!* That would cause her nothing but trouble, no doubt. She wasn't going to give him any reason to think she was, in any way, available. She needed to get in control, whatever that meant. She stared down hard at the unseen pages of her magazine. She wanted to be invisible, bad. She wanted to crawl down a hole, deep enough where no one could find her. She wanted it so bad it hurt behind her eyes. She shut her eyes against him."It's time to leave." The smooth voice pierced the darkness. Christine opened her eyes to see him stand over her. "You were asleep."

Coming up from a fuzzy depth, she looked around, saw the other girls watching her and Paul. Watch him mark her as his.

He backed away, louder, to the room. "Time to go. Let's go."

The others got up, moved to the door, lined up. Christine fell in at the end of the line with Paul beside her, nearly touching her. The pain behind her eyes started to pound. Without another word, the line proceeded down the hallway. Paul remained at her side.

In a low voice meant for Christine only, he said, "At this time the girls go back to their rooms and prepare for supper. I am responsible for seeing that all of the girls are delivered safely to their rooms." He didn't look at her as he spoke. "Do you know which room is yours?"

She didn't. Mellon had taken her to a room with a few cots in it, had said that was where she'd stay because the other room, the "safe room", was occupied. But she didn't remember the room's number or how to get to it. Panic juiced the pounding behind her eyes. "I'm sorry, but..." She whispered so others wouldn't know. "I forgot the number. Could you tell me?"

He clucked at her. "You shouldn't forget these things." He grinned at her. "Don't worry, I remember. I'll take you there." He didn't tell her the room number.

> At the end of a second corridor, the girls in Christine's group peeled off into two separate rooms. Paul and Christine remained in the hall. Other girls approached from either direction, watched him marking Christine, then disappeared into a few nearby rooms. Suddenly they were alone. *Tell me where to go!*

"This is your room." He indicated the door next to Christine, with a smile.

You fucker! Pain roared in her head, a furious surf slamming against jagged rocks. He continued in a hushed tone. "I work until midnight tonight, and from noon to midnight the rest of the week. I will see you."

Christine said nothing. She escaped into her room: six cots, neatly made and six footlockers: one at the end of each cot, closed and latched. No other furniture, no items laid around. Fluorescent light high above. Nothing indicated which bed was Christine's. She really wanted to lie down, but didn't want to be found on someone's bed and piss somebody off. She stood in the middle of the room, waiting for whatever came next.

The door swung open and three laughing girls burst in, seeming to pass through the doorway all at once. They stumbled to an abrupt stop, still in a clump, when they saw Christine in their room. They quieted down, still smiling. "Hey, check it out, the beat up chick."

A spidery, lively eyed girl pulled out of the tangle. "Hey, I'm Elena." She stepped towards Christine. Throwing her thumb over her shoulder at her friends. "These two goofballs are Sara and Rachel."

They said, "hey."

She threw a "hey" back. "I'm Christine."

The three girls giggled. Christine smelled pot. Elena flopped on her cot. Sara and Rachel landed on another bed. All had their full attention on Christine.

Elena asked, "What'cha doing standing there?"

Christine flushed red. Before she could think of an answer, Sara piped up, "She doesn't know which bed's hers."

The three girls snorted, laughing.

Elena soothed, "Hey don't worry about it. That one you're standing next to, that's yours." She looked past Christine. "Where's your shit?"

Christine sat on the cot. "Don't have any, haven't been home since I got popped."

Elena asked, "Popped for what?"

"My boyfriend got busted for coke. I was living with him, so they grabbed me too."

The girls all nodded. Rachel took up, "That sucks. Same with me and Sar. boyfriends selling meth...got themselves busted."

Sara added, "Dumb asses. Making meth in the basement." "Wicked crazy, huh Sar?" Rachel laughed.

Christine laughed with the others.

"Yeah it was way out of control. Then bang! Busted." Sara said.

"Threw us in here bein' we were fifteen. Been a year now." Rachel explained. Sara finished, "Our tale of woe."

Rachel turned to Elena. "Elena Marantz, would you like to share with the group your tale of woe?"

Elena's eyes flashed with wicked humor. "Why yes, certainly. You see, I am a child of the streets, a victim of the drug scourge that plagues our nation. My mother is, or was, or is, a recovering heroin addict—"

"Except when she isn't, or wasn't, or isn't." Sara piped up.

Elena continued. "Who brought into this plagued world four beautiful children. A boy, Armand, when she was seventeen, whose whereabouts are a mystery to us all. I vaguely remember him as a kid before we were taken away by the state, split up, and I never saw him again. Then me—"

"This is where it gets good, right, 'cause you're losing me." Rachel tossed out.

Elena continued, "Fast forward a bunch of years. Ma's out of rehab, the boogers Carl and Tracey and me are all home with her, but she's a mess, strung out then banging again, and me I'm like trying to keep shit together 'cause the boogers are like seven and five years old and I'm like thirteen and making some cash helping my uncle hustle. And I get caught the first time with like a dozen bags on me and I'm doin' juvey probation, and I get popped again, few months later, this time holding like thirty bags. And they want me to rat out my uncle, but I don't. I don't tell them a thing, and they get all p.o.'d and throw me in here. And fuck 'em." Elena bit off a hard, dry laugh. "My tale of woe."

"What happened to your mother? The boogers, do you get to see them?" Christine asked.

Elena stopped smiling. "Ma? I don't know, haven't heard from her since I landed here. That was about nine months ago. My uncle says she went into rehab again, but skipped out with some guy and disappeared. He thinks she went down to Tennessee, but nobody knows for sure. The boogers...they're in foster homes. They write me cute letters, send me pictures, shit like that. Sounds like they're doin' alright. I miss 'em. Can't wait to get out of here and see 'em."

The room went quiet until Christine gently asked, "When are you getting out?"

Elena gave a small shrug. "There's no plans for me getting out, so I figure I'm here until I'm eighteen."

Christine turned to Rachel and Sara. "And you guys, when do you get out?"

They both shook their heads. Rachel answered, "Most likely here till we're eighteen. Haven't heard different. They're not gonna just let us go."

Sara smiled. "But we're not complaining, could be worse." Christine couldn't think of anything much worse than this hole.

Elena sat up, "Yeah, well enough about us. I gotta know Chris, how'd you get that big ass cut on your head?"

"Just clumsy." She said with embarrassment. "And stupid. I ran into a cell door with my arms cuffed behind me."

The girls let out a whoop. "No shit, you're kidding, right? What were you thinking?"

"I wasn't."

Sara laughed. "Ha, shit happens, right? Call you Crash."

"Speaking of shit happening, heard Paul's got a thing for you, yeah?" Rachel poked.

How'd she hear that? Christine blushed hard. "I don't know, yeah I guess he was kinda hitting on me. He can fucking forget it though, he's gross."

Elena let out a soft whistle, "Ooh girl, I don't think it's that easy, 'cause from what I heard, he was really into you, an' I don't think he's gonna take no for an answer."

Sara and Rachel nodded. Rachel added, "I don't think his girlfriend's gonna like it too much either."

"How's his girlfriend gonna find out?" Christine asked.

"She probably already knows. I'm sure someone went running right to her when they saw Paul being all goofy on you." Rachel responded.

"She works here?" The others laughed.

"Nooo, Julie Phelps, she's a resident. One of us." Sara clarified.

This is crazy. Christine blurted, "Wait a second, you mean to tell me that Paul's got this girlfriend who's an inmate in this place, and he gets away with it?"

The girls looked at each other. Sara answered, "Hey it happens. Not like they're the only ones doin' it."

"Yeah, there's Roy and Gretchen, Lydie and Leonard..." Rachel smirked.

"It's gross. The guys are pigs and the girls are stuck up bitches, goin' round like their shit don't stink." Sara clarified, again.

Rachel added, "Everybody hates 'em, but you can't do anything, seeing who their boyfriends are."

Christine shook her head. "Yeah, well I'm not Paul's. And I don't want to fuck around with his girlfriend. So you guys want to do me a favor and let her know I'm not interested. Really not interested."

The girls nodded. "You got it Chris." Christine believed them. "Thanks."

"Chris, maybe you better watch out for Minard, too." Rachel warned. "I heard she's been checking you out, you being new and all. She kinda likes to make a point of showing new residents who's the boss in here."

"Yeah, I saw her in the hall. Pretty intense."

"Intense? She's completely psycho is what she is. I'd stay away from her until she gets okay with you." Elena advised.

What the hell is that supposed to mean? "Yeah, I'll try."

Sara wondered, "That ugly cut you've got, she might be thinking you're some kind of badass. Maybe thinking she's got to take you down. We'll get the word out you're cool, maybe she'll lighten up."

This place fucking sucks! Christine whispered, "Yeah, I'd appreciate that."

***

Later, Christine thanked god for the dark. She lay in bed, beneath a thin blanket, thinking back on the rest of the night: joking around at dinner and watching *Dallas* in the community room with a bunch of other girls. Back in their room, before lights out, they had talked about boyfriends and partying and sex, what the days were like in this place, the crazy boring routines day in and day out. And how easy it was to get high and all the shit the kids got high on. How the losers huffed glue and anything in an aerosol can. And how sometimes you had to give a guard a blow job or let him play with your tits to get high, but it didn't mean you were his girlfriend or anything, so it was cool. And if you got your hands on something good, you shared it with your friends and anyone else, if there was enough to go around.

She heard about the counselors and the guards; the ones who had a clue and the ones who were there on some kind of mission to save lost girls and were clueless. And how much shit went down because the ones who had a clue had to let it happen or the place would blow up. Like how they let Minard beat up on the new girls, because that's the way things were. And how the clueless ones never understood what was happening, kept in the dark so they wouldn't make a lot of work for everyone else with disciplinary reviews and lockdowns and outside investigations and cops and lawyers.

Sometimes things went over the line, like an overdose or a serious beating. Everyone hated when that happened, then all hell would break loose with the investigations and all. So, the clued in staff paid attention, made sure things didn't get out of control. That's how it was.

Christine laid there wondering how bad it could get if Paul wouldn't let up. How bad his girlfriend was going to be, if he didn't let up. She had seen her talking to Minard at dinner. Rachel had pointed her out. The two of them stared back at her like they totally hated her. And Minard? Christine knew she couldn't stay away from her forever. She knew the girl was after her. How bad was it going to be when Minard caught up to her? Did anybody running this place know that any of this was happening? According to her roommates, some of the staff knew and they let it happen. The girls swore they'd talk to Phelps and Minard tomorrow, tell them she was cool. Christine weighed their words: *what good would that do?* She should call her lawyer. *And say what?* Most likely she'd be worse off if she did.

Tired of running that mess through her brain, Christine lay there and listened to the sounds of her roommates sleeping, their breathing and shifting; to the sounds beyond the room's walls, bodies passing in the hallway; murmurs from rooms up and down the corridor; to sounds from farther off, doors opening and closing, the building's faint mechanical humming. She heard what sounded like crying, distant, but she wasn't sure.

***

That night, before she went to work, Lynne carefully packed a suitcase: Christine's shampoo, her brush and comb, deodorant, new underwear and bras, her favorite jeans and T-shirts, some shorts and sandals. This, in case she didn't come home after court on Friday. There was no reason to think she would. Lynne wanted to visit

Christine before then, but caseworker LaValley had said she couldn't. She'd have to wait. She couldn't cry, so she focused on packing.

And if she did come home. She'd have to explain all this to the kids, She couldn't handle the thought of that. She'd do it. She finished packing.

CHAPTER 14

Thursday, July 9, 1987

If he doesn't get away from me I'm gonna scream!

Paul straightened up—he had been leaning over the oak table, where Christine sat in the reading room, asking her questions about Branford, about her friends, her boyfriend. "So, he's a criminal? You like the bad ones, eh?" His words mingled with the sick sweetness of his breath freshener. His questions hung there for the other girls in the room to take away.

The room shrunk around Christine, the air pressed against her skull. She didn't answer him. She put her head on the table, shut her eyes against him. *Just back off!* She had been in the study hall all morning. She would be there until lunch, until noon. It wasn't ten o'clock yet. She kept her head on the table. She would be there all day, Mellon had told her. She'd be there until she was assigned to a group, which might not happen for a couple days, according to Mellon. When she was placed in a group, she would be assigned chores, get some school instruction, have an outdoor recreation period, and time in the study hall. That's what her roommates had told her. She figured she wasn't leaving Stonebridge anytime soon.

Christine felt his heat as he came closer. She kept her eyes shut. She smelled his skin—like rotten eggs—before he opened his mouth to speak. Close to her ear, but loud enough so the others could hear. "You know, not all of the bad ones are behind bars like your boyfriend. Maybe one will come for you."

She pressed her eyes shut harder against him, pain flew inside her skull. *Jesus, shut up.* She'd do anything to get away from this guy. Her father came to mind. If he could get her out of this place, she'd go with him. She'd tell her lawyer that's what she wanted. Tomorrow, at court. Christine opened her eyes. Paul had moved away, was across the room watching her. *I've got to get the fuck out of here.*

She paid no attention to the suppertime noise in the dining hall, ignored her tray of boiled ham, potatoes and cabbage. Her roommates had just sat down and she wanted to hear what was going on, what was being said, because there were a lot of girls throwing looks at her—it had to be about Paul and the way he'd acted earlier.

Elena answered yeah, everybody was talking about Paul hitting on her, and how his girlfriend, Julie Phelps, was ripped. "She said she's gonna fuck you up. I told her she's got it all wrong, that you weren't into him, but she just said I was covering for you."

Shit. "What do I do?" She knew Phelps must be staring at her, the way the noise shifted. The talk died down. The clatter of eating eased up. *Enough.* "I've got to talk to her, straighten this out." Christine began to get up.

Rachel grabbed her forearm. "No, not now, not here. She'd bust on you if you went up to her with her girls around. Let me talk to her later. She's okay with me when there's not so many people around. I'll tell her you want to talk...get things straight."

Cold fist in her gut, "Yeah, sure. So, when?"

"The community room, after shower? Before it gets crowded. Just you two." "Okay." Christine nodded.

Christine laid on her cot, stared at the door, waited for Rachel to return. It had been less than ten minutes, but it felt a lot longer. The door finally opened. Rachel and Sara came in. Christine asked how the meeting with Phelps had gone.

"She said sure, see you at the community room. After shower. In like twenty minutes." Rachel answered her.

"She say anything else?"

Sara said, "No, not really. She was acting friendly, like it was a good idea."

It's a setup! "You guys do me a favor and come with me? Wait outside, make sure everything's okay?"

The two girls said they would.

Good. Christine had twenty minutes and her first chance for a shower since she'd been arrested. *Yes!* "Hey Sara, you got some clothes I can borrow? I've been wearing this stuff since Monday."

The other girl popped over to her trunk, pulled out a T- shirt and a pair of sweatpants, tossed them to Christine. *A shower and clean clothes!* She couldn't imagine anything better.

***

Mark attacked, "You want to tell me what the hell is going on?"

Lynne froze, she held a dish towel in one wet hand, and the phone away from her ear in the other.

"I get home tonight and these court papers are waiting for me! Chris living with a drug dealer! Someone's dead! She's assaulting people in some detention center! What the hell is going on, Lynne?"

She bit her lip and choked out, "Mark, I'm sorry."

"Sorry? Sorry doesn't come close. Did you know anything about this? Christine living with this guy?"

Lynne made herself answer, "Yes."

He raged at her. She was irresponsible, pathetic, worthless, a lousy mother, a fucking idiot; she'd pay for what she'd done. Lynne held the receiver against her chest, but heard most of it.

He paused. She had to speak, "Mark, something's wrong. I think Christine may be in trouble where she's at..." She had to continue, "She may need you. She may need to stay with you if they don't let her come home."

Mark exploded. "Oh no you don't, Lynne. Don't go playing some guilt trip game with me. You screwed up and feel bad, so you're dragging me in to fix things. I don't think so. As soon as I read these charges, I called my lawyer and had it all explained. He said you've screwed up so bad there's no way they're going to let

Chris go back to you. He said I could probably have her come live with me if I wanted. But you know what, I thought about it and there's no way I'm going to step in and clean up *your* mess. Chris has been off doing god knows what. Who knows what condition she's in, and you're asking me to have her show up at my doorstep, strung out or whatever. Not gonna happen. She's safe where she is. She's being cared for by professionals who know how to handle girls in her condition. She might not like it. I'm sure she doesn't, but she's just going to have to take her medicine. Hopefully, a little scare will straighten her out."

Screw you, prick. Lynne tasted the blood from her lip. He had to see Christine, see her battered face. Maybe then he'd take her. "Mark, it's just...I understand what you're saying. Maybe she needs to hear it from you directly, for it to mean anything... when she's at court, tomorrow."

Mark looked across the den at the clock on his desk. Nearly six – thirty. The news would be on soon. He wanted to end this conversation, but she might have a point; Christine needed him in court to make sure she got what was best for her. There wasn't anything pressing at work tomorrow. "I'll be there."

***

No one was in the changing room. Christine stripped off her clothes and its four day old stink, threw them on the concrete floor. She set the clean shirt and sweatpants on the wooden bench, which ran along the faded pink cinder block wall. She heard water running. Steam clouded in from the shower entry. No sounds of other girls. Christine tensed. No staff person. She looked at the clock high on the wall; six thirty, there should be a bunch of people there.

She entered the shower through the steam. Three girls stood at the far end, water streaming over them. They weren't washing themselves. They were facing her. *Minard!* Christine looked away, reached for the nearest shower knob, turned the water on, and lifted her face to the water. If she ran, they'd chase her down. She knew. The hot water pelted her. Two girls, not Minard, came up to her, stopped so close that the shower stream struck them also. One of them reached out. Her shoulder pressed against Christine's bicep. The girl shut off the water. Christine turned to the girl, looked into cold black eyes. The girl stepped back, went over to the shower entrance. The other girl joined her. They blocked the entrance. Christine listened for the sound of people in the changing room. She heard nothing.

Minard spoke, "Bancroft, come here."

Christine took a step towards the hulking, naked girl at the back of the shower. Her heart pumped like a fucking maniac. Six feet away. She saw muscle jerk beneath Minard's slabs of flesh; the body nearly six feet tall, and wide. She saw red swollen hands clench and unclench. She smelled cabbage and ham.

"You know who I am?" Minard stepped through the shower flow. A foot closer.

Christine, completely still, said nothing. She watched the other's eyes, set close in her heat splotched face.

"I'm your nightmare." A long moment followed. The only sound was water slapping the wall. "Do it!" Minard commanded.

In one instant, a girl came up behind Christine to the right, grabbed her right wrist, whipped it up and slashed a razor, which was strapped to a toothbrush handle, across Christine's knuckles. She felt no pain. No fear. She didn't cry out.

What happened was done. What happened next was all that mattered. She looked at the blood screaming red from her hand, splashing on the shower floor, thinning as it washed to the drain. Time stopped, Christine took everything in: the sound of her pounding heart, blood pounding in her ears, the water against cinder block, against skin; the taste of her adrenaline like sprayed acid;

Minard's rank viciousness and surging bloodlust; she smelled the reek of wet hair, crotch, flesh and crevices, of rotting teeth. She watched Minard's slate gray eyes wildly flare, blood ribbon to the drain; the feel of her warm blood mixing with the steam and the spray and the sweat and the fear over her skin, dripping against her leg, her foot and the pain rising from her slashed knuckles, sharp, red, throbbing with her pulse. Everything extreme. Waiting.

Ready for what was coming.

"Get her a towel." Minard ordered. One of the girls slipped away. "You're pretty fucking stupid, pissing people off like you been doin'."

Christine said nothing; she stood with her right hand raised shoulder high to slow the blood loss. Brilliant red flowed down her forearm. She wasn't going to scream for help, she wasn't going to run—it wouldn't do her any good. Everything was clear.

The other girl left, returned quickly. She stepped past Christine, brushed against her. Handed Minard a wooden plunger handle. Minard held it with two hands, in front of her. Looking down at it, she growled at Christine. "You've gotta learn." Her head whipped up and she thrust the handle at Christine's belly, stopping inches away.

Christine didn't flinch.

Minard smacked the handle into the palm of her hand. She shifted from one foot to the other. Her face cracked into a broken smile, "I've got a better idea."

Christine watched the girl read her four feet away.

"You go down on me, go down on me good, and I'll cut you a break." The face cracked wider. "You gotta make it good though." She threatened, then quickly thrust the handle at Christine, at her vagina. Minard's eyes were wicked. In a few minutes it was over.

***

Christine savagely assaulted Minard. She rose off Minard's body, still quivering on the shower room floor. When Christine staggered toward the other two girls, they parted to let her pass into the changing room. She was approaching her clothes when Rachel and Sara rushed through the door, stopped short, stared at their naked bleeding friend. "Oh my god, Chris!"

She heard their thin voices sound from far away, didn't answer. She watched them.

Rachel handed her the T-shirt. "God we're sorry Chris, as soon as we heard that Phelps sent Minard."

Sara went to the shower entrance, looked in, saw Minard, and whispered, "Jesus."

The changing room door slammed open. Rachel and Sara spun to face the noise. Christine glanced up to see Flo, one of the night staff, fill the doorway.

"What's going on here?" The wiry black woman marched into the room, straight to Christine, grabbed her forearm and held her bloody hand up, quickly looked at it. She fired at Minard, who stood naked with a split lip and bloody nose, at the shower entrance. "Get dressed and get your ass to your room. I don't want to hear a word out of you. I'll be down soon's I get this girl straightened out. You're on lockdown. Nobody in or out of your goddamn room, you got that?" Minard and the two other girls grabbed their clothes and fled. Flo radioed the other staff person on duty about the three girls, said they'd been ordered to their rooms and were en - route.

"What's your name, child? You new? 'Cause I don't recognize you."

She felt the woman's deep brown eyes search her. She was safe. She floated free, held at the wrist by the woman's bony fingers. "I'm "Christine." The words seemed to flit from her mouth.

"Christine, huh, what room you in?" She couldn't answer, she didn't know.

"She's in our room, room 223." Rachel offered from Christine's side.

"Any of you know what happened?"

They didn't. They had been in the community room and had just gotten there.

"No idea, huh? That's what I thought. Help your friend, here, get dressed and back to her room."

Christine couldn't stand any longer. She sat on the bench, leaned her bare back against the cool cinder block. Sarah and Rachel eased her into her clothes. *My friends.* The clothes felt good, warm. She had been naked for too long. As they helped her dress, her friends asked questions about what happened, but their words were scraps of sound blowing by. Still dazed, she didn't understand what was being asked. She didn't answer. She felt the pulsing from her right hand, saw the bleeding had mostly stopped. The crimson gash leered at her. She looked away.

She traveled with her friends' help down the corridors, past nervous looking staff, to her room. She lay down on her cot and the room swirled violently from a point in the pit of her stomach. She retched into a wastebasket. Elena held under her chin.

Minutes later, Flo stood over Christine, looking in the waste-basket. She sniffed, "You been drinking? I don't smell it. Look at me."

Christine gazed up at the brown eyes.

"Drugs? You on somethin'?" To Christine and the room, "Naw, I don't think so.

Just shook up, huh?"

Christine nodded, what the woman seemed to want her to do.

"Let's get you cleaned up, squared away." To Sara, Rachel and Elena. "Go get a couple wet washcloths and another towel. You see anyone you tell me. This wing's on lockdown and they all know it."

The girls left.

"It don't look so bad. Nothing deep." The woman gently took Christine's hand, applied antiseptic gel to the cut. She wrapped the hand in a gauze bandage. Christine watched the woman's lined face in the hard light. As she dressed the hand, Flo spoke quietly. "What happened tonight is you slipped in the changing room, your hand caught the edge of a locker when you were falling. That's what I'm writing up, and I'm saying that's what you told me." She stopped, looked Christine in the eyes, "It won't do any good to make a big deal out of this. Minard will still be here in the morning, and after she gets disciplined, she'll come lookin' to get back at you. This way it's done, it's over with. I know what I'm talkin' about." Inspecting Christine's bandaged hand, she continued, "I don't know what happened, and I don't want to know, but you must have put some kind of hurt on that girl 'cause she's pretty shook up. Can't say as I've ever seen Minard shook up like this before. Just don't go bragging on it, if you want this to be over."

Christine nodded. She wanted it over. She wanted a deep hole, far away, where no one could reach her.

CHAPTER 15

Friday, July 12, 1987

She had slept at the bottom of a black sea. She woke to the throbbing bandaged hand. She remembered she had been in a fight, in the shower, Minard. She had been cut. She couldn't remember more—her head pounded. She sat up, saw her roommates getting dressed.

Sara spoke to her, "Hey Chris, you better get a move on, you'll miss breakfast."

Sara was there last night. Images surfaced: Minard lying on the shower floor, naked, blood flowing into the drain, Minard staggering past Flo. *What the hell happened?* Flo had said it was over – *what was over?* Her head pounded. She had slept in Sara's clothes. *After the fight.* She remembered she hadn't had clean clothes.

Christine was quiet while walking with Rachel, Sara and Elena through the corridors to the dining hall. The other girls said nothing. Everyone they passed looked at her quickly, then looked away. *Because of the fight.* Nails scraped behind her eyes. They stopped at the entry to the dining hall. Faces quickly turned to Christine, then away. She saw Minard, her back to the doorway. The hum from the room swarmed as Christine entered.

Paul came up beside her and hissed close to her ear. "You are disgusting. Someone should fuck you good, whore."

Go away! She saw him through the blinding, scraping pain in her skull. She saw Julie Phelps beside him. *His girlfriend.* They had to leave her alone. The two faded into a haze.

***

She lay on her back with her eyes shut and heard, "She came in here with one of the staff from the dining hall, complaining of headaches, maybe fifteen minutes ago. We gave her some Tylenol. She must have fallen asleep."

Christine didn't know who spoke. She opened her eyes and saw Julie Mellon over her. Another woman stood next to Mellon. She must have been the person who spoke. There was no one else in the room. Maybe she was the nurse. Christine looked past the two women; the room had posters of different body parts and exercise slogans on the wall. She tried to figure hour she had gotten there, as she lay on a hard cot in a very bright room.

"Okay Christine, you need to get up and get yourself ready. Court today.

The sheriff will be here soon." Mellon looked at the bandaged hand and asked the nurse. "She say anything about the hand?"

The nurse shook her head, no.

To Christine, "The note in your file says you slipped in the changing room last night and cut yourself, is that right?"

She nodded.

Mellon didn't ask any more about the injury. "See that she gets back to her room, I'm late for a meeting." To Christine, "You're in your room until someone comes to get you, understand?"

She nodded, and Mellon was gone.

***

Christine shifted in the back seat of the cruiser to escape the sunlight beating against her. The sight of trees, cars, people and buildings flew by, and made her nauseous. She closed her eyes against it. Her head throbbed. Her hand throbbed. The reek of Minard's body came up her throat. The hiss from Paul's threat that morning, coiled in her bowels. She fought against the nausea and instead, focused on the good scent of Sara's clothes. When this court thing was over, she knew they'd bring her back to Stonebridge. A wave of black passed through her. She couldn't go back. She opened her eyes. Her father could get her out of there. *He could.* She had to reach him.

***

In a small conference room, next to the courtroom, Lynne saw her lawyer and Christine's lawyer. She also noticed the guardian ad litem waiting for someone to answer her question; if Christine wasn't allowed to come home with her, would the judge let her go home with her father today?

"Christine told me it may not be what she wants. "Simmons answered. Fitzgerald interrupted. "Do we even know if he's entered an appearance?"

Lynne didn't know what he meant but she responded, softly, "Maybe it would be better if Christine were with her father rather than in that place. He said he'd be here today."

Just then, the bailiff opened the conference room door and announced, "The judge says we're running late. We're going to start as soon as the juvenile gets here."

"Christine needs to tell him herself that she needs him. Otherwise he won't agree to take her." Lynne looked to both lawyers.

"Lynne, we'll have to do that after the hearing, get SRS in on it. They'll have to do a home evaluation before they place Christine with him." Fitzgerald explained.

Simmons added, "We'll work on getting LaValley, the caseworker, to place Chris somewhere else until you or her father are approved."

Lynne understood Christine was going back to Stonebridge once she left the courtroom. She shook her head, no.

"The transport's arrived. The judge wants everyone in the courtroom." The bailiff interrupted from the door.

***

Hot and humid, the air was so much thicker in Branford. Christine felt it swamp the cruiser when the door opened. It draped over her as she shuffled, shackled, from the cruiser to the courthouse entry. Passing through the courthouse's narrow back passages – with the broad shouldered sheriff leading and the female sheriff following from behind, Christine steeled herself. She had to explain to everyone in that courtroom how it would be good, if they let her stay with her father. The lead sheriff stopped at the door she knew opened to the courtroom. The female sheriff removed the handcuffs and the ankle cuffs. *Help me, god.*

Jesus Christ! Mark watched Christine enter. He stared at her, at the purple-green bruise that spread from her forehead's thick-stitched gash to her red rimmed, sunken eyes. He gaped at her bone thin frame, draped in oversized clothing, her bandaged hand, cradled against her ribcage, her shuffle between the two officers. Her eyes caught his and burned into him. He averted his eyes. He couldn't see her like that, so damaged.

She saw her father with that same stupid, horrified expression she had gotten two days ago from the rest of them. She pressed on a smile as she searched his face, tried to say "hi, dad" with her eyes. But she couldn't make them twinkle that way. She slipped. Instead, her eyes accused. *Are you going to take care of me? Because I need you. Now!* He looked away and didn't look back. *Fuck you!*

Lynne noticed the bandaged hand, then the rage in Christine's eyes. She saw her daughter in danger. She heard the judge talking, the lawyers talking, that miserable caseworker LaValley talking, but she wasn't listening. She intently watched Christine.

Christine ignored the court and instead, watched as her father stared straight ahead. The judge would listen to him. He was the key. She stared at him, pleaded silently.

C'mon, say you'll take me! Take me! His lawyer spoke to the judge, "Your Honor, as you can well imagine..." *He's not going to do it!*

She stopped looking at her father. Her eyes half focused on some middle distance away from him, as the words droned past her. The lawyer depicted her father's concern and heartbreak, his trust and hope, his humility and gratitude to the State for rescuing his troubled daughter and expertly caring for her at this difficult time. The judge nodded his approval of the father's gratitude.

Her insides crashed. She had to do something, she didn't know what.

> Leaning into her lawyer, Christine asked, "Can I say something to the judge?" Simmons nodded, yes.

When it was her turn to speak, Christine rose slowly, unsure, feeling cold sweat everywhere, her ears rang. She began as her eyes met the judge's glower. "Your Honor, thank you. I just wanted to say that I know I did some stupid stuff, and I can understand why some people might think I'm out of control, but they don't have to worry because I'm not. Really, I'm okay. There's no need to have me locked up. I can behave myself, no problem. At my mother's or, if people are uncomfortable with that, then with my father."

In that next frozen moment, she saw her father look up at her, his steel blue eyes spiked with annoyance. She had to tell him. "Everything will be fine, dad. Really."

Mark turned away, jaw clenched. With the courtroom as silent as a stone, Christine heard the blood pound in her ears. She sat down. She didn't raise her eyes. She wouldn't let them see her cry.

"Miss, you may not like where you are now, but your father is right, you need to be cared for by people who know how to handle girls like you." The judge scolded her. "I've read what happened in Burlington, and I've heard the parties' arguments about your custody while this case proceeds and I agree with the State and your father that you should remain in the custody of the Commissioner of SRS, who shall be responsible for where you are placed. And that is the order of this Court."

Everyone stood, the swirl of bodies, her mother a distance away. Christine tried to hold on, tried not to lose it. She kept her tearful mother in sight. Her father disappeared. She knew he was furious with her. She had put him on the spot in front of all these people. She had questioned his judgment. She saw him in her mind, rimmed in black, in control.

In the conference room, her mother, the lawyers and the old woman guardian—asked if she was okay. Asked if anything had happened to her and how she hurt her hand. There was nothing to say. She couldn't explain what had happened, nor what was happening to her. She said she was fine, that she was tired, that she had slipped and cut her hand. She tried to smile. No one smiled back. Her father would never save her now. She had angered him. She fought back the bile rising in her so she could be present with her mother in that small room. The lawyers explained to Lynne and Christine what came next: the merits hearing. This would be when the judge would decide whether Christine was abused, neglected or unmanageable. The lawyers said there was no sense disputing the merits since Christine had been found living with a cocaine dealer far from home. The issue in this case was custody and control over Christine. The lawyers explained how the law mandated the court's primary concern was in the best interests of the child, Christine. The thinking was to return a child to her home as soon as possible. Their job was to also convince SRS and the judge that something like this—Christine getting involved with drugs and drug dealers—wouldn't ever happen again. Lynne asked how they would do this.

"We work with caseworker LaValley on a plan that makes them comfortable sending Christine home." Fitzgerald said. "Things like drug and alcohol screening, some substance abuse counseling, probably a parenting course. Then you and Christine follow the plan."

"How long will that take?"

"It's hard to say. Sometimes weeks, or months. It depends on the plan and how well you do with it."

That can't be right! Lynne looked at Christine, read the fear in her eyes.

Weeks! Months! Christine pushed down her panic.

"That's why we've got to get going right away with LaValley, starting with a home visit, so she can check out your living situation. Start turning you into a real person in her mind. I mean she hasn't even interviewed you yet, has she?" Fitzgerald asked.

Lynne shook her head no.

Christine rasped, "I could be there months?"

"Not necessarily." Simons responded. "Until the judge approves your return to your mother, we're going to push your caseworker to find another place for you to live."

Christine stared at the table. *I'm fucked.* A black river roared through her.

"Christine, it's time you headed back." LaValley said from the door, with the sheriffs just behind her.

Christine stiffened, looked up to see the broad faced woman grinning at her. *No!*

She felt arms around her shoulders, her mother's. She felt her mother press her cheek against the top of her head. She heard, "I'll be up to visit tomorrow. I'll bring some things for you." She felt warm tears on her scalp. She stood up. She had to go.

"Tomorrow." Christine whispered. They kissed each other's wet cheeks.

When they separated, Christine felt a body close in behind her. She felt strong fingers wrap around her forearm. She jolted, nearly tried to break away. She caught herself in time. Dread swarmed through her. She left, quietly.

Lynne and the others watched in silence from the conference room as the sheriff, towering over Christine, pulled her arms behind her and handcuffed her in the hallway. Lynne's heart ripped open.

LaValley broke the silence. "Lynne, we should set up a time when you can come in." The caseworker rummaged through her shoulder bag, as Lynne watched Christine disappear through the doors at the end of the corridor.

"Hold on Rose." Simmons spoke. "I want to know what is going on with Christine up there. The bashed head? The hand? Is there a problem you're not telling us about?"

"What? No! She's had a couple accidents." LaValley stammered.

"A couple accidents! You're kidding, right? Something's going on, what is it?" "We don't have any information..."

Simmons cut her off, "So you're just going to sit back and wait? Until when? Until..." The lawyer stopped.

Lynne stood between the two women, shaking. LaValley didn't respond.

Simmons demanded. "I want Christine out of there. Now."

"Are there any foster beds available, Rose?" Fitzgerald asked.

"Maybe one, opening up Monday. But it's not an intensive placement, so I don't think..."

Fitzgerald interrupted her. "Why does this need to be an intensive? Basically, this is an unmanageable kid case. Slap some conditions on her like 'restricted to the premises' or a 'daily piss test.' Let her know, if she screws up, she's back at Stonebridge. That should be enough to hold her. Who's the placement?"

LaValley named the foster parents. Fitzgerald smiled. He knew them. He said they were more than capable of handling Christine, that they had handled a lot worse over the years. He looked to attorney Simmons, who nodded in agreement.

"Alright, I'll call them when I get back to the office."

"So Christine should be there Monday?" Simmons asked.

LaValley said yes, most likely. She'd try to reach the foster parents that night. Lynne smiled weakly. *Thank god.*

***

Back at the detention center, Christine slumped in a chair, in Julie Mellon's office. She stared at nothing. The woman from across the oak desk talked at her. "Alright, we have the court's order now, so it looks like you're going to be staying with us awhile. That means we need to get you into some programming. It's late, so we won't get started today. But Monday, I'll meet with staff and set something up and on Tuesday, we'll have you up and running."

The voice sounded like bubble gum. Fake. She didn't care what Mellon said.

"How's that sound?" The woman asked again.

Christine didn't look at the woman, didn't say anything.

"In the meantime you get to relax in the study hall. I'll have a staff member take you down there."

Christine dug her fingernails into her thigh.

When she arrived at the study hall, Paul looked Christine up and down, while she searched the room for a place to sit, a place where she could shut her eyes against him. Against the rest of them, staring at her. The only seats available were the wooden chairs at the table. She slid into one of the chairs and put her head down. She heard a chair scrape against the linoleum, from the area where Paul had sat. She smelled his cologne approaching.

Go away, go away, go away. He bumped the table. She squeezed her eyes to keep them shut. If she opened them, she knew she'd see his thick crotch just above table level, a couple feet away. Pain scraped behind her eyes. He would keep banging the table so long as her head rested on it, she knew that. She sat up, her eyes open—he wasn't in sight. The girls on the couch across the room looked at her, then past her at him. He brushed her from behind, brushed her chair with his hip, as he passed her by. Christine froze. She heard the sound of his chair scrape the linoleum floor. She got up, went directly to his desk, blood pounded at her temples. She watched herself from a distance say to him in a fervent whisper, "You have to leave me alone."

His lewd grin reached her through her black rimmed vision. He spoke slowly, "You... have... to... fuck... me... first."

No! Christine shot down the vast hole that burst open in the center of her chest.

Somehow, she returned to her chair.

***

Back in her room, alone after study hall, she sat on her bunk with her back pressed against the wall, her knees drawn up to her chin, her arms wrapped tight around her shins. She saw nothing. Suddenly, the door swung open. Elena tripped across the room, flopped on her bunk. Rachel and Sara were quick behind her. Rachel swore she'd never pick another weed, so long as she lived.

Spotting Christine, Sara asked, "Hey, we didn't know if you'd be coming back, so how'd court go?"

Christine watched the girls scramble around, chatting away, from the bottom of a deep well. They were dirty and sweaty and she could taste them in the air. They were good. She surfaced, watched herself answer. "I'm here, right?"

Elena laughed. "No shit. How's the hand?"

Christine looked at her bandaged hand and answered softly, "It's alright."

"Yeah? That's good. Minard, though, she wasn't doing so good today, all weirded out."

"Pounded D'Orio when she asked what happened last night." Rachel remarked. "Staff took her away.' Sara added. "They were gonna put her in segregation, but came back twenty minutes later 'cause someone's already there on suicide watch." "Big ol' Minard was looking crazy." Elana hooted.

The girls' words reached Christine, muffled, from a distance. They kept talking. They advised her to stay in the room after dinner, promised to stay with her and warned her to stay away from Minard. She heard their concern. They were good friends. She smiled, grateful for them.

***

Windham County State's Attorney Howard Petrie loosened his tie and checked his watch, as his call went through. It was just past 4:30. Ray Dugan picked up on the other end.

"Ray, Howard Petrie. I got your message. So the boyfriend hung himself?"

"Yeah, they found him this morning, in his cell.".

"That's a real shame. You get anything out of him about what happened the night that...?"

"No, nothing. That's why I'm calling about the girl. I'm hoping she's got something for me, some names. What's happening with her down there?"

"She was in court today. Overbeck ordered her to remain in SRS custody. They've stuck her in Stonebridge."

"Good place for her. I'll get my investigator down there sometime next week to see what she's got. Listen, Howard, do me a favor and make sure she doesn't go anywhere until I'm through with her."

Petrie heard the hitch in Dugan's voice. He couldn't imagine losing one of his kids that way, or any way. "Yeah, Ray, sure. Give my best to Janice. Hang in there, okay? Anything you need down this end you just let me know."

Dugan's voice was hard. "Just make sure she stays locked up."

***

The clatter and the roar reached Christine before she arrived at the dining hall. Maybe it wasn't a good idea to go there. She entered and a balled, crazy energy flew at her. Everyone's eyes followed her to the food line, where she grabbed her tray and silverware. The silverware glowed bright. *Where's Minard?* She searched the tables until she spotted the girl's broad back. The others at the table looked at Christine as they spoke. They were all talking about her, she knew that: her and Minard.

As they moved forward in the line, Christine's friends were talking to her, but she didn't hear them. Their words blended into the room's clamor. The food looked grotesque—some kind of dead animal in brown liquid, white starch, drowned vegetables. Her tongue swelled and her throat tightened. Maybe there was soup somewhere. She could swallow that. Maybe some crackers. The line moved very slowly. Food piled on plates, the smell reached her: dead food. Minard was still seated in the same place. No sign of Paul—*where is he?* She searched. He had a way of sneaking up on her. Not like Minard. Christine could see her. She would know when Minard was coming. But Paul, well he'd find her, sneak up on her. He had said so. Thank god they had chicken noodle soup and crackers. Christine followed her friends, with their piles of dead food, to a table across the room from Minard. She could see the girl from where she sat.

Bent over the bowl, the warm smell rose and filled her. She swallowed the hot broth, not listening to the girls at her table, intent on filling herself with the good soup. Suddenly someone stood beside her, held a tray while she spoke. Christine pushed through the noise to hear the girl who had come from the other table. She hadn't seen her approaching! She'd been distracted eating! All she needed to know was where Minard was, and she had slipped! She looked, saw Minard, still seated. The fist that had seized her heart released it.

The girl was still there, still speaking, her words lost again. Christine fought to hear her, "...and she's really pissed off about it. Because you..." She didn't understand what the girl was talking about. She looked back to her soup. The girl left. Christine quickly glanced at Minard. She was still at her table.

Christine asked Rachel beside her, "Where's Paul?"

Rachel answered he had gone for the day, he wouldn't be back until tomorrow. *Good. But Minard is really pissed off.* Christine no longer wanted to eat, she couldn't eat. She asked Rachel, "Can we go back to the room now?"

"Yeah, soon as I'm done."

Christine saw the half eaten dead food on the plate and Rachel talking with her mouth full.

"You alright, Chris? You don't look so good." She heard Rachel ask.

Sara, sitting across from Christine, spoke. "I'd be pretty upset, too, I mean D'Orio basically just said that Chris is fucked. I think we should tell Flo or someone."

Rachel shook her head. "Just make more trouble..."

More trouble.

"...besides, Flo knows something's up, she saw D'Orio come over here..."

Something's up.

"Lot of good that did last night." Sara argued.

Rachel snapped back. "Last night was different. Last night was before all this shit happened. Now she knows."

Christine watched Minard get up. She pleaded, "I want to go back to the room now." The black rimming pain brutally amped up.

Back in the room the three girls tried playing gin rummy, but Christine couldn't.

She didn't know what she was supposed to do with her cards, unable to read their cryptic meanings. She mimicked her roommates awhile, then quit. She sat on her bed with a Seventeen magazine she wasn't reading. She flipped through the pages a couple times, but they were a blurred confusion. She watched the door. God, her eyes hurt, her head hurt. Someone outside in the hall banged the door hard—all three girls jumped. Christine cringed inside. *The door has no lock!* She got up and put a foot locker in front of the door. She refused to leave the room to brush her teeth or wash up. The other girls took turns washing up, never leaving her alone.

Lights out. Christine sat in bed, unblinking. Bits of memory surfaced—pieces of last night in the shower, Paul leering and hissing in her ear, her father staring with hatred at her that morning – all careened through her mind. She tried to stop the fractured stream by sitting motionless. When she moved, the images became angry. She conjured up images of her mother holding her, crying with her, promising her tomorrow. Tomorrow was something. Tomorrow was nothing. She could not shut her eyes because ...*why?* In the darkness, Minard would get her, Paul would get her.

Awake alone. Elena sniffled, twitched in her sleep. Rachel and Sara in the same bed, silent, entwined, asleep. Sleepless, the red nail rimmed Christine's skull. She refused rest, to keep them from getting her.

CHAPTER 16

Saturday, July 13, 1987

Through the long night, Christine weakened under a siege of vicious scenes from the past few days, shards twisted from her recent memory, until she surrendered to a violent sleep the hour before the sky began to lighten.

She is in a round room somewhere. Light, empty, rows of tall windows. She doesn't know where the room is. Now there are many people. The room is no longer light. She can't see the windows because of the people. She can't tell who the people are; they're faceless. Murmuring, they walk around her in single file. She is in the center. She thinks she knows then but cannot recognize them.

She sees her mother at the fringe, moving with the others, all moving in the same direction. She doesn't try to call to her mother; she doesn't have enough strength. She has no arms. She hears crows, but won't look up. If she looks up, it will be bad. Now they are landing on her head and shoulders, picking at her hair, tearing her skin with their talons.

Where are they coming from? She can't look up. None of the people are helping her; they are still doing the same thing, moving around her. She can't see her mother any more.

Someone brushes against her, flesh on her flesh. She can't see who. Another brush. Who is it? The other people aren't saying. Again. This time the flesh presses against her longer. The flesh is clammy. She must be naked. The people she can see are wearing clothes.

Her head is bloodied from the birds. The tufts of hair they take away are blood tipped. She can't look up to see where they are going with her hair. She had beautiful hair before this. None of the people seem to notice. She catches a glimpse of her mother in the crowd, then she is gone again.

Touched again. More flesh brushing up against her. It's disgusting. As soon as she thinks that, the people stop moving, no more birds appear. She feels the pain from the wounds to her head. Maybe someone will help, now that they have stopped moving.

Where is her mother?

The touch of flesh again; loose, clammy flesh. She can't see who it is. She is always looking in the other direction when she is touched, and can never turn her head in time to see who is touching her. This time, when she turns, a swollen penis and a torso loom inches from her face. She can't look up, something bad will happen if she does. The penis and groin are so close she can't see anything else. The groin is hairless. Someone has to help her.

She has to take the penis in her mouth. There is nothing else she can do. It's disgusting. As soon as she thinks that, the penis swells so that she is choking on it; it is forced down her throat and she can't breathe. She can't push away because she has no arms. She hears a loud humming. She can't breathe. The penis is even larger and further down her throat and she can't even gag. She has to look up.

The torso is smooth and has arms. The head is high above, she can't see the face.

Who is it? She is desperate to know. If she knew then she could breathe. The penis is rocking in her mouth. She is terrified of what might happen. The rocking – deeper, faster. She can't breathe.

She sees Jimmy. She gasps for air. Everything is gone except Jimmy - - he floats above her a few feet away, very sad, in the room where she was in the beginning. She can't understand what he wants, he wants something. Suddenly she is very cold. She is terrified.

Christine bolted awake, her sheet and blanket twisted around her legs, her T-shirt drenched in sweat. Jagged shreds of nightmare cut across her mind, her racing heart fueling the scenes. She had to slow it, her heart. She tried to slow her pulse, her breathing, but couldn't.

The day was beginning. Christine sat upright on her cot. A blasting agony rose in her skull and smothering the dreamed images. Through the violence, she made out a slight hum from a great distance. She desperately focused on the faint vibration to hold on to something beyond her pain.

Through burning eyes, she watched her roommates wake up, each awakening a miracle. *Miracles of life*. She watched in awe as they roused themselves and rose. Christine knew they were angels, each of them. Her awe intensified, filled her breast and lifted her to jangling heights. She rose with her roommates and shared the sacrament of dressing and washing with them. She said nothing, not wanting to interfere with the sacredness of these moments. It had been a long night, and the blessedness of the day was upon them.

At the dining hall table Christine sat board straight with a blissful smile as she deliberately ate corn flakes.

Elena questioned her, "Hey Chris, you get into somethin' good this morning?

What's with the shit eating grin?"

Christine smiled more broadly, she felt she could barely contain the powerful joy tumbling inside her. Words couldn't express it. She said, "Oh, nothing." *Who wouldn't be full of joy, sitting with angels.*

She swung her head around to see Paul walk into the room—*the dark one!* She swung back to the table abruptly, hoping he wouldn't find her.

Rachel asked, "Hey Chris, you alright?"

Her euphoria was unraveling; the hum of her surroundings took on an ominous pitch, becoming a vast noise in her head. She tried to smile; it hurt.

She whispered, "I think so. I don't know."

Rachel leaned in close. "Chris, what have you been doin'?"

What does that mean? I know my angel is trying to help, but what is she saying?

"I don't know." She whispered. Elena softly, "She wigging?"

Rachel spoke to the other girls, "Listen... let's get Chris back to the room. We can figure out what to do there."

Christine liked the sounds of that; her angels were going to take care of her.

Sara added, "Good thing it's Saturday, just have to make it through morning lecture then kite the rest of the day."

As the girls left the dining hall, Paul approached them from behind. Christine whirled around to face him. Her face contorted. She spat, "Stay away from me."

The other girls froze. Paul stood there with his wicked, unflinching grin.

Rachel murmured to Christine, who stared knives at that grin. "Jesus Christ Chris, you wanna knock it off."

Sara spoke to Paul, who kept his eyes locked on Christine. "We were just goin' back to our room. We'll be fine. Be back in a few minutes. For lecture."

He ignored Sara and instead, spoke to Christine, his words riding a silk scarf to her ears. "It's alright. I can understand you would be upset. I myself just heard that your boyfriend hung himself yesterday." He paused, reset the grin.

Christine's eyes violently flickered.

His smile broadened before it disappeared completely for the cold, final words, "If there's anything I can do, help in any way, let me know."

Through the clanging, blind to everything, Christine stood mute. "C'mon Chris." Sara took her by the arm, the girls escaped.

They laid Christine down. Rachel checked her temperature. No fever, but her skin was damp. She looked into Christine's eyes—dilated pupils. Her breathing was rapid and shallow. Her heart beat hard and fast. Sara put wet paper towels on Christine's forehead. Her eyes flitted around.

Through the clanging and the burning within her, Christine begged. "Save me!" Rachel commanded. "She's tripping. Get orange juice, as much as you can."

Elena left.

Sara considered, "Maybe we should bring her to the nurse."

"No, let's see if we can't get her straight first. Save her a shitload of trouble."

Christine saw her angels chittering, caring for her. The crashing let up; *they will save me.*

Elena returned with a quart of orange juice. Christine gulped the drink from the container, then laid back with her eyes shut. A few minutes later, her eyelids had stopped twitching, her breathing steadied. The clanging softened.

Rachel, sat at her side. "She seems better. Chris, how you doin'?" Christine heard her friend, saw her hover over her. "Better."

"Yeah? Listen, we have to go back to the dining hall. You o.k. with that?" "Are you guys going?" Christine mumbled.

"Yeah, all of us."

"Chris, baby, what'd you take?" Sara asked.

What does she mean? "I don't know." The noise increased, tinged ominous. The pain began to fragment and careen.

Elena whistled through her teeth. "You don't know? Shit, it could be anything." "We've gotta go." Rachel said. "Chris, hang tight, we'll get you through this." Christine nodded, the craziness leveled off. *We will.* As they walked down the hall, Rachel spoke to the other girls. "We have to keep Paul away from Chris, he's freaking her out."

The other two girls nodded. Christine watched her protectors make their steely plans. *They are good.* She had no idea what they were saying.

At the dining hall doorway, the energy from the room tore into Christine. Word had spread that she was freaking, and nearly all the girls were trying to get a look at her. The staff in the hall hadn't heard and wondered what was going on. Paul knew. He watched Christine from the far end of the room.

Through the fierce noise Christine screamed to herself. *Who are these people?* She couldn't see faces. *What do they want?* She locked stiff.

Rachel held Christine's rigid arm and whispered. "This is a bad idea. Let's go see the nurse."

Christine turned to the soft voice that reached her through the chaos, saw Rachel.

My angel.

"You four! What are you doing back there?" The words boomed from the front of the room, from the small woman who stood at the podium, leaning into the microphone.

The sound slammed the room, slammed Christine—*oh my god, save me!* She looked up, through the blast, to face her destroyer. There, floating before her, all else having disappeared, was Jimmy. *Why?* Needing her to be with him. *No!*

"Get away, get away, get away!" She screamed, flailing at the vision. The roar inside Christine burst from her. Then oblivion.

***

"Jesus Christ, what's going on here?" The shift supervisor marched into the nurse's office. The nurse stepped forward. The supervisor looked past her to see a girl sitting on the floor, in a corner, knees drawn up to her bowed head, matted hair covering her face, rocking. Two staff workers stood on either side of the girl. Without waiting for the nurse to say anything, the supervisor asked, "Drugs?"

"Probably. She's non responsive, hallucinating." The nurse answered. "You given her anything?"

"No, I don't have any medical release paperwork in the file from SRS." "Goddamnit! Don't give her anything. Get her in restraints before she hurts somebody. And get an ambulance here ASAP to take her up to Waterbury. I'll get something from SRS in the meantime to get her admitted." The supervisor wrapped her cardigan tighter around herself, then left.

Christine faced howling, scorching winds. No angels. The wicked circled to feast on her. *Jesus save me. Jesus save me. Jesus save me...*

SECTION 2

CHAPTER 17

"I'm here, Chris." Lynne whispered, bedside, at the state hospital. She pressed her wet cheek against her daughter's, tried to send the motionless girl every particle of love she had ever known. She offered her warmth, mingled their breath, not knowing what reached her. Christine lay hollow eyed beneath the thin hospital blanket. Lynne knew she would give up her soul to save her daughter. A whisper of her daughter's breath passed her ear. The shimmer of her pale heat rose to Lynne's cheek. Straightening up, rising from a swoon, Lynne evoked another formless prayer.

How she had arrived at this place—Waterbury, the redbrick state psychiatric hospital—was a blur. When she had gotten to Stonebridge earlier, for her visit with Christine, a woman in a sweater at the front desk had told her Christine had been taken to Waterbury a few hours before. The woman had said there had been an emergency. Lynne had panicked. She demanded to know what had happened, but the woman had said she had no other information, then gave her directions to the hospital.

At the reception area, she had asked where she could find Christine. The stolid woman had telephoned someone and had given Lynne the name of the building and the room number. Lynne found Christine in the room where they now sat. Lynne studied her daughter's stillness.

Someone quietly came up beside her; a stocky man with white hair tufted around his ears and a shining bald crown. Ruddy faced and not much taller than Lynne, he introduced himself. "Mrs. Bancroft? I'm Dr. Hawkins. I admitted Christine."

Lynne nodded. "What's happened?"

The doctor turned to her. "Christine appears to have suffered a psychotic break." Lynne didn't understand but didn't ask for an explanation.

"She was hallucinating when she arrived. She's sedated now."

"Does she know I'm here?"

"Perhaps."

Lynne saw slight twitching at the corner of Christine's eyes, watched her lips slightly move. "How long will she be like this?" She asked.

"It's hard to say. This may be a brief, acute episode, or it may be the onset of a longer term, chronic condition. Right now we can only monitor Christine's symptoms until we have enough information for a diagnosis."

Lynne wanted more. "Why?"

"We don't have enough information leading to the cause of Christine's break. We may never know."

There are no answers. Lynne felt oddly light. All she could do was love Christine completely. Nothing more, nothing less.

***

In the dense gray fog of Christine's mind, fragments of blasted scenes slowly appeared occasionally, dull toned, before sinking away. A constant thrumming rose and fell in small measures, with the appearance and dissolution of those fragments. Once the fog thinned, everything lightened a few shades. The thrum pitched higher and Christine glimpsed her mother at the fringe, gazing at her. She held that image, precious, until the fog reclaimed it.

***

Mark escaped into the hospital building, drenched by the sudden July downpour. A thunderclap exploded as the automatic door swished shut and the air conditioning swept over him. With the black sky and sheets of rain behind him, he saw ahead the brightly lit corridors beyond the well-lit empty waiting area. It was Sunday afternoon, the day after he had gotten a call from some social worker in Vermont.

"Can I help you?" The black woman behind the desk asked.

"Christine Bancroft."

The woman looked down at something Mark couldn't see, then answered with his daughter's room number.

He went and stood beside Christine's bed, chilled water trickling down his neck, wet shirt clinging to his shoulders and chest, wet slacks clinging to his thighs. He shivered. He looked down at the unmoving body, lying straight, beneath the white bedspread, arms along her sides. Her damaged face, still. *Jesus Christ.* His Christine, in a state mental hospital.

He spoke to her. "Honey, it's me. Dad." He touched her shoulder, quickly took his hand away. It seemed wrong to touch her. He thought he saw her eyelids flicker. The doctor had said she would more than likely be unresponsive. He had mentioned she was heavily medicated.

Mark watched his daughter, thinking *that's what they do, just dope them up*. The doctor basically had said she lost her mind. Other than that, they didn't know anything. So they were just going to dope her up and leave her in a room. She'd been there two days and nothing had changed, according to the doctor. *Ridiculous!* They had no idea what they were doing – *just dope her up and make money*. He looked down at Christine's twitching face. He couldn't stand it and left without saying anything.

***

A storm rose black and red in Christine's mind. Violent clouds churned from all points on the horizon. She couldn't breathe. The sea beneath her churned dark. Indistinct images rampaged. He was there, her father. The turmoil lasted long in her mind, but she didn't know time. She didn't know the beginning or the end of it. She suffered the threat as long as it lasted.

CHAPTER 18

Nearly a month after the date Christine was arrested, Lynne entered the same courtroom, where she had seen her battered, handcuffed daughter. She remembered Christine's smile signaling her not to worry. Now her daughter was in a hospital, barely speaking. Lynne's throat tightened. She sweat through her light cotton blouse. She looked for Mark, although her lawyer said he wouldn't be there. Attorney Fitzgerald appeared at Lynne's elbow.

"I'm not clear what we're doing today." Lynne began.

"We're supposed to schedule the merits hearing to determine whether Christine is unmanageable, but the lawyers have agreed to ask the judge to put the hearing off until Christine is better."

"Why am I here?" Lynne murmured.

"To show the judge you're committed to Christine. It could help bring her home." Lynne noted the empty chair next to Christine's lawyer. *When will that be?* But Christine had been talking a bit, saying some things that made sense. Lynne saw small changes every few days, when she was able to get to the hospital. She said to Fitzgerald, "She's improving."

Judge Overbeck entered the courtroom, took his seat. He spoke to the state attorney. "Do you have a stipulation to the merits to present to the court?"

The young lawyer stammered, "No, your Honor. We thought... you see... the juvenile has suffered some sort of psychological, um, breakdown, I guess. She can't really..." The lawyer looked to LaValley for help as she continued. "She's at Waterbury. She's not really communicative."

The judge interrupted. "What's that got to do with anything? I've got a clear cut case of unmanageability in front of me, so where's the parties' stipulation to merits?"

Lynne didn't understand. She touched Fitzgerald's elbow.

"The judge wants us to concede that Christine was unmanageable, and skip the hearing." He whispered.

Christine's lawyer, attorney Simmons, stood. "Your Honor, we were all under the impression that this would be a status conference..."

The judge barked. "It didn't say 'status conference' on the hearing notice, did it?" Fitzgerald stood up.

Overbeck cut him off before he had a chance to speak. "Before I instruct the State to begin putting on its case, I want to know a few things. I want to know whether there will be any evidence that the juvenile was not sixteen years old when she was arrested in Burlington at dawn in the apartment of an adult male, in the bed of that man at the time she was arrested. I want to know whether there will be any evidence that a felony quantity of cocaine was not located in that apartment at the time the juvenile was arrested. And I want to know whether there will be any evidence that the apartment in which the juvenile was arrested, was not located more than a hundred miles away from the home of her custodial parent, her mother." Looking at Lynne as he spoke, "If you don't have evidence refuting those points then you are wasting my time and the time of this court. Because those facts overwhelmingly point to the unmanageability of the juvenile, and most likely, neglect by the mother." Lynne burned with shame.

Overbeck paused, looked from one lawyer to the next. "You all know the drill; the parties stipulate the child was unmanageable, we move on. We focus on what the child needs. I'll call a five minute recess."

He stood and left the bench without giving the lawyers a chance to respond. Lynne, Simmons, Mrs. Fromme, and Fitzgerald gathered in the small conference room off the hallway, outside the courtroom.

Fitzgerald started. "I don't like it. Christine should have a chance to explain what happened, but Overbeck's already decided."

"We don't have anything that's going to change his mind and, to be honest, we don't want to drag out what happened in front of Overbeck." Simmons said. "We do a full merits hearing and it's going to get really graphic."

Lynne stared at her feet. She understood: the arrest, the drugs, that boy's death.

Mrs. Fromme nodded. "It's sad isn't it."

"Christine is getting better." Lynne insisted. The room went silent. Simmons spoke. "We should stipulate that Christine was unmanageable."

Fitzgerald and Fromme agreed.

Lynne went along with the others, because they seemed to know what should happen. She didn't realize she was crying when she said, "We're not bad people."

> She felt an arm around her shoulder. It was Christine's lawyer.

A few minutes later they were back in the courtroom. Judge Overbeck sat in his chair and the lawyers took turns explaining to him that they all shared the position that Christine had been unmanageable. The judge asked Mrs. Fromme if she agreed, and she said she did. He then issued his finding that Christine was "unmanageable and therefore a child in need of care and supervision." He ordered that she "remain in the custody of the Commissioner of the Department of Social and Rehabilitation Services, until further order of the court."

Lynne couldn't lift her eyes to face his condemnation.

***

On the very day the judge ruled she was unmanageable, Christine was able to sit up through most of the day and had taken a short walk in the small garden outside her wing of the hospital. She noticed the sun through the trees and felt a slight breeze while she walked. She smiled.

***

Lynne stopped in the hospital hallway, her Nikes squeaked on the waxed floor that shined up at her. She spread her arms to stop her children, to keep them behind her. They were racing to see their sister, her room midway down the corridor. It was their first visit and Lynne didn't want them barging in on her.

She took a deep breath. "Alright you two, you have to settle down. We have to take it easy."

Matt nodded, Charlotte answered yes. They shuffled where they stood, Matt shifted the presents in his arms while Charlotte stared down at the cake she was holding. Lynne followed her gaze to the pink and white "17" candle.

August eighth, it had been a gorgeous day, the day Christine was born. Lynne could never forget her magnificent daughter, pink and strong, being handed to her moments after her birth. She remembered her heart expanding as if she contained the world when she held Christine to her breast. That feeling echoed throughout her as she stood in the hospital corridor.

"Okay?" Lynne lowered her arms. She didn't know how this was going to work out, even though the doctor said it should be fine. She led her two younger children to Christine's room.

When they walked through the door, they quietly called out "Happy Birthday." Lynne saw Christine's face shine brighter than she had seen in a long time, long before the breakdown. She watched Christine beam as Matt bent over to hug her in bed, as

Charlotte proudly announce she had made the carrot cake from scratch.

For the next ten minutes Matt and Charlotte stayed at Christine's bedside as they peppered her with stories from home, about their friends, about Matt's job bagging groceries at the Finast, about the Liszt piece Charlotte was learning at her piano lessons, about the neighbor's dog pooping on their lawn. Lynne watched from the end of the bed, smiling. When she noticed Christine's eyes start to lose focus, she suggested it was time to open presents.

Christine rallied. She opened the T- shirt from Charlotte and the mug from Matt hich both stated: *Best Sister Ever!* She goofed along, "Ya really think so? Well I have to agree." Everyone laughed.

Lynne handed Christine her present. Before she had it completely unwrapped, Christine could see enough of the book's cover to blurt out. "Oh mom!" She pulled at the wrapping with shaking hands. Lynne leaned over and helped. "Mom..." Christine's eyes welled up. She hugged the book of Audubon prints to her chest before she released it and showed her brother and sister.

Lynne shared, "I saw it in the bookstore window, and I had to get it. For you."

She had seen it earlier that week while walking home from court, miserable after everyone had agreed that Christine was "in need of care and supervision." In that dark moment she had found something beautiful for her precious daughter.

Lynne noticed Christine's smile grow weary. "Are you feeling alright, sweetie?"

"I'm...fine." Christine shut her eyes. "I'm fine." She didn't open them.

"Tell you what, we'll give the cake to the nurses and tell them to save it for when you're a little more rested."

Christine opened her eyes, looked at her mother at the foot of her bed, at Matt and Charlotte next to her. She didn't speak. She closed her eyes.

Lynne kissed her on the forehead and whispered. "It's time for us to go."

Matt and Charlotte both squeezed Christine's hand. Lynne saw that each had teared up.

***

It had all been fine until the pounding overcame her. Christine didn't know what it would be like, seeing Matt and Charlotte. She had been worried they might be scared or something, seeing her in the hospital like this. The air thrummed nervously before they got there. But when they did, it was okay—a lot of static flew off them, but it was good static, and she could see them pretty clearly for the most part. Things got harder and louder and fuzzier after a while, but it was okay. She knew she was with her family, and it was her birthday, and they were happy to be with her. And she was happy to be with them. And grateful for the beautiful book of birds. The mist that night was thin and light, the tone was gentle.

***

A few mornings after her family's visit, Christine rested on the edge of the bed. It had been another gentle night, light and easy. Like the night before. The orderly was at the door. "Time to see the doctor, Chris."

She had eaten and dressed, and was ready. Christine had seen the doctor before, one time maybe, but she couldn't remember him. She left with the orderly. They walked the long corridors, past the community room and the door leading outside to the lawn and garden, past the dining hall, past the nurses' stations and damaged people of all ages who stood in the corridors or sat in wheelchairs. They continued, under fluorescent lights that scoured deeper into Christine the longer they walked. She was losing strength, her head buzzed, her eyes burned. She had been taken to the doctor's office in a wheelchair the previous week.

"Where are we going?" She asked. "To see Doctor Vrabel, remember?"

"Oh yeah." The name didn't mean anything to her. They padded along the buffed, high gloss linoleum. Christine desperately needed something to drink.

They arrived at an office. It was cooler than the halls, with gentler light. A man in a button down shirt and flowered tie sat behind a desk. He welcomed her. "Christine, how are you?" He smiled at her. It was a pleasant smile, it fit his words. Christine had seen him in her room a number of times. She remembered she had been in this office before, with him: *Doctor Vrabel.*

She asked, "Can I have a glass of water?"

The orderly brought her a glass of water. She sipped it as the doctor began. "It's been a big week for you, since we last met. Happy birthday." Christine thanked him.

"Your mother visited, and your brother and sister, too. A little party?" "Yes." She smiled, remembering the visit.

"How did that go?"

"Good."

Vrabel glanced at a folder on his desk. "Staff mentioned you went right to sleep that night, that's good."

Christine didn't say anything. Maybe she was supposed to, she didn't know.

"I'm told you haven't mentioned any nightmares from these past few nights. Is that right?"

"Yes." The nightmares. *Jimmy. And the big girl in the water. And the snake.*

Vrabel was talking, "I see you went to the community room for the first time last week, and a couple times after that. How was that?"

They had taken Christine to the community room and tried to get her to do activities with other patients like play cards, exercise. The others were too messed up to talk to or do anything with. Many of them were close to her age, but they were wasted. Their burnt out eyes made Christine feel lousy. Then there was this intense girl, Suzanne, who had bugged out eyes and really quick hands. She talked a lot, sparking and spiking like crazy. She asked Christine all kinds of questions, including where she could get some pot. Christine couldn't get away from her, and nobody came to take her away. So, she sat and watched television like the rest of the vegetables. The whole community room thing sucked. She answered, "I like being in the garden better."

"Why's that?"

"I don't think I'm ready for all those people."

Vrabel smiled, nodded, wrote something down. "Do you feel the nightmares are getting better?"

"I don't know. They're kind of always there, in my head."

"What's always there?"

Christine shifted in her chair, felt the heat where her body touched the wood and answered. "Thoughts of Jimmy. Him being dead. Other stuff." She didn't want to talk about this.

"What other stuff?"

The buzzing got worse, the girl in the water appeared. "Just stuff. Sad stuff. My head hurts." She squinted against the room's light.

"Sure. Maybe someday you'll want to tell me about it."

Surfaces churned, the doctor faded back into the rising haze. "Maybe."

She heard him say, "Well, you're doing great, keep it up." She had no words. The fog swallowed her.

CHAPTER 19

Lynne hated this building, the state office building. She hated it because it was so ugly—a huge, orange brick block surrounded by asphalt parking and a few diseased saplings in concrete planters. She hated it because it was where she had to go to apply for food stamps, when she had first separated from Mark, and unemployment benefits when she was laid off from her nursery job at the preschool, when the kids were much younger. She had hated waiting for hours with needy people waiting to see their pissy caseworkers. She hated this place now. The SRS offices were in this building, and she was there for a meeting about something called Christine's Case Plan. Her lawyer had said she had to be there, that it was very important. It was about deciding Christine's future. He had said he didn't know whether Mark would be there, but that he would have received notice of the meeting. She doubted he'd be there.

Lynne, and the others involved in Christine's Case Plan meeting, entered the conference room and took seats around a long, laminated table. The air in the meeting room was stale with the sweat and laundry soap smells of the group that had just left. She looked to the windows to see if they could be opened to let in some fresh air – they couldn't. The central air conditioning slowly worked against the thick mid-August humidity. Lynne hoped the door would at least stay open for air.

After they were all seated, LaValley shut the door, took her place at the head of the table and asked everyone to introduce themselves and state why they were there. Lynne, attorney Fitzgerald, attorney Simmons and Mrs. Fromme introduced themselves. A woman identified herself as "an impartial observer" from the SRS central office, there to monitor the meeting, which was done at all Case Plan meetings. A man named Stan Derosia from the state's attorney's office was also there.

When the State's Attorney identified himself. Fitzgerald asked, "Not to be discourteous Stan, but what the hell are you doing here?"

"The State has a particular interest in this case." Derosia answered. "We have a pending homicide investigation, and Miss Bancroft may be a witness. I'm here to keep track of her circumstances."

"Stan, I've never heard of anything like this." Simmons challenged. "This is a Case Plan meeting. We're talking about Christine's treatment issues, her placement alternatives, things like that."

"Exactly. And these may affect her suitability and availability as a witness."

Fitzgerald shook his head. "You're kidding, right?" He turned to LaValley. "He's kidding? You invited him to the Case Plan?"

LaValley answered. "The state's attorney's office always gets a copy of the Case Plan and notice of Case Plan meetings, as they represent the State in the CHINS proceedings."

"Yeah, I know, but sending someone from their criminal prosecution division?"

The observer spoke. "There's nothing in the regs that says who the state's attorney can or can't send. Nothing that says that an attorney from their juvenile division can't go back to the office and share information from a Plan Review with the criminal division. I'd say it's allowed for a prosecutor to attend. Now, can we get started?"

Fitzgerald sat back from the table. "This isn't right, and you know it. I'm getting on the phone with the defender general as soon as we're done and reporting this." He turned to Lynne, "I'd leave right now, but they'll continue without us and put on the record that we refused to participate, which could be used against you later in court. At the end of this meeting we'll write our objection into the plan, along with any other objections that may come up."

LaValley uncomfortably shifted her bulk and asked if everyone had received a copy of the Case Plan and had had a chance to read it. Lynne had gotten her copy in the mail the day before and had read it. She nodded. The others also nodded.

The caseworker continued, "For those of you who are new to this process, SRS is required by law to come up with a plan for returning a child who is in state's custody back to their parents, so long as it is in the best interests of the child. We want children returned to safe, supportive, nurturing homes."

Lynne looked blindly at the report as LaValley kept speaking.

"That is why we have these sections called Goals and Objectives for Christine and her parents. These point out needs that must be addressed for Christine to be returned to her parents. If these needs aren't adequately met within a reasonable amount of time, typically no longer than eighteen months, then the State will file an action to terminate the parental rights to the child, freeing the child up for adoption."

What did she just say! Lynne looked at Fitzgerald for some explanation.

He nodded, indicating the caseworker was correct.

She whispered to him. "Why does she keep talking about 'the parents' when Mark has nothing to do with Chris?"

Distracted, LaValley continued. "There will be scheduled Case Plan Review meetings set up like this every three months. This is to discuss progress on the Goals and Objectives and any changes in the Goals and Objectives that are needed because of changing circumstances. Any questions at this point?"

No one spoke.

"Okay then, we'll go through the Case Plan, starting with the Background Information. Do I have the parents' information correct?"

Lynne's age, address, occupation were correct. The names and ages of Matt and Charlotte, their school, their grade levels were all correct. Lynne wasn't sure about Mark's address, but it looked correct. His age, birth date, phone number were all correct. She wasn't sure who his employer was.

Lynne murmured. "Looks about right, although I don't know about Mark."

LaValley said that was alright, a copy of the Case Plan had been sent to him, and if he felt there were any changes needed, he could let her know.

Lynne had a question. "You say Christine is enrolled at Branford High School, but I don't think..."

LaValley interrupted, "I know. It's unlikely Christine will be matriculating at Branford when school starts, considering her condition and the fact that school starts in about two weeks, but that is the school she was last enrolled at, and we consider her enrolled there until she is taken off the rolls by the school administration."

The cold answer slapped Lynne.

"We don't have a detailed education plan for Christine, considering her current condition, which is why the Plan merely states 'Return to Branford Regional High School.' We can also regard that as a goal for now. Under the Health section, the Plan at this time is that all of Christine's medical and dental needs are being met at the Vermont State Hospital in Waterbury. This obviously will change as Christine's condition changes. However there are no plans to move her at this time, or to change her treatment."

LaValley flipped the pages of the Case Plan on the table in front of her. "Attached to the Case Plan is a report from Doctor Vrabel, Christine's treating psychiatrist, dated August fourteen. It describes Christine's current medical condition and the progress she's made."

Lynne and the others turned to the report.

"As you can see Doctor Vrabel reports Christine has apparently suffered a psychotic break, and is being treated for psychosis symptoms with Trilafon and with Prozac, an antidepressant. He reports Christine has shown marked improvement since she was hospitalized, and has recently attained sustained orientation to time, place and her identity. Incidents of delusion and hallucinations are now infrequent and her traumatic nightmares are becoming less frequent. In the Recommendations section, Doctor Vrabel reports Christine may be suitable for placement in a therapeutic group home setting if she continues making progress, but he can't say when that will be because progress in cases such as this can be erratic. His conclusion is that Christine should remain at the hospital. For now." LaValley looked up and smiled at Lynne. "We look forward to her continued recovery."

Lynne didn't smile back at the sweating woman. She was thinking about Christine, slumped and speaking weakly in her hospital room a few days ago.

LaValley spoke to the group. "Presumably, Christine will continue to get better, so there will come a time when we need to decide whether to return her to her parents. Before that happens, we need to see Christine meet certain objectives set out in the Goals section of the Plan." She paused to make sure everyone was at the right place.

Lynne found the section.

Continuing, "The first requirement is that Christine will undergo a drug and alcohol assessment and participate adequately in any treatment plan recommended in the assessment. Second, she shall abstain from drugs and alcohol and shall submit to screenings as are deemed necessary to ensure compliance. Third, she is to attend school or otherwise further her education in an approved manner. Fourth, she is to live an orderly life."

Lynne interrupted, "All these things that Christine is required to do, who decides what's adequate or necessary or orderly. I mean what does 'orderly' mean, anyway?"

"Those determinations are made by me, in consultation with my case manager, and based on input I receive from people like Christine's teachers, her drug counselor, people who are working with her. And from you and Christine, of course."

She suddenly saw the caseworker clearly: this overworked, poorly dressed, uncomfortable woman was going to oversee Christine's life, judge her, write 'plans' for her, evaluate her, report to people who would control Christine's future. Like that horrible judge.

"How long does this go on, this Case Plan?" She wanted to know.

LaValley smiled. "As long as Christine is in SRS custody." Lynne hated that she smiled. There was nothing to smile about.

"Lynne, these requirements are pretty routine for a case like this. Christine's medical condition makes it more complex, but this is what kids face when they've gotten into this kind of situation." Fitzgerald shared.

Lynne looked at attorney Simmons, who nodded. "Christine will be asked to do things that may be hard. But she has me, and you have attorney Fitzgerald to argue if the Plan isn't reasonable or if Christine's behavior or performance isn't being fairly assessed. We can challenge an unfair Plan in court."

Simmons' words weren't encouraging. Lynne remembered Judge Overbeck's harsh glare. The air in the crowded room pressed against her.

LaValley resumed, "So no objections to this section of the Plan?" No one spoke.

"Moving on to Goals and Objectives for Lynne. There shouldn't be any surprises here either. Lynne, we're asking you to undertake individual counseling related to parenting issues, and become involved in a support group for parents of children with substance abuse problems. I expect, if things progress, we may also require family counseling, but we'll hold off on that for now."

Lynne watched LaValley read from the Plan and thought, *When am I supposed to find the time to do all this?*

"We also want to address the issue of adequate supervision of Christine, and the other children for that matter. Clearly Lynne cannot adequately supervise the children if she is working between eleven at night and seven in the morning. This is a significant contributing factor to Christine's delinquency. So, the Plan requires Lynne to change shifts or jobs so she is home when the children are out of school, or make arrangements that ensure there is adequate adult supervision of all of the children when she is not home."

Overwhelmed, Lynne blurted, "You can do that? You can make me do that? I mean how am I supposed to find a new job. I'm an LNA, I can't just change jobs. We barely get by as it is, and you want me to what, quit my job? I have to do that before you'll let Christine come home?"

Fitzgerald placed his hand on Lynne's forearm, signaling her to stop, to let him speak. "I think Rose is not necessarily saying you need to do that, are you Rose? The issue concerning SRS is that Christine be adequately supervised. There are different ways to address that issue. Rose, would you state that Objective in broader terms, allowing Lynne some leeway in meeting that important need?" "I don't know. I think Lynne needs to know..."

"I think she understands what's needed here." Fitzgerald interrupted. "Let's change this language so it doesn't appear that you are requiring Lynne to quit her job. Restate the objective to read that Lynne shall make arrangements for adequate adult supervision of the children at all times."

"I'm not saying..."

Fitzgerald held his ground. Simmons supported him and LaValley relented, agreeing to change the wording.

Lynne saw her chance. "And all those therapy sessions you want me to go to, are they really necessary? I mean, how am I supposed to do all that, and work full time, and raise a family?"

Annoyed, LaValley shot back, "There are issues here, Lynne, that need to be addressed. You need to take a look at what happened, and I really think you might need professional help seeing your role in Christine's problems and preparing you to parent a child who has demonstrated serious behavioral issues."

Lynne burned red.

"Rose, that's not necessary..." Simmons pushed.

"Maybe it is. If Lynne does some work with some professionals and they say she doesn't need any help parenting a troubled teenager, then we can revise those requirements. But for now they stay." To Lynne, "I work with a lot of single working mothers who take on more than this. You can do it if you make the commitment. That's what we're looking for, commitment."

Lynne saw a mean spirited woman glaring at her, who was all about lecturing and bringing down consequences on people. And she was talking at Lynne like she knew her type already.

LaValley straightened and sat back before continuing. "Finally, the Goals and Objectives for the father."

Lynne wondered again why they were even talking about Mark. She looked at the Plan: the only thing he was being required to do was take part in the support group for parents of children with substance abuse issues.

"Rose, it's not stated in the Plan that Lynne is Christine's custodial parent. That needs to be added." Fitzgerald mentioned.

Simmons agreed. LaValley said she'd make the change.

Fitzgerald, "I understand that the father needs to be included as a potential placement and custodial parent by law..." He looked at Lynne to emphasize the legal requirement, "but I think we need to make it clear he has not, at this time, indicated any intent to have Christine placed with him, or to take custody of Christine."

LaValley said she'd include that information in the Plan. He wasn't finished. "I think we also need to note in the Plan that Lynne has been in contact with Christine at least twice a week since she was taken into custody, including since she was hospitalized. While at the same time, the father has visited Christine just once."

"I don't think..."

"Rose, of course it's relevant." Simmons wasn't letting go. "Under your Goals and Objectives for Christine, you state she needs to establish and maintain healthy relationships within the family. This information is important on that issue and should be noted so we can track progress in subsequent Plan Reviews. Put it in, please." Simmons wasn't asking.

LaValley shrugged, agreed. She looked at her watch. The next Plan Review was scheduled to begin five minutes ago. "Okay, so if there are no more comments, I'll generate a revised Case Plan with the changes we agreed to, and ask that you sign it and get a copy back to me." She concluded.

The caseworker closed Christine's file, rose from her chair, and left the room.

Lynne had had enough of the woman. She stood up at the table. As Fitzgerald gathered his materials beside her, she felt like she and Christine were being forced into a chute. She watched the prosecutor slip out and shuddered.

***

The window air- conditioner blew quietly, cooled Miranda Howe's office, providing Lynne relief from the day's steaming heat. The sheen of sweat on her skin chilled, although her summer dress still clung to her. She smelled Miranda's familiar lavender and relaxed into her chair. Throughout this miserable summer, she had come to this place every other Friday afternoon, as if it were a calm island.

Once Lynne settled into her chair, Miranda asked, "At our last session, you had mentioned some big things were coming up, Christine's birthday and the Case Plan Review. How did they go?"

Lynne smiled. "Christine's birthday was wonderful. Matt and Charlotte were excited to see their sister. And she was glad to see them, too, but they kind of wore her out. She's doing great, though. The doctor says she's really coming along."

"That must be good to hear. Any word on how much longer she'll remain in the hospital?"

Lynne shook her head. "No. I guess it's hard to predict."

"Is that difficult for you, not knowing?"

She paused to think about the question. "Not really. She's getting better and she's safe, that's enough." She saw her therapist smile, slightly.

"Good. Have there been any discussions about where Christine might go after her hospitalization?"

Lynne clasped her hands. "Some kind of group home. A therapeutic group home? What exactly is that?"

"It's a place for people who aren't so sick they need to be in a hospital, but aren't quite well enough to be living on their own." Miranda explained. "Christine would be living with others transitioning like herself, and professionals who are trained to support them."

The answer reminded Lynne of the Plan Review. She mentioned, "The caseworker at the Case Plan meeting was saying Christine is going to have to go to therapy, and I'll have to get parenting counseling and join a parents' group. It feels like she's asking an awful lot." Lynne rubbed the arms of her chair.

"Perhaps. Do you have the Case Plan with you?" She didn't.

Miranda suggested she bring a copy the next time they met, then added, “The difficult things we’ve been talking about this summer, the tough issues you’ve been working on, like figuring out what Christine needs and how you can give her what she needs, that’s what your caseworker has in mind when she’s requiring you to get some counseling. You’re already doing it, here!”

A smile broke across Lynne’s face. “Okay, well that’s good. I can do that.” “Have you told the caseworker you’re seeing me?”

Lynne blushed, shifted in her chair. “No. It’s just...the way she comes at me, digging into everything. She never asked and so I didn’t tell her. I don’t really want to.”

“Why not?”

Lynne didn’t answer.

“Because you’re sharing personal matters with me, matters you wouldn’t want the caseworker to know about?”

“Yes.”

“Okay, that’s important. You need to feel you can speak freely in therapy for it to be effective.”

Lynne smoothed her dress.

“Your work with me would most likely meet the counseling requirement. But our sessions could be open to some scrutiny by SRS and any others involved in this case. That would be true of any counseling you got involved in, if its purpose was to meet the requirement.”

She nodded she understood.

“I’ve been involved in many cases like yours and Christine’s. I know how to honestly tell caseworkers and lawyers how a client of mine is doing without sharing my client’s personal details. If you want to use our therapy sessions to meet this requirement, let me know when you’re ready and we can talk about it some more.”

A knot in Lynne’s chest dissolved. “Thanks.” She then asked Miranda what she thought about parenting groups.

"They can be very helpful if they're done right. You get the chance to hear what people like yourself are going through, how they handle issues that you're also facing. A parent who has a teenager in the legal system, a teenager who's been involved with drugs, that's a lot to be dealing with alone. It's a good idea to have all the support you can get. I know a woman who moderates a group for parents of troubled teenagers. Her name is Sally Peck. She's been running groups like this for years out of Family Support Services. She does a great job." Miranda offered.

Lynne couldn't imagine talking about her problems in front of a bunch of strangers. She didn't say anything, didn't nod. Her mouth felt chalky.

"I can give you her phone number if you're interested. When you're ready." She wasn't ready, but she thanked Miranda just the same.

***

Friday evening, Mark arrived home from work to a quiet house. Nancy's note on the counter stated she and the baby were at her sister's and they'd be home around seven. *In an hour.* He filled a tumbler with Johnny Walker Red and a couple of ice cubes, gathered the mail from the kitchen counter and took it down to the den to sort.

Settled into his easy chair, Mark slit open the bills and checked balances due as he sipped his scotch. Nothing out of the ordinary with the bills. He decided to ignore Nancy's VISA statement. Friday evening, after a long week of work, was not the time to think about her spending problem. The next envelope was from Vermont, the Department of Social and Rehabilitation Services. It looked like another one of those Plans he got a couple weeks back. He read the cover letter saying they had their meeting and as a result some changes had been made: the portions added were underlined and the portions deleted were scored.

Mark read the revised Case Plan. *Goddammit!* There were all kinds of changes; making a big deal about how much Lynne had been seeing Christine and how little he had, talking about him like he didn't matter! He slapped the papers on the desk. *What do they expect from me?* She'd been in a freaking coma or something. Did they expect him to travel three hours just to stand around waiting for her to blink, for Chrissakes?

Fine, I'll go see her. Annoyed, but he got it: It was important he keep in touch with Christine, important for her health. And it was important because he had a say in what happened with her, that's what his lawyer had told him. He could even have Christine stay with him if he wanted. But that wasn't going to happen. She was too much of a goddamned mess.

He took a long sip of scotch. This Plan said they didn't even know when she was getting out of the hospital. So, there was no sense thinking about her living with him and his family. He should go see her, though. He'd check for himself how she was doing.

Mark leaned forward in his recliner, scanned the desk calendar and saw that next weekend was Labor Day. He'd have Monday off. He could visit her then. He'd call and let the SRS woman know he was going, make sure she gave him credit. He checked the cover letter that came with the revised Case Plan; the phone number was right there in the heading. He settled into the recliner, drained the remaining liquor, enjoying the heated glow as it went down. *See how she's doing. Good.*

CHAPTER 20

Sitting by herself, on a flimsy folding chair in the sun blasted community room with a dozen other patients and some staff doing whatever they were doing, Christine put the modeling clay on the newspaper, spread over the card table. A photocopy of the northern barred owl print she had found in her Audubon book, lay flat at the far corner of the table. A couple days earlier, she had asked a staff member make the copy. Two patients stood nearby, but not too close. They watched her Christine didn't notice them.

She worked the clay, felt the surfaces yield to her strength, felt them warming against her palms and fingers. She flattened the clay, pressed and rolled it and felt how it worked her arm muscles. The air was thick. She kept her eyes down against distraction.

Suddenly, she knew to look up. Her father was in the doorway. She stopped handling the clay. He crossed the room to her. She didn't move. He was smiling, and his smile hurt her. She saw only him. The rest of the room was a blur. Patients and staff faded into the background. He approached. She would not look at his eyes. They would tell her something she didn't want to know.

"Hi honey! Good to see you." He was so close, his words were so loud. He stopped and held his arms open.

Christine didn't move. Her hands hovered above the clay. She said, "Hi."

He dropped his arms. She felt the air swish violently. He continued to smile, it continued to hurt her.

He asked, "What are you making?"

She didn't answer, just stared at him.

What's wrong with her? He took a step back, noticed the photocopied owl, asked "Thinking of making a bird?"

He wanted something from her, she gave him an answer. "Yes."

An orderly came up beside him, came out of the shadows to speak. "Christine, your dad is here to visit. Would you like to show him the garden?"

The woman's voice was pleasant. The garden was always nice. "Yes."

"Okay, then." To Mark, "Christine really enjoys spending time in the garden. There's a bench in the shade she particularly likes. I'll show you." Back to Christine, "Shall we show your father the bench under the pines?"

"Yes."

Mark and Christine sat in cool shade, with the bright summer heat beyond the shade. They sat on a bench, two feet between them, what seemed the right distance. Christine watched the dead-headed daylily stalks shimmer in a slight breeze. She felt the breeze, saw maple leaves flit on nearby branches. She watched flying insects dart in and out of the light. She heard the insects and the shimmering plants. She heard footsteps crunch on the gravel walkway.

Mark heard the footsteps too. He asked, "How are you doing?"

Christine didn't have an answer. She said, "Fine."

"Do you like it here?"

"Yes."

"It seems nice."

She didn't have an answer and said nothing.

After a moment Mark commented. "I can see why you like this garden."

She didn't understand what he meant. A rough buzz snatched away the garden's shine and glow. His buzz. Now there was nothing but him, beside her. The rest didn't matter, everything stopped shining.

She sat without speaking. He said some more things. Ten minutes later the orderly came and told them it was time for Christine to come in and clean up her table. As they walked back to the building, three sets of feet made cruel noise in the gravel.

Christine heard the orderly say to her father, "I don't know what's come over her. She usually isn't like this. At least she hasn't been for a while." Their footsteps loudly crunched.

They returned to the card table in the community room. The room's tones mixed in the thick air: sick and sad and angry and confused. Everything was a dirty gray backdrop, with shapes that moved or didn't. He was beside her. He was in front of her. He was smiling, and the smile had a sick tone.

"Listen," Mark started, "I should be going. It was good to see you, honey. I loved your garden."

He watched Christine's eyes dart from point to point, somewhere beyond him. He watched her lick her lips and lick them again, for no obvious reason. He stepped up to her, put his arms around her, and squeezed her gently. He stepped back and said, "You take care of yourself. Get better."

Her eyes rolled to the back of her head and she began to collapse. The orderly leaped forward, caught Christine under her arms. She spoke over her shoulder, "Perhaps you should leave now."

Confused by what was happening, Mark left as he was told.

***

He had stepped up to her, pressed himself against her, wrapped his arms around her. His man smell had swarmed over her. He had deeply bruised her. She felt pain everywhere he had pressed against her. The dark fog rose. She heard him, he was there. She let go, she dropped, into darkness.

***

The evening of the second Tuesday after Labor Day, Lynne arrived at the church early. She wasn't sure which church downtown was the Congregational Church. She didn't know which room inside was the vestry, wasn't even sure she knew what a vestry was. So she arrived for the meeting early. She also didn't want to walk into a room where everyone was already seated and have strangers looking at her, as she took her seat.

Inside the side entrance of the church, Lynne heard sounds of a person moving around, coming from the direction of a dimly lit corridor. She followed the corridor to a room where a woman was carrying an old wooden chair. It appeared to be heavy.

The woman noticed Lynne. "Hello, here for the parenting group?" She put the chair down.

Lynne understood now that the chair was part of a rough semicircle of eight various chairs. She answered, yes.

The woman—middle aged, average sized, with short black hair and bright green eyes—approached Lynne, her arm extended for a handshake. "I'm Sally Peck, the group facilitator. You've come to the right place."

Lynne shook the woman's hand. "Lynne Bancroft."

"Right, we spoke last week. Your daughter is Christine?" "And I have another daughter, and a son. Charlotte and Matt."

"Okay. Glad you could make it." The woman turned away from Lynne, headed for a doorway at the other end of the room. She stopped, asked, "Want to give me a hand?"

Lynne followed her to the next room, a kitchen of sorts. Peck took a half gallon bottle of apple juice and a half gallon bottle of water from the refrigerator. She handed Lynne the water and asked her to grab the two boxes of supermarket muffins from the shelf Lynne stood next to.

As Peck grabbed paper cups, paper plates and paper napkins out of a cupboard, she asked, "Do you think it makes sense to have refreshments at these kinds of meetings? I mean, it's so typical. On the other hand, I'd hate it if someone was distracted because they were hungry." The two began walking back to the vestry as Peck spoke. "I guess the food can be a little distracting, too, but in a good way, if there is such a thing. Sometimes things can get a little intense. So sure, maybe some distraction isn't so bad, break things up a bit."

Standing at a side table against a wall in the vestry, Lynne opened the package of napkins.

"I'm looking forward to working with this group." Peck continued. "Usually I have a group that's been going awhile, or a mixed group of old hands and newcomers, but we have a brand new group starting today. You'll all get to enter this process together. I'm very excited."

Peck looked past Lynne to an older couple, maybe in their seventies, standing at the entry. "Hello, are you here for the parenting group?" They nodded yes. She headed for the couple with her arm extended.

Lynne was very uncomfortable, as she sat on a padded folding chair and waited for the meeting to start. The elderly couple, who had been the next to arrive, sat next to her and introduced themselves: Pat and Marcelle. They didn't have anything else to say and neither did Lynne. Her stomach fluttered as she waited.

She didn't want to talk about herself, or about what Christine was going through. But she had to come. When she had seen Christine the previous weekend, laying there all drugged up and out of her mind, Lynne fell apart. It was too much, seeing her like that again. She had been getting better, she had been doing so well. The doctor had said something like Christine's recovery would likely have relapses. Lynne hated him for telling her that. She wanted Chris healed and there was nothing she could do. She wanted to smash things, anything, and everything. Instead she had called this woman, Sally Peck, like Miranda suggested, and here she was.

When the meeting started, Lynne's nerves settled down. Peck had told them there were no rules, except that they each deserved respect; that it was likely they were each going through something very difficult, and to be kind to each other. She then handed out notecards and pencils. She asked that they write a brief introduction about themselves. They could express anything they wished, but had to include at least one sentence on why they had enrolled. When they were finished they would introduce themselves to the group, using the cards to help them if they wanted.

Five minutes later Lynne was the first to speak, "My name is Lynne. I'm the mother of three wonderful children, Christine, Matt and Charlotte. I'm a single mom and I work as a nurse assistant in the maternity ward at Branford Regional. My oldest daughter, Christine, turned seventeen last month and I'm here because I'm having a really hard time dealing with what she's going through." Lynne paused. She wiped her hands down her sides, then continued. "She got involved with a boy... and drugs and was arrested back in July." She took a deep breath, continued. "She was sent to a detention center and while she was there she had a mental breakdown. The doctor calls it a psychotic break. She's been in the state hospital for nearly two months now. She was starting to get better. Then she completely fell apart again. Now she doesn't know who I am or where she is....and it's very hard. I heard about this group, where I can talk because I don't how to deal with this. So, here I am."

When she finished, Lynne looked up from the spot on the floor she had been staring at. She saw the seven others giving her their full attention, their faces each showed concern. She shut her eyes, relieved. The others told their stories. They were brief, but Lynne heard a lot of suffering.

Pat and Marcelle were caring for two teenage girls aged fifteen and thirteen, their granddaughters, whose mother was last heard from over a year ago when she abandoned the girls. The girls were acting out in school, with boys, with alcohol and maybe drugs. Another couple, well dressed – the father wore a tie, might have come straight from work - had one daughter, seventeen years old who had tried to commit suicide in the spring and was now in a recovery center in upstate New York. A single mother about Lynne's age had a fourteen year old son, who was in a detention center for violently assaulting an elderly neighbor during a robbery. An African American woman, a single mother as well, had a fifteen year son and two daughters. The son was always high and running with a crowd she suspected was selling drugs, and the oldest daughter, eighteen, had recently told her that her stepfather, the father of her youngest daughter, had sexually molested her for years. Lynne nearly cried during the last introduction. Each speaker sounded like his or her heart was breaking. *I'm not alone.*

Peck then had the members of the group discuss instances that had been particularly difficult for them. Lynne described the time she thought Frank was going to hit Christine that morning last winter, *just a few months ago.* Peck gently congratulated Lynne for making Frank leave, and the group silently nodded in recognition.

At the end of the meeting, Peck asked the group to stand. She went to the end of the semi-circle and stood beside Keith, the man in the tie. She instructed, "Put your hand on the shoulder of the person to your right."

Lynne put her hand on Janice's shoulder, the African American mother. The elderly man, Pat, rested his hand on her shoulder.

Peck continued, "Shut your eyes."

Lynne did. She felt Janice's thin muscle and the bone beneath, felt the muscle receive her touch. She felt the gentle weight of Pat's hand on her, felt herself receive his touch.

Peck said softly, “Take a moment. Take a breath.” Tears streamed down Lynne’s cheeks.

“When we meet next week, I’ll ask you to sit between different people. You can open your eyes.”

***

Doctor Vrabel had decided to resume Christine’s therapy sessions. He had heard she was sitting up and was responsive to the staff again. She had been brought to his office in a wheelchair. He spoke to the girl slumped in the wheelchair. “Christine, would you please take a seat.” He indicated the chair across from him.

She slowly rose from the wheelchair, walked the few feet to the office chair and flopped into it without looking at him. The doctor made a note in her chart that she understood his simple request. It was September sixteenth. He checked Christine’s charts: two and a half weeks since her relapse. He noted that the increase in her Trilafon dosage seemed to have addressed the pronounced dementia characterizing her relapse.

“Do you know where you are, Christine?” He asked.

She looked up at him, her head tilted sideways, one eye open, her voice flat; she answered. “No.... your office.”

“Do you know who I am?” “No.... the doctor.”

“Yes, I’m your doctor. Doctor Vrabel.”

Christine recognized his voice, and the name. She looked harder at him, his face blurred, but there. The haze thinned some more, so she could make out the framed pictures and diplomas on the wall. The clamor in her head lessened.

“I’m in the hospital.” She mumbled.

“Yes. Can you tell me who is in the room?”

Christine strained to sit up, straighten her head and look around. She turned her head a bit to the right, then the left; the haze thinned where she brought her focus, so she could see the bookshelf and the floor lamp and the window. She saw no one.

She answered, "Just us." Her head began to ache, the clanging stepped up. "Good. Can you tell me how you slept last night?"

She couldn't. The haze thickened darkly, the man who was talking became a smudge. His words came from far off and turned into sounds. Through the fog... she felt them press against her. Thick, wet. She went deeper to get away.

The doctor watched the orderlies position Christine in the wheelchair as she murmured "get away from me." She weakly writhed, her face twisted, her lips moving for words that came out and words that didn't. When she was gone, Vrabel wrote in her charts: 'C demonstrated brief period of cognition, aware of place, presence. First cognition observed since relapse of 8/ 31. Continue Trilafon at current dosage.'

***

I take my pill. The lights dimmed in Christine's room. She recognized the orderly who came with her sedative, the same orderly who had wheeled her to the doctor's office earlier. She didn't remember what happened after she arrived at the office. She had crawled away, into cover. She was safe in this room, her room. In her bed, with the woman in the other bed, whimpering. She had lifted herself from the blackness. She was here now in her dim room. There had been a man who wanted to fuck her. He sniffed her and leered at her. She couldn't remember his face. And there were girls. She couldn't remember their names or faces. There was a shower. She was in the shower, and there was a terrible smell. Christine stared at the dim lights. That place, where the shower was - dark, green, stone – hummed wickedly. She remembered these things. They weren't dreams or images. She did not slide beneath the waves to escape her memory but remained present until her pill lowered her to sleep.

CHAPTER 21

Standing in the doorway of the community room, Lynne clutched the sweatshirt she had brought, one of Christine's favorites, gray and worn smooth. She watched her daughter, sitting alone at a card table, small, busy at something. The orderly had said Christine was back to working on "her figures" that week, after being away from them since her Labor Day relapse, more than a month ago.

Lynne approached quietly, spoke softly, "Hey, sweetie."

Christine looked up, "Hi mom" She didn't smile, her eyes didn't shine. "What are you making?"

"A bird. An owl." She pointed at the copy of the Audubon print of a barred owl, taped to the corner of the table. The clay shapes were two connected ovals lying side by side.

"It's lovely. The picture, is it from your book?" Christine nodded, looked at her hands resting by the clay.

"I brought you this, it's getting cooler." Lynne held out the sweatshirt. Christine reached to touch it, stopped, looked at her hands. "I can't."

Lynne tore off a few sheets from the roll of paper towels on the table. "Here."

Christine wiped her hands, but couldn't get all the clay residue off. She kept wiping, harder and faster.

"I think they're clean enough, Chris." She held out the sweatshirt again. Christine took it, felt its warmth, smiled up at her mother. "Thanks, mom."

The rare small smile lit Lynne's heart. She asked, "It's a beautiful day out, want to go to the garden?"

A choppy breeze knocked the brilliant maple leaves from their branches, sent them hurtling along the ground before resting. It snapped at Lynne and Christine as they slowly walked the gravel path. They were in no hurry, they had no destination. The wind filled their lungs and raced past their skin. Patches of clouds scudded across the sky, rapidly throwing the world into shadow and light repeatedly. It was cool for early October. It was just going to get colder. Winter was coming.

A few minutes into the walk Christine spoke first, "Am I going home soon?"

The air swirled. Lynne calmly answered, "When the doctor says it's time." She remembered the Case Plan and added, "You might need to go to a group home first, but after that...the idea is for you to come home."

The wind snatched the words from Christine's mouth, "Whose idea?"

Lynne tried to shape her answer correctly. "There's a plan the caseworker made, with your doctor that says it would be a good idea if you went to a group home after you leave here. To help you get better."

Back there. Darkness swarmed Christine. She couldn't speak. The garden disappeared. Her mother disappeared.

Lynne noticed her daughter's skin go white, her eyes roll back and her legs sway.

She steadied her daughter, set her down on the pathway. She frantically looked around for an orderly, for help. *Oh god!*

That night Christine struggled against the twisting sheets pulling her down. She kicked free and woke, heaving air. Slung from sleep, she began to recognize where she was in the thin predawn light: the room, the woman in the nearby bed breathing loudly, the sheets kicked to the floor. She reached down to gather them, her mind spun; it had been the same nightmare, now scattered. She covered herself with the sheets and bedspread. Their weight contained her, held her. She ran her shaking hands along the bedspread's smooth, familiar surface.

She remembered—the pressing, clammy flesh, the stench, her hair being pulled viciously. Alone. No one coming to save her. She ran her hands hard along the covers, her eyes shut, tried to calm her breathing, calm her heart. She remembered—a naked woman, thick skinned, water poured over her, the woman held a stick, stared at her full of hate, wanted to hurt her.

No! This wasn't a nightmare, or a hallucination. It was a memory of something real. Christine was certain. A real woman with a large head, round shoulders, hanging breasts. At that place. *The Plan.* The deep black surged to swallow her thoughts.

***

Vrabel observed Christine as she sat across from him, bundled up in a gray sweatshirt, a set of deep eyes watching him. She had walked, assisted, to his office. He expected she would have been wheeled in, after reading the staff report on Christine's incident, during her mother's visit four days earlier, and her withdrawn behavior since then. Staff reported she had barely eaten the past three days, that she spoke very little.

Yet, what she did say, indicated she was present when she spoke. There were no indications of delusion or hallucination. He had talked to Lynne on Monday. She had told him that they had been speaking about Christine's future after the hospital stay, right before she collapsed. The conversation may have induced trauma. He had increased Christine's dosage of Prozac on Monday.

He began, "Hello Christine, how are you today?"

The girl said nothing, only watched him.

"Did you see your mother last weekend, did she come and visit?"

She said yes, barely audible, then, "I have to tell you something." The man across from her was her doctor. "I've remembered something. I remember this girl, she was my age." Christine shut her eyes, recited her memory, "she was big. Naked. She was in a shower..." she went deeper, "she's wet. She's holding a stick and staring at me. She wants to hurt me." She had nothing more. Christine opened her eyes to look directly at Dr. Vrabel, her voice clear, "This happened."

Shortly after the session ended—after Christine had shut her eyes and stopped answering his questions—Vrabel paused before he entered his notes into her file. A girl in the shower. *Perhaps Stonebridge?* When he had asked her if anyone else was present she had said she didn't know. When he had asked her what else happened in the shower, she stopped speaking.

Vrabel considered; if the incident occurred at Stonebridge, there may be some notes in her file concerning it. Scanning Christine's intake records he found a brief injury report by a Stonebridge staff person: "3 inch superficial laceration across the knuckles of C Bancroft's right hand. Stitches not required. Disinfectant applied, wound bandaged. Bancroft reports the cut resulted when she slipped in the shower. Her explanation was confirmed by others present." *Something happened in the shower.*

The date of the accident? The report was dated July 10, the time of injury reported as the night before, July 9. Vrabel searched the file further: Stonebridge staff first observed or reported symptoms of psychosis in Christine on July 11. She was admitted to Waterbury that same day. *Trauma induced psychosis?* He went back through the earlier records: no other entries described any significant events. *Except* the trauma of her arrest and incarceration. July 6; admitted at Stonebridge with a reported head wound; immediate suicide watch; complaints of enduring pain from the head wound. *Beaten during her arrest, while resisting arrest?* Pieces from five days in this young woman's life. *Compound trauma.*

Vrabel rubbed his temples. He wrote nothing in Christine's file, except that she "recounted an indistinct threat from her past which disturbed her." He would not put anything more on record. If anyone who read her file found an entry about a suspected assault in the Stonebridge shower, all hell would break loose, with investigators, police, and lawyers tearing into everything: him, the hospital, Christine. He wasn't going to go to go through that or put her through that until he had something more substantial. *Then it would be worth it.*

***

Another day. The day after Hallowe'en, Christine lay in her room, the wacko roommate still asleep. The grated window. Get up, get dressed, leave the room. That's what she did, like every other freaking day. Down the hallways leading here, leading there. The only way to get anywhere. Narrow, long, fluorescent, suffocating hallways. Anywhere: the dining hall with plastic chairs welded to plastic tables—filled with dreary, pasty patients, with their dead eyes swallowed in their skulls, or the scary ones, with eyes on fire, hair sparking so you can smell their brains frying. The food: bland shit day in, day out, so that eating was senseless, like the entire place, except when it was pathetic. Pathetic was when someone tried, and called it "special". Like ice cream sundaes with insanely colored toppings or staff dress up days. The worst. Like Halowe'en, yesterday.

It was better when the staff just didn't try, better if they kept as senseless as everything else. Everything else: pills, the doc, the community room, the grounds, her room, the night. The grounds were just very sad with the leaves down, with dead scattered brown leaves blowing around. Bare trees were too pathetic, scraping the sky for no reason. Even more pathetic were fallen leaves, nothing but dead, blowing around, the deadest nothing brown. Everything knows the winter is coming and everything is scared shitless because it's the starving time. It's too fucking pathetic inside and too cold outside. Another afternoon in the community room and she would rather drink Drano, but that would be too pathetic. Do that and she'd never get out of this place unless she got it right and died, but somebody would save her and throw her back on this endless loop that keeps bringing her back to this same spot, this exact same spot, again and again, until she got it right.

The nights, a different kind of worst. Alone. Before the last pill of the day kicked in, when some part of her brain came alive. Through a chink in the deadening wall came pieces of her other life—there was another life. Not her mother and her brother and sister in Branford, and the rest of the world, but the place where her pieces of memory came from. Stonebridge. The way the pieces streamed through the chink before the last pill took effect. The way they waited for her when she woke, before the day's first pill did its job. Pieces of the other world; the naked, wet girl holding a handle, wanting to kill her, water streaming from showerheads, blood in the water washing down the drain. Her blood. Crazy, crazy shit. She had told the doc she had memories, but maybe some of it was her imagination. She didn't know. If they were memories, *then what happened*? She didn't want to know. Something very messed up. It could have been what broke her mind. When she thought too much about it, the blackness took over.

She remembered more from the other life. Jimmy: his face close to hers, his eyes pulling her in, smelling like death, cocaine cooking on a spoon. Jimmy: terrified, being hauled away by the cops. And some leering guy she didn't know, white powder around his mouth, in his eyes. And the guy who wanted to fuck her at Stonebridge, hands all over her, eyes all over her. *Fucked up shit*. She needed to disappear, when too much rushed through those chinks when she slipped into sleep, when she woke up, until the drugs took over again and the next senseless day began.

Later that day, the day after Hallowe'en, she was in Vrabel's office. She watched him do his usual stuff, waited for him to ask, 'How are you feeling today, Christine?'

She hadn't told him any more about the memories. He was part of this senseless place, so why should she? His job was to decide when to ship her back to Stonebridge. That was his part of the Plan. Everybody knew that terrible shit went on at that place, and they still sent kids there. They were sending her back. That was sick.

She usually spent her sessions with Vrabel telling him about her stupid senseless days, answering his worthless questions, thinking he might do something more that would make this place a little less pathetic. But nothing changed, so what was the point? This time though, she'd had enough.

He began, "So, Christine, how are you doing today?"

"Same. Listen, I want to know, when are you sending me back to Stonebridge?" She leaned forward, sat on her hands, feeling like her chest was going to explode.

Vrabel met her stare. "You're not going back to Stonebridge, Christine. I would never allow you to be sent back there." He held her stare.

Christine broke her eyes away, *he said…!* A jagged smile tore across her face through painful tears. "No shit?"

"No shit."

CHAPTER 22

Sitting in Miranda's office, Lynne rubbed her hands again, the warmth slowly returning to her. She wasn't ready for the cold, she never was. The second week of November and she still hadn't gotten the winter clothes out, but she never did this early. And she always froze. The kids needed everything new, too. They always did. She had no idea how she was going to afford it all. She had just paid for the first fuel oil delivery, there was no money left. The kids were good with sweatshirts for now. They didn't need boots yet, although Matt needed shoes. Next paycheck. They'd be geared up by Christmas. Mark always got generous about the kids' need for winter clothes halfway through December. Then she thought, *Christine, what does she need?*

The heat from the cast iron radiator eased into Lynne's chill. She settled into the stuffed chair, breathed in the lavender. She left her thoughts of winter needs. Miranda sat across from her and asked how she was doing.

"Really good. Last weekend I saw Christine. You would not believe how well she's doing. She was alert, sitting up, chatty. She's been making things with clay, she made me a little heart. She still gets worn out though. Don't get me wrong, she's doing so much better."

Howe asked if Vrabel had given Lynne an explanation for Christine's improvement.

"He said the medications seemed to be having an effect. No hallucinations for a while now. I guess she's been suffering from depression and he said the Prozac is starting to help with that. And he said she's starting to talk about things that might be troubling her."

"That sounds like good progress." Howe smiled.

"Yeah. He says Christine should be ready to leave the hospital soon and that she should be going someplace that can help her get ready to come home. Not Stonebridge. The caseworker, Rose, was planning on sending Chris back there, but Doctor Vrabel said no. She said she doesn't have any other place to send her, so my lawyer argued that she should send Chris home with me and let her do therapy from home. But then, Doctor Vrabel said that wasn't a good idea at this time and Rose said no way. We're supposed to talk about this at the Plan Review next week."

"What do you think about bringing Christine home now?"

Lynne pressed her palms against her thighs. "I don't know. I want her home so much, but you know...I understand if it's not time yet. I mean, I hear all these stories in Sally's group about kids getting better for a while, then backsliding and ending up worse. I just want Chris to get better, whatever it takes. She can come home when the time is right." She paused then, "You'll help me know when that time comes?"

Miranda smiled. "Of course."

***

Lynne sat at the conference table, at the same place where she sat at the last Plan Review, three months ago. She noticed everyone sat in the same place as the last time. There weren't any new faces. They nodded to each other as they took their seats.

Christine's lawyer touched Lynne's shoulder as she passed behind her, which was nice. Attorney Fitzgerald said it was great how well Christine was doing, which Lynne also liked.

LaValley started the meeting. "This shouldn't take as long as our first Plan Review, being mostly updates. So, let's begin. First off, Christine's legal status. Obviously, she is still in state custody. There is a court date set for December third, regarding the Disposition hearing. I understand the court will be setting the date then for a contested hearing, is that correct?"

The lawyers agreed it was. State's Attorney Derosia explained that SRS believed Christine needed to remain in its custody, and that the lawyers for Christine and Lynne had taken the position she should be returned to her mother's custody, considering her medical improvement.

LaValley addressed Fitzgerald and Simmons, "I don't see how you can take that position. It's clear what Christine and Lynne need to accomplish. It's spelled out in the Case Plan and they are nowhere close to achieving those goals. I know this is what you lawyers do, but it would just make so much more sense if you stopped wasting court time, and concede custody of Christine to the State."

Neither lawyer answered the caseworker. Lynne couldn't believe what she had just heard, *wasting time? Concede custody to the State?* And no one was saying anything. She looked at her lawyer who shook his head slightly, dismissing the comments.

LaValley returned to the material, an edge in her voice. "So, let's take a look at that progress. Regarding Lynne, since our last Plan Review, she has been attending a parents' group led by Sally Peck. Sally reports that Lynne attends regularly, nearly every week and is a valued member of the group. Congratulations, Lynne. Are you finding the group helpful?"

Surprised at the sudden question, Lynne stammered yes, it was helpful. "But you haven't taken up individual counseling, yet? Is there a reason?"

Lynne still didn't know if she wanted to tell this woman, and these other people, about Miranda. She answered, "I don't know, I just haven't."

"And you're still working third shift, and still leaving your children alone at nights without supervision. That needs to change if Christine is to be allowed to return home, you understand that, don't you?"

All she could do was say, "Yes."

LaValley turned the page of the Case Plan. "Alright. Regarding the father, nothing's changed. Which brings us to Christine. You all have a copy of Doctor Vrabel's letter attached to the Review? A lot of what he says is incorporated into the Plan. Such as Christine's current health and treatment. He reports that aggressive treatment with antipsychotics and anti-anxiety medications has resulted in significant progress with Christine's psychosis. He notes there have been no reported incidents of delusions or hallucinations for some weeks now. But, he also reports that she is suffering from ongoing depression, occasionally acute, perhaps chronic. In any event he has been treating Christine with anti-depressants and she has been functioning at a much higher level recently." She looked up from the report. "However, he warns Christine is at a guarded place in her recovery. She will continue to need to be treated for the depression into the foreseeable future, and for debilitating bouts of anxiety. He states she no longer needs the intensive level of services, which the hospital provides, but does need to be placed in a safe, therapeutic setting. Definitely not in the general population at this time."

The others nodded, they had read the report and were familiar with Doctor Vrabel's letter. Lynne nodded along with the others.

LaValley cleared her throat. "I received a call this afternoon from Waterbury. This isn't in the Case Plan. They need Christine's bed, and because she no longer needs that level of treatment, they will be discharging her by the end of next week at the latest."

Does that mean Christine's coming home? Lynne looked to the others for some confirming signals, saw them shifting in their seats. No one looked back at her.

"I've been calling around, haven't found a bed yet. You all know how hard placements are to come by."

What is she talking about? Could she send Christine back to Stonebridge? *Despite everything Christine's doctor had said?*

***

Christine watched Dr. Vrabel arrange himself behind his desk, placing her file just so, placing his pen on the notepad beside the file. The usual, although it seemed more deliberate—maybe it was her imagination.

He began, "Christine, how are you?" He sounded different. The usual words, but different.

She was feeling pretty good. Sure it sucked that it was cold out, and walks weren't very enjoyable, and everyone was a moron. But she had begun talking to a couple of the staff, and they weren't so bad. One of them had a daughter a little older than Christine, who sounded fun. She was making progress on her owl sculpture, working on the wings, which she enjoyed. So why was the doc looking at her like that, like he was trying to look inside her head? Did he always look at her like that? *Maybe.* She realized she was starting to notice things more. She answered, "Good."

He asked about her sculpture, about her visit with her mother last weekend. The usual stuff. Christine watched him take notes, look away from her, then back.

"Have you spoken to your mother lately?" He asked.

The unusual question caught Christine. "No, why?"

"I didn't think so. There's some news I expect she would have shared with you by now. Good news, I suppose. Good news because of how well you're doing..." *What is he talking about?* "...it's not necessary that you remain here. You'll be leaving, next week. It's still unclear where you will be placed..."

Static crackled in the air around his words, Christine's stomach tightened. She interrupted him. "Does that mean I could be going home?"

"It's up to your SRS caseworker, but it doesn't sound like that is likely." The static started to thrum, grow deeper. "Then Stonebridge?"

"No."

She didn't believe him, "How can you say 'no' when it's up to the caseworker?"

Vrabel rubbed one hand over the other as he answered, "Because of what you told me a few weeks ago. The memory you had about the girl in the shower. I looked in your records; something happened in that shower. You were injured, a cut. The report said it was an accident. I think it wasn't, based on the memory you described to me. You've been hurt there, badly. I won't let them send you back to Stonebridge."

Minard. Christine remembered the name of the girl in the shower. The room was swirling. He had dug into her life. "How are you going to do that?" She asked.

"I'll tell your lawyer my concern, and she can fight your return to Stonebridge. I can tell the judge that the place seriously traumatizes you without getting into specifics about what happened to you. He hears that and he won't send you back there." Vrabel looked down briefly, then back up at Christine. "You've been through a lot, you've done really well. We're going to keep you safe."

A dam within Christine collapsed, two streams of tears burned down her cheeks. She shut her eyes. The room was silent, but she didn't shrink into the black. A few moments later she opened her eyes.

"We'll make sure you're sent to a safe place." Vrabel said.

Christine wiped the side of her nose with her sweatshirt sleeve. She nodded. She didn't believe him. *Safe how? From what? From myself? I'm not safe. Jimmy wasn't safe.*

"I've recommended that I continue seeing you in therapy, to keep up on your road to recovery. See that you get better. Does that make sense to you?"

It did. She wanted to keep seeing him, she answered yes. She needed him.

"I expect that Ms. LaValley will agree. It's a fairly routine suggestion."

She remembered the caseworker, the strange woman. "Have you told anyone about what happened in the shower?"

"No." Vrabel shook his head, "You don't need to go through all that now." Christine didn't understand what he meant by 'all that.' She didn't ask.

He fixed his gaze on her. "You've talked about that girl and what happened once with me. You may remember more. You may feel the need to talk about what happened, what you remember. If you do, you can talk to me about it."

He looked at her so seriously. She nodded. What she really wanted was to forget that place forever, to save herself.

CHAPTER 23

The tires hummed, the asphalt highway stretched ahead, gunmetal clouds hung low above the bare November hillsides. Christine slipped in and out of wakefulness, exhausted. Everything had happened so quickly. Yesterday she had been told she was leaving the hospital to live in a foster home way up north, somewhere in the woods, with two sisters and some messed up kids. It sounded terrible, but her lawyer called and assured her it was okay. And Vrabel said it was okay. Christine didn't have any say. She had been told to get ready to leave the next morning.

Her mother had been at the hospital that morning to see her off. Doctor Vrabel had stopped by her room and made a big deal about her progress and her future, while her mother stood there, tearing up. Christine had said goodbye to some staff she liked, packed up and hit the road with the weird SRS woman, Rose LaValley.

At the beginning of the trip. LaValley tried to make conversation, but it wasn't just conversation—she was sneaking in questions about Christine's home back in Branford, and how her mother took care of her and the other kids. She told Christine she was still in State's custody because her mother hadn't made her home a safe place to live.

Shut up. Christine closed her eyes, leaned her head against the window, felt the temperature as the gray light dimmed the further north they traveled. She asked how much longer would they be travelling.

"An hour, maybe an hour and a half."

With her head resting against the cold glass, Christine drifted off to sleep.

The car turned off of the paved roadway, tires crunching onto a dirt drive.

"Here we are." LaValley piped up.

You're kidding me, right? Christine, bent over the barely functioning heat vent, glared through the dark at the social worker looking bizarre in the dashboard light. She turned away from the freak, stared hard at the driveway ahead. The last ten minutes had been quiet. Christine had grown more uneasy, as the last leg of the trip seemed to go on forever - the last seven miles down a two lane back road. The bitter cold day had quickly darkened. The two women sensed an approaching storm. The dark green conifers and bare limbed silver birches silenced them.

The driveway was long and narrow, with the house nowhere in sight. Tree branches nearly touched the slowly moving car. The shock absorbers and universal joints squealed as LaValley maneuvered the Civic over the gouged and rutted drive. A couple sudden, unseen runoff troughs scraped the undercarriage hard.

LaValley exhaled her tension. "Just about there."

Christine wanted the woman to shut up and concentrate on her driving. Or turn around, because they must be lost. A quarter mile down the trail, around a hairpin turn, past a boulder larger than the Honda, the lights of a house shone through the deep darkness.

"Your new home." LaValley proclaimed.

Christine ignored her, tried to make out what they approached: an older two storied log home with dormers and what looked a new aluminum roof that cast some reflected moonlight. Pulling beside a parked Jeep Cherokee, LaValley turned the car's engine off and the sudden stillness surrounded the two. *Where the hell are we?*

The front door opened and two figures appeared, silhouetted against the light beaming from within the building. Christine thought of a scene from a science fiction movie.

LaValley chirped, "Well, let's go meet your foster parents." She shot Christine an idiotic smile. A voice inside Christine spoke: *It's going to be alright.*

When Christine got out of the Civic, her senses sparked, alive to her surroundings. The scent of wood smoke, evergreen needles, the oncoming winter storm, roasting onions and meat fat reached her. The wind gusted through pine tops, tree limbs creaked. Forms took shape from the dusk: a monster Jeep Wagoneer sunk to the floorboards in old mud to Christine's right; large vehicle parts and a fifty gallon drum nearby; a long, solid woodpile along one side of the house, this patched with light from the windows; fingers of white birch trunks, faint against the deep forest beyond the house. So much! She took a deep breath. Her head spun.

"Well, let's go." LaValley said.

Christine grabbed her duffel bag and the clay owl sculpture she had been working on in the hospital. She walked towards the two women waiting in the doorway twenty yards away. The women didn't move from the entrance. As she approached, Christine could see them more clearly: older women, maybe in their late fifties or early sixties. One was about six feet tall, large boned and strong looking, with a broad face, short salt and pepper hair, thick lips and piercing blue eyes. She wore men's clothes; canvas pants and a green plaid flannel shirt. The other one was shorter, about Christine's height—five foot six. She was rounder, softer. Her gray hair was pulled back into a bun, her face broad like her sister's, but her lips thinner. Her eyes shone blue. She wore a flower print shift.

When she reached the women, Christine held out her hand, "Hi, I'm Christine." The taller sister took Christine's hand in her large, calloused hand. "Rosemary. And this is Kathleen."

"Please come in." Kathleen smiled.

Rosemary asked Christine if she had anything else to bring in.

She answered that she didn't.

Kathleen invited LaValley to stay for supper, but she declined, saying she wanted to get back on the road before the storm hit. Kathleen then insisted that she take a thermos of coffee and a couple banana muffins with her. "In case you get stuck somewhere."

As Kathleen went to the kitchen, Christine was left standing a few feet inside the entryway, her senses jumping as she took in the rich aroma of the food that cooked in the kitchen, as well as the interwoven odors of bodies, soaps, wool, flannel, leather, old and new wood ash, wood smoke, cook smoke, the scent of a dog long gone, lingering in the oval rag rug in the living room. From the living room, to her right, yellow light shone from lamps with faded lampshades on end tables which bracketed an overstuffed, worn couch across the rag rug from the wood stove. She looked further into the room and saw two solid stuffed armchairs on either side of the woodstove, each with an old floor lamp that was turned off, leaving the end of the room, dim. To her left, through a wide archway she saw the dining room with a length of the dining table visible. Sitting at the table were two children, a younger boy and a girl, staring at her, motionless, grim. Her vision shimmered for a moment. *It will be alright.*

LaValley was at the door, thanking Kathleen and Rosemary, shaking hands, making vague comments about Christine. Then she was gone. The door blew shut behind her, leaving behind the aroma of the strong coffee she carried and a cut of the night's wet cold. Leaving Christine behind, alone with these strangers in the middle of nowhere.

Rosemary spoke to the children in the dining room. "Marshall, Hannah, would you please come here. I'd like you to meet Christine."

The boy heaved back from the table, nearly upsetting the tablecloth and place settings. He scrambled across the space to Christine, bumping into Hannah along the way. Christine figured he was about seven years old, Wiry, wild haired, clean, rippling energy, he looked up at Christine, made brief eye contact, then looked away. His eyes darted from one thing to another, sometimes settling at her ribcage two feet away from her face.

"Christine, this is Marshall. Marshall has been with us a little over a month now. He is very helpful with the animals." Kathleen said.

The boy quickly looked up at Christine. "I feed the chickens and the ducks. And I gather the eggs. So, why are you here? You're a teenager."

Rosemary corrected, "Marshall, that's not polite."

Christine wanted to answer that she didn't mind, but decided she better not in case it was the wrong thing to say. She spotted Hannah, who had slipped silently next to Kathleen.

"Hi, I'm Christine."

The, girl, about ten years old, didn't say anything and looked down to the floor.

"Hannah joined us just last week." Rosemary offered.

It sounded like an explanation. The girl didn't look up. Christine wanted to hug her. But again, she didn't know if that was allowed.

Kathleen announced supper was ready to be served and suggested that Rosemary show Christine her room, while she and the children got the food on the table.

She smiled at Christine, a genuine smile. "You can unpack later."

The steps to the second floor creaked when Christine stepped on them. At the top of the stairs, a small hallway led to four closed doors. Rosemary opened the first door to the right. "This is your room."

The room was colder than the hallway. Rosemary flicked the switch by the door and an overhead fixture lit the simple space.

Two single beds, one along the wall to the left wall, one along the wall to the right, both neatly made, were separated by a green and blue oval braided rug. At the far end of the room was a window, with a dresser to the right of it. A closet opened on the left wall beyond the bed. Over one bed hung a picture of Jesus, pointing to a shining heart bursting from his chest. Over the other bed hung a print of a New England fishing dock scene.

"Your bed is the one on the left. The top three drawers in the dresser are yours. There are some hangers in the closet if you need them."

Christine nodded she understood, dropped her bag on her bed, carefully placed her clay owl on the dresser and followed Rosemary down to supper. She noticed the grate on the floor, closed. *They keep it closed to keep the heat downstairs.* She somehow knew the grates would be opened when it was time for bed.

Christine and Rosemary arrived to a table piled with steaming, fragrant foods: a five pound meatloaf, a huge bowl of roasted carrots, potatoes and onions, a basket of fresh baked biscuits, two tureens of deep brown gravy – all untouched. Kathleen and the children had waited for Rosemary and Christine to join them. Kathleen sat placidly at the far end of the table. Marshall squirmed at the place to her left. Hannah, waited, head bowed, to her right.

Christine took her seat and waited for the others to begin eating. The sisters made the sign of the cross, the boy imitated them. Together they recited: "Bless us oh Lord for these thy gifts, which we are about to receive, Amen." Marshall and Christine repeated, "Amen." Kathleen served large helpings of food for all, except Hannah, who took only a biscuit and a bit of meat swimming in gravy. When all were served, everyone began eating. Hardly a word was spoken as the food quickly disappeared. This was perhaps the best food Christine had ever eaten, certainly better than the hospital slop she had been stuck with for the past three months. While they

"Good, you're not easy to track down. I spoke with Mrs. LaValley today and she gave me your number. So, how do you like it, being out of the hospital?"

The question was stupid, but she answered. "Good."

"And you like where you're at? Are they treating you alright?"

Stupid questions. "Yes."

"I looked at a map, you're way the hell up there, almost at the Canadian border.

"Cold up there?"

What does he want? "Kinda." "Get any snow yet?"

She wanted to stop talking to him. "No."

"Yeah, well it shouldn't be long. So, some good news. I spoke to that Mrs. LaValley about coming up and visiting. Not this weekend, but next, after Thanksgiving. Whaddaya say, good news, huh?"

The room quivered. "Yeah, that'll be great."

"Great. Listen, I've gotta go. Can't wait to see you. Love you." "Love you too." The words escaped past her lips. The line went dead. Christine held the receiver, regained her focus, saw Kathleen looking at her.

"Why don't you give me that?" Kathleen reached out for the phone. "Go have a seat by the fire and I'll be in with some tea."

Through a clouding darkness, Christine answered, "Thanks Kathleen."

***

God, it was like pulling teeth from her. Mark caught himself, remembered she was sick. Still, she sounded like a zombie. *She's probably all drugged up.* He'd see for himself. God, it was a long drive though for one of these visits. He wouldn't be making a habit of it.

***

Christine looked into the fire with one thought; *why can't he leave me alone.* A wet log hissed in the stove. The household was quiet. The children were in their rooms, where the sisters were reading to them. Their tones, but not the words, reached her through the wide plank oak boards. Like a chant. The heat of the room, the droning chant. Christine felt herself slipping under the black waves. She fought against the rising tide, raised herself from the swallowing chair, and stumbled out the kitchen door into the dooryard. She gulped the air, turned her face to the sky; felt the wind sting her forehead, her cheeks, and her closed eyes. *Why can't he stay away?*

Rosemary heard the door thrown open, rushed downstairs to find Christine facing the weather, a few feet into the night. She held back at the doorway, watched the motionless girl, asked, "Are you alright, Christine?"

No answer.

Rosemary stepped up beside her. "Are you alright?"

Christine heard the voice, turned to the woman beside her, the woman who put her arms around her. She buried herself in Rosemary's arms, buried her face in Rosemary's flannel covered chest, with no understanding what was tearing at her, except that she did not want her father there.

***

Sitting behind his black walnut desk, Blum rose when Mark entered his office. He didn't extend his hand. A thin young woman, wearing a navy suit and a thin gold chain necklace, stood when Mark entered.

"Mr. Bancroft, my associate, Felicity Knowles. You spoke with her yesterday about the matter of your daughter."

The woman took a step towards Mark, hand extended. He hesitated before shaking it, then sat when Blum indicated for him to sit. Knowles sat in the straight back chair to the side of the lawyer's desk.

"Felicity has told me you have questions concerning how your daughter is being treated in SRS custody. What questions?"

"The state people have shipped my daughter off to some foster home way up by the Canadian border. I spoke to her on the phone last night and I have to tell you, I'm worried. She didn't sound right. At all. They've sent her to this place, right from the hospital. After I got off the phone with Chris, I took a look at that Case Plan they drew up, that's supposed to say what's going to happen with Chris, to see if they should have sent her to this place. Reading it, I realized they're planning on sending her back to her mother's." Mark paused leaned forward and looked at Knowles then back to Blum. "Am I missing something here? I mean, her mother is a lying druggie who has no idea how to handle a teenager. They must be out of their minds, if they think I'll let Christine live with her again." Mark sat back. "I'm thinking it might be best if she came to live with me and my family. Get her out of that screwed up state. Keep her away from her mother and her druggie friends." He paused briefly, resumed with a more deliberate tone, "This is where I need your advice. How do I go about doing that? I think Chris needs to be evaluated first to see what kind of drug problem she has. Then after she's done her treatment and we're pretty sure she's no longer dangerous, she can come live with us. Me and my wife. We'd love to have her, so long as she's clean and sober. Does what I'm saying make sense?"

"Mr. Bancroft," Blum began, "I remember your daughter from court last summer. You said she was in a hospital?"

"Yes, up in Waterbury. She had some kind of mental breakdown. Spent the summer there. Just got out."

Blum said he was sorry, that he appreciated Mark's concern. He paused, "You have described two issues: your daughter's current placement, and her long term custody. These issues need to be addressed through different means."

He signaled Knowles to take notes of what he was about to say.

"Regarding Christine's current placement...the caseworker, this Rose LaValley, she needs to know that you disapprove of the placement and specify the reasons. I have heard your concerns and I will have Felicity communicate those concerns to Ms. LaValley, together with your expectation that a more appropriate placement will be obtained for Christine immediately. We will handle all communications with Ms. LaValley."

Mark didn't mind, the woman drove him nuts.

"Regarding your opposition to Christine's return to her mother, and having her placed with you, there are two ways to handle the situation. Because the mother is Christine's custodial parent under the terms of your divorce decree, you could file for a change of custody on the basis of the mother's unfitness to raise this child. Then, as the custodial parent, you would be named in the Case Plan as the parent with whom Christine would eventually be placed. It would be expensive, engaging in two legal actions simultaneously; the CHINS proceeding and the change of custody action. And it involves some risk if Christine is not prepared to be placed in your custody rather than her mother's. But, I expect this approach would destroy the mother, and likely diminish her strength as an adversary in future proceedings."

The lawyer leaned back and paused to let his words sink in. Mark liked what he had just heard but wanted to know the alternative.

Blum continued. "The second approach has a greater likelihood of success in terms of Christine living with you under more favorable circumstances, and at less expense to you. This approach involves Christine remaining in SRS custody, but placed with you after she has completed any recommended drug treatment. While she is placed with you, you can strengthen your relationship with your daughter and concurrently diminish her mother's importance. Or you may learn during this time, a trial period so to speak, that it may not be the best outcome for you or Christine that she live with you permanently. In which case it would be up to SRS to place her elsewhere. If things work out however, you will be in a much stronger position to obtain permanent custody of your daughter."

Now we're talking! Mark smiled, stretched his legs out.

Blum was not finished. "Another distinct advantage to this approach is that as long as she's in state's custody, the State will pay the expenses of her evaluations and treatment, with some contribution expected from you. Whereas if you were to obtain custody right off, you would bear all of those costs on your own."

He didn't have to say any more, Mark got it: go with Option B. It was settled. Blum told Mark, Knowles would lodge the complaint about Christine's placement and begin the process for having Mark considered as an immediate placement option. Blum would provide oversight and become directly involved as necessary. He left Mark with no doubt he would prevail.

***

Christine made her way through the hospital hallways, without needing any help or directions. It was strange to be back after only five days but it felt like it had been months since she had left. She asked Rosemary if she had ever been to Waterbury before.

"Just once. To drop off a child."

When they reached Doctor Vrabel's office. Christine went in and Rosemary took a seat in the waiting room.

Vrabel sat behind his desk as usual, when she entered. Christine mixed up their routine by asking, "So, doctor, how have you been feeling?"

He smiled, "Very well. I'm looking forward to eating too much turkey tomorrow, which is good. Tell me, how's your new home?"

Christine spent the next ten minutes describing the farm, Bixby, the sisters, Hannah and Marshall, the food, the sculpture she was working on, the chores and the hikes, especially the morning she was pelted with the ice tubes. She watched him make several notes as she spoke.

"It sounds like the placement is working out pretty well, I'm glad to hear that. Any problems? Anything you want to complain about?"

Immediately, "I miss my family, my mom. I mean Rosemary and Kathleen are okay, but I want to be home."

Vrabel nodded, "Of course. Hopefully soon, but these things take time."

What things? She remembered, "My father called Monday night. He said he's visiting me next weekend."

"How do you feel about that?"

The light dimmed, her vision smeared, "I don't know. Not good."

Quietly, "Why is that?"

"He just...he's a jerk. He doesn't care about anyone but himself."
"He's coming to see you..."

Christine flashed, "That doesn't prove anything!" "If you don't want him to visit..."

Lurching forward in her chair. "He's got it all worked out with the SRS woman, he's coming."

"You don't think you can stop that?" Challenging him, "Can I?"

Vrabel closed his eyes for a moment before answering, "For being a jerk? I'm not so sure. Maybe he's concerned about you, maybe ..."

"Doubt it."

“Or maybe you can tell me how the visit goes and we’ll figure out a way to deal with him.” Vrabel wrote a note.

She stared at the doctor, her head throbbing, “Yeah, maybe.”

He asked Christine whether she was having any problems sleeping; any problems getting up in the morning: hearing any voices, problems with her sight, headaches or feelings of emptiness.

The night her father had called, she had a hard time going to sleep. She felt like she was crawling out of her skin, her head pounding, pounding lights, threatening noises, something threatening out there, something in her head, ready for her, something dangerous. She didn’t get to sleep for a very long time, not until dawn Tuesday morning, yesterday morning. She was tired, scared, yeah. No one could protect her, help her, not really. Look at Hannah, look at Marshall, all the shit they must have been through to be stuck in a cabin out in the middle of nowhere. If you weren’t empty, you were hurting. Christine didn’t say any of this. That kind of talk might get her sent back to the hospital. *And there’s no way.*

She answered no to all of his questions and she saw him watching her as she answered. She didn’t care if he believed her or not.

“Is it alright if I speak to Rosemary about how things are going?” He asked. *She’ll tell him about Monday night, finding me outside. Whatever.* “Yeah, sure.” “Do you think it may be hard to have your father visit?”

Christine didn’t answer at first, quieted herself enough to feel, “Yeah, it’ll hurt.”

CHAPTER 25

"C'mon girls, we have a lot to do today. Let's go you lazy bumpkins. Happy Thanksgiving!" Rosemary stood at the bedroom doorway, barely lit by the new day.

Christine pulled herself out of a deep slumber. She didn't remember falling asleep last night. Maybe it was the pill: Vrabel had given her a new prescription they had filled while she was at the hospital. Before Rosemary left the bedroom, she asked Christine if she had slept alright. She answered, yes. Vrabel must have told Rosemary to ask. *That's okay.* Her bare feet hit the cold plank floor. *First things first: get some socks on.*

There was a lot to do. The sisters' niece, a woman named Eileen, was expected at noon and the sisters wanted everything ready by then. They had the meal to prepare, and Rosemary and Christine were going to the homeless shelter to deliver the pies, Indian pudding and applesauce they had made last night.

When they finished their breakfast of sausage gravy and biscuits, the children brought the potatoes, onions, butternut squash and a stalk of Brussels sprouts up from the root cellar. Christine and Kathleen then made the stuffing while Rosemary, Marshall and Hannah brought in the firewood. The damp cold seeped in and wrapped around Christine's ankles as she stood at the counter. She glanced out the window over the sink to see the raw gray sky, glad to be in the kitchen's heat and warm aroma.

An hour later, with the turkey stuffed and in the oven, it was time to deliver the desserts. Christine and Rosemary drove to the far edge of Bixby's village, to a rambling old clapboard house on a large town lot. Inside, Christine saw about twenty people gathered in the hallway and in the community room off of the hallway watching television, older people and parents with children, along with the shelter's director and her assistant. She smelled turkey cooking. The director came up to take the Indian pudding from Christine, and the apple pie from Rosemary. He thanked them.

Rosemary responded, "There's more in the Jeep. We could use a hand."

A woman and her son, about thirteen years old, stepped forward and they all went out to the car to retrieve the last of the food. On the way Christine said Happy Thanksgiving to the boy walking beside her.

"Thanks, you too. Thanks for the pie and stuff." He replied. "Sure. You live here?"

"Yeah, for now."

Christine looked at the boy, could tell he was ready to make it through whatever he and his mother were facing. She said, "Good luck, then." She meant it, from the heart.

When Christine and Rosemary arrived home, the food was ready except for final preparations. The table was set, there was nothing that needed to be done. Eileen wasn't due for another hour. Christine got Rosemary's approval to spread some newspaper on the rug before the woodstove and make some things out of clay with Marshall and Hannah.

A collection of thumb size turkeys and lanky Indians and Pilgrims were assembled on the rug before the living room wood stove, when Eileen came through the door carrying a gallon jug of cider and a quart jar of cranberry relish. Christine watched Rosemary and Kathleen rush to the young woman to unburden her, take her coat, touch her, hug her; saw the brimming love in their eyes, in each gesture. She felt a twinge, vague jealousy, as she roused the kids off the floor so they were standing when Kathleen introduced Eileen to them, "our lovely niece from Michigan" who had been having Thanksgiving dinner with the sisters since starting college at the University of Vermont three years ago. Eileen stepped forward to shake Christine's hand first, then Hannah, who responded tentatively, then Marshall, who shook back very enthusiastically.

"Nice to meet you all." She had a sweet smile.

The dinner was delicious. Christine leaned back in her chair, stuffed, after two healthy servings of everything, except the Brussels sprouts. The gravy was especially delicious. She had made it with Eileen, who shared what Kathleen had taught her. The table was spread with dirty plates and half-filled serving dishes.

There was a brief lull. "For this we are thankful." Rosemary offered.

Christine swelled, *Yes.*

The day rolled along with a meandering hike after cleanup then back home for pies and pudding, coffee and hot spiced cider, and a rowdy game of Parcheesi, won by the team of Marshall and Eileen. The cold gray outside dimmed to dusk. Eileen brought her suitcase in. She was staying the night.

That evening, the house was quiet with the younger children upstairs when the telephone rang. Christine answered it, "Happy Thanksgiving to you too, Mom. How's it going down there?"

"Just fine, we're getting ready to eat. Your brother and sister just got home from the football game. Sounds like Branford got whupped. How about you, sweetie, how's your day been?"

Good, really good. Rosemary and Kathleen's niece, Eileen, is here. We've already eaten and the food was great. I made the gravy. And this morning we dropped off some pies at the homeless shelter in town."

Lynne smiled. "Listen honey, let me get things done here, we haven't eaten yet. I'll put your sister on the phone, she's right here. Love you. I'll see you Saturday."

Christine imagined her mother's kitchen in clear detail: pots on every burner with potato water boiling over from one; the small round kitchen table crammed with different serving dishes, waiting to be filled; her mother scrambling around the open oven door siphoning grease from the drippings, checking if the rolls were done, checking the pop up timer on the Butterball turkey. She imagined Charlotte and Matthew hanging back, watching. Like she used to.

A hole in her, spreading, she answered, "Yeah, see you then."

Charlotte came on, then Matt. They sounded good. Christine loved hearing their voices. The hole spread, deepened. The call ended.

Later, as Christine and Eileen finished a self-declared bonus serving of pie a la mode in the kitchen, the phone rang and Christine answered. A woman on the other end said she wanted to speak to Marshall. She sounded drunk. Christine didn't know what to say, only, "Hold on a minute." She found Rosemary reading to the boy upstairs. Rosemary took the call and explained that Marshall was already in bed, and that she would tell him that his mother called. Christine watched her face, resolute, as the mother kept talking. Suddenly Rosemary said, "I'll tell him you called." She hung up, then took the receiver off the cradle. To Christine, "Leave the phone off the hook for a while."

After about a half hour, Christine hung up the receiver. Soon after, it rang again and interrupted Christine and Eileen as they played cribbage. Rosemary and Kathleen were still upstairs with the children. Christine answered. The woman on the phone introduced herself as Hannah's grandmother and asked to speak with Hannah.

When she delivered that message to Kathleen, Kathleen brought the girl to the phone. From the dining room Christine could hear Hannah asking how her mother was, how her sister was. She heard the girl say, "When you see them, tell them I love them. And I love you too Gramma. Bye." Hannah passed through the dining room, past Christine, looking at the floor. Kathleen followed her. Christine wanted to say something, wanted to hug her. She knew Kathleen would give her what she needed.

Christine forgot about the game as she stared through the steam from her cup of tea, thinking. *These kids have their shit, I have mine.*

Eileen broke through the silence. "It's always like this, every time I've been here for Thanksgiving...or Christmas." Christine fought her darkening mood as the woman continued. "But it sounds like you had a nice call."

Christine closed her eyes. "Yeah, it was alright."

She wanted to be left alone. She needed the phone to stay silent - her father hadn't called yet, she couldn't deal with him tonight. She chatted with Eileen, barely listening, finished her tea. He didn't call. She felt alone. She waited for her medication. She waited to go to sleep. She slept dreamlessly.

***

The Saturday after Thanksgiving, Lynne arrived early for her first visit with Christine at the foster home. After a flurry of introductions, conversation over coffee, and touring the house and the animals, Christine took her mother on the trail that she'd been dying to show her. They headed up into the hills, through the birch and evergreens, gray clouds scudding overhead.

They chatted about small things as they walked. When Christine mentioned she had just finished "One Flew Over the Cuckoo's Nest," Lynne said she thought the book was depressing.

Christine disagreed, "Nah, they're kind of like heroes the way they stood up to nasty Nurse Ratched."

Lynne didn't reply. She didn't want to point out how all the characters suffered horribly because they stood up to the nurse. A mile into the hike and her feet were killing her. Lynne asked how much further before they reached the place Christine wanted to show her.

"It's a ways." Christine answered. She noticed her mother's flushed face. The road would get steeper before they reached the glen. "Maybe it's too far..."

"Slow down a little and we'll get there." Lynne wanted to see it.

"Sure."

As they walked, Lynne told Christine she liked Kathleen and Rosemary. "They're really good people." She agreed.

Lynne nodded.

Christine looked up the trail. "I love this hike." "Why?"

"Because so much goes on in these woods. I've seen all kinds of things." Lynne smiled at her daughter.

She knew they arrived at their destination before Christine said a word. Lynne took in the stunning glen, a tree lined bowl of quartz and granite, tall grass lying tan beside a small brook that flowed beneath the rock outcropping, stone fences running along the hillside contours.

Christine took her mother's hand. "Come on, I want to show you something."

They followed one of the stone fences into a steep gully to a square stone square wall about two feet tall and twenty feet to a side. Within the square, the flat surface was sunken several feet.

As they stood beside it, Christine explained. "It's a cellar hole. Someone's house about a hundred fifty years ago, maybe longer. I've found all kinds of things here. Pieces of old glass, chipped pottery, a spoon. I'll show you when we get back to the house."

They decided to rest. A thin mist clung low to the ground. The wall's flat stones were cold to sit on, but Lynne didn't mind. They ate buttered bread and drank some of the cider they had brought.

"Does Kathleen bake all your bread?" Lynne asked.

"Yep, pretty great, huh? She's teaching me how to bake, too."

Lynne managed, through a tinge of jealousy, "That's nice."

Christine heard the tone in her mother's voice. "I'm glad I'm here mom. But I really miss you guys." Gazing into the cellar hole, "Has anyone said when I'm going home?

"Not really. There are things that are supposed to happen first..." "Like what?"

Lynne turned to Christine, her voice soft, "Well, I'm in a parenting group, that's one thing...and I see a therapist, that's another. And they want me to switch my work hours so I'm around at night to supervise you kids. And they want you to recover some more."

Her mother was doing a lot. "Sounds like I should be home soon."

"I don't know Chris, it's not up to me. There's a court thing next week. I'll know more then."

Christine shifted on the cold stone and sipped some cider. "What court thing?"

"I don't remember what it's called, but they'll be looking at our progress, talking about what happens next."

They both imagined strangers picking over their lives. Christine leaned over, took her mother into her arms and whispered. "It will be alright mom. I'm alright."

Lynne held her daughter tightly, whispered back. "I know."

CHAPTER 26

Lynne watched the courtroom door as she waited for the hearing to begin. Fitzgerald had pointed out Mark's lawyer—the young blonde woman in the tailored suit at the other table. Mark hadn't arrived by the time the judge, a middle aged woman, took the bench. Lynne was surprised, thrilled it wasn't that nasty judge who had presided the last time. Fitzgerald explained that Judge Susan Hamilton was on rotation in this court.

After making note of those present for the record, the judge addressed Mark's lawyer. "Ms. Knowles, I understand you represent the father. I see that he's not with you at the table, will he be present?"

Knowles stood up. "Your Honor, Mr. Bancroft will not be attending. It is our understanding that this disposition hearing will be continued. He lives and works in the Albany, New York area and he's very busy with his work as an engineer. I am fully aware of his position on the issues we need to take up today."

Hamilton pursed her lips, a small rebuke. "Very well."

To the state's attorney representing SRS, "Is that correct Mr. Derosia? The court clerk has scheduled this as a contested disposition, to be continued. Is this matter still contested?"

"That's correct, your Honor."

"Okay, so how long will the parties need to prepare. How much time do you think the hearing will take?"

Derosia raised the point that Christine needed a drug and alcohol assessment, the state needed to complete a home study of both the mother and the father's home, and they needed a comprehensive psychological evaluation of Christine. He explained that the caseworker had not yet been able to schedule a psychiatrist to perform the evaluation, but he believed that eight weeks should be sufficient time to get all necessary evaluations completed. He finished by saying the hearing should last two days. As Derosia was speaking Lynne felt her lawyer's agitation. The judge asked Fitzgerald if he had anything to add.

Fitzgerald spoke as he rose from his chair, emphatic. "First off, your Honor, I have to ask why SRS is calling for a home study of the father when he has not indicated that he is willing to have Christine placed with him."

LaValley, from her seat, "Your Honor, last week Mr. Bancroft, through his lawyer, informed me that he is interested in having his daughter live with him, which of course is his right."

Lynne looked up at her lawyer, bile rising in her throat. *Oh my god, he's trying to get Christine!*

Fitzgerald continued. "Your Honor we were not told that until just this moment. In fact, two weeks ago at the last Plan Review, there was no mention of placement with the father..."

The judge interrupted and addressed Christine's attorney. "Ms. Simmons, were you aware of the father's position concerning placement?"

"No, your Honor, not until just now."

Judge Hamilton, stiffly. "Mr. Derosia, you shall refrain from springing important matters on the other parties in open court. That being said, I will allow time for the father's home study to be completed. Mr. Fitzgerald, anything else?"

"Yes, your Honor. "On behalf of the mother, I strongly disagree with the proposal to have Christine's comprehensive evaluation done by someone other than her treating psychiatrist, Dr. Vrabel. Christine has a complex set of issues that needs to be adequately reviewed before any placement or disposition decision can be made. According to her records she has suffered psychotic breaks, bouts of acute depression, severe anxiety, and perhaps chronic depression. Dr. Vrabel understands better than anyone what factors may aggravate or mitigate Christine's condition. Anticipating that the state would be requesting a comprehensive evaluation. I spoke to Dr. Vrabel. He said he could complete his evaluation in six weeks."

The judge raised an eyebrow. "I trust he is including the parents in this evaluation?"

Lynne glanced at Fitzgerald then back to the judge.

"Yes, your Honor. He feels it is essential to assess the family dynamic in determining what is in Christine's best interests. That would involve one or two interviews, preferably two interviews, with each of the parents, to get a sense of their respective abilities to meet Christine's urgent and challenging needs. And in light of this news that the father is interested in having Christine placed with him, it appears even more important that the complete family dynamic be properly assessed."

Hamilton nodded. "I agree. I'm familiar with Dr. Vrabel's work, the quality of his evaluations. I don't see why there would be any objections" She looked at the State's table.

Before LaValley or Derosia had a chance to respond, Knowles was on her feet, "The father has an objection, your Honor. A strong objection. While Dr. Vrabel may be a qualified psychiatrist, I am concerned he would be inherently conflicted if he were to be asked to provide an objective, unbiased evaluation of a subject who he is treating in therapy..."

The judge interrupted, "I don't understand your point, counselor, this is common and accepted practice."

Knowles' face reddened. She looked down for an instant then straightened up, "My point, your Honor, is that Dr. Vrabel clearly expresses a bias against my client and in favor of Christine's mother... as evidenced by some of his treatment notes. In fact, this past week he has attributed Christine's recent anxiety to her father's upcoming visit, and he has increased her levels of Prozac to deal with that purported anxiety."

Lynne closed her eyes against her rising dread.

Simmons quickly rose. "Your Honor, if Ms. Knowles thinks she can direct my client's treatment, she is way out of line."

The judge to Simmons, "I think that is a bit of an overreaction. However, she does have a point, Ms. Knowles. Let's allow Dr. Vrabel to do his job unless there is a specific reason to believe he is failing to do so."

"We're concerned, your Honor." Knowles started. "Mr. Bancroft expresses his wish to be involved in his daughter's future. He sets up a visit with her and suddenly she's being treated for heightened anxiety? My client has to wonder if he will be treated fairly in an evaluation by Dr. Vrabel."

"She...Christine, has suffered severe aggravation of her symptoms on other occasions following contact with her father..." Simmons said tersely.

Knowles interrupted. "According to Dr. Vrabel, who seems to have formed an opinion about my client without ever having met him..."

"Enough!" The judge told the two women to be seated. She addressed the guardian ad litem. "Mrs. Fromme, do you have any concerns that Dr. Vrabel would be unable to prepare an objective evaluation of Christine's psychiatric condition?"

Surprised by the sudden question, Fromme blurted, "No, I don't think so."

Hamilton thanked the guardian ad litem then added, "I'm not going to open a full evidentiary hearing into the appropriateness of Dr. Vrabel's treatment of Christine. Suffice it to say I have been put on notice of the father's concern. Nonetheless, Dr. Vrabel is the professional most aware of Christine's psychiatric needs. At this time he would seem to be the best qualified to render an opinion on that central issue. For that reason I will order that he prepare the evaluation."

She turned to attorney Knowles, "Which is not to say the father can't hire his own expert to review Dr. Vrabel's methodology or his conclusions."

"Ms. Simmons, as Christine's attorney I expect you will take care to see that those who are providing services to Christine are not inadvertently causing her harm or prejudicing the rights of others. This evaluation is not to be outcome determinative. By that I mean, the conclusions are not to be determined first, then filled in with evidence supporting the predetermined outcome. I expect Dr. Vrabel will not do such a thing."

Judge Hamilton looked to Fitzgerald, "And back to you, attorney Fitzgerald, do you have any other concerns?"

Fitzgerald rose. "Yes, your Honor, like the matter of the father seeking placement of Christine, we had no knowledge until just now that he has resumed visitation with Christine, and that there is a visit planned for some time soon, apparently. The mother would like to know when visits with the father are scheduled to occur."

Simmons from her seat, "As would I, your Honor."

"Ms. LaValley, when is the father scheduled to visit Christine?" The judge asked. LaValley stood. "Next weekend."

"And are there plans for future visits?"

"We're considering alternate weekends with the mother."

Fitzgerald, "No consultation with the mother, none with Christine, apparently, or her psychiatrist. This is outrageous!"

Judge Hamilton had had enough, "Ms. LaValley you are required by law to serve the child's best interests, make sure that you do. Mr. Fitzgerald, Ms. Simmons, if you have some specific, articulable objection to Ms. LaValley's conduct that denotes specific, articulable harm to Christine, then bring it to my attention in the form of a Motion sanctioning that conduct. Otherwise, alternate weekend visitation, on its face, is reasonable."

The judge concluded the hearing by ordering that Christine undergo a drug and alcohol assessment, and that Dr. Vrabel conduct a comprehensive psychiatric evaluation of Christine, all of which would be presented at the disposition hearing. She ordered that the parties present their evaluations, witness lists and exhibits lists, no later than February 1, discovery to be completed February 15. The disposition hearing was scheduled for February 22. Two days were allotted for the hearing. As the judge left the bench, Lynne stood up together with the others. Overwhelmed, she followed the attorneys out of the courtroom.

In the hallway, Lynne asked Fitzgerald and Simmons, "Can he do that, can they do this? Give him visits every other week? Didn't the judge hear his own lawyer say that Doctor Vrabel believes he's harming her? I don't understand!"

"Lynne, alternate weekend visits is a typical arrangement." Fitzgerald tried to explain. "The judge was telling us she needed a specific opinion from Doctor Vrabel about the visits causing Christine harm before she decides to cut them off."

Simmons added, "Christine sees the doctor once a week. I'll make sure he knows our concern and I'll ask him to let me know immediately if the visits need to stop. He's a good doctor. We have to trust him."

Lynne worried. "I don't think she knows he's coming. Someone has to warn her. I'll call her tonight and tell her."

"Be careful what you say, Lynne." Fitzgerald warned. "I don't want you accused of undermining Christine's relationship with her father."

What is he talking about? "What relationship? What's he doing? Showing up, making trouble?"

Fitzgerald, "I don't know. But he has the right to see Christine until he abuses that right."

Lynne fumed. *The right to make Chris miserable!*

***

Christine was doing homework at the dining room table, with Hannah watching, when the phone rang. Kathleen left her knitting to answer it, returned to tell Christine it was her mother and handed her the receiver. She took the phone and asked her mother how she was.

"I'm fine sweetheart. What are you up to?"

"Homework. Can you believe it? Rosemary's got me doing algebra, this math package the school sent. Nothing hard, kind of review. I guess when I get through this part it will start to get harder. Court was today, right? How'd that go?"

Lynne hesitated "It was alright. They went over all of these tests and evaluations they want to do. Your doctor Vrabel is going to evaluate you, me and your father..."

"Dad? Why?"

"Well, according to the caseworker, he wants you to live with him."

Christine leaned against the dining room wall in shock. "No! He can't."

"I don't know honey. That's what she said, and his lawyer said the same. He wasn't there."

"He doesn't even show up and he's telling people what he wants?" Christine's breath was shallow as she spoke. "Do I even get a say in any of this?"

Lynne wasn't sure. "Doctor Vrabel will be asking you, I would imagine. And if he feels it would be harmful for you to be with your father, he's supposed to let your lawyer know. She told me that herself. And that goes for these visits he's going to be having with you. You let the doctor know how it goes with your father."

Christine wrapped the phone cord tightly around her wrist. "What visits? I just know about the one coming up this weekend!"

"Yes, every other weekend."

Pacing the room, Christine shouted, "Well what if I don't *want* to see him? Anybody think of that?"

Lynne murmured, "Then you should tell Doctor Vrabel. Or your lawyer. I'm supposed to stay out of this, my lawyer told me."

Screaming, "Fine! You do that!" Christine slammed the phone down and ran to her room.

Lynne stood in the kitchen's gloom, hung the phone up, her brain pounding.

She'd do anything to make it all stop. Standing in the half-light, she remembered she was seeing Miranda tomorrow. And she had her group. *I'm not alone.*

Christine lay in her bed, her head pounding out pain. She fought off the black. The pain lessened. After a while, Rosemary came up to her room and told her Kathleen had a cup of mint tea for her.

"Thank you." Christine rose and followed Rosemary downstairs, knowing that hot tea would help.

***

The lavender scent didn't soothe Lynne, the radiator heat didn't warm her, but when Miranda smiled at her before she spoke, Lynne's wracked mood shifted for the better. The therapist began by asking how the visit went with Christine.

"The place is great, two sisters run it. They're teaching Chris how to cook. She's hiking a lot. She's even started schoolwork."

"All of this sounds very good Lynne. So, she seems happy there, you think?"

Remembering her daughter screaming at her on the phone last night, "Yes and no. She likes it there, a lot, but there's so much going on. We had court yesterday and Mark has visits with her now, starting this weekend. His lawyer said he wants her to live with him."

"I forgot you had court. That's a sudden change from him, isn't it?"

Lynne looked at her hands on her lap. "Nobody knew. And Christine's all worked up about it, yelling at me ..."

"Why is she yelling at you?"

"She wants me to do something to stop it. But I can't. I told her that. The lawyers told me to stay out of it."

"They're right, still that must be hard for you. I'm sorry."

Lynne nodded. "He's upsetting her. She's sick, and he's upsetting her."

"And he's upsetting you, too."

Lynne's head bowed, tears started down her cheeks.

Miranda softly, "It's a lot, it's sudden and it hurts, but I want to ask you why it hurts."

The room was quiet, except for the clock on the mantle. Lynne couldn't answer.

She took in a deep breath. *He'll get her.*

She choked out, "If he wants, he will get Christine. She'll be forced to live with him, if that's what he wants. And it will be terrible for her."

Quietly, "Why will it be terrible?" "Because he's a bastard."

"Do you think Mark will follow through and do what is needed for the judge to allow Christine to live with him? Or will he lose interest before then, based on his history of abandonment?"

Lynne wiped at her eyes, "Maybe." *That would be like him.*

"You focus on what you need to do to get Christine back. Working with me. Your group."

Lynne straightened. "I'm going to tell the caseworker that I'm seeing you."

Miranda nodded, agreed that was a good idea.

"Then all I've got to do is stop working nights. I've got to put in for a different shift at the hospital. Next week. If I get off nights they should send Chris home." *Meanwhile, he's going to be seeing Chris*. Lynne whispered, "He's going to hurt her."

A moment passed. Miranda responded, "Christine has you and Doctor Vrabel and her lawyer watching out for her. Protecting her."

CHAPTER 27

Christine heard the stove door clang downstairs, smelled the word smoke that had escaped the stove. The day's light pressed against her closed lids. Her face cool, she pulled the blanket to her eyes. She didn't want to get up. Last night had been terrible—she knew she had nightmares, but couldn't remember them. The sheet was still twisted around her ankles. She was exhausted. Her father was coming today.

Doctor Vrabel had said he wasn't going to prescribe her stronger medication at this time. He had said they should see how this visit went. Christine was jumping out of her skin: *Why? He's a jerk, so what.* The doctor had asked her why she thought her father was coming all this way to see her. She didn't have an answer. But last night, lying in bed completely awake, she had told herself that maybe he loved her. She could imagine Vrabel nodding. Maybe he was just a jerk who loved her. Maybe it was part of her illness, or the meds, or her crazy life that had her all worked up. Whatever, She had to get out of bed.

That morning, she tried reading the paper, working on the owl sculpture, sketching some fir cones, all with no success. She thought Rosemary would suggest that she do some extra chores to take her mind off things, but she didn't. So she sat on the couch, listened to the burning wood shift in the firebox, ignored the brilliant winter sunshine pouring through the windows. Marshall brought her a book, 'Tom Sawyer', which Rosemary had been reading to him at bedtime. Christine began to read to him, Hannah joined them. Soon after they started, she heard a car approaching then stop. She looked at the clock on the living room wall: 11:40. She finished a paragraph, barely seeing the words.

Just as Christine was about to open the front door, he pounded on it, calling out, "Hello?" Everyone inside jumped. She opened the door. There he was in his ski jacket, Icelandic wool hat, new Sorel boots—looking like he arrived from another civilization.

He spoke before Christine had a chance to greet him. "There you are. I didn't know if I had the right place. That driveway, jeez. You should put up a sign or something." He was in the house, past Christine.

Kathleen welcomed him. "Mr. Bancroft, I'm Kathleen Murphy. I'm sorry you had trouble finding us."

"I nearly missed it completely." He unzipped his jacket, turned to Christine, "Hey, honey. Wow, what a trip. I've been on the road since eight. Now this is the middle of nowhere, officially."

"I like it here." Christine blurted.

"I'm sure you do. After the hospital, anything's bound to be an improvement." Christine burned with embarrassment.

Kathleen asked, "Mr. Bancroft, can I get you some tea or coffee?"

"Some coffee would be great. And call me Mark."

"Certainly. Mark. Christine why don't you take your father's jacket. Marshall, Hannah, you go off and play."

Mark watched the two children leave for the living room, without saying anything to them. Kathleen called them back, apologized, and had them introduce themselves. Mark shook their hands, and explained he was Christine's father from a faraway place called Albany. Then they left.

By the time the coffee was brewed, Kathleen had filled the table with a platter of cold ham and a wedge of cheddar, jars of pickles, sliced rye bread and some cold apple cobbler. Mark said he was starving. Christine helped Kathleen serve the food while he told them about the trip and how different it was 'way up here' compared to civilization. She sat next to her father, who was building himself a thick sandwich.

As Kathleen brought the coffee and took her seat, she explained. “Rosemary should have been back by now. She just went into town for a few groceries. Probably remembered something she needed at the hardware store. Wouldn’t surprise me.”

Mark asked through a mouthful. “Rosemary, that’s your sister, right? Just the two of you run this place? Amazing. You have a man help you keep the place up?”

“No. Well, some things. Like the new roof. Otherwise we keep the place going.”

Mark looked at her, trying to figure if she was kidding him or not.

“They grew up here, lived here nearly their entire lives.” Christine said. Kathleen smiled, “Rosemary and I are fourth generation Murphys here.”

“You don’t really know anything different than this? How about your kids, are they going to take over when it’s time?” Mark inquired.

Christine winced.

Kathleen lost her smile. “We’ve raised dozens of children, but none of our own, no.”

He seemed to ignore the uncomfortable response and continued to ask Kathleen questions about living on this land. Finally, she suggested Christine take her father on a tour of the house and the property once he finished eating.

As Christine showed her father the first floor, he asked where the television was. She showed him her room, and he asked if she was happy. She responded, yes. He didn’t ask her why. Outside, she showed him the woodpile and he said it looked like it would be fun to split some wood. He grabbed a maul and split a couple chunks into kindling, while Christine watched without speaking. He leaned the maul against the woodpile, breathing plumes into the bright day, sweating a little. "This is great. I can see why you love this place."

Christine wasn't sure whether he meant what he had just said. She wondered what to do next. The forest trail was so far off. It didn't seem worth the effort.

She gathered the kindling to take inside. Mark watched her, talking about the cold and the clean air and good appetites, and the crazy driveway and the damage it must have done to his car. He wanted to take a look at his car. She put her armload of kindling down and followed him around the house to where his Audi was parked.

Mark commented over his shoulder about all the stuff lying around, "It's like a miniature junkyard."

"Rosemary probably has her reasons for keeping it." Christine suggested.

He didn't answer, was already on the ground, peering under the car, "Jeez, scraped up pretty bad. I better have my guy check it out when I get home." He glanced up at Christine. "Gonna cost a fortune, probably."

She was looking at her feet, she didn't answer.

He said, "Let's take a walk down that drive...see what caused it."

Around the bend, past the glacial boulder, with the house out of sight, the thick evergreen canopy surrounded them, a shroud against the light. Christine and her father walked in silent shadow. He studied the contours of the roadway. She walked a few feet behind, watching him.

"Here, this is what I'm talking about." He shouted as he turned to her.

Christine's heart jumped.

"Look at this. Come here and look at this."

She came and stood next to him. She didn't want to be there. She couldn't hear any sounds except his accusing voice as he pointed at a gouge in the road.

> "It's got to be six inches deep. Looks like runoff caused it. You'd think they'd get this fixed." They were close, he was facing her. She didn't know what to say.

Suddenly, the sound of groaning, squealing metal on metal came at them from down the green shadowed drive. They both looked in the direction of the noise. The swaying, swerving Cherokee appeared from around the bend ahead of them, less than thirty feet away, fast approaching. They jumped back, to the forest's edge. The Jeep bucked and rattled to a sudden stop beside them, three feet away.

Rosemary's face appeared in the rolled down window, "For crying out loud, I almost hit the two of you!"

Mark stepped forward, introduced himself as Christine's father. "You must be Rosemary."

She looked at him like he was a fool, asked Christine what they were doing.

"Just taking a walk."

"Studying your driveway, so I can safely navigate it home tonight." Mark added.

Still looking at him like he was a fool, "Alright. See you back at the house." She shifted the Jeep into gear and the vehicle lurched down the road.

Mark laughed, "Not very friendly is she?"

Christine shot back, "She was upset. She wasn't expecting us on the road."

"No, I suppose not."

They walked further down the drive.

Mark abruptly said, "You know honey, I'm glad you're doing better. It's sure been rough, huh." She said nothing.

"I don't know how long they plan on keeping you here, but I want you to know, if you need to, and people say it's okay, you can come live with me and Nancy."

Christine stopped. Her face burned. "No."

Her curt answer surprised Mark, "It's just...in case you need someplace..."

"The plan is that I go home with mom."

"I thought..." He broke off, then suggested they head back because he should be getting on the road soon. "After all, I have a long drive ahead."

They walked back to the house without speaking. A bright clarity filled Christine's silence. Mark's annoyance rendered him speechless.

At the house, Mark said goodbye to Kathleen and Rosemary, said nothing to the children. He refused Kathleen's offer of a thermos of coffee and fresh baked lemon pound cake. At the door he told Christine, "I'm glad you're better. See you in two weeks. I'll try to arrange for you to visit us in Albany. Nancy would love that and you'll get to see the baby."

Christine said nothing. He hugged her stiff body. She smelled him, felt him, fought against him. Her head swam in the winter light. Then he was gone.

Mark turned onto the blacktop, putting that place behind him. *God, what the hell is she doing way the hell out here? Those sisters are strange, and those kids are seriously damaged. This can't be good for her. The way she acted, telling me about 'the plan', like she's programmed. That's what they're doing, programming her. Way the hell out here, no human contact, not even going to school. Got to get her out of there. Get her back in the normal world. Take her shopping. That might change her mind about things. About living with her mother. That's the programming talking, 'the Plan'. I've got to talk to Blum.*

Mark didn't notice he had made the wrong turn out of the Murphy's drive until twenty miles later, when he reached the Canadian border.

After he left, Christine went to her room without speaking to anyone and struggled against the rising black until, exhausted, she fell into a deep, troubled sleep. She slept through dinner, through the evening, until she woke in the middle of the night fighting her nightmares, sweating in the cold dark room, trying to purge the vivid stalking from her dream recollection, and failing.

***

That Wednesday, after her father's visit, Christine took her seat across from Doctor Vrabel. On the edge of the chair, leaning forward, she began before the psychiatrist had a chance to speak. "You want to know how I'm doing? Not so great. These past few days, since my father came to see me, I've been having a real hard time sleeping. Nightmares about Stonebridge...remembering stuff. And my dad, I've been thinking a lot about him, like why is he back? He told me he wants me to live with him. I don't get it. He left us, went off and got married, had a kid, and now he says he has a place for me, if I need it. Well I don't!" She shook her head. " I don't need him. I'm doing fine without him. He said I'll need a place when they make me leave Rosemary and Kathleen's. I thought the idea was that I'm going back home after their place. I mean, when I talk to my mom, it sounds like everything's working out. But nobody's saying I'm going home for sure, or when I'm going home. I know the Murphys are just like an emergency place, and I'm not supposed to be there too long. So what are they going to do with me after that?" She threw her hands up. "Nobody's telling me. And then he shows up and tells me he'll be visiting every other week, and that he's going to have them send me down to his place. And what about mom? Nobody's talking about me going home to visit her. It's like he knows what's coming and nobody else knows. That's the way he is—he always knows what's going to happen. Well, I want to know what's going to happen to me."

Vrabel watched Christine throw herself back in the chair when she finished her rant. "You see your father as very powerful." He observed. "A person has a lot of power because people let him control them. You know, I've been asked by the court to evaluate your psychological needs. That will include an opinion on where you might live, who you might live with. Your mother has said all along she wants you to return home, and your father has recently said that he would like you to live with him. I'll talk with your mother, I'll talk with your father, and most importantly I'll be talking with you, listening to you about what you need. I'll write that up, and my report will hopefully help the judge make the best decision about what is best for you. So, a lot of the control over your future will be coming from what you tell me. The power is in this room." "You said last time that maybe he's showed up because he wants to help me, how could you say that?"

"I was just saying that might be an explanation."

"He said he's going to have me visit him in Albany. I don't want to, but he made it sound like I had to."

Vrabel assured her, "You're not ready to do that. I'll let your caseworker know I think that's a really bad idea."

"And what about the visits, what if I don't want to see him at all?"

"Did something happen during last weekend's visit?"

Christine rubbed her nose and glared, "No, just that he was rude and a jerk." "You're upset about your father planning to have you live with him, about the visits. What else?"

"It's just that he's so weird, the way he acts and everything. I didn't like it, the way he treated Kathleen and Rosemary and the kids. I won't ever like the way he treats people. I hate being around him."

"And the way he treats you?"

The way he treats me? She had no words for that strange pain.

Vrabel told her there was nothing he could do to stop the visits at this time; that they'd work on ways she could cope with his annoying behavior; that her father was part of her life so she should learn how to deal with it. That's what he was there for, he said, to help her deal with annoying shit.

She had a better idea; how about if he helped her keep the annoying shit out of her life. She didn't say that to him. Instead she asked why couldn't she go home over the holidays?

He said something about her not being ready for that either, that her caseworker most likely wouldn't allow it at this time.

Yeah, tell me about all the power I have.

***

That evening after her session with Vrabel, Christine fiddled with the clay at the dining room table, not really working on her owl sculpture, thinking about what her lawyer had said earlier. When she had gotten home from Waterbury, she called and left a message on attorney Simmons' phone saying she was really upset about having to go to her father's in Albany, and she wanted her to talk to Dr. Vrabel about what they could do to stop that from happening.

Her lawyer had called back. She had spoken with Vrabel and she would stop the visit, even if it meant she had to get a court order. Then right before dinner, Simmons called and said that the caseworker admitted she was wrong and that there would be no visit in Albany at this time.

She should have been feeling good—standing up to her father, or whatever she had done—but she didn't. It wasn't like that. She smoothed a patch of gray clay on the figure with her thumb. She felt odd, realized she was hoping they hadn't been mean to her father when they made him change his plans. She thought that maybe he just wanted her to have a nice time with his family. And that it was a very long trip for him. And that it must be really strange for him to see her in a place like this. The phone rang. Christine didn't notice, until Kathleen came to tell her the call was for her, that it was her father.

Mark told Christine the caseworker had called him at work. "She said you aren't really ready for a visit here in Albany. I understand. It was just wishful thinking, I guess. I thought, here we could...You're right, we need to take things a step at a time."

Christine listened in silence.

"Bottom line kiddo, is I love you very much. You've been through a hell of a lot. I don't want you hurt anymore. That's what I'm thinking when I say I want those social workers to keep me in mind if you need a place to live." The words were soft. "A lot of water's gone over the dam, maybe it's time we made a fresh start."

"Maybe it is." Christine said gently. Then she slid into a sudden, deep sadness. "Something to think about."

"Sure." "Love you."

She needed to say it, "Love you, too."

After the phone call, for the remainder of the evening, Christine tried to make some sense of her father and what he meant to her. The sisters watched her, quiet in the night, until it was time for her medication and bed. Sleep took her mind to rest.

The next morning, Rosemary brought Christine on a long hike into the hills, hours in frozen quiet. When they returned for lunch, Christine devoured the lamb stew and biscuits Kathleen had made. She was truly grateful. After lunch, she brought out the owl figure.

She didn't think about her father. Her hands worked the clay and the afternoon passed. She left the owl and began another shape.

***

That Saturday Christine gazed out the window after breakfast, worried that the roads weren't safe for her mother to make the trip up. The snow had stopped an hour before. It had snowed through the night. Her mother had called and said they'd only gotten a few inches in Branford, that the roads were getting cleared and the interstate shouldn't be bad, except for the skiers. There was less than a foot of snow in Bixby. The roads would be cleared in time. Rosemary was plowing out the drive, already.

As she waited for her mother, after shoveling paths to the cars, the henhouse and the woodpile, Christine painted clay farm animals -—a couple cows, a horse, a couple pigs, some ducks and chickens—she had made for Marshall's Christmas present. She'd been working on these figurines the past few nights, after the children had gone to bed. Hannah and Marshall were away for the weekend, staying with family. It was a good opportunity to finish their presents. Christmas was coming Friday, six days away. After her visit with her mother, Kathleen was going to help her make a doll for Hannah.

Christine then remembered she hadn't had any nightmares for a few days, since her father had called. Things seemed pretty good. She wasn't even upset that the other kids got to go to their families for Christmas and she hadn't. It didn't matter, really. The caseworker had told her lawyer that her mother's home was not regarded as safe for her. She didn't know what that was supposed to mean, but she didn't fight it. She was celebrating Christmas with Rosemary and Kathleen. On New Year's Day they'd have a party – Kathleen had promised a holiday party—when her mother, Matt and Charlotte would come up to visit. She carefully daubed yellow on a tiny clay duck.

When Lynne arrived, Christine was still painting the figurines, and they decided it was a good day to stay in. Her mother would help her finish the figures after they had lunch. Kathleen suggested they might work on Hannah's doll also, which seemed like a great idea to Christine and Lynne. After a lunch of split pea and ham soup and sourdough bread, Kathleen and Rosemary searched the house for materials for the doll, and Christine and her mother decorated little animals and drank hot cocoa, while they shared what had been going on with each other. They were comfortable, it was good.

The sisters brought scraps of cloth, buttons, felt, yarn, scissors, thread and needles to the table. The four women began designing the doll and its outfit, and planning how to assemble it. It became clear to Christine that a lot of work was going to be involved, especially sewing. She had a hunch she would know how to sew by the time this project was completed. She watched her mother, Kathleen, and Rosemary huddled over the table conferring on whether to use felt or buttons for eyes and mouth. And she was happy.

A few hours later, Lynne noticed the light outside fading; dusk falling. The doll was nearly finished, but she had to go. It was a long drive ahead, dark and cold. She didn't want to get home too late. As she was putting on her coat, saying her goodbyes, Lynne felt the small box in her coat pocket. She interrupted Kathleen, who was pressing her to take more cookies home with her. "Oh wait a second. Honey... there's something I brought for you." Lynne held the box out. "An early Christmas present."

Christine received the gift with a beaming smile, "Thank you!"

"Open it."

Christine carefully took apart the wrapping. As she opened the palm sized box, her breath escaped, "Mom, it's beautiful!"

Lynne shone as her daughter slowly withdrew a brilliant red necklace. "I've had this a long time. Since before you were born, even before I met your father."

Christine slowly ran the necklace through her fingers as her mother spoke. The beads were exquisite; translucent cherry red glass encased a white ceramic center, the white exposed at each end of each cylindrical bead, each bead no longer than a pencil point, no wider than an apple stem. They seemed to glow from within and shine on the surface at the same time. There was a purity to them, a power and a beauty.

"They're called 'white hearts,' beads made like that. The red with the white centers."

"Where did you get it?"

Lynne touched a distant memory. "A boy gave them to me, a young man really. His name was Charley Springer... the summer before I went off to college. Not long after that, he died. In Vietnam. I wore them for a while. Then I met your father and it didn't seem right...so, I put them away." Lynne watched the drape of the necklace shift in her daughter's hands and added, "They're too beautiful to sit in a box."

"They are." Christine slipped the mid length necklace over her head and pensively fingered the beads laid over her collarbone.

"They look lovely on you. They're yours now."

Gently, "I love them, Mom. I promise you I'll wear them."

"I should be going." Lynne gathered up the tins of cookies: pfeffernuss and snickerdoodles Kathleen and Christine had baked. She again thanked Kathleen and Rosemary for the New Years' plans—they had talked over some more details about the party, such as what everyone liked to eat and when they would arrive.

Lynne looked at her beautiful daughter for a long second before hugging her goodbye.

In that moment Christine sensed her mother through the beads: a strong, young woman. Her mother's life, before her spirit began dying. She swore she would never die like that.

CHAPTER 28

Christmas Eve: Matt and Charlotte charged downstairs when they heard Lynne come through the kitchen door. They scrambled into the kitchen, before she had a chance to unload the bag of Chinese takeout, a Christmas Eve family tradition, going back three years.

"Christine called while you were getting the food. She said you don't have to call back, she'll talk to you tomorrow." Charlotte reported.

Lynne watched her children eat chicken chow mein noodles, while she thought about her eldest daughter. Christine had called every night since Saturday's visit. They had been easy conversations, about everyday things. Matt and Charlotte had also spoken with her during the week, and they were excited they were going to see their sister on New Year's. Even though she was far away, Lynne felt like Christine was more present in their lives than she had been in a long time.

***

Christmas Eve: *Jesus Christ, is every maniac in the world in this mall?* Mark looked at his watch: *after six*. Nancy wanted to be at her sister's by now. She knew he had some last minute shopping to do. *What did she expect?* He couldn't worry about it, she'd figure it out and go without him.

He just had to grab a couple things for Charlotte. He found Kohl's. They'd have girls' clothing and that should take care of it. He had already gotten Christine a gift certificate for some running shoes and running gear at the sporting goods store, where he knocked out most of Matt's gifts. He was in good shape. As he headed into the department store, he remembered Christine saying something about wanting some collection of poetry, some poet she was reading and liked. He couldn't remember who, but it didn't matter because he doubted they sold books at Kohl's, and when he was finished there, he was done.

***

Christmas Eve. Elbow deep in hot soapy water, Christine scrubbed the last of the dinner plates. Kathleen chatted beside her. "We usually go to the dawn service, but we figured the midnight Mass would be more lively, more interesting to you. Of course it hasn't been midnight Mass in years. Too late, too exciting, if you know what I mean. So, they hold it at ten now, and it still counts for Christmas."

Christine smiled, content filled with minestrone soup, fresh baked bread, applesauce cake and cider. Kathleen explained she liked to make a simple meal on Christmas Eve. "Because a baby's birth is a humbling thing. I think about Mary waiting to have her baby, scared. Just like every mother who's ever been."

While they ate, Kathleen and Rosemary had reminisced about some favorite Christmas moments from their childhood and more recent celebrations. Christine joined the reverie and described some of the best times she could recall: her first bike parked next to the tree, her sister giving her a big kiss for her potholder present, baking sugar cookies with her mother while Matt dipped into the icing, and of course, Chinese takeout on Christmas Eve.

A few hours later, Christine and the sisters traveled through the clear, starlit night to a town down the valley from Bixby, where the Catholic church and two other churches on the commons were brightly lit up for their Christmas Eve services. It was more than lively. A loud throng of flush faced people greeted each other with hugs, kisses and handclasps, at the entryway of the Catholic Church. The scent of alcohol and cologne mingled and stirred with each gust of wind. Rosemary and Kathleen greeted a few from the crowd, introducing Christine as "living with them," which seemed to make sense to the sisters' friends.

Christine entered the church with Kathleen and Rosemary, and they slipped into a pew in the packed church. She felt the crowd's great murmuring anticipation. Then, the massive organ in the choir loft issued forth great waves of notes beginning *Hark! The Herald Angels Sing.* It was the first of many familiar and unfamiliar hymns and carols to be sung boisterously, earnestly by the full throated congregation and choir. A priest and two altar boys walked down the center aisle to the altar in order to begin the Mass, which itself was mysterious to Christine; both solemn and joyous with incantations, ranks of lit candles, billows of pungent incense, tinkling bells, a hearty sermon, and more boisterous singing. The celebration filled the building and spilled out into the winter's night, proclaiming the birth of mankind's Savior.

Christine preferred Kathleen's take on the birth of Jesus: a baby born to a scared, poor couple. Since then, the Christian world had been celebrating this birth like crazy. It made sense, sure, at the darkest time of the year to fire up the lights, push back the winter hunger a few more days. She glanced over to Rosemary, singing a hymn devotedly and a bit off key, and silently thanked her and Kathleen for the comfort and shelter they gave her.

***

Christmas Day was brilliantly sunny and frigid. The temperature wasn't expected to go above ten degrees. Christine split and brought in extra wood—they would be burning a lot the next few days. Meanwhile, Rosemary and Kathleen packed jars of jams and pickles, breads and cookies, and a few presents for Kathleen to take later that day to their aunt and her neighbors in a nursing home in Saint Johnsbury. Usually both sisters went, but Christine was in their home for Christmas, so Rosemary would stay behind.

When Christine finished bringing in the wood and sat at the kitchen table to drink some warmed cider, Kathleen and Rosemary presented her with a package wrapped in tissue paper. "Merry Christmas, dear."

Weren't they doing presents on New Year's Day?

Kathleen would have none of it. "You need to get a little something on Christmas morning, that's the way it's meant to be."

Christine slowly removed the tissue paper and uncovered thick maroon and fuchsia, hand knit woolen mittens. "Kathleen, they're beautiful. But when..."

"After all you children were asleep." A mischievous smile shone from the woman, pleased with her surreptitious ways.

She threw her arms around Kathleen. "Thank you."

The telephone rang. Christine offered to answer and both sisters nodded in agreement. On the other end of the line three excited people shouted "Merry Christmas!" Matt and Charlotte then took turns rattling off the presents they had received and had given their mother. They wanted to know what it was like for Christine, up there, this Christmas. She told them about the Mass, and the freezing temperature, and her stunning new mittens. There was a pause. Christine thought: *they can't imagine, but they're trying.*

"You'll get to see all this next weekend, see for yourself and get to meet Kathleen and Rosemary. You'll love them." She said.

When Lynne got on the phone, Christine repeated what she had just told Matt and Charlotte. She listened to her mother express cheerful things about Christmas and the upcoming New Year's Day. It was good and all but kind of sad, like something more, something bigger should be said. It was weird, but Christmas was like that, it always seemed like something bigger was supposed to happen. On top of that, this was her first Christmas away from home. Christine told her mother she was really looking forward to seeing them all, which was definitely true.

Rosemary and Kathleen joined Christine in the kitchen, got on the phone and wished the Bancrofts a happy Christmas. Christine took the receiver back and said again she couldn't wait to see everyone, and goodbye.

Kathleen left. The house was suddenly too quiet. The only sounds were the burning logs popping in the woodstove and the floorboards creaking as Rosemary moved about. Christine needed to walk, alone.

The forest was glorious. Each snow crystal sparked color, tree trunks squeaked from the bitter cold. The iced air singed Christine's nostrils and burned her lungs as she snowshoed the logging trail. Her muscles heated up against the cold as she rose into the higher woods, her red cheeks chafing. After trekking hard for nearly a mile, she slipped into focus on the immediate presence of the deep evergreen forest, the radiant blue sky. A vast pleasure filled her. As she gathered a few pine cones for a gift she was making Matthew, Christine realized that the shape she had been working on the past week, a pair of hands, would be her mother's present. But they were far from complete, so she turned around and headed home to work on it.

She spent the rest of Christmas day sculpting intently, stopping only to eat. That included sharing a large bar of Belgian chocolate Rosemary had given her as a "little Christmas something." What she had in mind did not come easily, but by nightfall, as the dusk tinted the snow lavender outside the window, Christine felt she was starting to get it right. After a dinner, consisting of leftovers, she continued to work on the figure at the dining room table. She was shaping the hands to hold something. *What?* Were they her mother's hands? She wasn't sure. She just wanted them to be beautiful.

It was getting late, the hours had passed quickly, silently, in the mid-winter dark. Kathleen had returned. Pulling up from her work, Christine noticed the time, 10:30. She remembered it was

Christmas and realized she had not spoken to her father—she should have called. *No, that was something he should have done.* But he hadn't, which didn't bother her. *Whatever.* It was late and time to sleep. Christine took a last look at the clay hands: the fingers still cumbersome, the palms not in right relation to the fingers or each other. She would work on it tomorrow.

***

The day after Christmas, Mark barreled up the interstate through the brilliant winter glare, pleased with the morning so far. Matt and Charlotte had grown so much taller. They both seemed glad to see him. Lynne had been civil. There hadn't been much time to catch up with what was going on with the kids, but that was okay. The visit was about exchanging gifts, spreading holiday cheer. *So, alright.* An hour and a half later, he turned onto the Murphys' drive, amazed again at what a god forsaken place this was.

Christine greeted Mark at the door. *She looks good.* Her hair was brushed back in a clean ponytail, she had a nice sweater on. She gave him a smile when she said, "Hello, dad."

Mark stepped inside and held his arms open for a hug, "Merry Christmas, dear."

Christine hesitated, her smile stiffened before she stepped into her father's embrace. A sheet of cold lightning flashed through her as she smelled his familiar scent, felt his familiar arms around her, his breath on her. "Merry Christmas." She managed.

He released his hold. Light headed, Christine fell back a step.

"Happy holidays, Mr. Bancroft." Rosemary and Kathleen stepped forward into the living room, which surprised him. Of course they would be here, although Mark had briefly struck the Murphys from his mind upon seeing his daughter. He looked at her for a moment longer before turning his attention to the sisters,

"Mark, please. And happy holidays to you." He brushed past Christine to shake the women's hands.

With her father's back to her, Christine tried to compose herself. *What next?* She and the sisters had planned for the visit to take place in the most comfortable room in the house, the kitchen. Christine stared at her father's back.

Kathleen initiated, "Mr. Bancroft...Mark, it's such a long trip, you must be terribly hungry. I've made some gingerbread if you'd like, and some coffee or cocoa."

The group moved to the warm, sweet smelling kitchen and fell into small talk, mostly about the weather. Rosemary and Mark went on about how much colder it would get, how much longer the cold would last, how much more snow would be coming, and so on, while Kathleen bustled about getting food and dishes together. Christine absently helped. With everything on the table, Kathleen hastened, "Sit, sit."

Christine watched her father talk and eat. She couldn't think of anything to say to him. He barely addressed her. She figured he was probably at a loss, too. There was only so much local history, local weather and local economics he could ask about, *then what?* Finished her slice of gingerbread, Christine peeled a clementine orange, which she had taken from a bowl on the table. The fruit's tart aroma snared Mark's attention, he looked over at Christine. It was then that he noticed the red bead necklace, subtly radiant around his daughter's neck. It contributed to what made her beautiful that day. He smiled. She offered him an orange, which he accepted.

She felt he wanted her to speak. She offered, "I'm feeling a lot better these days. Still not a hundred per cent, that's for sure, but the doctor has me on some medication that's really helping."

"Good, I'm glad to hear it. You seem much better..." Mark sputtered.

Christine couldn't think of what else to tell her father. She didn't know what he would want to hear.

He couldn't imagine what to ask about Christine's odd life or her illness. Instead he said cheerfully, "What do you say we open some presents?"

The compass Christine gave her father, seemed meager in his hands, even when she explained the joke. "Because you're always saying you're afraid of getting lost up here." The inscription in the hand-made card she gave him sounded weak when he read it aloud. "Here's wishing us many Happy Christmases." He didn't say anything about her wish. She didn't remember him saying thank you.

After he read the card, Mark simply handed his present to Christine. "Hope you like it." It was a pink running suit that he explained. "Will be great, with all the trails you have up here."

Pink! She had never worn pink in her life, and never would.

He then handed her an envelope. "These stores are everywhere, you won't have any problem finding one." It was a gift certificate for running shoes from a sporting goods store. The closest store was probably in Burlington, over an hour away. He sat back, no other presents apparent.

That's it? Christine forced a sincere sounding. "Great Dad, thanks." "Let's see it on you." Mark encouraged.

Christine stood up and tried the running jacket on. The sleeves went past her knuckles and the hem fell far past her butt. Grinding her teeth, "I love it, thanks a lot."

She wasn't going to try the pants on. She sat down, wearing the jacket, and rolled up the sleeves. She simmered; *what about the Emily Dickinson collection I asked for? Or any poetry? Or any book that has anything to do with what I've been telling him I'm interested in? Or anything that has anything to do with anything I'm doing? Or something that goddamn fits me? Or that looks like something I'd wear? Does he ever hear a word I'm saying? Does he have any idea what I like, what I want, who I am? He's completely lame.*

The gifts exchanged, there was nothing else to do. Mark glanced at the clock on the kitchen wall and said, "Look at the time, it's getting late. I've got a long drive ahead of me." He had been there less than an hour.

Christine's heart ached. There had to be more than this. Something, anything. There wasn't. She walked him to the door, the sisters following. Christine and her father hugged stiffly. It didn't disturb her this time. They said goodbye.

Mark gave his daughter a kiss and a last look, *so beautiful,* before leaving. He drove home pleased with how gracious Christine was becoming.

Christine stared out the dining room window the rest of the afternoon, declining Rosemary's offer to join her for a hike. *Does he have any idea how lame he is? Would it kill him to get me the one thing I asked for? One thing. Is that asking too much? How can you love someone who is that out of touch? Out of touch, all the freaking time. He says he loves me? How's that work? Learn to cope, the doc says. Why should I?*

As the sun was setting, Kathleen asked Christine how her sculpture was coming. It needed work, a lot of work. She brought the piece to the table and began reshaping the hands, working into the night except when she broke for dinner. It was still not quite right when she stopped, to go to bed.

***

The second day after Christmas, Sunday: The bitter cold pressed into the house, the wind whipped around the corners; the woodstoves burned hot, pushing back against the winter. Sitting at the dining room table, Christine didn't notice. She almost had the hands right. She gently pressed into the clay.

Kathleen brought her a cup of tea, "to keep your hands warm." Christine stopped, leaned back, felt how cold the room was.

She asked, "When do Hannah and Marshall get back?"

"Marshall should be back this afternoon, before supper. Hannah's having supper at the foster parents."

"Foster parents?"

"Yes, the Halperts. Hannah may be going to live with them. This was their first weekend together. Nice people. They're a long term foster home. They have another daughter, Lisa, who stayed here. They adopted her a few years ago. And a boy they adopted, who's in college. If things work out, they'll likely adopt Hannah as well."

A lump caught in Christine's throat. "She's not going home?"

"No. It's sad. Her mother's not in a good way, and it isn't that she'll change anytime soon. I hope the Halperts work out, they'd be good for Hannah."

Christine wrapped her hands around the cup. "I hope so too."

"She's going to come back pretty confused. Kids usually do at this stage, early in the adoption process, their feelings get caught up in two worlds."

"Yeah, I can imagine." She couldn't. She asked where Marshall was.

Kathleen answered that he was staying with his grandmother and likely had a supercharged weekend of rambunctious cousins and huge quantities of junk food and television. "He's going to be a handful. He always is when he comes back from his gramma's. Can you believe they let him have soda for breakfast? For the next few days he'll be asking for Mountain Dew with every meal, until he figures he's not getting it."

"Will he be going home, soon?" "To his mother's?"

"Or his father."

"I don't think they've seen his father since he was born. And the mother, she's not able. It sounds like the mother's family, along with the State people, are figuring out who he can stay with. We'll see."

Christine's heart clouded.

That afternoon Marshall tore into the house wild – eyed and demanding that he go back to his grandmother's, back to his cousins. He couldn't sit still for a second and refused to help Rosemary bring in the firewood.

Christine sidled up as he slouched in a kitchen chair, kicking his heels against the rungs while complaining that he was "really, really, really, really bored."

"Hey Marshall" she started, "want to play this game I learned while you were away?"

They went outside, to the dooryard, and spent over two hours throwing chunks of firewood, seeing who could throw the farthest, the closest to the fencepost, the highest, the best mid-air wood chunk collisions, which were Marshall's favorite by far. The games ended when they were called for dinner as a sliver of a moon rose in the pink dusk sky.

"Let's go in and wash up. You can sit with me, and after we're done eating, I'll give you your present." Christine promised. The boy nodded yes to his good friend.

Hannah arrived after dinner with Mrs. Halpert. The woman went to the kitchen with Rosemary. Hannah didn't move from the front door, didn't take her coat off.

Looking down, she didn't speak. Kathleen welcomed her home, but before she could say anything more, Marshall ran up to the girl shouting, "Hannah, Hannah, look what Chris gave me!" He thrust his arms at her with two fists full of clay animals. "She gave me all these, and we're gonna make a barn!"

Hannah looked at the boy's busy hands without smiling.

Christine stepped forward. "And I have something for you. Come on in, I'll go get it."

When Christine returned from her room, she found Hannah at the kitchen table with Mrs. Halpert seated beside her, the two of them munching on pfeffernusse cookies. Marshall was at the table, spreading his new toys out for everyone to see. Hannah looked up and watched Christine approach with her hands behind her back. When they were side by side, the doll appeared, with its bright felt face smiling from a round satin head. It wore a homemade dress and apron and had brown yarn hair, which streamed from beneath a cloth cap. Hannah's eyes danced.

"She doesn't have a name yet." Christine explained. Hannah burst out, "She's Rosie!"

Christine leaned down, close to Hannah's ear and whispered, "She's a special doll. You can tell her anything you want, just like a best friend, and she'll always listen."

Hannah stared at the doll, intently, then hugged it to her face, her eyes shut.

Christine straightened up...heard the small, "Thank you."

That night, after finishing the ornaments she had made for Charlotte from forest scraps, Christine lay in bed and, before she slipped into sleep, she heard Hannah whispering, as if to someone else in the room. "Goodnight, Rosie. I love you."

CHAPTER 29

New Year's Eve: With the day's last light gone, the night pressed against the window panes, frigid air radiating into the dining room. Christine sipped heat from her steaming cup of tea. Rosemary read the paper in her chair by the living room stove. Kathleen was in the kitchen baking a couple of pies. The children were gone again, Hannah with the Halperts, and Marshall at an aunt's. In the quiet, Christine considered the sculpted hands on the table, which she had fired that afternoon in town, at the kiln belonging to a friend of the two sisters. The woman with the kiln, Judy, had told her she could come back anytime. She loved the idea of making pottery and hanging out with Judy.

The hands could be better. Christine wanted them to be strong, but they seemed fragile. She wanted them to be caring, but they seemed to need care. They could be better but they were good. The rustle of a newspaper being turned broke into Christine's thoughts. She felt the cold and the near quiet; here she was. *New Year's Eve,* nursing a cup of tea in some cabin *in the middle of nowhere with two old ladies.* No way could she have predicted any of this happening. *Too freaking weird.* A year ago, she was getting ready to go out, half wasted already. She could have been with Jimmy this New Year's. She couldn't think about him, she refused. It didn't matter and it would be too depressing. The wind rattled the windows, moaned through the walls. *All that shit happened like forever ago. And now I'm here.*

"Rosemary," she asked, "what's it like having all these messed up kids come live with you?"

Rosemary set the newspaper down on her lap. "It's hard sometimes, sad sometimes. Mostly it's good, though, helping the children."

"Do you think the kids end up better off?" "I'd say so, most of the time."

"Even the older kids?" Christine stared at the sculpted hands. "I think so, yes."

Not quite believing her, "Yeah, but anything must be an improvement over what those kids have dealt with."

"No, I'd say every child who's lived with us could have ended up much worse than when they came in."

A stream broke loose in Christine. "I really screwed up."

Rosemary asked what she meant.

"I ran off with Jimmy, you know...to Burlington. Just to get out of Branford because it sucked so bad there. But it sucked with Jimmy too." Her eyes cast away. "He was way into cocaine. Buying it, selling it, shooting it up. I was like, 'hey this is not okay'. But he didn't stop. He got busted...I got busted. Because some guy he knew OD'ed. They threw me in Stonebridge." Christine closed her eyes, after a long moment, she continued, softly, "That place is terrible." She held up her scarred hand. "I was jumped I thought they were gonna kill me...I took the girl down. Then...I flipped out. I...Jimmy killed himself."

Rosemary had moved to the table, was sitting beside Christine. She took the girl's icy hands in her chafed hands. Christine recoiled at the touch, dark images pushed in on her.

"It sounds like it was very hard." Rosemary approached Christine's loss, gently.

The words reached Christine through a rising fog. She sent an answer back. "It was." The night moaned. Pushing against the darkness, she struggled. "I still have nightmares."

The dense aroma of baking blackberry pies swelled into the dining room. Christine returned to the room, returned to her body, the darkness thinning, to find Rosemary beside her. She was safe.

Her voice hoarse, "I can't go back." "No, I don't think that will happen."

Christine looked into her cup, swirled the tea weakly. "Why can't I go home?

They'll let me go with my father, won't they? I think he wants that." Not looking away from her tea. "That would kill my mother."

"What do you want, Christine?" "I want to go home."

"Alright then."

***

New Year's Day, 1988: Christine woke up groggy, having slept in a dense, woolen haze—Rosemary had given her an extra dose of medication before she had gone to bed. But her mind cleared with breakfast. All morning she thought she heard her mother's car coming down the drive, looked out the living room window several times, only to find nothing. This time there was no doubt, she picked out the sound of her mother's creaking Corolla as soon as it rounded the last curve. She raced to put her boots on and dashed into the drive as the car pulled into the parking space beside the Cherokee.

Matt and Charlotte tumbled out of the car. Matt looked around, proclaiming, "This place is wild." Charlotte, twirled where she stood, laughed at the strange setting. Lynne watched her kids, smiling.

Christine grabbed her brother and sister with a wide armed hug, laughing too. "Yeah, this is it." With one arm swung over Charlotte's shoulder, she turned towards the house, to Kathleen and Rosemary who stood on the front steps and shouted. "Rosemary, Kathleen, this is my goofball sister Charlotte, and my goofball brother Matt."

Kathleen called back. "Nice to meet you two, and good to see you, Lynne. Happy New Year! Now, are you all going to stand in the driveway the rest of the day, or are you coming in?"

The six of them settled in the dining room and stories flowed throughout the afternoon. Lynne's family had so much they wanted to share with each other, the things that had happened in their lives recently: Matt's first school dance and his wrestling try out, Charlotte's piano recital, Christine's firing at the pottery kiln with her new friend Judy, the triplets born on Lynne's shift last week, Charlotte's growing friendship with another girl in band, Lynne's fender bender in the supermarket parking lot, and Christine's marvelous hikes in the woods. Rosemary and Kathleen added bits about their lives and about Christine: her helpfulness, her prowess with algebra. On it went, all of them laughing at silly details, and admiring the recounted moments of accomplishment or grace.

The conversation rolled into a late afternoon supper. The sisters and Christine served up ham from a local smokehouse, yams and mashed potatoes, green beans, buttermilk rolls and apple sauce. The Bancrofts devoured the food, heaping gratitude on Kathleen and Rosemary. Kathleen pointed out that Christine had a hand in the meal, having made the apple sauce and the mashed potatoes.

"You're kidding." Matt joked.

"No, your sister is actually a very good cook." Kathleen answered.

After second helpings, thirds for Matt, Rosemary suggested they take a walk before dessert and presents. Bundled up, they headed to the woods under the low clouded sky. The sun had just set, the smell of snow in the air mixed with the scent of the evergreens and wood smoke. As they walked, Christine pointed out ridgelines and stone fences, bird and squirrel nests, chipmunk and chickadee chatter, cones and pods and seeds she had learned to identify.

Charlotte was captivated, Matt intrigued: this was their sister like they had never known her. Lynne listened, watched her confident daughter. This was her place. Christine was making her own life, away from her; growing away. She wanted to be happy with that thought, but couldn't, not then. *And that's okay.*

As it grew dark, the group turned back towards the house. Tumbling back in the house in tufts of frosty air, Lynne and her children were met by the warmth that only a wood stove could throw off, and the aroma of blackberry pie. With chilled cheeks reddened from the heat, the family stretched their cold fingers over the stove. While watching her brother and sister stomping by the stove, Christine smiled to herself, *they're having a great time.* It was so right.

The Bancrofts and Murphys decided to exchange gifts before dessert, and seated themselves in the living room. Kathleen had knitted wool mittens for Lynne, Matt and Charlotte, which they loved. Lynne gave Kathleen a French country cookbook, and Rosemary a tape of Acadian fiddle tunes, which thrilled them both. Rosemary presented Christine with a hard bound book of poetry, Mary Oliver's "American Primitive", which she knew Christine would love. The sisters reverently touched the nativity scene figures Christine had made for them. Matt and Charlotte marveled at the ornaments from their sister, and in return they gave her a tape of Charlotte playing Debussy's *Clair de Lune,* along with a tape of Matt reciting from Walt Whitman's, *Leaves of Grass*, which she adored.

In a brief lull of gift giving, Christine unthinkingly touched the red beads at her chest.

Lynne remarked. "The necklace looks very nice on you."

Christine bowed her head to the necklace. "I wear it every day."

"Good."

The two smiled and handed each other their gifts simultaneously. "Mom, it's perfect, how did you know?" Christine showed the others the complete collected works of Emily Dickinson. Inscribed on the inside cover, "*To my wonderful Christine, Happy Christmas, 1987. With all my love, Mom.*"

"Well, I remembered you said you liked her poetry a lot, so..."

Christine threw her arms around her mother's neck. "Thank you mom, you're the best." She drew back. "Now open mine."

Lynne carefully tore the tissue paper away. "Christine, my goodness, it's beautiful." She held up the sculpted hands for all to see—simple, strong, holding a fragile glass ball. The hands were brilliant. She looked at her daughter a long moment across the small distance. "Thank you very much, dear."

Lynne suddenly ached, realized in this moment they were as close as they might ever be, but there was still a distance between them that would never disappear completely. No matter how much love they shared, her daughter was growing away.

Christine sensed the undeniable space as well. A shadow passed through her for an instant in the deep memory of how vast that distance had once been, knowing how vast it could be. She smiled through. "Love you, mom."

Kathleen announced, "Time for dessert." And they all made their way to the dining room table. The pie was warm, served with vanilla ice cream dolloped on each slice. When they had finished eating, the Bancrofts and Murphys decided, regrettably, that the day better end as well. A big snow was coming and it was a long drive home. The hugs were long because none of them, Lynne or her children, wanted this feeling to end, ever. Lynne and Christine held each other last, trying to press their separation small.

When they released, Lynne whispered, "Love you, always."

Christine nodded. "Always."

CHAPTER 30

The Tuesday after New Year's Day, Rosemary took Christine back to the pottery studio. When Christine had fired her hands sculpture the week before, she and the potter, Judy, had talked about her returning and learning how to throw pots. In exchange, Christine would watch Judy's two daughters, Chelsea, age four, and Mariah, age two, for a couple hours while she got work or chores done. Her husband, a welder, had just left for Alaska and she had said she could really use the help. It sounded like a great idea to Christine, and Rosemary and Kathleen approved. They knew Judy Repchuk and her family, knew they would be kind to Christine.

Judy's home was in a glade just off the road, heading up into the mountains, at the far end of Bixby. The first thing Christine noticed, when she approached the studio, was the smoke that poured from the home's main chimney and from the chimney of the addition, where the kiln was located. She felt the heat as if she were already inside.

As they pulled into the parking space off the road, Rosemary asked, "You're sure you don't mind caring for the two girls? You don't have to..."

"No, they're great. They're really sweet. Besides, Judy could use the help." Christine remembered Chelsea taking her around the house the week before; explaining where the food and toys were kept, showing off her bedroom and her pet rabbit. "No, I don't mind at all."

Judy stood at the open door, holding Mariah on her hip with Chelsea standing beside her, clinging to her mother's long skirt. Judy called out to Christine and Rosemary, as they got out of the Cherokee. "Hey, good to see you. The girls have been excited all morning."

It was a just before noontime. Christine imagined that little kids could make for a very long morning when they were wound up. She called back, "Hi girls, good to see you."

Chelsea's face broke into a huge smile, and Mariah smiled shyly, her face buried in her mother's shoulder.

Judy invited Christine to have some barley soup for lunch, after Rosemary left. The girls joined them at the table. As the soup warmed up, Chelsea peppered Christine with questions: how old was she; did she drive a car; did she go to school; did she have a boyfriend? Christine simply answered no to the last question.

Judy gently broke in, "I'm glad you're here." She suggested that Christine watch the girls after lunch while she fired some mugs, then she'd help her put the girls down for their naps in about an hour. With the girls asleep, Judy could start Christine on her wheel.

Chelsea interrupted, "Mommy's going to teach you how to make cups and plates."

"I know. I'm very excited."

The girls liked that.

Not long after the lunch cleanup, Mariah nestled into Christine's lap, sucking her thumb, as Christine read *The Pokey Little Puppy* for the third time. Chelsea quietly played house with her dolls. They were settled in, the long afternoon stretching ahead of them when Judy entered the room. All three looked up.

"Hi, mom, we're playing." Chelsea said. "I can see that."

Fifteen minutes later, Christine and Judy left the girls in bed with Mariah asleep, and Chelsea looking at her Winnie the Pooh picture book.

In the workroom, Judy pointed to the sleeping bag and blankets piled in the corner. "Chelsea will most likely settle in here in a bit, if you don't mind."

"No, of course not."

Christine sat at the potter's wheel. She learned to throw, the moist lump of clay spun. It felt magnificent in Christine's hands. It fascinated her how its shape changed between a slight shift in her touch and the foot pedal.

Judy leaned in. "Just get the feel of it for now."

That was fine with Christine as she enjoyed smoothing the spinning surface, creating dips and hollows.

"Bend your hand like this." The potter placed her hands on Christine's—a bowl took shape! Just as suddenly the shape was lost.

"Try again, and feel the pressure you need to hold the shape." She did. The shape held, wobbled, distended. "Try again, start over. Control the speed at the foot pedal. You're doing really well."

I am.

The hour passed like seconds. Chelsea had come to the room and settled in and fallen asleep, as Judy had predicted. No sounds were heard from Mariah over the baby monitor. Christine was fully in the moment, where her fingers touched moist clay. At the end of the hour, four bowls she had made rested on the shelf beside the wheel.

A murmur from the monitor. Judy responded, "Mariah's getting up. Next time I'll show you a couple glazing techniques. How did you like it?"

"Loved it."

"Good. You have a really nice touch." Christine glowed.

Judy continued, "If you want, I'll throw a couple pots, and I'll explain to you what I'm doing, while I'm creating." Mariah's call for her mother reached them through the monitor. "She's still sleepy. We can bring the rocker in, and you can hold her while I work."

For the next twenty minutes, Christine held the quiet two year old, as she watched the potter shape three small pitchers, instructing her all the time on what she was doing and the effects she was creating. Christine could feel what was being described, within her own hands. It was amazing. But Mariah grew restless, her sister woke up, and the lesson came to an end. Christine imagined it could have gone on forever, or at least much longer.

Judy poured green tea into two mugs, while Christine filled two bowls with vanilla yogurt and sliced bananas for the girls. She admired the bowls, but Judy dismissed them as seconds. Christine drank out of a deep azure colored mug, the glaze etched with leaf patterns. She said it was beautiful. Judy repeated, "Second." She showed Christine the minor imperfections: a tilt in the base, a ding in the lip.

"You can't sell something like this, not to paying customers. Friends, they'll take them for free." The woman smiled.

"How many pieces do you make that can't sell?"

"A good amount, you'd be surprised. They have to be perfect though." "That's got to be hard..."

Judy laughed, "It's alright."

"How long have you been doing this, selling pottery?" "About a dozen years. Since I moved up here with Skink." "Skink?"

"Yeah, my husband, that's what he's called. His last name's Skibnowsky." Christine asked "Where'd you move from?"

"Philadelphia. When I met Skink he was still in the Navy, working at the shipyard. I was in college, Penn. Met him, dropped out, and eventually got into pottery. After a while, Skink had to get out of Philly, so we headed up here. This place is an old hunting camp he fixed up. It belonged to his uncle. Some friends came up too, stayed awhile, a couple years. They left. Too cold."

"And now Skink's gone to Alaska?"

Judy looked at her oldest daughter, who had been following the conversation, "Yes, he went to find some work, and send us money." She smiled for her daughter. Christine read the smile: there was more to the story.

Judy returned her attention to Christine. "I like it here. We're alright."

That evening, during the drive back to the house, Rosemary asked her how the afternoon had gone. Christine looked over at her foster mother. "It was wonderful." She answered. She then described how much she liked Judy, the girls, the work, but she couldn't find words for that connection she had made with the clay, or the way she felt Judy working through her. As they turned into the drive, Christine asked, "Two afternoons a week, that's the plan?"

"Yes. So long as you keep up with your schoolwork and your chores at home." "No problem." Christine decided she'd try to get three afternoons as soon as she proved she could keep up with her studies. Besides, she was sure Judy would appreciate the extra help. Bumping along the rutted drive, suspension creaking, the overhanging firs and hemlocks leaning in, she smiled to herself—even two days a week would be fantastic.

Around the last bend of the driveway, Christine and Rosemary saw the lights of the house shining on a Vermont State Police cruiser. Dread and panic seized them both. *What's happened?* Rosemary braked, before completely pulling into the parking space. They ran to the house.

Kathleen opened the door as Rosemary's boots hit the front steps. "Nothing to worry about." She said immediately. "Come in."

As they entered, Christine saw two broad shouldered troopers standing in the living room, facing her. She saw the two children, very quiet, at the dining room table, looking back at her, wide eyed.

Kathleen spoke, her nervousness showing, "Christine, shut the door behind you. This is Trooper McNally and Trooper Frechette. They would like to talk to you."

What?!

Kathleen, in quiet command, "Officers, please make yourselves comfortable in the living room. Rosemary, I'm going to take the children to the kitchen, would you keep Christine and the officers company?"

The troopers took a seat in the living room's two easy chairs. Still wearing her coat, Christine sat on the edge of the couch. Rosemary sat beside her.

Trooper McNally began, "Christine we're here to ask you some questions. Concerning James Connell."

Fuck! Bile burned up Christine's throat. The room darkened.

Rosemary sensed Christine stiffen beside her. She spoke, "Isn't Mr. Connell dead? I don't understand..."

The troopers looked at each other. "Ma'am, we're conducting a criminal investigation." Trooper Frechette started. "We believe that Miss Bancroft may have some information relating to the death of Edward Dugan last summer. Circumstances leading up to that death involved Mr. Connell."

Christine found Rosemary's hand, took it for protection. Rosemary held her hand, answered, "A criminal investigation into a death? Shouldn't Christine have a lawyer present during questioning?" Frechette snapped, "Not if she *wants* to speak with us."

Rosemary shot right back. "She's a minor, did you know that? I think it really isn't for her to decide whether she speaks with you...."

McNally jumped in, "The paperwork we have says that approval to the interview was given by SRS down in Branford..." The trooper shuffled through some documents in a folder he held. He slowed his delivery, while he searched, "Seeing that she's in the custody of the Commissioner of SRS, and under the specific supervision of the Branford District Supervisor, that approval should suffice."

Rosemary didn't flinch. "It's curious that neither Kathleen nor I were notified of this clearance, and we are the foster placement directly responsible for Christine's care and wellbeing."

Christine heard Rosemary fighting for her.

She wasn't finished. "There may very well be a mistake, your being sent here to question Christine, without her attorney present. A serious mistake."

Rosemary looked McNally in the eye, then Frechette. She raised her arm to check her watch. "It's past five. I'm sure there is no one at the SRS office who will answer the phone. I'll call first thing tomorrow morning to clear this up."

"Ma'am, we're here to conduct an interview." Frechette insisted.

"I understand that, but not tonight..." She stood up to indicate to the men that it was time to leave. "Perhaps another time."

Rosemary!

McNally stood, stared down at Christine for a long moment. She watched the men leave as she slumped back into the couch. She didn't hear what Rosemary said to them as they left, but it was harsh. Rosemary returned to Christine and promised, "We'll find out what's going on. I'll call your lawyer first thing tomorrow."

Weakly, "Thanks, Rosemary."

Christine didn't eat, and barely spoke the rest of the night. She had one thought: *they came to take me back to Stonebridge*; they could do that, they had permission; there was nothing to stop them. She went to bed early and lay still, awake in the cold night. *They'll take me away. Just like that.* She held on against the darkness that threatened to envelope her. In the long hour before dawn, she captured some sleep.

***

Christine fell into the chair across from Vrabel. She buried her face in her hands. She felt like shit.

"I didn't sleep last night." She didn't look up.

"I heard. Rosemary told me. She said some troopers came to interview you yesterday. About Jim."

She didn't answer. It didn't matter what she said, what he said: if they wanted to take her away they were going to. Whenever they wanted.

Vrabel asked, "You want to tell me what has you upset?"

Was he fucking kidding? She scooped her necklace in her right hand and pressed it hard against her closed eyes.

"Rosemary told me your lawyer has spoken to SRS about canceling the interview. I'll support that in any way I can." She ground the beads against her face. He stopped talking. She had nothing to say.

A couple minutes passed, Vrabel asked, "Nightmares?" Christine nodded.

"Stonebridge?"

She nodded again, her face still buried in her hand. Vrabel referred to her file, "I'll increase your Prozac dosage a bit. And I'll prescribe something that will help you sleep. *Something to help me sleep.* The darkness was swallowing her.

"We'll get you through this, okay? When you're feeling better I want to hear about last weekend, your family's visit. Rosemary said it was a very special time. And I heard about your pottery lesson yesterday. That sounds good."

Christine rubbed the beads, remembered the feel of the clay. "It is good." She looked straight at the doctor. "I don't want them to take me away."

***

The next night, Thursday night, Lynne called Christine after dinnertime. She hadn't spoken to her daughter since last weekend and the New Year's Day visit. When she had called Tuesday night to ask how the pottery lesson had gone, Rosemary had said Christine had gone to bed early, that she wasn't feeling well. Then yesterday, Fitzgerald had called her and told her the State Police were trying to question Christine about the young man who had overdosed, and that Christine's lawyer was trying to stop it. He had called again today, and said she had to be interviewed but that she'd have a lawyer present. The interview was taking place tomorrow.

"Hey sweetie."

Christine didn't want to talk. "Hey mom."

"How are you holding up? My lawyer told me what's going on with the police. How are you doing?"

She didn't want to talk about it. "Not so good." "No?"

"No. People are saying it will be okay, though." Her words hung limp in the air. "They're not going to take me away, are they? Away from here?"

"I don't think so. Mr. Fitzgerald would have told me if they were. They're just going to ask you some questions, and you'll have a lawyer."

Silence, then, "What happens after that? They're not going to let me stay here. This is just temporary."

Hurting, "I don't know, honey." "Why can't I come home?"

Lynne choked out. "I love you, honey."

That was all, and it wasn't enough. "I love you too, mom. I've got to go."

When bedtime came, Christine took her pills. She watched Rosemary put the pill bottles away in the top shelf of the kitchen cupboard, then lock the cupboard. She was tired. She watched Rosemary pocket the key. *The pills let me sleep*. They kept the black from swallowing her. Her mother loved her. But that wouldn't keep them from taking her away. Christine slept through the night, through the nightmares.

***

Christine's plea, '*Why can't I come home?*' repeated in Lynne's mind throughout the miserable night. No matter what, she couldn't stop it.

CHAPTER 31

On Friday afternoon, in Burlington, Christine arrived at a squat red brick building where the State's Attorney's office was located, where the State's Attorney and the State Troopers waited for her. She and Rosemary found the office. She was sent to a small conference room, where she sat at a table with a small man wearing thick glasses - her new lawyer for this thing—who told her she had to talk, she had to answer all their questions.

Someone had explained to Christine why she needed a new lawyer. She didn't remember the explanation. She had called her real lawyer, Mrs. Simmons, who had told her to call if she had any problems. Mrs. Simmons had said they had fought it, her being questioned. She had said that she, and Doctor Vrabel, and her mother's lawyer told some judge she shouldn't be questioned, that it would be too hard for her. They didn't convince him. *It doesn't matter. I'm here. They're going to do what they want.* She stroked her beads.

The new lawyer talked at her, without saying much. He told her that no harm would come to her because the state's attorney was giving her "qualified immunity," which would protect her from everything. Unless she lied. If she lied, she would be in big trouble. Christine wanted him to shut up. He said a judge was ordering her to answer all the state's attorney's questions because she now had "qualified immunity." She wanted to scream: it didn't matter what this guy said. She had a thought, a good thought. "Can Rosemary be with me?" She asked.

"I don't see why not. And of course, I'll also be present."

Christine looked at him. He looked back, her court appointed lawyer.

They went to another conference room. A lot of people were already in the room, sitting at a large table, waiting for her. No one wore a uniform, but they all looked like cops. She was told where to sit. Rosemary sat at her left, her lawyer at her right. The man across from Christine, detective somebody, explained he would ask her the questions. He explained a lot of things about the questions that sounded like a lot of legal stuff. She said she understood. She heard him say, "Just tell the truth and you'll be fine." She didn't believe him.

A woman with a tape recorder, placed her under oath. The detective started asking questions. Where did she live? Who did she live with? How long had she lived there?

Christine had trouble answering these questions. She didn't know the Murphy's' address; she couldn't remember the name of the town; she wasn't sure how long she'd lived there, maybe a couple months. "Since around Thanksgiving." Something like that.

Was she on medication? "Yes."

What?

Christine couldn't remember exactly. "Prozac and something else, and something to help me sleep. Three pills."

Did she understand she was sworn to tell the truth? She did. Did she understand that what she said wouldn't be used against her in court? Yes. Unless she lied, then she could be charged with perjury, did she understand that? Yes. She understood.

He was so serious, this was serious. She had to answer his questions.

Her lawyer spoke. "Of course, if you don't know the answer, it's alright to say you don't know."

She said she understood.

The detective resumed. Where had she lived before the Murphys? "The hospital." Before that? "Stonebridge." Before that? "With Jimmy Connell in Burlington." What address? She didn't know.

The questions seemed to come faster. How long had she lived with Mr. Connell? She wasn't sure, not long, last summer. After school let out. How old was she? Sixteen then, seventeen now. The man stopped, looked at a paper in front of him. Christine looked to Rosemary, gave her a tight smile.

Why was she living with Mr. Connell? He was her boyfriend. How long had he been her boyfriend? She wasn't sure, they met that spring, a few months. Did she have any knowledge that Mr. Connell used or possessed drugs or illegal substances? Yes.

What drugs? Cocaine, pot. Did she have any knowledge that he, Mr. Connell, sold drugs? Yes. What drugs? Coke. Did she ever use drugs or illegal substances? Yes. What drugs?

"Objection, getting beyond the scope..." The lawyer surprised Christine. The detective smirked, "This is an investigation, but I'll let it drop."

He asked how she knew that he sold drugs? She had seen him. How many times? A few times, maybe more. Where had she seen him sell cocaine? At the apartment, at some bars. What bars?

Christine's memories rushed forward, "I don't remember, just bars."

The detective told her, "If you withhold information, you're impeding an investigation, which is also a criminal offense. Now let me ask you again, what bars did Mr. Connell sell drugs in?"

Somebody stop this! "I'm not sure."

What bars had she been to with Mr. Connell? She didn't remember their names. Describe them, describe where they were. She did, she had to. Had she been in those bars when Mr. Connell sold cocaine? Yes.

People were going to get in trouble because of her. She shook inside, felt sick.

He asked, did she know any of the people who came to the apartment? No. Were they friends of Mr. Connell's? Sort of. Did he do things with them other than sell them drugs? Yes, they did cocaine together, there at the apartment. They went out drinking, clubbing. These friends, what were their names? She didn't know. Didn't he introduce them to her? Sometimes, not always. Where did he know them from? She said she didn't know. She didn't tell the cop about the guys Jimmy worked with. He asked Christine if she wanted to take a break, get some water. She did.

In the hallway, Christine sipped water from a paper cup, her hand shook. This was not good, she was screwed. They were going to nail her. Rosemary came and stood beside her. She asked Christine if she was alright.

"Yeah, I'm okay." She wasn't. She was screwed and there wasn't anything Rosemary could do to help her.

The lawyer said something lame like, "You're doing fine." He didn't know shit. The cop asking the questions knew. And there he was, "We're ready to resume."

Back at the table, the room reeked of her fear. She knew the cop smelled it, he knew what fear and desperation smelled like. It's what he did for a living.

He began: could she remember the names of any of Mr. Connell's friends or acquaintances? She couldn't. Did she know someone by the name of Eddie Dugan? She thought so. How did she know Mr. Dugan? She remembered the cop saying his name when he was busting her. She said she met a guy named Eddie at a party down in Branford, a friend of Jimmy's, then she saw him again in Burlington, at the apartment. Then, when they were busting her, the police showed her a picture of him dead.

When he came to the apartment, was he alone? No. Who was he with? She didn't know their names. The party in Branford, who was he with? She didn't know. Did she see Eddie Dugan the night before she was arrested? Yes. Who was he with? She didn't know. She remembered the faces, but she didn't know their names, they were just a bunch of scumbags. She didn't say that. Instead, she said, "I went out that night with a friend a little after they got there."

Were they using cocaine before she left? Yes. Who? All of them. And when she returned? No one was at the apartment. What time was that? Between eleven and midnight. Did she see Eddie Dugan again? No. When did she next see Mr. Connell?

"It was about dawn when he came home."

She wanted to tell the cop that she hated the whole thing, she hated what they were doing, Jimmy and his scumbag friends, how fucked up it all was, but she didn't. She was too scared, too medicated, too intimidated, too something.

Did she know where Mr. Connell obtained the cocaine the night before she was arrested? No. Did she know where Mr. Connell had ever obtained cocaine or any other illegal substance? No.

Her memories raced: JT, the guy on the motorcycle, the place in the North End on the way to Montreal. She was drowning. She felt the sweat, she touched her necklace. She saw the detective watch her touch the beads.

She changed her answer, "I mean yes." She had to give him something. "There was this time down in Branford, last spring, before I moved up, some guy Jimmy met at a restaurant, a Chinese restaurant. He rode a motorcycle."

Any other times? Once, in Burlington, some place in the North End. She couldn't say where exactly. Did she meet the person who sold Mr. Connell the drugs? No. He went in, she had waited in the car. What drugs? Cocaine. Would she recognize the place if she saw it? She didn't think so, it was a little house that didn't look much different than the others around it, and she was new to Burlington, she didn't know the street name.

Were there any other occasions when she was present when drugs were bought or sold? No, not that she could remember.

"Well if you should remember, you need to contact me. If I should find out you were present or involved in transactions that you haven't described, I would consider your testimony as perjured, or worse, obstruction of justice, impeding an investigation.

Understand? Now, I'll ask again, were there any other times when you were with Mr. Connell when he purchased drugs?"

"No."

"Do you know the names of any person—first name, last name, nickname—of anyone who Mr. Connell bought drugs from?"

She wasn't going to name JT, "No."

"Alright, and you can't recall the names—first name, last name, nickname—of anyone who Mr. Connell sold drugs to."

"No." She blurted, "I hated him selling drugs."

The detective stopped. He reached into his jacket pocket and pulled out a business card. He handed it to Christine—*Detective Carl E. Schumer*.

He said, "If you remember anything later, don't be stupid, call me."

Christine took the card. It was over. She could leave. They weren't taking her away. She shut her eyes. It would never be over.

***

At the same time that Christine rode home from her interrogation, Lynne passed through the streets of Branford in the dim, sleeting dusk. She walked past her car, her head bent against the weather. The light from the store windows guided her. She didn't feel the cold or the stinging sleet. She had to see attorney Fitzgerald, she needed answers. What did she have to do to get Christine home?

She had gone to the personnel director at the hospital that afternoon to inquire again if any positions were available, in any department, for first shift. She had tried not to sound desperate. The young, tight faced administrative assistant had said there were no first shift openings. Lynne then asked if anyone had been hired or transferred to first shift since she had submitted her written request, weeks ago.

The administrative assistant had responded with cold cruelty, "Yes, we filled a first shift position in the pediatric unit last week. Perhaps another position or two, I can't remember. When did you say you submitted your request?"

Stricken, Lynne had left without another word.

She was fortunate she had caught Fitzgerald in his office on a Friday afternoon, especially with the storm that was coming down. He welcomed her, but said he couldn't talk long because he had a brief he had to complete and get in the mail. Standing in the lawyer's office, water running down her coat, Lynne rasped, "I've got to get Christine home."

Fitzgerald told her there was a lot that needed to happen before Christine came home. All those evaluations they had talked about in court, and the thing about her work shift.

Lynne broke in, "I was just at the hospital and the personnel director's secretary told me they've passed over me a few times. I don't know what to do."

"That doesn't sound right. Do you have a copy of the hospital's personnel manual?"

She didn't.

"We'll get a copy and see if there's some process spelled out, something they violated when they passed you over. Even if there isn't, we'll get their attention. I'll call there now and tell them you're on your way to pick up a copy of the manual. Bring it to me Monday and we'll see what we've got."

He called the hospital. When he hung up he told Lynne, "The office closes in twenty minutes. If you hurry, you'll make it."

On the street, Lynne didn't feel the sleet stinging her face. She checked her watch. She'd make it.

***

Christine awoke slowly from a great depth. At first she didn't recognize where she was, still lost in the dream that she couldn't remember, that left her feeling she was drifting dangerously, unattached. But she was in her room, in the home of Rosemary and Kathleen. *Thank God.*

She looked over to Hannah's bed—she wasn't there. It was Saturday. She was at the home of her new foster parents for a long weekend. She would move in with them soon, within the next couple of weeks, according to Kathleen, as soon as the paperwork cleared. Hannah didn't know yet, in case something fell through. Kathleen had also told Christine that Marshall most likely would be going to live with his grandmother, as soon as they lined up some social services for her. Marshall didn't know either. In case things fell through.

Christine felt strange watching these kids go through their daily routines, knowing their future when they had no idea what was being planned for them. It felt kind of wrong. But she was no different than them. She didn't know any more than they did what was being planned for her. There were people making arrangements regarding when she would be taken from the Murphys, and where she'd be sent. Nameless, faceless people.

A few hours later, Mark was perched in Rosemary's easy chair, across from Christine, who was sitting on the couch. The bitter cold still clung to his clothes and his skin, he leaned into the heat coming off the stove. The house was quiet. Marshall had left for his grandmother's, Rosemary was off on errands, Kathleen was rolling out pie crust in the kitchen. Christine fingered her necklace, watched her father. A log hissed in the woodstove. All he had talked about so far was how cold it was. She had agreed along with him. She didn't want to talk about anything. He asked her how she was doing, she said fine. She was medicated, drifting, and here he was. She didn't care enough to ask about his week.

Mark straightened in the chair. "I passed a pizza place in town, you hungry?" "Sure." She lied. It didn't matter.

"I'll see if it's okay." He went to the kitchen to ask Kathleen.

Waiting for him, Christine thought, what did he have to do with all of this, her situation? Why was he here; what did he want?

He popped back into the room, "We're good to go." He grinned like they were heading for an adventure. Christine could gag on the bullshit. *What does he want?* She gave him a cracked smile, "Great."

The day, with its brilliant sunshine, was painful. The cold biting through her clothing and scouring her exposed skin was painful. The frigid air banked on the pizza parlor floor was painful The sickening oily heat blasting from the air vents was painful. Sitting in a brittle plastic booth with her father, knowing that it would be at least fifteen minutes before the pizza arrived, was very painful. Christine threw out conversation bait: how was the baby, and Nancy; what was he up to at work; what did it mean when a load of concrete didn't meet spec? Her father seemed to devour the opportunity to fill the time with details from his life. She watched him go on. *What does he want?*

Was he coming all this way to claim her? To be a hero? To beat her mother? To mess with her head? Maybe he was there because he loved her. It seemed crazy, that he loved her. Maybe it shouldn't seem crazy. *Isn't that what Vrabel said?* And if it was crazy, she could deal with it. She had her shrink. And her pills. She'd dealt with worse.

If he loved her, then he'd help her with all the shit she had going on. Because the cops weren't done with her, and they'd throw her away when they were. Who was going to stop them from dumping her in some shithole worse than Stonebridge when they were through with her? She watched her father talking through a mouthful of pizza, not listening to his nonsense. *Would he stop them?* Because her mother couldn't, she was useless; she couldn't handle the tough shit. If he loved her, he would stop them. *He could stop them.*

She waited for her father to swallow the lump of doughy cheese before asking, "Dad, you know what I'd like? I want to come down and visit you at your place, with Nancy and the baby. What do you think?"

A real smile spread across Mark's face. "That would be great, I'd love it."

They agreed, next visit at his place. Christine twinkled her eyes at him. Mark's smile spread throughout his body – his daughter was returning to him!

CHAPTER 32

The Cherokee crawled through Rutland along Route 7, past miles of strip development. The road was choked with cars, driven by people from Connecticut, New York, Massachusetts, New Jersey. People pushing to get to their ski weekend, clogged the intersections, ignored the traffic signals and blew their horns for no apparent reason. Rosemary inched along, rattled by the unfamiliar traffic.

Christine shut her eyes against the lousy view and the stupid behavior around her. This sucked on so many levels. Besides being stuck on this crappy road, she had to miss her pottery lesson. She wanted to be with Judy and her girls throwing pots. But no, here she was on her way to be interviewed by some guy about her drug history. She kept reminding herself, *this guy can screw me as bad as the cops*. He'd have his hands all over her future so she had to put on a good show.

She sat in the windowless meeting room of the Rutland County SRS office and stared across the table at the sweating man. Joe somebody was explaining that he was doing a report for the court about her substance abuse and a treatment plan; *blah, blah, blah.* The man's body stunk like an old can. He had a fresh mustard stain on his shirt and a darker stain on his tie, and the top button of his shirt was unfastened to make room for his chin. He had a kind of fervor in his gray eyes, like she was a pagan and he was a man of God, and she disgusted him, and his disgust got him worked up. He didn't take his eyes off her. The creep was going to send his "evaluation" of her to court, so a judge could decide what to do with a screw - up like her. Christine straightened, broke a little smile—not too much, not like she was a freak or anything, just to show she wasn't hostile—because this asshole could nail her to a cross. She had to make this work. She was sweating.

Joe Benson had read Christine's arrest report and her SRS file. He had come across dozens of girls like her in the fourteen years he had been a probation officer and his three years as a drug and alcohol abuse screener. This report wasn't going to be much different than the others he had written for the courts over the years: patent drug abuse history; denial of any trouble arising from drug or alcohol use; insincere pledge to correct lifestyle to avoid drug - alcohol related issues in the future. The only difference would be in the details. He'd be out of there in half an hour, mail the report to SRS by the end of the day and earn his three hundred and fifty dollar fee.

Benson rattled off one question after another at Christine, like he was reading from a paper, but the entire time he didn't take his eyes off her. Watching her every flinch, squirm, sigh. He wrote quick notes, not more than a couple pen strokes, after each response. When he took his eyes off Christine to write, she could see the marks he made at the end of each line, going right down the page. She was sure it didn't matter what she said, he just filled out the form while she talked. She could say anything and he probably would be disgusted by her, probably thought she was a druggie before he even started.

Fuck him! She was going to answer his annoying questions and not worry about it. What was there to say? It was simple: she had used drugs, she didn't use them anymore, she didn't miss them. End of story. She'd had it with this guy.

He kept asking his questions: Pastimes? Interests? Usage history: Marijuana, hashish, cocaine, methamphetamine, barbiturates, appetite suppressants, quaaludes, LSD, psilocybin, mescaline, heroin, opium, beer, whiskey, wine, glue, aerosols, valium, cold medicine? First time? Last time? How often? With whom? How much? On and on, as he studied her. She concentrated on presenting answers that appeared sincere. She lied, she told the truth; she was going to say whatever it took to keep him from labeling her a degenerate.

He asked, "And so, do you believe that you have a drug or alcohol problem?"

She answered, "Like I said before, I haven't touched anything since last July, and it's not a problem. I don't miss it at all."

"You've been in an enforced setting since last July, do you believe you would have no problem with abstaining from drugs or alcohol if you were returned to the general population?"

"You mean like falling in with kids who are using? I don't see that as a problem. By the time I was arrested, I was sick of the whole situation. I've moved on. Definitely."

The room was suddenly silent as Benson looked at Christine. *He thinks I'm bullshitting him.* The silence intimidated her, she continued, "I've got a life now. I'm learning all kinds of cool stuff at Kathleen and Rosemary's. I'm doing really good with my schoolwork. I started doing pottery with this great woman in town, which I really love. And I've gotten a lot of help from my psychiatrist, Dr. Vrabel. He's really been helping me deal with a lot of stuff. I'm even getting along better with my father."

She stopped. He was watching her, not writing anything down. He didn't want to hear it. He was finished. He completed the form questions, the comments section. He looked at his watch: just less than a half hour. He was going to write what he had expected he would write before the interview had begun. His conclusion was that this girl has no concept of the severity of her problem or the depth of her denial, and furthermore that she has no apparent skills, background, education or support in place that would lessen the probable likelihood of her return to substance abuse upon release to the community.

Christine sat sweating in the windowless room, as the guy went on about when he'd complete the evaluation and when he'd send it to SRS. It didn't matter, she knew she was screwed. She rode home in a fierce silence, staring out at the ugly city, the ugly people, and the empty winter countryside. *The cops, now this guy*. She was going to be dumped somewhere terrible. *Maybe worse than Stonebridge.* At one point Rosemary touched her hand, reaching Christine through her thoughts. Rosemary and Kathleen were taking care of her now.

She whispered, "Thanks."

Back at the Murphys, the house was quiet, with the two children already gone for the weekend. Christine took out some modeling clay and worked at it aimlessly: poking it, pressing it, shaping it. Unseen hands were working her. She pressed harder. She had to get her father to fight them: the drug guy, the cops, everyone who was out to screw her over.

***

Saturday morning, waiting for her mother to arrive for her visit, Christine finished feeding the chickens, chopped and hauled firewood and cleaned up after breakfast. She couldn't sit still inside so she stood in the dooryard, watching her clouds of breath. She didn't want to spend the day cooped up in the cabin. She didn't want to make small talk with her mother for hours. She wanted to be someplace else. She remembered Judy talking about Lyndonville on Tuesday; how there was a college there, with restaurants and stores. She went inside and asked Rosemary how far Lyndonville was. A half hour's drive. She wanted to go. She had to get away.

When Lynne arrived, Christine immediately asked if she wanted to go to Lyndonville and see someplace different. Lynne hesitated. Before she could ask how much more driving it would involve, Rosemary offered to pick Christine up when the visit was over. This way, she wouldn't have much more driving overall. She agreed to go and Rosemary gave her directions.

They found Lyndonville's Main Street, then found the Lyndon State College campus. The streets were filled with people Christine's age and people who didn't look like they had just finished milking a cow. There was an Indian restaurant, pizza parlors, a couple taverns, and the diner Rosemary had mentioned. There were two bookstores and a clothing store. Lynne asked if Christine wanted to get something to eat. She wasn't hungry. "Not yet."

"Then let's just get out and explore."

Lynne pulled into the next parking lot, a half block away. The two of them walked through the campus, along paths that passed purposeful buildings and crossed open commons. They walked with students who moved through the chill damp weather. Christine imagined the bare trees leafed out, the snow-covered lawns green, the students relaxing in warmer weather.

"This seems like a nice place, Chris." Lynne said. "Have you been thinking about applying to go here?"

Christine answered short. "No."

"Well maybe you should. You've been doing really well with your schoolwork, I think you'd do well in college. You love biology. And your pottery. Maybe art school."

Christine stopped suddenly. Lynne stood beside her, with people passing them in the middle of the walkway. She glared at her mother, furious at the fact that she could think something so stupid. "College?" She spit. "You're kidding me, right? I don't even know where I'm going to be next month, and you think I'm thinking about college? Get real, mom. I'm just worried that they're going to throw me back in Stonebridge or some place worse. Anytime now."

Lynne gulped air. "Don't say that, honey. That's not going to happen."

Shouting, "How can you say that? How can you be so sure?" Christine decided she wouldn't say any more. Not about the police interrogation, or yesterday's questioning by the drug guy. Or about her hope that her father could save her, or her plans to visit his home and new family. She wouldn't hurt her mother that way. Her glare weakened, then broke like a wave. "I'm scared." She admitted.

"I am too."

Christine stiffened. *What do you have to be scared of?*

A light, chilled drizzle had begun. "Let's eat." Lynne suggested.

Christine nodded. They left in the direction of the restaurants they had seen when they first came into town. They walked in an awkward silence.

Lynne decided she wouldn't explain to Christine that her lawyer was fighting the hospital for passing her over for the first shift positions. She decided not to mention that she had applied for jobs at the Walmart, the Stop n Go and the Cumberland Farms, jobs that would have her home at night, even though she would make a lot less than she did now. She would not bring up the fact that she didn't see how they would get by if she got one of those jobs, but she'd figure how—food stamps if she had to. It was all too much. She just wanted to hold her frightened daughter. She took Christine's hand.

Christine flinched at the touch. She had been walking in silence with her betrayal. If she told her mother that she was thinking of living with her father, it would crush her. She'd have to tell her sometime, when it was sure to happen, but not before then. She held her mother's hand and they walked in the light rain.

They stopped at a coffee shop. Before they placed their order, the young man at the register asked Christine, "Hey, Branford, right?"

She wasn't sure if she recognized him. Branford was another planet, long ago. She answered. "Yeah, right."

"You go to school here?" "No, just visiting."

"Thinking of going here?"

She glanced away then back to the boy. "Maybe."

"That's cool. I'm in my second year. It's not bad here."

When he handed Christine her latte and scone, he smiled and added, "Maybe see you, if you end up here. Nice necklace."

She touched the red beads. Her fingers lingered at her neckline for a moment, "Thanks. Yeah maybe." She watched his eyes fall to her hand, the scar across her knuckles.

"My name's Jonah." He offered.

It felt like he wanted to see her again. She hadn't been looked at like that since Jimmy, except different. The boy at the counter seemed uncertain. Maybe the scar spooked him. Maybe he could see Jimmy's shadow over her, *and all the other shadows*. Still, he had a kind of sweet, kind of not so innocent thing going. She smiled a little, didn't try to be coy when she answered, "Okay. Christine." It was weird to be looked at like that. It was weird that it was weird.

Christine and her mother sat at a small wrought iron table against a burnt orange wall. Over her steaming cup of coffee, Lynne teased, "He's cute."

"Yeah, kinda."

They went quiet. The narrow store channeled a dozen students and townspeople to the counter and out again, or to small tables and booths through a steady clamor of conversation, laughter, clattering dishes, rattling silverware. Bob Marley could be heard on the sound system, weaving through it all. The air was ripe with the scent of coffee and baked goods.

It was too much, all this, all these people her age, living like this. It was like an insult. Like a punch. Christine didn't taste her scone. She only felt the coffee's heat. She listened for the reggae through the clutter, she heard, *'One Love, One Heart, let's get together and feel alright.'* She wanted that. That feeling, lifting her. She wanted it so, so much it hurt. She had to leave, she told her mother they had to leave. Lynne called Rosemary to come get Christine.

***

The next morning, restless, Christine ate and then finished her chores. She caught up on her algebra homework, but her mind kept drifting back to the coffee shop. She tried to read, but couldn't. She poked at some clay. The Marley tune kept lilting in her head, *One Love, One Heart….* She wanted that sweet music. The only thing they listened to was Vermont Public Radio, classical music all the time, except bluegrass on Saturday night. She wanted something that made her feel alright. The cabin's silence ridiculed her. The hissing log in the stove pissed her off.

"I'm going for a walk." She called from the door, didn't wait for an answer. She marched off into the lead gray day, wearing snowshoes, headed for the deep woods. Before she had reached the forest's edge, she had already unzipped her coat—the warmth of the January thaw steamed her to a quick sweat. The top few inches of snow were slush after a couple days of melting temperatures and rain. Hard hiking. She soon tied her coat around her waist.

She took the abandoned logging road, past the fork to the right that looped back to the house a mile away. She continued at an unbroken pace for a couple more miles, beyond the furthest point she had ever been, on this ancient road. She was lost to distance or time. She only wanted to keep going, to move, to push her body hard. She wanted no Marley, no loss, no confusion. She wanted no fear, no desperation. She kept going, hard. She wanted no mother, no father, no cops. No holding cells, no detention centers, no hospitals, no Jimmy, no woman in the shower. No queer little cabins, no future.

Streaming sweat, her muscles strained against the heavy, wet snow—her body sworn to moving forward. She slogged beneath the low banked clouds she did not see, through the whispering evergreens she did not hear.

Until she stopped, panting. She collapsed to her knees at the edge of an ice lined stream, cupped a handful of snow and ate it ferociously—cooling her burning throat, her raging thirst. She tasted pine. She cupped more snow, sunk her face in her hands, and breathed in halting gasps, then heaving sobs. She had not reached the place she wanted. Some place she didn't know, a world far beyond all her shit.

Barehanded, double fisted, she pounded against the snow. *Why can't...* furiously pounded the snow, the ice crust; pounded buried rock and buried log and frozen earth... *my life...* with bleeding, raw fleshed fists, with every piece of her *...be normal!*

Heaving, kneeling, Christine bent low in the thick spread of her devastation; her face inches from the earth, from her knees sunk in the slush. Exhausted, but not released. There was more. A roar from her heart wracked her body, exploded full throated from her mouth. She howled in the deep woods, howled until there was no more, moaning at the end.

Emptied, she heard the silence. Small sounds of the winter forest returned to her: The stream splashing and echoing the contours of the pebble bed, a distant call and response of a pair of chickadees, the rustle of fir needles in a moist stirring of air. She breathed in the air which carried the scent of rain. She had to go back.

The rain swept in on a gust of cold wind. It came in sheets, pounded at Christine's back bent, water streamed down her neck, chilling her instantly. She pulled her coat over her head, stood. *The way back?* She followed her tracks, her only choice—she had no idea where she was, or how she had arrived there. No trail in sight. Fighting the sodden snow, head down against the storm, she could only think on the next few steps ahead of her. A couple miles later, straining through her exhaustion, the hard rain and the nightfall, to find the next footprints, she didn't see the beam of light. Rosemary, walking into the gale, didn't see Christine until they were thirty feet apart, at the far reach of the flashlight's range. She called to her through the storm.

Christine heard, looked up. *Rosemary!* They reached each other. There, beside the trail, beneath the scant shelter of a clutch of wild grapevine, Christine shook violently as Rosemary wrapped her in the wool blanket from her knapsack, then she drank strong tea from Rosemary's thermos.

"We were worried."

Christine felt the tea's warmth spread within her, "I'm sorry."

The woman looked at the girl, barely visible in the last twilight. "No need to be." She corked the thermos. "Let's be going, we've a long way ahead."

That night Christine plunged into a sleep deeper than her nightmares.

CHAPTER 33

Christine sat across the desk from Dr. Vrabel. He asked how she was, what was new since the last time they met. She told him she had gone to another pottery lesson that went really well and that she would bring him one of her bowls next time. She told him she and her mother visited the Johnson State College campus last Saturday, that it was nice to get away, that maybe it was a good place to go to college. She didn't tell him she and her mother had fought that day, or that she thought it was ridiculous to be thinking about college, or that she had raged in the forest on Sunday. She didn't tell him that, since Sunday, she felt more clear headed than she had in a long, long, time.

She told him about her interview with Benson. "I don't think he believed me when I said I wasn't into drugs anymore."

"Why do you think he didn't believe you?"

"Just the way he acted, like he wasn't listening at all." She shifted in her chair, "What bugs me is that his opinion matters so much, and he's got it all wrong."

Vrabel suggested they wait and see what the evaluation had to say. She might be surprised. And if it was bad, she could talk to her lawyer about it. Christine sat back, irritated that her doctor obviously didn't hear her just tell him she was screwed. *Like he couldn't care less.*

Vrabel pushed some papers across the desk, towards Christine. "Speaking of evaluations, this is a draft of what I've prepared. I want you to take a look at it, tell me if you have any questions."

This is it. She took the papers.

Vrabel spoke as she began reading. "I want you to have a chance to comment on what I have to say about you before I submit it to the court and the other parties."

Christine scanned the Background section: her home and family; her school and education; her relationship with Jimmy, the arrest; her detention, hospitalization and placement with the Murphys. So much pain boiled down to a few sentences, a few dozen words. Her background. She didn't like this.

She kept reading. He used all kinds of words to describe her: "intelligent", "articulate", "engaging", "generous", "recovering", "psychotic", "trauma", "depressed", "acute", "chronic", "precarious", "anxious", and "disorder". It hurt to read, but she continued. She had to because this was what everyone was going to read about her. *The judge and everyone.*

Vrabel had written that he did not think Christine's psychotic break was drug related, as there was no evidence to support that diagnosis. He had written it was likely due to some trauma that had induced her psychosis. That the precipitating trauma could not be specifically determined, but that it was clear she had suffered significant distress from her relationship with Jimmy, the circumstances of her arrest, her experience in the detention center, Jimmy's suicide. He had written she presented notable anxiety and depression around those events.

The evaluation said her anxiety and depression compounded and intensified around her relationship with her father and the uncertainty of her return to her mother's home. It stated she considered her father unreliable, and she believed her mother may not be able to satisfy the requirements imposed by SRS for her return home.

She stopped reading. It was much more complex than what he was saying. It would take pages to tell it right. These people, the judge and the rest of them, were going to read this and think they knew all about her. This evaluation, and the drug guy's evaluation, and the cops, were all going to tell the judge what to think about her. She was getting screwed, and Vrabel was only making it worse.

She looked at him. He asked if she was finished, if she agreed with his recommendations.

She told him she hadn't gotten that far, and found the "Recommendations" section. It said that her intent and desire all along has been to return home to her mother; that returning home may cause her some anxiety, but with continued therapy, closely monitored medication, and the continued support of her mother, she should be able to manage the challenges; that her mother was equipped to provide Christine with the support she needed, as Lynne was engaged in meaningful therapy and an active parent support group; and that her father, although expressing concern for her wellbeing and an interest in taking a more active role in her life, had yet to provide her with the consistency she urgently needed, and should not be considered as a placement option.

He's got it all wrong! Was he completely ignoring all that stuff SRS said about her mother not providing enough supervision? She tried to scan back through the parts of the evaluation she hadn't read, but couldn't focus on the blurring words. And what about all the time they spent talking about her father loving her, and how it was normal to feel crazy about it? *Doesn't he get it*? No one was going to let her go home. It didn't matter what he said about her mother caring for her. *Everyone knows that already. They've known since the beginning, but I'm still not home, am I?* They, the judge and everybody, were going to blow off this stupid evaluation if it recommended she go back to her mother. She had to make it work for her, so she didn't get dumped somewhere terrible.

Christine put the evaluation on the desk, "Thanks doc, I appreciate what you've done. Y'know, though, things have changed for me, I think. All that talk about getting my feelings straightened out about my dad, stuff you said we can deal with in therapy. I've been thinking a lot lately that it might be best if I went and stayed with him." *You hear what I'm saying?*

Vrabel was surprised. “I didn’t know we were talking about you living with your father. I thought you were trying to manage how to let him back in your life gradually.”

“Yeah it was like that, but it’s more than that now. With the state people so down on me living with my mother, they’re never gonna let that happen. And they seem like they’re okay with me living with my dad, so I’m okay with that.”

“You want to live with your father?”

“That’s right. I’m just saying it wouldn’t be so terrible. I mean you yourself said, and I agree it’s gonna be really hard for me to go back to Branford. Maybe we should consider my father’s as a place to live. That’s what I want. Can you write that in your evaluation?” She held the doctor’s gaze.

“I can include your thoughts in the report. In fact, I will try to use your exact words. But I can’t recommend that you live with him. Not at this time. Not from what I’ve observed, and your history. I think there is a risk of harm to you if you went to live with him now. Maybe over time, you and he can develop a trusting relationship, but now I feel you need...”

Christine jumped out of her chair, leaned over Vrabel’s desk, “Don’t go telling me what I need. I know what I need, and that is someone who I know will take care of me. And that’s my father. He’ll protect me...” She leaned back, tried to calm down. “I mean, he’s got it together. He’s got a good job, a nice wife and kid, a nice place to live.

It’s pretty clear he can take care of me. The judge will let me live with him. We’d have to work some stuff out, and I think we can. I think I can, with your help.”

Vrabel nodded, “I think I understand. I’ll write up your concerns. And I’ll refrain from a placement recommendation one way or another.”

Good enough. “That’s all I’m asking.”

***

Christine lay in the dark, her muscles ached from throwing pots, but she didn't mind. She had gotten a lot of time on the wheel, and loved every minute of it. Finally, a Friday working in clay, rather than being grilled by bastards turning her inside out.

Maybe she was done with that stuff, now that she had made it clear that her father would be taking her. She felt strong, laying there.

It had been a nice evening, too. Kathleen and Rosemary had thrown a little going away party for Hannah. She was moving in with her new foster family tomorrow, and the Murphys had a special dinner of her favorite food; spaghetti and meatballs, chocolate cake and ice cream. They had given Hannah presents. Christine had forgotten about the party, but fortunately she had brought home a few bowls she had made and had given Hannah the one she thought was the most beautiful—deep blue with scalloped edges.

When she gave Hannah the present, she had said. "I want you to keep very special things in this bowl and keep the bowl someplace where you'll see it, so you can find your special things and look at them anytime you want." Hannah promised she would.

"Will you miss me?" The small voice reached Christine through the night. "I mean, tonight at the party, Kathleen said she was going to miss me. Rosemary said was gonna always remember me. I'll always remember them. And I'll always remember you."

"Yes, sweetie, I'll always remember you." She was certain Hannah was smiling. "Good."

Christine heard her nestle into her bedding, otherwise the room was silent.

Hannah whispered, "Christine, don't be sad. You're going to a good place, too." Christine struggled to breathe, she whispered back, "If I'm lucky. Like you."

Hannah would be gone tomorrow, to people who would care for her and protect her. She had a child's blind faith that things will be good. She didn't understand that she would still be living with the mess that took her away from her mother and sister.

Christine prayed for Hannah, from her heart, that someday she would be free from her past.

She whispered into the dark, "Goodnight Hannah, love you."

She prayed for herself. Prayed to be safe. Prayed to be freed someday from all the shit she was dealing with. She prayed to her father.

Hannah's soft words returned, "Love you, too, Christine."

Love like a small candle flame.

***

Descending south and westward towards Albany, through the day's dawning, Rosemary and Christine rode silent with their own thoughts, sipping coffee. Christine tried to imagine what she and her father would talk about, what his wife would say, what they would do for the day. She came up with nothing. The sun broke over the hills, distracting her from her silence. She asked Rosemary to stop for a bathroom break. When they pulled off the highway at a diner just north of Albany, Christine realized how far they'd come. Her father was close, waiting for her. They were early so, they decided to have breakfast at the diner. They should arrive at his house before nine – the time he was expecting them.

A half hour later, they were back on the road. The directions Mark had given Rosemary led them to a vast tract development. Block after block of the same basic houses, the same front lawns, the same driveways and garages. Christine had never seen anything like it.

"This place is kind of strange." She said.

"I wouldn't want to live here, but there's many who do." Rosemary agreed.

Guess so. Christine read the directions to Rosemary. They turned onto another street, turned again. The Cherokee slowed, the two scanned the house numbers, all located to the right of the front door. As the numbers uniformly progressed, they both knew which house was their destination from half a block away. Pulling to the curb, Rosemary said. "292, this should be it."

Christine examined the split level ranch like it was a mystery to be solved. There was her father's Audi in the driveway, along with a late model Ford Explorer. *There he is.* Her father at the front door, Christine didn't move.

"Are you going to get out?" Rosemary asked her.

Mark strode down the front walk and beamed at his little girl. He was pumped. Today was going to be great; a chance to show his daughter what he had to offer. He arrived at the end of the driveway smiling, but his smile froze as he watched Christine and Rosemary get out of the dented, filthy Cherokee. They both wore worn flannel, jeans and boots, and reeked of wood smoke and forest. Were they trying to embarrass him? He saw nothing smug on Christine's face. *She doesn't know what she looks like, how she smells.* They'd go shopping, he'd get her some appropriate outfits. He already had planned on going to the mall. Now he had a clear purpose. *Good.*

He stepped up to Christine, threw his arms wide and welcomed her. "Honey, it is so good to see you here. Finally."

She stepped into his arms. "Dad." His scent, his feel, his strength swept over her.

She pulled away. "It's great to be here." She patted his arm, looked past him to the indistinct woman holding a toddler on the other side of the storm door's glass panel: his family.

Mark brought Christine and Rosemary inside and gave them a brief tour of the first floor, after he had introduced his wife Nancy and his "little guy," Charlie. Passing through the house, Christine noticed there were no smells, except for what came off of her and Rosemary. She corrected herself; there were odors, from the chemicals that made the place seem spotless. Nancy and the baby followed behind them. Christine's father blabbered on about nothing. Nancy didn't say much. The baby was really cute.

In the kitchen Mark asked, "Some coffee, Rosemary, before you go? Christine, get you something?"

Christine observed no utensils or food except a pot of freshly made coffee sitting on its perch in the Mr. Coffee coffeemaker. "I could go for some coffee, dad."

"Yes, thank you Mr. Bancroft."

"No, Mark, please. Here we like to keep it casual. Grab a seat."

He gestured to the glass topped table with four white wrought iron chairs in the corner of the all-white kitchen. He looked to his wife. "Honey, you want to join us?"

Nancy had been standing at the doorway, jostling the baby on her hip. She entered the room. He went to the cupboards for some mugs. Nancy retrieved a jar of Coffee mate and a plastic bag of Sweet 'n Low packets from another cupboard. She sat with Rosemary and Christine. The child immediately began to fidget, stretching for the sweetener packets. Christine tensed; this was the kind of thing that could piss her father off. She looked at Nancy, who appeared tired.

Mark stepped up to the table holding four mugs, two in each hand. "Here we go, steaming hot cups of Joe."

Nancy held the baby and lurched forward as Mark put the mugs down with a clatter. The child squirmed in his mother's lap, trying to reach what was on the table. Rosemary dangled a couple sweetener packets, made them dance in front of Charlie. This seemed to please him. Nancy didn't touch her coffee. She couldn't, without losing control of the baby. She apologized, and abruptly left with Charlie, to go find a toy.

Awkward conversation followed. Christine contributed while barely paying attention. Instead, she kept her eyes on her father. She watched her father, proud and possessive he was in this place, in his immaculate kitchen with its white walls, white linoleum floor, white tile countertops, and blonde wooden cabinets. Nancy returned with the baby and a bright plastic teething ring. Christine watched Charlie gnaw and drool on the soft ring, watched Nancy dab at the baby's chin, preventing drool from touching anything. She watched how Nancy kept looking to her father, how her nervous eyes flickered. She watched her father's smile go brittle, his eyes darken. *Why?*

She drank her coffee, but didn't taste it. She listened to her father go on and on. She could handle this place. *It's weird, but so what.* Life was weird. Besides, the state people would love this whole setup. No one would take her away from here. She noticed that her father was speaking directly to her.

"The mall? Yeah that sounds great, dad." She answered.

***

Christine shut her eyes. It had been a long day, and it was going to be a very long drive back to Bixby. Her father asked her something about the song that played on the radio. She said she didn't know. She had given that answer a lot throughout the day, whether she knew an answer or not, whether she heard the question or not.

She had paid enough attention to give her father some real answers now and then, so he didn't think she was completely retarded. But really, stuff about Michael Jackson, about the weather, about the "latest fashions"? She could only spew so much.

It had been an endless day at the mall and the back seat was filled with clothes she either didn't like or didn't want. It had been crazy—he kept picking stuff off the racks, asking her what she thought, telling her to try it on. At first she had said she didn't like what he chose, but he kept insisting that she try the things on anyway. Finally, she figured if she said she liked something, then he wouldn't make a big scene about her trying it on and he would just throw it in the cart. The whole afternoon had been that way. She got maybe two things she really wanted: a Talking Heads T-shirt and a pair of regular Levis, unlike the three other pairs of designer jeans he bought that she would never be caught dead in.

On the long drive home, her father jabbered away, or sang along with the Top 40 hits. The music was idiotic, the DJs were idiotic, the commercials were idiotic, and the radio stayed on the entire time. After a while, it seemed to Christine that her father had forgotten she was there. It didn't matter, it was easier that way for both of them. It just became noise, and she fell asleep. She slept until they were just outside of Bixby. When they said goodbye, her father hugged her tight as she stood at the door. She didn't mind. And he didn't seem to mind that she had fallen asleep. She thought he might be angry about it—he would have gotten angry a few years ago. *Good sign.*

CHAPTER 34

The day after her visit with her father, Christine hummed as she did her chores and wrote a social studies essay. Rosemary had suggested she finish her homework that morning because a new child would arrive that afternoon. It was weird to have another kid moving in the day after Hannah moved out. *That must be the way they do things.* The house was quiet. Marshall was still at his grandmother's. Kathleen had said he might be there a few days, that the State people wanted to see how the boy and his grandmother managed.

Throughout the morning Christine thought about her visit, about Nancy and the baby, about their house. The whole thing felt kind of strange but okay, like she was in a foreign country and didn't understand the language yet.

Christine was setting the table for lunch, when the new girl arrived with an SRS caseworker. They were early. The young girl, Anna, stood motionless at the doorway with a full Hefty bag set beside feet: her belongings. The caseworker stood on the other side of the girl. Anna didn't look up. She clutched a stuffed bear. She was small, thin, and pale. She couldn't have been more than seven years old.

Kathleen stepped forward. "Hello dear, we were just sitting down for lunch, would you care to join us?"

Anna didn't speak or move.

The caseworker answered, "That would be nice."

Christine quietly set two more places at the kitchen table.

The girl said nothing during the meal. She ate none of the bean soup and instead, drank a couple sips of milk. After lunch, Rosemary, accompanied by the caseworker, showed Anna her bedroom. She explained which bed would be hers and which bureau drawers she could put her things in. Anna didn't respond to anything Rosemary said.

After the caseworker left, Anna didn't move from the front door. She watched as the woman disappeared, the woman who had been with her since she had been taken from her home that morning. She started screaming. She screamed for her mother, her uncle, her dog. She shrieked to go home. She tore at her clothes. Kathleen quickly went to the girl to calm her. Rosemary went to the phone and sent Christine outside.

When the caseworker returned Rosemary's call, two hours later, she told the sisters she had no medications for Anna. There would be none until the next day, Monday. That's when they could get her to a doctor. She told the sisters there were no other placement options. Rosemary insisted that Anna needed hospitalization, but the caseworker said there were no beds available anywhere. They were it. She told Rosemary, Anna had been sexually assaulted, most likely repeatedly, by the live-in uncle. She said she knew the sisters could handle it: Just get the girl stabilized until the next day. They'd done it before. And if they couldn't, they should take her to the emergency room. Anna screamed for hours. She tore at her skin. She shit all over the bathroom.

Rosemary called Judy Repchuk to ask if Christine could spend the night, but there was no answer. Christine remembered she was out of town for the weekend. Kathleen remained close to Anna, trying to soothe the child and protect her from hurting herself. Christine stayed away, but heard the sisters talking: they'd call the state hospital themselves if they had to; they'd call the state police if they had to. They would not let Anna harm herself.

Night fell. Kathleen got Anna to eat a bit of bread with butter. She was winding down to trembling tears. Kathleen rested her hand on the back of the girl's head and said, "Dear, dear Anna, it will be alright. We're here to take good care of you."

The little girl looked up at the woman speaking to her. Christine, who had just entered the house after her second long hike, witnessed the moment.

Rosemary fixed Christine a cup of tea and explained it could be a rough night, that Kathleen would sleep with Anna in Christine's room and Christine would take Kathleen's bed. Dinner would be leftovers.

Meanwhile, Kathleen went upstairs gently helping the girl wash up and change into a pair of pajamas. She would read to her, and hopefully the exhausted child would fall asleep. The low sound of Kathleen's voice was all that Christine heard from upstairs.

Mark called that night and rattled on about what a great time he had the day before, and how much Nancy enjoyed having her visit. That visit seemed a universe away from where Christine was now. She said she had a good time also, and thanked him for the nice things he bought her. She told him she loved him. She heard him say he loved her, too.

Lynne called also. Christine didn't tell her mother about Anna; it was too raw to share. She didn't tell her mother she had visited her father, because she didn't want to get into that either. They spent a few minutes of small talk: life in Branford, what Christine was reading, the weather. Then Christine said good night.

"Love you, dear."

"Love you too, mom." It felt like a lie. Covering up the visit to her father's was a lie. She hated it, she hung up.

Anna's whimpering and intermittent shrieks during the night, woke Christine several times, and kept her awake until she slipped back into a thin sleep. The girl's agony spawned vicious nightmares, which roamed within Christine, threatening her the entire raging night.

***

The next day, Anna was prescribed a strong sedative, but her trauma kept on. She was sullen, silent. She constantly rubbed herself and masturbated, sometimes when Christine was nearby. The girl smeared her shit on the walls. All of it freaked Christine out. Kathleen had to take Anna to the psychiatrist in Burlington three times that first week. On Monday morning, Rosemary arranged for Christine to spend each afternoon with Judy Repchuk, except Wednesday when she would see Dr. Vrabel. On Tuesday, she stayed at Judy's for dinner.

Marshall didn't return from his grandmother's. The SRS people decided it was best if he moved there. Christine wished she could have said goodbye to the booger. She had really liked him and his wild boy energy.

The days and nights with Anna were a constant, exhausting struggle. Christine stayed away from the child. *There's nothing I can do. I shouldn't crowd her.* Kathleen was with Anna most of the time; comforting her, limiting her, protecting her. Rosemary and Christine cooked the meals, which weren't nearly as good as those Kathleen made, but they certainly were good enough. The kitchen didn't gleam, but they kept it clean.

Deep in the night, Christine's nightmares worsened. There were people coming at her, unidentified yet somehow distinct—she felt their breath, she smelled their rot. They were going to do something terrible to her, but she always tore herself out of the dream before they did.

During the afternoons, Christine and Rosemary would go for hikes or head downtown together. Christine noticed the strain in Rosemary's eyes. Sitting in the Bixby diner for lunch on their way to her appointment with Dr. Vrabel, she asked Rosemary why Anna had been placed with them.

"Sometimes a child needs to be taken out of a situation immediately, and there's no time to find the ideal place. We're one of the choices that are available in such an emergency."

"It must be really hard."

Looking absently at her hands, Rosemary responded. "It can be. We do what we can."

"How long will Anna be staying?"

"It's hard to say. She'll be moved when a bed at a care facility opens up. She's going to need a lot of care. Could be days. Or weeks. Can't really say." Rosemary swished the coffee in her cup.

Weeks! "How's Kathleen doing?"

Rosemary looked up, "She's alright. Sometimes it's easier to be close and involved with the child than apart, as we are, you and I." She touched Christine's hand, "Kathleen will get some relief, even if it's just for a day, by the end of next week, I'm fairly certain."

Christine told Dr. Vrabel about Anna and her nightmares in detail. She told him about her visit to her father's home, too. She explained that if she was with him she wouldn't have to deal with Anna, wouldn't be having the nightmares, and wouldn't be in a place where people like Anna were sent. She complained that Anna could be at the Murphys' for weeks. Then, she asked Vrabel the date of her court hearing. He looked in her file. "February twenty - second." It was January twenty - seventh. *It'll be over in a few weeks.*

CHAPTER 35

Thursday afternoon, Lynne sat motionless in Fitzgerald's office. She had received the evaluation from Dr. Vrabel the day before, and the drug and alcohol assessment earlier in the week. She decided she had better contact her lawyer right away. She didn't know what to make of the reports. Neither of them seemed to state Christine should be returned to her. That couldn't be right, she must have missed something. Fitzgerald would tell her what they meant.

She waited, on edge, as she watched him skim Vrabel's evaluation. He had explained he hadn't had a chance to read it before she arrived and apologized. She slipped her coat off and draped it over the back of her chair.

Fitzgerald reviewed the "Testing Results" and "Treatment History" sections: above average intelligence; scored well on tests of receptive and expressive language, on measures of verbal reasoning and comprehension, and on mathematical analysis, *impressive*; is current with academic requirements for graduation from secondary school in the spring of 1989, *good*; psychotic break, no relapses since released from the state hospital, *good*; no evidence supporting a diagnosis of schizophrenia or schizophreniform disorder, *good*; repeated bouts of acute depression, abated, but still at risk, exacerbated when anxious, *makes sense*; anxiety and depression symptoms correlating to Christine's experience of the legal process, her placements at Stonebridge and the hospital, and the uncertainty of her future placement, *makes sense*; possible development of chronic depression if these issues are not resolved, particularly the need for Christine to be placed in a supportive environment. Fitzgerald penciled a note in the margin beside this entry, *'support = mother'*.

He continued to read: "Christine has expressed her wish to return home to her mother and her desire to be placed with her father. This deep ambivalence appears to arise from Christine's perception that her mother will not be deemed 'good enough' by those responsible for her placement decision, and therefore has abandoned that goal, despite her mother's consistent involvement in her care and rehabilitation since being taken into custody. Her need for certainty, concerning her future placement, has led Christine to express her wish that her father be considered as a placement option, despite her past reports of his failure to consistently support her emotional needs, causing her undue stress and anxiety." Fitzgerald circled the passage and added an exclamation point. Lynne anxiously watched the lawyer mark the page, wondering what had drawn his attention.

The section concluded by stating that, despite Christine's history and the conclusions contained in the Benson drug and alcohol assessment, Vrabel was convinced she had abstained from intoxicants for the eight months she had been in the State's custody. He found there was no evidence of her physical or psychological dependence on intoxicants, other than possible susceptibility to peer pressure, and there was no need for a residential treatment program. He recommended Christine continue therapy to address her pronounced psychological issues. *Good, negates the Benson report.*

Fitzgerald continued to the "Parent- Child History and Resources" section. The first part concerned Lynne. Vrabel referenced the SRS home evaluation in writing that Lynne was adequately providing for the two other children, who remained at home. He then stated Lynne had consistently shown appropriate care and concern for Christine throughout the time her daughter had been a patient of his, *good,* that Lynne's support significantly contributed to Christine's recovery, *nice*; that she had been engaged in individual counseling and group therapy designed to address issues of parenting children with histories similar to Christine's, *good;* and that Lynne had consistently expressed her dedication to meeting her daughter's needs, *very nice.* Fitzgerald couldn't ask for more. However, he thought it was curious that Vrabel didn't mention the matter of supervision that was so important to SRS. He would have to ask the doctor his opinion on that issue.

And the father? Citing the SRS home evaluation of Mark Bancroft, Vrabel stated that Christine's father was meaningfully employed, had a wife and infant son, lived in an adequate home in suburban Albany, and was a suitable placement for Christine. Vrabel also wrote that the father reported to him that he was most concerned about protecting his daughter from drug abuse and people involved with drugs, which were the cause of Christine's problems. The father had told Vrabel that Lynne 'has neither the physical nor personal resources' to protect Christine from further harm*, bastard*. The father had also told Vrabel he was concerned that he had not had a chance to assist more in Christine's recovery, but he was fully committed to seeing she got what she needed, *a real bastard.* Fitzgerald thought the doctor should have challenged the father on this rhetorical crap and kept the father's opinions about Lynne out of the evaluation. That was the kind of garbage that got into people's heads and influenced their opinions. *Not good.*

Lynne grew more anxious as Fitzgerald continued reading to himself.

He read on to the "Conclusions" section. Vrabel stated that the most important goal was to place Christine in the setting which would most likely meet her need for security and support while reasonably, considering her opinion on how to meet those needs. "No placement will succeed in the long run if Christine does not invest herself in that success." *Can't argue with that. He leaves it wide open, though.* Fitzgerald didn't like it, something was up. He'd seen Vrabel reports before, where he'd come out squarely in favor of a particular placement. Not here, even though the father was a complete jerk. Reading between the lines, he figured it was all about Christine's "deep ambivalence". She had weighed in, even though she was really confused, and Vrabel had reported it. Fitzgerald understood: Vrabel had to document Christine changing mind. He was telling them she needed the mother's consistency, while not alienating his patient and risking her resistance to future treatment by excluding the father as a placement option. Fitzgerald noted this point in the margin.

The lawyer realized this kid was really going through hell, torn between her parents like this. Before the hearing commenced, he had to convince LaValley that Lynne was a safe option and that she could keep Christine safe too. Christine needed to know she was heading home.

Fitzgerald told Lynne what he thought of Vrabel's evaluation. By the end, she was bent in half, her face buried in her hands, devastated by Christine's desire to be placed with Mark. She murmured. "Why would she say that?"

"I'm not sure, scared perhaps."

Straightening up, "Scared of what?"

"The chance of being returned to Stonebridge, or being sent to a drug rehabilitation center, something like that." Fitzgerald offered.

Lynne recalled her daughter's behavior over the past few weeks. "She's been thinking about this hearing. She *is* scared. She's told me as much, maybe not in those words, but the way she's been acting ... the way we've been fighting..." Lynne's heart tore open—*he'll just hurt her.* "If I don't get that shift change, they won't let Chris come home, will they?"

Fitzgerald hedged, "It makes it more difficult. But if that doesn't work out, I think there are things that can be done, that we can offer, that would address S.R.S' concerns."

"Like what?"

"Random urine samples, N.A requirement..."

It sounded so desperate. "I don't think she'd go for that." Feeling the sweat under her clothes, Lynne broke out. "She won't do anything like this again. She made a mistake, and she knows it. I'll take good care of her. Just like I take good care of her brother and sister. I feed them, keep a roof over their heads, get them to school. What more can I do, really? What do these people want from me?" Tears streamed down Lynne's cheeks. She didn't want the lawyer to see her like this, but she couldn't help it.

Quietly, "I understand. We'll make it clear that you're a good mother and that Christine should be home with you."

She wiped away her tears with Kleenex from his desktop. "I'll find another job next week. That's what they want." *Promises won't bring her home, though.* She had to make this happen.

***

Friday afternoon, Mark sat in Blum's anteroom, leg tapping. He had gotten these evaluations and he had to know what his lawyer thought, what they were going to do to get ready for the court thing coming up. He glanced at his watch. He'd been waiting ten minutes. He was fortunate enough to have a lag in his project schedule so he could take time off to see this guy. He looked at his watch again. As he waited, Knowles briefed Blum on the Vrabel and Benson evaluations.

Mark had barely sat down in Blum's office before he started speaking. "The reason I wanted to see you is, I need to know how this thing works. I know we talked, back before Christmas, about Chris coming to live with me, and you recommended she stay in the State's custody ... get treatment for her drug problem first, before coming to live with us. And that all makes sense. But I've been seeing more of Chris, and I read the reports. The ones where her shrink says she doesn't have a big problem with drugs and the other guy says she should go to rehab." Mark sat forward. "I don't know what to think. Yes she might have a problem, but she doesn't have to go into treatment. I mean, there are programs she can do without going off to one of those places." He sat back. "Because, to be honest, she goes into one of those places and the people she runs into there...she's going to come out a whole lot worse. Seeing Chris, knowing she's been clean and sober all this time, I'm thinking she doesn't need to go into rehab. She lives with me and I can guarantee she'll get the treatment she needs." He looked back and forth between the lawyers. "Like you said back then, if she stays in State's custody, while she's living with me and things don't work out, then they can deal with it and take her off my hands. What do you think?"

Blum cleared his throat. "Very well. From what you've told us, and what I've read in these evaluations, I'm confident the State will place Christine with you, while continuing to keep custody of her. You can let the caseworker know that is what you want, or we can. It would be best coming from you though. You need to do that next week because there are only three weeks until the disposition hearing, when the judge will determine who gets custody of Christine and what kind of rehabilitation she should receive. If possible, we should push to have Christine placed with you before the hearing. It would strengthen your position considerably if that piece was in place."

Chris coming home sometime in the next couple weeks?

Looking at Knowles, Blum continued. "Also, we want to determine the outpatient drug treatment programs, treatment support groups, AA and NA locations and schedules in your area, so that Christine can access those services immediately, upon being placed with you. Ms. Knowles will have that information for you and the caseworker by the end of the day, Monday." Looking back at Mark, "We will see to it that she is made fully aware of the resources available to you and Christine."

Mark understood. It was perfectly clear. *I'm getting Chris back*!

***

Saturday afternoon, Christine and Rosemary stood on the sidewalk outside the coffee shop in Lyndonville, looking in. It was as crowded and noisy as it had been two weeks before. It was alive, and it was away from Anna. Christine was relieved that her mother had agreed to come back here for the visit. She was glad Rosemary was there too, getting a break from Anna. After waiting a few minutes for Lynne, they decided to go in.

As they got in line, Christine heard some Afro-Cuban jazz through the clamor and remarked, "I love this place, what do you think?"

"It's nice, I like it."

Christine noticed the exhaustion in Rosemary's eyes: she was just there and didn't appreciate the place at all. It didn't matter, they were here and Christine was glad they were. When they had been served, she led Rosemary to a table that seated four. They sat with their coffee and scones and watched for Lynne.

Lynne arrived twenty minutes late. She apologized as she struggled out of her coat—her arm was stuck in the sleeve and she didn't have enough space to maneuver because the tables were so close together. She finally got the coat off, put it over the back of her chair and the chair fell over backwards, into another customer, causing the woman to spill her chai. Lynne stared at her coat on the floor. She picked it up and apologized to the customer, who was spreading napkins over the spill. She retrieved the chair with her free hand and sat.

Christine thought her mother looked like a mess; her hair was a dried out tangle, her eyes red rimmed, and her skin pale and splotchy. Rosemary offered to get Lynne something. She answered, "Just a coffee, cream, sugar. Thanks."

When Rosemary left, Lynne asked, “So, how are you doing, Chris?”

Christine thought it was a peculiar question, the way it was worded—kind of impersonal. She answered, “Hanging in there. This stuff with Anna is really hard on everyone, but we’re doing okay. How about you?”

Lynne looked at a point a few feet away. “Getting by. Nothing new.”

Her mother was acting really strange. Probably exhausted, *like everyone*. She didn’t want to hear why; she watched the people and listened for the music. They didn’t speak until Rosemary returned with the coffee.

Lynne looked down into her cup, as the three of them talked about meaningless things; flooding down south, a missing girl out west and gas prices. The noise around them began to sound tinny, unreal to Christine. The people laughing and chatting around them felt trivial. *Living in their fake, little worlds, all happy and shit.*

Rosemary finished her coffee and left to return home. Christine wanted to get out of there. She watched her mother drink her coffee.

They walked. The day was indistinct: Not cold, overcast without a threat of anything. Wordless, Christine walked hard, but not so fast that Lynne couldn’t keep up. She was angry because everything basically sucked for every reason and no reason, and there was nothing to say. They crossed the campus, went down residential streets.

Lynne thought, *I’ve had enough!* “Where are we going?” “I dunno. I just feel like walking.”

Lynne stopped. “Why are you doing this?” Christine glared at her. “What?”

"Why are you doing this to me?" Christine snapped. "I'm just walking." Lynne snapped back. "No, all of this." *Say it!* "All of what?"

All of everything! Since reading Dr. Vrabel's evaluation with her lawyer Thursday, Lynne could not understand how in god's name Christine could possibly think about living with her father. After all she and Christine had been through, always there for each other, through everything and she was blowing it away. Like it was nothing, like it was dust. Lynne hadn't slept last night, worried about Christine. *What the hell could she be thinking? Doesn't she know he's going to hurt her? What's he said to her?*

Lynne answered through her teeth. "Dr. Vrabel's report. Where you say you want to live with your father." She forced the words out. "You can't. We'll get you home. You can't go live with him."

Shaking, Christine unloaded on her mother. "No! You don't get it, do you?

They're not going to let me go home with you. They're sending me somewhere, and it's not back to you." Her eyes flashed furious, "They're not locking me up! I'm not going back to juvie. Or the hospital. Or some bullshit treatment center. That's the plan, right?

Not gonna happen. If I've got to live with dad to stop that from happening, then that's what I'm going to do." Her voice cracked. "If that's what I've got to do... You've got no idea, no fucking idea what..." Christine's head pounded viciously behind her eyes. "You have no idea..."

The two women stood apart, in a sudden vast silence, in wholly separate worlds of pain. Lynne managed to say, "I'll take you back to the Murphys."

As she rode to Bixby, rimming, red pain scraped Christine's skull. Jagged images leaped behind her eyes, clawing. She pressed her head against the cool window glass and felt the air rushing past. The pain eased as she kept still, eyes shut, holding on.

Lynne had no answers, had nothing to say. She drove the highway, hollow and alone, with no idea how Christine was suffering in the seat beside her.

When they arrived at the Murphys', Lynne promised. "I love you, Christine. I'm going to keep trying."

Christine heard the words, but they were useless. "I love you too." She answered.

***

Monday evening, Kathleen was upstairs, reading to Anna. Rosemary was taking a long walk under the nearly full moon. Yesterday, Christine had hiked all day, alone, surrounded by the deep forest quiet, returning late by the moon's light.

Christine sat at the dining room table with newspapers spread out, lumps of modeling clay on the paper. She had rolled out some clay and carved into it with the X-acto knife Judy had given her that afternoon. She was going to practice some of the shapes that they had made in the cups they threw that afternoon: various leaves and seashells. Instead she carved without intent, unconsciously. Whorls, slashes, wavelengths.

Christine's clay wasn't allowed around Anna because the feel of it overstimulated the child to frenzied rubbing. But it was Christine's time now, and this was what she wanted; to feel the clay yield to her knife any way she chose. She didn't want anything else. She balled up the clay and spread it again with the heel of her hand, when the phone rang. Last night, she was in the forest when her father and mother had called. She hadn't called them back. The phone rang again, she had to answer it.

It was her father. "Honey, how are you?"

"Good, dad. I was shaping a bowl when you called."

"Nice. I've got some great news. I spoke to Rose LaValley, the woman from the state, today about you coming to stay with me and she thinks it's a great idea..."

His words landed on Christine like a massive wave.

He was still talking. "...of course they have to do get some paperwork together with people here in New York, but she said that was just a formality..."

Christine's heart pounded.

"...shouldn't take too long, a couple of weeks at most, in time for the court hearing. In the meantime, she said you could visit here this weekend and, get this, you can stay overnight. Whadda ya think?" Her father's voice pitched with excitement.

Trying to match his pitch, she answered, "Sounds great, dad."

"I knew you'd be happy. Nancy and I are looking forward to having you here." "Yeah, me too." Straining, she fought to keep her voice from trembling.

"Well okay then. I'll let you go. Talk to you later in the week with more details." "Okay." Pounding inside, she trembled by the phone. *This is what I wanted.*

CHAPTER 35

Saturday in Albany, Rosemary drove Christine to her father's, arriving late that morning. He was home when they got there. Nancy and the baby were out. He didn't explain where they were. Rosemary left immediately and Christine was alone with Mark for a few minutes, before he suggested they go to the mall.

The mall was as stupid and ugly as it had been two weeks before. Her father made her try some clothes on at a couple stores and he bought her an ugly sweater and some leggings because he didn't want her to "freeze to death up there in God's country." After they bought the clothes, Christine said she was hungry so, they got a couple of slices of pizza at the food court. As they ate, she watched the kids her age go by in clumps, acting like morons. The girls wore way too much makeup and dressed in some kind of messed up mix of Flashdance and New Wave, getting it all wrong. The guys looked like idiots, drooling and pawing their stupid girlfriends. *A million times more pathetic than Branford.* She couldn't imagine ever hanging out at this mall, or any mall.

Christine half listened to Mark going on, something about Oliver North being a persecuted freedom fighter. She wasn't going to respond to that. She sipped her Coke, zoned out. She could retire as a vegetable here. This would be her home soon, isn't that what her father had said?

She interrupted, "Dad, the other night, when you called and said that the State people were going to let me come live with you, how's that supposed to work?"

Mark smiled, "The woman at SRS, Rose, said she was willing to place you with me as soon as the New York people get me into their system. She said it shouldn't take long, two weeks at most. Then we're all set, you can move right in."

"They can do that? Don't they need mom to agree, or the court to say it's okay?" "No, the way they're going to set it up is that you will still be in SRS custody, but they will place you with me, so they don't need anybody's approval." "So that hearing coming up, that's not happening?"

"No, that's still on. Your mother is fighting with the State to get custody of you. That's what the hearing will be about. If the State wins, and they probably will, then they can send you to live with me."

"Yeah, but they could take me away from you, because they have custody, right?" "They could, yes, but the way my lawyer explained it is that the law favors kids living with parents, so long as the kid doesn't mess up. If you mess up, then they have that power to place you somewhere else."

Christine's throat tightened, "I won't screw up, dad."

"I know you won't." Mark looked at his watch, "Nancy won't be home for another hour, want to do some window shopping?"

As she watched her father clean up his trash, Christine said, "Thanks, dad."

They wandered the mall for an hour. When they came to a music store, Christine wanted to go in and get some Marley and a Walkman, but decided against it; reggae might be too druggie for the people in charge of her. She wasn't going to give them any reason to worry about her screwing up.

They came to a Barnes and Noble. Christine asked her father if they could go in. "What's with you and books?"

Inside, she found Louise Erdrich, Toni Morrison, and some of her other favorite authors. She skimmed the inside flaps, decided against asking her father to buy her anything. He didn't need to know what she liked to read, didn't need to get concerned over nothing. It wasn't worth it. She didn't want him to have any concerns about her, or at least no more than he already had. They left the store after a few minutes.

Outside the bookstore, Mark suggested they leave and take their time driving home so he could show Christine where he worked. That was fine with her. They drove for about a half hour through the suburbs to an office park, where they turned off of the four lane throughway and entered the campus of four story tall buildings spread across acres of turf and asphalt.

Passing the fifth identical glass paneled block, Mark announced, "This is it." "Nice." What else was there to say?

They followed the drive in a broad loop, no other cars on the road, until they reached the exit to the throughway. Forty minutes later, after passing unbroken stretches of tract housing, strip malls and shopping centers, they reached Mark's development, identified by a sign at the entrance: Elm Heights. A couple minutes more and they arrived at her father's home.

Christine tried to remember the names of the streets they were on, how they got to his house, but could only manage the last street, Tulipwood. Which she already knew. *That's okay, I'll get it straight soon enough.*

Nancy and the baby were home when they arrived. As Nancy began to prepare dinner, Christine joined her in the kitchen and watched Charlie. Mark went downstairs to the den. A few minutes later, she could hear the sounds of a television coming from that direction. Nancy removed a pale red tomato from a cellophane package, while the baby crawled around on the immaculate linoleum. "Is there anything I can do to help?" Christine asked her.

"No, thank you. Well, perhaps. If you could rinse some lettuce for the salad?" "Sure."

Christine ran the leaves under the faucet as Nancy chopped a bright green bell pepper. Standing close, she saw her father's wife in detail now. She was much younger than her mother, maybe twenty – eight. She wore her highlighted hair in a way that made her appear younger, pulled back in a high ponytail. She had a thin figure and hands that didn't show veins or hard wear. Nancy thanked Christine when the lettuce was washed and dried. Their eyes met. Christine found her eyes to be sad, like they were new to sadness, confused by it.

What does she think about me being here, moving in with them? She must be freaking this woman out, her husband's crazy daughter arriving in her home. Christine suddenly thought, *maybe he hasn't told her what was going on*. She looked into Nancy's eyes, didn't see any deep questioning. *She has no idea what's happening!*

"I'm almost done, why don't you go join your father." Nancy said as she unwrapped three thick, bright red steaks from their cellophane and Styrofoam packaging.

"I can watch the baby..."

Charlie was sitting on the floor, mashing a teething ring.

"No, he's fine." Nancy's voice was soft but determined, like she had spent enough time with Christine.

"Yeah, sure."

Christine heard the television news anchor's important voice before she reached the den. She felt Mark's presence before she entered. She stopped at the doorway, saw him in his recliner with a half empty tumbler of Scotch on the table beside him. He was facing the television, unaware she was there. She watched him for a moment in his place, his territory. Light headed, she willed herself into the room. He looked away from the television; interrupted, annoyed. But when he saw it was his daughter, his eyes brightened. "Honey, come on in. I was just watching the news."

The dinner conversation was quiet, restrained. Mark and Nancy recounted their day with little detail. Christine added some comments, the baby gnawed on a zwieback. No one mentioned that Christine would be moving in soon. Christine didn't taste the food. After the meal, she helped Nancy load the dishwasher. Nancy then took Charlie upstairs, and Christine joined her father in the den to watch television for a couple hours. Nancy did not join them. Mark explained that she liked to read in bed.

Christine felt she had nowhere she could go except the den. Her father filled another tumbler with Scotch, which lasted him the rest of the evening. She watched the mindless shows, the stupid commercials. She stopped caring as time wore on. Once in a while, Mark would comment on what they were watching, and she would give him an answer that fit what he said.

After the ten o'clock news, he folded out the daybed. Together they spread a fitted sheet over the thin mattress. He handed Christine a pillow and a cotton blanket. He said it had been a wonderful day, and he was very glad she was there. He seemed to mean it.

"Yeah, it was great. I'm glad I'm here, too."

Mark leaned into Christine for a hug, a kiss. "Good night, honey."

Her body stiffened as his odor and his power swelled over her. She went blank as he pressed her to him and kissed her forehead with wet lips, then released her.

He whispered, "Good to have you back."

She heard herself answer, "Good night."

Then he was gone, but the room was still filled with him. Christine retreated to the small bathroom off of the den, sat on the toilet breathing fast and shallow. She calmed herself down, didn't move from the toilet. *What the fuck?*Why did he make her feel like that? She thought about the way the liquor smelled on his breath; the way his skin smelled; the way his wet lips felt on her skin; the way his arms pinned her to him. She knew what all these things felt like, from when they had lived together. *I can handle it.* She washed and changed into sweat pants and a T-shirt. She took her pills. She stepped out of the disinfected bathroom, back into the dimly lit den, that wore her father's presence like an animal hide. He wasn't there, but he was.

She turned the lights out, lay on the daybed and talked herself through the day and her upcoming life: *I can handle it.* She tried to rest, but couldn't. She tried to sleep, but couldn't close her eyes. She stared into the darkness as the bed frame dug into her, as the night chill seeped into her.

She eventually reached sleep, despite being folded over the metal bar that bisected the mattress, her body twisted. Her dreams ran very deep. When she awoke, she had no memory of the dreams, but there had been something in the black. She woke with her body screwed hard against itself, pain firing from a dozen fists of knotted muscle. *God, this bed sucks.*

"About time sleepy head. I thought I was going to have to go down there and drag you out of bed." Mark had a smile pasted on his face, but she knew he was irritated. He sat at the kitchen table with a half-finished cup of coffee.

Christine's eyes burned as she looked for the kitchen clock, couldn't find it, asked, "What time is it?"

"Already past ten. I've been up since eight, always up at eight on weekends. Already went and got the paper, read it. On my second pot of coffee, want some?"

"Sure. Where's Nancy?"

"Off to church with the baby, praying for my soul and the souls of the damned."

Pain scraped behind Christine's eyes, a red rimmed violence. The room tilted. "I've got to sit down."

"Okay, and as soon as you're ready we can head out...hit a Denny's and grab some breakfast on the way. Sound good?"

Through the jangling in her brain, "Yep."

Trying to keep it together, she shut her eyes, got no relief. *I can do this.* She stopped listening to him—he rambled on. She felt the cool glass of the tabletop with her fingertips. She just wanted to be speeding down the highway home.

***

Christine shifted side to side in the chair in Vrabel's office. She had to talk. She wanted him to hurry up and get started, to stop shuffling papers.

"You spent last weekend at your father's, how'd that go?"

Now that he asked, she didn't know what to say. "I don't..." But she continued, "It was weird, but that's no surprise. It's strange down there. I figure I'll get used to it."

"Weird, how?"

"Well, the houses, his house. All perfect and spotless and everything right..." "Not like Bixby?"

A quick laugh popped out, "Not at all. It's not bad or anything, just kind of intense. Like at the mall, no one seems real. The way they act doesn't make sense."

Vrabel nodded. "I think I know what you mean. How about your father and his family, what was it like to be with them?"

What to say? "Yeah that's really different, too. Pretty boring. A lot of TV. I'll figure it out. It'll be okay."

"They'll need to get used to you, also. Over time you can develop some routines that work for all of you, I would hope. Do you see that happening?"

"Yeah, sure. Except he's got to get me a better place to sleep. He had me on this fold out bed that nearly killed me."

"Did you tell him that?"

Embarrassed, "No. I will though."

"And your feelings about living with your father, did the visit change that?" "No, not really. It'll be okay."

A cloud crossed Christine's mind. She didn't want him asking questions about her feelings. Things had to be alright, so there wasn't anything to talk about. She sat still, waiting for him to continue.

"And how's life at the Murphys? Anna doing any better?"

"She's a little better, but not much. I mean she is *really* messed up." "She's in a living hell, Christine."

"Yeah." She had heard something like that already. She told Vrabel she could tolerate Anna better now that she spent so much time out of the house with Judy and her girls.

"Good. And the nightmares? Any better?"

The nightmares. Pain immediately rimmed Christine's skull. "No, not really." The scraping pain. "They're worse."

"Since last week?" "Yes."

Vrabel observed Christine whiten, her eyes glaze off to a middle distance. "How are they worse?" He asked.

From deep within her. "A lot more painful. Like nails in my head. And flashes that hurt, really bright, kind of like explosions. There's this feeling that I'm gonna get hurt. That others have been hurt somewhere. I haven't seen it, what happened, but I know. There's crying somewhere near. I know it's going to be bad. I can feel it coming, the thing that's hurt everyone. Like the ground is rumbling. A noise that I can't describe, just something I know. And a wind starts blowing so hard. I'm like fighting the wind, trying to understand what's happening. And stuff is blowing into my face, like sand and trash, and it stings and makes it so I can't see, and I don't know what is out there. And sometimes I think I recognize something or someone, but I'm not sure. Maybe it's someone from the juvie hall or the hospital, or maybe even Jimmy, dead. Then see my mom or my dad or other people I know, but everything is swirling around me, so I can't be really sure. And it's so hard to see and hear it makes my head hurt and there's the flashes and shit..."

She stopped, suddenly, rigid. She was there, in her doctor's office. She saw him across the desk.

"Christine."

She had said a lot, she knew.

"Christine, you haven't described your dreams to me before, not like this. Is something different?"

She blinked, "Yeah, I've been remembering some of it lately, when I wake myself up to get away. I just lay there remembering. It really freaks me out." Her voice sounded like a thin reed. "There's more that I don't know. I'm scared."

Vrabel made quick notes in Christine's file. "How long have you been having these nightmares?"

"This bad? Since the weekend. The past few days. Every night. It's hard to sleep."

Vrabel wrote, 'since overnight visit w/ father'. Then he added, 'custody hearing less than 2 wks'. The psychotic ideation concerned him but he already had Christine on a high dosage of Trilafon. He decided to increase the dosage on her sleeping pills; undisturbed sleep might help reduce the symptoms.

"I'm going to give you something that should help you sleep better, help with the nightmares. But you need to let me know if they continue or worsen, immediately. It's important, don't wait until our next session. Call me if they don't get any better in a couple of days, by Saturday."

Christine nodded, grim. *Sleep isn't going to help.* The nightmares would continue until she truly felt safe. She didn't say anything.

***

Saturday morning, the snow fell like a silent curtain. It had fallen heavily throughout the night. Christine awoke to the silence. She lay in her bed with no nightmare memories. She hadn't woken up during the night. Her eyes didn't burn, no pain scraped her skull. Her mind was sweet, thanks to the sleep. Laying there, she remembered she wouldn't be seeing her mother today because of the storm. That was good. She wouldn't be seeing her father. *Just snow*. That was all and that was all she wanted.

The morning proceeded in a lazy way. The quiet of the snowfall blanketed the house. Kathleen made stacks of blueberry buckwheat pancakes and a platter of thick slab bacon. Anna helped measure ingredients and stir them into the batter. Christine noticed the girl's steady hand and focus. She watched Kathleen's gentle guidance. After breakfast, she went out to feed the chickens. Rosemary joined her and they shoveled a path to the henhouse. They worked silently, each listening to the sound of the snow landing across the fields and hills as they cleanly removed a foot of light- weight snow. The steady stream of white fell, no wind. The hills beyond the barn were barely visible, just dark shoulders hunched against the pressing snowfall.

Later in the morning, as Christine sat at the kitchen table working on algebra problems, and Anna practiced her multiplication, a dull roar, like a muffled freight train, startled the girls. They looked to the window.

"That would be the snow sliding off the barn roof." Rosemary explained.

Christine noticed the snowfall was coming down lighter. "It looks like the storm's ending."

Rosemary disagreed. They were expecting another day, day and a half of snowfall - it was a nor'easter. The storm would ease up some as it headed out to sea, where it would pick up moisture then swing back with more heavy snow in a few hours. A huge roar shook the house and a cascade of white snow poured past the window. Anna screamed.

"Makes a lot of noise, doesn't it? It's just the snow coming off the roof." Rosemary reassured the child.

"Want to go out and see?" Christine asked the girl.

Anna looked to Kathleen for permission. She said it would be fine.

The two girls bundled up in snow pants, coats, knit hats, mittens and boots. By the time they had all their gear on, Anna started to get agitated and Christine was glad when they swung out into the dooryard and into the cooling snowfall. They both held their faces up to the sky and felt flakes softly land on their skin. Neither spoke, until Christine suggested they venture over to the side of the house to see what had come off the roof. Christine plowed through the foot deep snow, while Anna followed in her path.

The snow along the side of the house was over four feet deep, and compressed. The girls climbed the pile by the kitchen window and peered in. They watched Kathleen peel apples and Rosemary read a National Geographic at the kitchen table. They smiled at each other, tickled with their spying. Christine slid back down the mound, lay in the snow bank, her body tilted towards the sky. Anna slid down beside her. Comfortable, they nestled into the white fluff.

"I like it here." Christine smiled. "I do, too." Anna responded. "Good."

"If you listen carefully, you can hear the snow falling on the trees up in the hills." The gentlest patter reached Christine all the way from the forest. She loved those hills.

Anna whispered. "I can hear it."

Christine believed her. "That's good."

They lay there listening for quite a while then went in, calm.

CHAPTER 36

After stomping the snow off their boots, Christine and Rosemary entered the cabin through the back door, into the kitchen and the sweet smell of pork ribs and sauerkraut cooking in the oven. Anna was sitting at the table waiting for them.

Christine slipped her boots off and greeted her. "Hey, sport." Anna smiled back.

Christine knew she would be waiting. Rosemary had told her Anna had been asking for her all day. Halfway through the afternoon, Rosemary had called Christine at Judy's and asked if she could pick her up early. Christine understood. During the weekend storm, she and Anna had spent hours together outside, quietly laying in snow banks watching the weather, or building snow people while describing the lives of the figures they created.

During the drive home Christine had agreed she would spend only four days a week at the potter's, four hours a day. It would be a great help, especially for Kathleen, if she spent more time at the Murphys'. She didn't hesitate to say yes to Rosemary's request.

Anna headed for Christine. "Wanna go out and see my snow fort?" It was just after four o'clock, with only an hour of daylight left. "Sure."

The two girls were putting on their winter gear, when the phone rang. Rosemary answered. "Why hello Lynne, yes, she's right here."

Christine cautiously took the receiver. It was a strange time for her mother to call. "Hi mom, what's up?"

"Chris, honey, I had to reach you right away. I just got off the phone with personnel—they can move me to first shift next week, in the intensive care unit! How's that for fantastic news?"

Fantastic? How? Flatly, "That's great, mom."

Lynne expected more excitement from her daughter: Their problems were over now, the path clear for her to come home. *She understands that, doesn't she?* Then fiercely clear: *she's decided to go with her father!* Lynne's throat tightened. "This means you can come home now."

"I don't know, mom. I don't know what it means." Christine's head pounded. *Everything's supposed to be different now?* "I'm meeting with my lawyer tomorrow to get ready for this hearing coming up, and I'll tell her."

Her words slapped Lynne. "Sure. Do that. I have to call my lawyer, too, tell him the news." She had to hang up. "I love you...I'll try to see you before the hearing."

A week away. Christine said nothing. They hung up.

***

Sitting in the anteroom of some law firm, in some town halfway between Bixby and Branford, Rosemary and Christine waited for attorney Simmons. She was running twenty minutes late. While Rosemary flipped through a copy of *Vermont Life*, Christine sat with her hands clasped on her lap. She didn't want to be there. It was Wednesday, her day to see Dr. Vrabel. She needed to see him badly. She needed help sorting this mess out, where she should live and all that. But this was the only time her lawyer could meet with her to prepare for the hearing, to figure out what she would say. She clasped her hands, harder.

Simmons charged into the room, struggling out of her raincoat as she said. "Terrible weather huh? Sorry I'm late."

The receptionist led the three women down the hall to a conference room. When they were seated, Simmons began. "Nice of these folks to let us meet here. Friend of mine from law school." She flipped open her notebook. "So Christine, it's been awhile, how are you?"

"Okay, I guess."

"I had a chance to talk with Dr. Vrabel earlier today. He says you've been having a rough time lately..."

"I'm doing better." "The nightmares?" "They're better." "The meds help?" "Yeah I guess so."

Christine liked that her lawyer wasn't wasting time.

"He said you recently spent the weekend with your father, how was that?"

The more she thought about the weekend, the stranger it felt, but she didn't want to get into that. "Okay."

"Yeah? Good. In his evaluation, Dr. Vrabel wrote that you want the court to consider your father as a placement option." Simmons opened the file, flipped some pages, stopped. Christine saw the open page, noticed some text underlined in red pencil.

"He said you feel placement with your father can provide you with some stability in your life." She looked up at Christine. "That sound right? The doctor get it right?"

I don't know, yeah I said that. "Maybe."

"Maybe we need to talk about what you want. What you're going to tell the judge you want. Make sure the judge understands."

"Okay."

"You want things to be certain, where you're placed and all, and that makes a lot of sense. In a way we all want things to be certain, so you're no different than the rest of us."

Christine's nerves grated. "Yeah, well the rest of you haven't been thrown in juvie for something you didn't do...and get screwed for something you didn't do...and lose your mind. And live with all kinds of freaking nightmares, have you? I'm trying not to lose it, understand? I'm scared shitless they're going to send me someplace that will really mess me up. So when he says I want some stability, it means I can't wipe out again. That can't happen. That's what I want. I have to be safe." Christine glared at Simmons.

Simmons chose her words carefully. "I understand it's been very hard for you, what you've been through. It makes sense what you're saying, why you want to be protected from more harm..."

Christine interrupted, "Like that drug report...it says I should be going off to some treatment center. But I haven't touched anything since I was arrested. I don't care if I ever touch drugs again. But that's not the way *they* see it, and now they're going to throw me in with a bunch of losers, and that would suck..."

The lawyer smoothed the pages on her notepad. "I don't think that will happen. You've been clean for quite a while. You've been doing really well since moving in with the Murphys." She gave Rosemary a nod. "You have a lot going for you. There are a lot of good reasons to expect you'll stay clean. We'll tell the judge that. I think he can appreciate how well you've been doing. Considering how serious things were, he might want some supervision in place, maybe some N.A., but I seriously doubt he'll be sending you for treatment. Okay?"

"Yeah." Christine unclenched her fists, saw the marks her fingernails left in her palms. She believed her lawyer.

Simmons continued. "And Stonebridge...I know something happened to you there. I don't know what exactly, but from talking to Dr. Vrabel, it's clear you can't go back. And there's no reason you should. Your mother's lawyer, along with Dr. Vrabel and I, will fight tooth and nail to keep you from being sent back. You're not the scary threat they locked up six months ago. We'll make sure the judge sees you as the accomplished, kind, young woman you really are. He'll have no reason to return you to Stonebridge."

"Yeah, but the Murphys' is temporary. They're going to send me someplace soon, probably someplace lousy. If I go to my father's, I don't have to worry about any of that."

Simmons allowed a moment, "Can I ask you a question? I read Doctor Vrabel's report. I've spoken with him, and it seems like your mother has been an important part of your recovery. If you felt fairly certain you could return and stay with your mother, would you want that?"

Christine felt a frozen bolt in her gut. "How could I be sure?"

"Well, your mother has always done a good job of providing for you and her family, and since your arrest, she has worked really hard in therapy and in a family support group to understand the challenges she'd faced. Ms. Howe, her therapist, and Ms. Peck, the woman who runs the support group, both have wonderful things to say about your mother. Things the judge should hear. Your mother's come a long way since last summer. Now that she got on first shift, she'll be home for you and your brother and sister, so that should take care of SRS's concerns about supervision. But most of all, she's been by your side through everything, supporting you. That is why attorney Fitzgerald and I believe we can convince the judge it would be best for you if you were allowed to return to her. That is, if that's what you want."

Christine had silently listened. Warm tears rolled down her cheeks by the time Simmons finished. Rosemary reached for Christine's hand. Crumbling inside, she whispered, "That's what I want." *I want to go home!*

"Then let's get ready for Monday.

***

Several hours later, as soon as she got back to the Murphys', Christine called her mother. "I told my lawyer I want to come home, mom." They laughed and cried and whooped: she was going home! It felt right and strong and clear.

Just after she hung up with her mother, the phone rang. "Hello?"

"Hey honey, looking forward to our visit this weekend? Nancy and I can't wait to see you again."

Mark's words rattled like dry bones and a dark fear rose in Christine. She pushed through. "I won't be coming down, dad. I can't."

Agitated, "Why not?" He immediately lightened his tone. "It doesn't matter, we'll have all the time we want after Monday, anyway. Are you spending Saturday with your mother?"

She said clearly what she had to. "I've thought about it a lot, dad, and I think it would be best if I went to live with mom...I'm going to ask the judge to let me go home." Her words flew from her, unable to be retrieved. She didn't breathe.

Hard edged, "Christine, I won't let you make that mistake."

She heard no love in his warning. He wasn't promising her protection; he was forbidding her to refuse his protection.

"You'll be better off with me."

She heard no love in his offer. He wasn't sending her comfort; he was telling her he was better than her mother. Light headed and with quiet firmness, she answered him. "I don't think so."

"The judge will think so on Monday." He threatened.

Christine wouldn't let him hurt her, she hung up.

SECTION 3

CHAPTER 37

"Ah, jeez." Fitzgerald flopped into the swivel chair at his desk, leaned back, and opened a can of Coke he had purchased on his way back from court. "Long day." He gulped down some of the soda.

"No kidding." Simmons slouched in the chair across from him, popped open her can of Diet Coke.

They had been in court all afternoon together, along with most of the defense attorneys and prosecutors in the county for Thursday afternoon criminal court calendar call, sorting out before the judge which cases on the docket were to be pleaded out and which were going to trial. As they waited their turn, Fitzgerald had shared with Simmons the news that Lynne had landed a first shift position at the hospital. Simmons had heard the news, having met with Christine the previous day. She then updated Fitzgerald that Christine clearly wanted to return to her mother, which he already knew from his phone conversation with Lynne that morning.

"So what do you think? I think we've got a pretty good case." He asked.

Simmons liked that about Emmett Fitzgerald, always upbeat. Unlike him, she was a worrier. They worked well together. She replied, "Yeah, pretty good. It's no cakewalk, though. I'm not sure what Art is going to make of our clients."

Judge Arthur Greenleaf was scheduled to preside over Christine's Disposition Hearing, and he was hard core old school. He didn't know the difference between an ounce of cocaine and an ounce of marijuana, and it didn't matter because all those people were degenerates in his opinion, with their dirty babies and their rusty cars and their foul mouths. Also, he had just recently been appointed to CHINS cases because of the severe backlog of juvenile cases. Attorneys who had appeared in these cases before him, reported he was clueless and very abrasive.

Fitzgerald smiled. "No problem. I think Lynne and Christine will come off well."

Simmons smiled back ironically, "Sure, considering we have a failed single mother, her sexually active seventeen year old runaway, drug abusing daughter. And considering that we're up against Christine's decent god-fearing father, the god-fearing substance abuse evaluator, and the State itself, which is charged with protecting the fine people of Vermont from the likes of our clients...piece of cake."

Fitzgerald sipped on his Coke. "I spoke to LaValley this morning, brought her up to speed about the shift change, and Chris's wanting to return to Lynne. She wasn't impressed. Still thinks dad's the way to go. She's convinced he's the best bet for keeping Christine on the straight and narrow. Very impressed with dad's home evaluation, impressed with his line of crap about being the guardian of his daughter's virtue and all that." He sat back, shut his eyes, spoke more slowly. "I asked her what she thought about protective supervision. Give custody back to mom, but SRS can yank Christine for any violations. Not only drugs, but delinquency, truancy...whatever. She's not interested, said it's too risky. Thinks mom's home situation is too dicey. She said it would be wrong to set Chris up, have things fall apart, then yank her. Too much damage. So, I asked have you read Vrabel's evaluation, his notes? Have you even talked to Christine? I said she needs to go home, that it's in her best interests. I told her it's Chris's mental health issues we need to focus on. She didn't get it, it was like I was talking to a rock. With her, it's all about the drugs." Reading Simmons' reaction as he spoke, "Maybe if you talk to her tomorrow, really lean on her. I think your client could nosedive if we don't get her home."

Simmons agreed. "I got through to Vrabel during the afternoon recess. I forgot to tell you. Chris had her session with him today. He said she was great, the best he'd seen her in a while. Said she was very upbeat about her decision to return home, very solid."

"Alright, let LaValley know that. Tell her to talk to Vrabel if she doesn't believe you. And seriously pitch protective supervision." Fitzgerald shifted in his chair. "So, who does the State have for witnesses?" He opened the file on his desk, scanned a sheet, attached to the inside front cover: "LaValley, Benson and his substance abuse report, and some sheriff up in Burlington who claims Christine tried to escape back when she was arrested."

Simmons rubbed the bridge of her nose. "The sheriff, he could hurt us. Paint Chris as a lunatic. The only one who can rebut his story is Chris, but I don't know if we want to get into that, have Art ending up with an earful of craziness."

"You're right." Fitzgerald groaned. "But we don't want to make a big deal trying to keep it out – Art will let it in anyway. We've just got to take the sheriff's story apart, cross examine the hell out of him. Shouldn't be too hard, the guy probably can't remember half of what happened. Get him to say 'I don't know, I don't remember' until he's useless. You want to handle that?"

"Sure."

"LaValley, we pretty much know what she's going to say. Lukewarm rehash of the stuff in her files: mother's a risk, father's a savior. Why don't you cross exam her, too. Make sure you go after her about protective supervision. Use her to paint a clear picture for Art of all the safeguards that can be put into place like the conditions that can be imposed on Chris and Lynne, how easy it would be to yank Chris if they don't comply." Fitzgerald folded his arms behind his head. "Make him understand it's like probation. Screw up and you're back in lockup. He'll understand that." Simmons nodded. Fitzgerald continued. "Get him thinking that the State's coming down hard on Chris with protective supervision. Really pump up the requirements and the extensive oversight. Piss tests at the cop station, N.A. attendance sheets, all that. Fill his head with it. It's what he's going to want to hear."

"We better prepare our clients to hear that. I'll go over protective supervision again with Chris, make sure she gets it. She seemed okay with it when we talked about Tuesday. I told her that's what she's got to do, if she wants to go home."

Fitzgerald said he'd go over it with Lynne again, also.

The two lawyers agreed LaValley's testimony, concerning the drug screening and treatment components of protective supervision, should take some of the bite out of Benson's testimony on his drug and alcohol evaluation. They decided that they wouldn't attack his methods or conclusions directly, but instead, back him into validating protective supervision as an adequate means of addressing Christine's substance abuse issues as he saw them. Simmons said she'd get Benson to admit that Christine's interests and behavior at the Murphys were consistent with those of a person with a minimal risk of substance abuse.

Fitzgerald stood, walked over to his bookshelf, took a baseball from one of the shelves and absent mindedly rubbed it. "Then I put on Lynne's case: her supervisor from work, Miranda Howe...her therapist, Sally Peck from the parent support group and finally, Lynne. The supervisor can speak to Lynne's employment history: reliable, responsible, that sort of thing. Miranda should present well. She's done a great job documenting Lynne's progress in therapy. I met with her yesterday and she gave me Lynne's information in basic English. She's testified in these kinds of cases a number of times. I think she can get our point across to Art."

"So what will you have her say?" Simmons asked.

"How rough it was for Lynne when Chris was arrested and when she was sick at the State Hospital. How dedicated she was to her daughter's recovery. What steps she took to be the parent that Chris needed, understanding what she needed."

Simmons scowled, "Blah, blah, blah. Art isn't going to want to hear that. Lynne screwed up. He's going to want to hear why she screwed up, and why she won't screw up again. End of story."

"You're right. I'll have her come right out and say Lynne was wrong. Then get into why she screwed up? Miranda can say it was because Lynne was afraid that Chris would take off anyway. That way she kept in contact. The lesser of two evils. Why won't she screw up again? That's when she can get into the therapy stuff. I'll call her tomorrow, run it by her."

"Nothing about the father?" Simmons asked pointedly.

"No, it's not worth it. Miranda starts talking about Lynne's issues with the father and we could end up getting into the saga of their marriage. Art will likely side with the father's version of things and award him the trophy daughter."

Simmons disagreed, "I don't see how you can get into Lynne becoming a better parent without getting into how she has recovered from the father."

"Yeah, I don't want to get into her recovery story. I think it will work against us, Art won't like it."

Simmons shook her head.

"Next I'll put on the support group facilitator, Sally Peck. Basic stuff: Lynne's regular attendance, participation, et cetera. A quick description of the issues they addressed in the group. Nothing too deep, so we don't lose Art with too much psych talk after Miranda's testimony. I spoke with Sally last week. She presents well, lots of experience running these groups. I've seen her testify in a couple cases. I definitely trust her. Which brings us to Lynne."

"So can she do it? Can she say 'I messed up, I'm not going to mess up again. And this is why' So that Art believes her?"

"I'll firm up the testimony with Lynne tomorrow. She has to sell herself, convince Art that she's safe. She needs to understand that." Fitzgerald hesitated, "She needs to believe it herself."

Simmons wondered if Fitzgerald could get his client where she needed to be. She moved on. "So the father's case, who's he putting on?"

"Blum listed the social worker, the one who did the home inspection. And of course, the new wife."

"The home evaluator? For Christ's sake, those reports are usually stipulated!"

"Blum maximizing impact."

"So we tell Art we stipulate." Simmons responded

Fitzgerald shrugged. "He'll let her testify. Doesn't matter, she's not going to hurt us. I'll do the cross examination on her." He picked up the baseball. "Now, the wife, she could be interesting. She may be the joker in the deck, seeing how the father is such an SOB. Maybe she'll surprise all of us and give us a healthy serving of what he's really like. How about you handle the cross, see if you can get a sisterhood thing going."

Simmons smiled. "Sure. Which brings us to dad."

"Righteous dad. The deal with dad is to crack his mask, let Art see what he's really all about." Rubbing the baseball, "I'll handle his cross."

Simmons knew Fitzgerald could worm under a witness's skin without offending the court. Still, she cautioned, "Don't get too heavy, we don't want to lose Art because you mug the guy in broad daylight."

"Not to worry." Fitzgerald returned to his chair. "Then it's Christine's show. What have you got?"

"I've got both of the Murphy sisters, the potter, Vrabel, then Christine."

"*Both* sisters?"

Simmons wiped a bead of condensation off the soda can. "Well, yeah. I know I can get all of the information out through Rosemary, but she's a bit rough. Art might have trouble hearing what she has to say if she shows up wearing flannel. Kathleen's softer. I'll have her testify how Chris contributes to the household, cooks, does chores. And how she's cared for the other foster children too. Then Rosemary can talk about Chris's academics: her projects, the courses she's taking. That she's on track with her requirements to graduate. I think it'll work out. Humanize her after Art's heard all the bad news about her."

Fitzgerald agreed. "Didn't the sisters observe Chris nosedive after visits with her father? Are they going to testify to that?"

"I plan on having Kathleen handle it."

"We handle that piece right, it could make a big difference. Can she deliver?" Fitzgerald asked.

"I think so. She's clear, and her style will allow for Art to hear her." "She going to get into details?"

"She has to, if she's going to have the impact we need." Simmons answered.

Fitzgerald shut his eyes, leaned back. "I think you're right. And Blum will look like a monster, if he tries to beat her up. I'm thinking though, maybe have Vrabel follow the sisters, follow up on the father's effect on Chris. The testimonies supporting each other, a combined impact."

Simmons nodded. "And besides, if the doc crashes and burns we have the happy potter story to pull out of the ashes."

Both attorneys had seen what Blum could do to a psychiatrist.

Fitzgerald asked, "Is the good doctor going to score for us?"

Simmons thought so, although she knew Vrabel could be pretty heavy with the psycho-babble. Fitzgerald wanted to know if Vrabel could deliver the basic message that Christine was better and why she was better. And that she likely would not screw up if she went back to her mother. "Can you get that out of him, so that Art will believe it? He's the one witness who can speak directly to what Chris's best interests are. He's the key to the case."

"I'll call him tomorrow, go over his testimony again." Simmons noted.

"What about the potter?" Fitzgerald asked.

"Yeah, Judy Repchuk. It's pretty basic, uncomplicated. She teaches Chris pottery, Chris watches her girls. She can testify that Chris is dedicated, talented and doing a great job."

Fitzgerald finished his Coke. "Finally...there's Christine. Do we want her to testify?"

"She really wants to." Simmons responded.

"It's a big risk, you know. Art won't be interested in hearing what she wants. If she comes off with any attitude whatsoever, the case goes right down the tubes."

Simmons advocated. "But he'll want to hear from her that she's committed to living more responsibly. Art might think we're hiding something if she doesn't step up. If he suspects this, he'll disregard our entire case."

Fitzgerald didn't respond.

Simmons pushed "And she can sell herself better than any of the other witnesses."

"You're probably right. So long as she keeps it straight, no drama."

"She's got her story straight. I think she'll stay on target." Simmons assured.

"She's not going to say anything about who she wants to live with, or not live with, is she? Definite disaster. Art will hate hearing a kid pick one parent over another, especially over righteous dad. We can work her preference into the narrative on the sly—references to things that the mother did for her, some problems she's had with her father. Keep it subtle, though. We want Art to reach his own conclusions." Simmons made a note to follow through on Fitzgerald's suggestion.

Fitzgerald continued, "What about protective supervision? Can we get Chris to say she can live with all the requirements and conditions? Get into some specifics without sounding too scripted?"

Simmons said she'd work that up.

"Bingo, we close out the hearing on that note and we should be in good shape. But she's got to nail it. Unequivocally. Otherwise, forget it"

Simmons nodded. "We'll nail it."

Fitzgerald looked at the clock, Simmons looked at her watch. They both had the same thought: *Six o'clock, Thursday*. They had a hell of a lot of work ahead of them for Monday's hearing.

Both lawyers looked at each other with the same thought: they had a lot of work ahead of them before Monday's hearing.

***

Thursday evening, six o'clock, Mark heard the sounds of people leaving the office, as he waited for Blum to speak.

"Mr. Bancroft, because of the nature of this case I will be handling the hearing personally. Attorney Knowles will assist me. Your ex-wife doesn't have a case, but it will take a certain level of skill to make the judge understand that. It is clear from the drug and alcohol assessment that your daughter has ongoing substance abuse issues, for which you are most suited to help her address. I will see that this is established at the hearing."

Mark believed Blum.

"Of course, the judge needs to know you will make it clear to your daughter, when she lives with you, that you will report her to SRS if she should use drugs. And that you will make it clear to her that the State would then remove her from your home, and most likely place her in a drug rehabilitation center or a juvenile detention center."

Of course, "I will."

"And the judge needs to know that you will report your daughter to SRS if she does not fully participate in any recommended treatment program. Or if she engages in any illegal or delinquent activity."

Mark understood, he nodded.

"Good. This judge will appreciate your firm resolve." Blum looked at some papers as he removed them from a file. "Now, this matter of your daughter preferring her mother over you, despite the mother's failure; it's clear that the mother, SRS, and the foster parents, all actively prevented you from interacting with Christine. In addition, her psychiatrist clearly demonstrates a bias against you when treating your daughter. In fact his bias, and Christine's deprivation of meaningful contact with you, has exacerbated her psychological afflictions. It's right there in the doctor's notes. So, I want you to prepare a schedule of instances in which the mother, the SRS worker, and the foster parents prevented, impeded, interfered with, or impacted your relationship with Christine." Mark nodded. "I want as much detail as possible. Dates, descriptions, quotes if possible. In writing. To me, by tomorrow. Memorize that information and be prepared to testify about it on Monday."

Mark nodded. *Yes.*

Blum fixed his client with a firm gaze. "The judge must understand from your testimony how those people poisoned your relationship with your daughter. And that, if she is not placed with you, she will be deprived of your vital love and protection. Her life to date is proof of the harm that has been caused by the limits placed on your access to her. Do you understand? Attorney Knowles will prepare you for your testimony, tomorrow." He closed Mark's file. They were done.

Mark stood up. He felt a raw thrill, knowing Blum would control the hearing. "Thank you."

CHAPTER 38

Sunday night. There was only Christine and the night. No lights, no movement, the household was asleep. She lay awake, exhausted. She had worked her body hard all weekend: hiked deep into the forest to the ridge, then miles along the mountain ridgeline; split and stacked two cords of firewood; thrown dozens of pots for hours at Judy's; carved out paths in the snow with Anna, and sculpted bird figurines in the evening. But her mind couldn't rest. She hadn't been able to sleep the night before, and when she had slept she had no rest. The nightmares she couldn't remember wasted her. Earlier that night, after Anna had been put to bed, Rosemary had given Christine an extra half of a sleeping pill, telling her she needed her sleep.

Her mother had called sometime after ten o'clock, a wreck about the hearing. She had called to assure Christine, to have Christine assure her, that everything would work out fine tomorrow. They had worried over the threads of their testimony. They had practiced the words and messages they must deliver in a few hours, and had tried to fend off their dread. Christine tried to comfort her mother. She had to hang up eventually.

Laying in her still bed, Christine thought: *We can win. Our lawyers say we can win. I can go home if we convince the judge that I'll behave, if we convince him that mom will make sure I behave. I get to go home if I agree to piss in a cup whenever they want me to. If I agree to go to meetings and talk about being a druggie, about whatever fucked up things they want me to talk about. I can do that. I can do whatever they want. And the lawyer says not to make a big deal about how much I miss my mother. And don't say anything about how I can't stand my father. Sure, okay. Whatever she wants me to say. Fuck them, I'll do whatever I've got to because...*

Her eyes grew heavy. Images swarmed, partial thoughts: *Water sheen on cinder block, steam, shower heads, rancid hair, Minard, drowning, Paul leering circling marking tasting her, cock, scent, jagged pieces drifting in the fog, in the soup, the pills, the paper cups, dead eyes wild eyes, restrained, leather canvas sheets, grates, steel bars, cinder block, cops, gun barrel fucking coke, crystal, tongue taste flame spoon, Jimmy's arm, fucking needles, vein, leering, whacked, white walls white floors the dead the dying, wife, baby, him, him in the thick air filling her, devouring her.* Barely conscious: *never again!* She slipped beneath the black waves. But her father remained, threatening nightmares she prayed with her last light to forget.

***

Lynne lay wide awake. Mark slept.

CHAPTER 39

In the faint pink light of dawn, Christine stood naked before the mirror on her dresser and put on the red bead necklace her mother had given her, brilliant against her clear white skin. The beads' power lifted her, they would protect her, She then dressed in her nicest blouse and her best jeans.

***

Where is he? Christine and Lynne, entered the courtroom together with their lawyers, scanned for Mark: he wasn't there. The two separated with a brief hug and sat at their respective tables. They waited, both shaking with nerves.

Mark finally arrived with his lawyer and his wife, everyone in crisp new clothes. He walked to his table without meeting the eyes of either Lynne or Christine. He took his seat and positioned himself so he could glare at Lynne when the opportunity presented itself.

"All rise. Now commencing the Disposition Hearing in the matter of In re C.B., docket number 782-87, the Honorable Arthur Greenleaf presiding."

The judge requested the parties state their positions relative to the permanent disposition of the juvenile, Christine Bancroft.

Derosia, for the State: "The Commissioner's position is that the juvenile remain in SRS custody at this time, and specifically rejects the mother's last minute request that the Commissioner concede custody to her, in exchange for retaining protective supervision over the juvenile."

Blum: "The father agrees that SRS should retain custody of Christine, and he would gratefully accept placement of Christine, during which time, he will prepare to take legal custody of his daughter. The father has no knowledge of the protective supervision offer from the mother, but joins with the State in rejecting it as wholly unsuitable."

Lynne and Christine each desperately wanted to ask their lawyers what Blum meant when he said that Mark 'will prepare to take legal custody' of Christine.

Fitzgerald: "The mother respectfully submits that the best interests of Christine require that she be returned to the custody of her mother, and if there are any doubts that the return to her mother is in Christine's best interest, the mother, at this time, offers that SRS retain protective supervision over Christine, to ensure her wellbeing."

Simmons: "Christine joins with her mother, undeniably convinced it would be best if she were allowed to return to her mother's custody and agrees to remain under SRS's protective supervision for as long as is deemed necessary."

Judge Greenleaf nodded; what was all this talk about 'protective supervision'? They'd have to explain that to his satisfaction. And from what he had read in the case file, the mother and daughter had a lot of explaining to do.

The State called its first witness, Rose LaValley. Although she had testified dozens of times in these hearings, she was nerved up. She knew some lawyer was going to try to trick her and she usually ended up saying things she didn't mean to. Her safest course was to stay close to the text of the court filings and answer the questions as simply as possible.

Derosia began the direct examination and LaValley mechanically addressed his questions about how Christine had been taken into State's custody; the details of her arrest and purported escape attempt; and her placements while in State's custody, at Stonebridge, Waterbury State Hospital, and the Murphys'. When asked whether SRS sought to retain custody of Christine at this time,

LaValley answered, "Only for so long as it takes Mr. Bancroft to sort out his custody rights."

"Why Mr. Bancroft? Why not agree to Christine's immediate release to her mother?" Derosia asked.

LaValley recited the answer she had practiced with the lawyer. "Mr. Bancroft, Christine's father, has a very stable living situation. He has a wife who is a stay at home mother. He is meaningfully employed as an engineer. His home is well kept and orderly. But most important, he has professed a clear commitment to getting Christine the help she needs in battling her addiction to cocaine and other drugs, and in overcoming her self - destructive tendencies. The mother, on the other hand, is a single working woman with two other adolescent children, living with her. Her family routines are haphazard at best, bordering on the chaotic. And most importantly, she has not demonstrated a commitment to Christine's treatment for drug dependency."

Christine immediately, *No way. She's kidding, right?* Lynne burned angry. Fitzgerald and Simmons scribbled notes. Mark and Blum sat at their table, looking satisfied. They all watched LaValley's testimony reel out. All the attorneys surreptitiously kept an eye on the judge who nodded and seemingly accepted the caseworker's account.

Derosia continued, "Thank you, Ms. LaValley. Now there has been some talk about Christine returning home, with custody returning to her mother, yet SRS retaining protective supervision. Could you tell the court about that?"

This was the part that made LaValley nervous. "Sure. Just last week, attorney Fitzgerald called me and suggested that, in exchange for SRS allowing the mother to take custody of Christine, they would be open to SRS retaining protective supervision over her. Following this, on Friday, attorney Simmons called and made the same offer. Well, I didn't think it was such a good idea, and when I told my supervisor about the offer she agreed that I should reject it."

"And why is that?" Derosia asked. "Why did you and your supervisor reject the mother's offer?"

LaValley leaned into the microphone, "Well, like I said before, the mother doesn't seem capable of handling Christine. So, what's the point of having Christine go home, when we would have to watch her anyway? I mean, why not just have her go to her father's, where we can be much more confident that she would be safe."

Judge Greenleaf interrupted. "Explain to me what this 'protective supervision' is?"

LaValley squirmed. "Protective supervision is when a child goes home, the parent has custody, but SRS keeps an eye on the household to make sure things are safe."

The judge asked no additional questions. The State's attorney had no more questions.

Fitzgerald stood. "Ms. LaValley, has Christine's mother, Lynne, told you about the support services she has been engaged in order to assist her in addressing Christine's issues?"

"I'm not sure what you're asking me." LaValley responded.

Fitzgerald let her think for a moment. "Has Lynne told you that she has been participating in a parent support group?"

"Yes."

"How long has she been participating in that group?" Reddening, "I'm not sure."

"Have you spoken to the group leader, Sally Peck, or Lynne, about the work they do in that group?" Fitzgerald's voice cut clear.

"A little, with Lynne."

"What is your understanding of the work Lynne has been doing in that group?"

LaValley straightened up, "She's been learning about other parents' experiences dealing with disturbed teenagers, sharing her experiences of dealing with Christine."

"Has this group therapy helped Lynne deal with Christine's issues?" "Sure."

"What are Christine's issues, in your opinion?"

Cautiously, "I'm concerned about the substance abuse history. Her self-esteem issues. Peer delinquency. Safety and impulse control issues. Judgment concerns."

Fitzgerald hardened his tone. "Mr. Bancroft hasn't engaged in any family counseling to assist him with dealing with Christine's issues, has he?"

Surprised by the question, "No he hasn't. But he's clearly devoted to Christine."

"Wouldn't it be in Christine's best interests, "Fitzgerald continued, "which by the way is the legal standard that must be met in these deliberations, that the parent who has custody of a child be prepared to deal with that child's psychological and mental health issues?"

"Yes, of course."

Fitzgerald nodded, "And have you spoken to Lynne's individual therapist, Miranda Howe, about the progress Lynne has made in therapy this past year?"

She had, once.

"Did Ms. Howe inform you that Lynne has been addressing parenting issues related to Christine?"

"I think so." LaValley didn't know where this was going.

"Do you know Lynne's plans for continued therapy with Ms. Howe?" "She's told me that she plans to continue in therapy."

"Would you agree that Lynne is a more effective parent than she was last July, when Christine was taken into custody?"

She had to say, "Probably, yes."

Fitzgerald nodded, looked at his notes on the table, looked up and asked, "From the information that you've received from Dr. Vrabel, can you conclude that Christine's mental health has markedly improved these past few months?"

"I guess."

"And that Lynne's care and involvement has assisted Christine in her recovery?" LaValley resisted, "That's what the doctor thinks, I wouldn't know about that."

Fitzgerald sharpened his tone, "Well, have you taken the doctor's opinion into consideration when assessing what would be in Christine's best interests?"

Resisting, "Not really. I see the issue clearly that Christine is an untreated substance abuser, and until that issue is resolved, there's nothing much to talk about." LaValley heaved a breath.

"So you're saying that Lynne's critical involvement in Christine's mental and psychological healing to date, has no bearing on Christine's future ability to address her substance abuse issue?"

"I don't know, I think so. I'm not sure I understand the question."

Fitzgerald looked over at the judge, then back at LaValley. More slowly, "Are you saying that Lynne's involvement in Christine's mental health recovery this past year won't help Christine recover from any drug abuse problems she may have?"

She hated this, "I don't know, it's hard to say."

Fitzgerald shook his head, signaling that the woman's opinion was worth nothing.

He continued. "Turning to the matter of protective supervision, you didn't describe the entire offer in your previous testimony, did you?"

"Well, I thought I did."

"Weren't you asked to consider a protective supervision arrangement, whereby Christine would be required to report regularly—daily, weekly—as SRS sees fit, at the Branford police station or other appropriate facility, to submit a sample of her urine, which would be analyzed, at her mother's expense, for the presence of alcohol and controlled substances, and that if she tested positive or did not meet her reporting requirements, SRS would be able to take Christine back into its custody?"

She hated this, "Yes."

"And that way you would know immediately if Christine has relapsed, and you could step in and protect her by removing her from her mother's care."

"Yes."

"It's pretty much like an adult being on probation?"

"Yes, I guess so."

"And if Christine were taken back into SRS custody, what would happen to her? Where would she be placed at that time?"

LaValley stammered, "I don't know. Most likely a rehab center, if available."

Fitzgerald leaned slightly over the table. "Describe the drug treatment or counseling that Christine has received during the seven months that she has been in SRS custody."

Burning, "There hasn't been any."

Fitzgerald raised his voice, sliced the air with the side of his hand, "Christine has been in state's custody for seven months, you have had complete control and custody over her that entire time, but you have not arranged any treatment services for her, despite your huge concern about her drug dependency? Is that correct?"

"Yes, I mean no." LaValley faltered. "No, she hasn't received services. It hasn't been that long since she's been out of the hospital..."

Harshly, "About four months?"

She nodded, head down. "Yes."

Fitzgerald shook his head, "Christine has been drug free since the day of her arrest..."

"As far as we know."

"You have no information or reason to think otherwise, do you?" She didn't.

"And her psychiatrist believes that she is a low risk to relapse?" Burning, "That's what he says in his evaluation."

"And that Christine, through protective supervision, would agree to reporting requirements and treatment requirements to prove she can maintain her commitment to remain drug free?"

Crumbling, "That's what her lawyer tells me."

"You haven't spoken to Christine about her commitment to living drug free?" "No, I haven't."

Fitzgerald laced his tone with acid, "Tell me Ms. LaValley, how many times have you spoken with Christine to discuss the issues she has been facing in her life?"

Burning, "I couldn't say, I'd have to look that up."

Fitzgerald had LaValley's case notes marked as Mother's Exhibit #1, handed them to her, "Take your time."

She fumbled through the bulging folder. After a couple long minutes, she looked up, red faced, "Two, maybe three times."

"The dates?"

"I don't know."

"How many times in the past month?" Burning, "None."

Fitzgerald glared at the woman on the stand. "Nothing further, your honor."

Blum slowly rose to begin his cross examination. With mild voice, "Miss LaValley, I have just a couple questions. You say that Christine came into SRS custody after she was arrested in a drug raid of the apartment where she was living, in Burlington; was she criminally charged relating to that raid?"

LaValley relaxed a little, "No sir, she wasn't."

"However, was any contraband found in her possession at the time of that raid?"

"Yes there was a quantity of cocaine in her handbag when she was arrested."

"And you testified that a quantity of cocaine was found in the apartment. Do you know how much?" Blum asked.

"No, I don't. It was a felony amount."

"Where did you get the information about the quantity of cocaine in Christine's apartment?"

More confident, "From the affidavit charging Mr. James Connell, Christine's boyfriend. I read it as part of this case."

"And do you know if Christine's boyfriend, Mr. Connell, was charged with a criminal offense?"

LaValley leaned towards the microphone, "Oh, yes. Felony possession of cocaine, distribution of cocaine, and manslaughter."

Blum arched his eyebrows, raised his voice, "Manslaughter?"

"Yes, there was a man that Connell sold cocaine to. He overdosed."

"This was in the police affidavit?" Blum inquired.

"Yes."

Gently, "And do you know what has become of Mr. Connell."

Leaning towards the microphone, "Committed suicide in jail a few days after his arrest."

Judge Greenleaf peered at Christine. Christine avoided his condemning eyes.

Lynne cringed at the judge's lashing countenance.

Blum continued, "Miss LaValley, you testified that attorneys Fitzgerald and Simmons approached you last week with this idea about protective supervision just days before this hearing? Did that seem a bit desperate to you, being approached at such a late date?"

Fitzgerald, angry, "Objection." "Sustained."

"Miss LaValley, by your testimony at least two young men are dead as a result of the cocaine enterprise that was conducted in the dwelling place where Christine resided. If she were under protective supervision, even with the reporting requirements proposed by her attorney, could SRS stop Christine from abandoning her abstinence and injecting a fatal dose of cocaine?"

"No."

"Exactly. Thank you. Your Honor, I have nothing further." Blum took his seat with a

Smug expression.

Simmons and Fitzgerald watched Greenleaf. He seemed riveted by the testimony.

Christine saw what her lawyer saw: *Shit.* Mark was pleased with the way Blum had nailed it. Lynne was torn open, thinking about Christine dead from an overdose.

Simmons rose to cross examine, "Ms. LaValley, Christine is currently in SRS custody. Could SRS stop Christine from intentionally stepping in front of a car today?"

"No, not really."

"Isn't it true, Ms. LaValley, that the best that can be done to protect Christine, whether she is in SRS custody or in her mother's custody under SRS protective supervision, is to provide a safe environment and support?"

LaValley, bolder, "I agree, and I think the safer and more supportive environment would be with the father. As I said before, I don't regard the mother's home as either safe or supportive."

That wasn't the note Simmons wanted to end on, but she made the snap decision that she wasn't going to descend into a swamp of rhetoric parsing with this woman. She had to trust that Greenleaf would remember how Fitzgerald had taken LaValley apart, given the lie of her qualifications for determining what Christine needed, and establishing the father's complete lack of effort to date. "No further questions, Your Honor."

Fitzgerald looked at Simmons, tried to hide his surprise. Lynne expected more. Christine expected more.

Charles Benson was sworn in as the State's next witness. He testified to his credentials and provided a nearly verbatim recitation of his drug and alcohol assessment, concluding that Christine was in denial of her drug dependency and needed to confront her addiction if she was ever going to recover. Blum, leaving well enough alone, passed on cross examination. Fitzgerald, deferring to Simmons, chose to pass as well.

Simmons stood up and began her cross examination. "Mr. Benson, you say that you've been involved in the drug and alcohol recovery movement for twenty - four years?"

The thick man in the stained shirt sat erect as he answered. "That's correct." "And in that time, you have encountered individuals who have recovered from their addictions on their own, without the assistance of a formal drug treatment program, haven't you?"

"Of course, but very rarely." Benson admitted.

"Those people who succeeded without undergoing a formal treatment program, what would you say contributed to their success?" Simmons waited.

Benson grew wary, but he'd handled plenty of tough cross examinations and Simmons didn't look too tough. "Well, first off, they need to be living in a drug free environment. Second, they need a strong support system, people in their lives who support their efforts at sobriety. Third, I think it's really important that they have a reason for getting up in the morning, a purpose to their lives: a job, loved ones, civic involvement, church. Things like that."

Simmons nodded her assent then asked, "Christine has been drug and alcohol free for nearly eight months. If she had those components, you just described, in place...isn't it possible that she could remain drug free?"

"Of course it's possible," Benson agreed, "but I don't see that happening, not with her background. What I see here is a classic case of drug abuse, typical of young people today.

The current widespread addiction to cocaine occurs in a context of a generally hedonistic or nihilistic outlook on life, which leads them from one high to another, be that sex, drugs or violence, meaninglessly passing their days. The danger is that these highs they are pursuing, are addictive and destructive. We're seeing more and more of these wasted souls within our youth community."

Caught off guard by Benson's intensity, "Are we still talking about Christine?" "Of course we are. She's no different than the others: the sex, the cocaine, the rest of it."

Simmons had to attack this garbage. "How much time have you spent with Christine?"

Benson glared back at the lawyer. "Long enough to know what I see." "How long?"

"An hour, but I also read the police reports and the SRS notes." "Thank you, nothing further your Honor."

Christine wanted Simmons to destroy Benson, but she hadn't. Lynne wanted to have heard none of his testimony, but she had and she suffered it.

Blum rose to take advantage of Benson's testimony. "Mr. Benson, by Christine's own admission she had been consuming cocaine before her arrest?"

"Yes."

"How frequently?"

"She said that she had really gotten into it in the spring, before her arrest, particularly after she met the Connell fellow." Benson stated, nonplussed.

"He was the drug dealer, the man she was arrested with?"

"Yes."

"Did she say how much she did with him?" Blum asked.

"She said a lot, but nothing specific."

"Did Miss Bancroft say she used drugs before she met Mr. Connell?"

"Mostly marijuana, which is typical. Marijuana is what we call a gateway drug. It leads to harder, more dangerous drugs and the drug lifestyle. It sounded like it was a pretty big part of her life the year before her arrest." "Alcohol?"

Benson continued comfortably, "Not so much. She said she didn't really like it. But that's pretty common with youth heavily into the drug culture, especially females. They seem to prefer the drugs."

Blum asked slowly, "Did Miss Bancroft say when she began taking drugs?" "She said she first had marijuana when she was fifteen."

Blum nodded, "Thank you. Nothing further."

Christine wanted to scream at the freak.

Fitzgerald couldn't let Benson's testimony end on the graphic detail of Christine taking drugs at fifteen years of age. He led Benson to admit that there was no conclusive evidence that marijuana use actually leads to cocaine addiction. But Benson maintained that they were both psychologically addictive and part of the "drug lifestyle."

Fitzgerald had Benson state that Christine would have overcome any physiological symptoms of cocaine addiction withdrawal in the eight months since her last usage, but again, Benson maintained it was psychologically addictive, describing the "exquisite" cocaine high as a "siren's song" that torments its former users who go untreated.

Fitzgerald had to let it go; the judge was losing patience with this line of questioning, shifting distractedly in his chair. He'd have Vrabel take apart Benson's babble. "Nothing further, your Honor."

Christine looked at her lawyer: *this sucks, this is complete bull-shit.* Lynne was rocked by Benson's lurid depiction of her daughter as a wasted soul.

The next witness was the sheriff, to describe Christine's attempted escape. His testimony was dramatic, but there was not much to it. On cross examination, Blum heightened the impact, getting the officer to state that Christine was "wild," "acting crazy," "definitely unbalanced." Judge Greenleaf gave the witness his full attention.

Blum concluded, "Sheriff Brown, would you say that Christine's behavior was consistent with someone who was going through drug withdrawal?"

"Well, yes. I would say that."

Shifting anxiously in her chair, Christine seethed. Shards of memory sliced across her mind: the apartment door bursting open, being questioned while half naked, the cop's fingers probing inside her, the cell stench, the glimpse of her mother. Her insides slid, her balance shifted. She didn't hear attorney Fitzgerald's cross examination. Just his tone: his ineffective pawing at the man in the crisp uniform.

Fitzgerald didn't get any traction trying to establish that Christine had merely tripped, and that the idea of her attempting to escape was ludicrous.

The sheriff was glad to respond to that: a crazy person, a person strung out on drugs, was capable of nearly anything. "Why, I've seen times when ..." He told Greenleaf a few crazed druggie stories, and the judge appeared to appreciate them.

Simmons tried to knock the officer off of his testimony, but he was obtuse on details and quick with the "crazed druggie" explanation for most of the factual inconsistencies. Greenleaf heard the sheriff out.

The sheriff was the last of the State's witnesses. The judge called for a morning recess. Lynne, Christine and their lawyers somberly headed for a conference room.

When they were all gathered, Fitzgerald spoke, "Okay, the State's case is over. They threw their worst at us, the past. Now it's time to talk about the present and the future. That's where we're strong. The judge needs to hear that the past won't be repeated. And we're prepared to do that."

Christine stroked her necklace. Lynne watched her daughter, reached out for her hand. Christine took her mother's hand.

The hearing resumed with the mother's case. Fitzgerald announced Lynne's first witness: Mary Donato, Lynne's shift supervisor from the maternity ward. Donato quickly described Lynne as a conscientious, hardworking, responsible licensed nursing assistant. She was aware that Lynne's teenage daughter was in state's custody, but that never seemed to affect her work. She was glad to have had Lynne on her shift and was sorry to lose her to the pediatric unit.

The State passed on cross examination.

Blum did not. "Ms. Donato, have you ever had to supervise an employee with drug dependency issues?"

Fitzgerald protested. "Objection, relevance."

Blum snapped. "Your Honor that was obviously a foundation question. If I may be allowed some leeway, the relevance will soon be apparent."

Judge Greenleaf allowed the question. After being reminded of the question, the nurse answered that she had.

Blum continued, "And if an employee is drug dependent, does the hospital administration take any action?"

"Well it depends on how severe the problem is. If there is accompanying criminal activity, or if the dependency appears to be severe, then that employee may need to be let go. If the employee comes forward voluntarily, and their problem doesn't appear to be too severe, then he or she may be referred to a treatment program, or put on probation." Blum honed in. "Why would an employee, using drugs, be terminated, or referred to treatment?"

Fitzgerald started to object, but decided the judge would allow the question. "Because their drug usage could potentially affect their performance, putting patients at risk." Donato answered.

Blum, evenly, "And the patients that you and Lynne Bancroft work with are among the most vulnerable. Mothers in labor, giving birth, and their newborns?"

"That's right."

"Where a mistake can result in death or permanent disability?"

"Yes, that's a possibility."

"Did you ever have knowledge that Lynne Bancroft, the woman seated at that table," Blum turned and pointed at Lynne, "used illegal or controlled substances?

Drugs?"

Surprised at the question, "No, not at all." "Nothing further, your Honor."

Christine sickened; *what's he up to?* Lynne felt a trap coiling, her insides dissolved. Fitzgerald and Simmons decided against re-cross examination.

Fitzgerald called the next witness, Miranda Howe. After being sworn in, Miranda smiled slightly at Lynne from the witness stand. She looked over at Christine—the first time she had seen her—thinking that she was an attractive young woman. She felt the stabbing glare from Mark's table, felt the power of the two men seated there.

After the initial questions regarding Howe's occupation, credentials and experience, Fitzgerald asked about the work that Lynne had done with her.

Composed, she replied, "Lynne began seeing me last summer, just before Christine's arrest. We had one session before the arrest. She was having a hard time making ends meet, and Christine was acting out with a lot of challenging behavior."

"Was Christine's behavior an ongoing focus of your sessions?" Fitzgerald asked. "Yes. Especially after her arrest. Tragic events happened quickly to Christine, and

Lynne was extremely distressed at what was happening." "What events?"

"Well, the arrest itself. Christine's incarceration. The CHINS proceedings. Then the transfer to Stonebridge and her daughter's psychotic break shortly thereafter.

Christine was suffering terribly through those times, and Lynne was miserable seeing her daughter suffer. Throughout all this, she wanted to know what she could do to help Christine."

Fitzgerald, gently, "Did you work with Lynne on how she could help Christine?"

Howe spoke to the judge, she knew he had to hear this. "Yes, both directly and indirectly. There were immediate things she could do for Christine, like visit her as much as possible. But more importantly, she had to get herself in better shape to effectively meet the needs of Christine and her other children."

"What do you mean 'get herself in better shape'?"

Howe remembered that the lawyers wanted to keep Mark out of this. "When Lynne first came to me, she did not have a lot of self-confidence. She felt powerless, unable to fend for herself and her family. She needed to believe in herself, needed to find her strength."

"And has Lynne gotten into 'better shape', as you put it?"

"Yes, she's made great progress. In so many ways she has shown how much more capable she is." The therapist looked to Lynne, "She should be very proud, her progress has been truly remarkable."

Lynne smiled back at Miranda.

Fitzgerald paused, letting the statement stand-alone, before continuing. "Can you give some examples of Lynne's increased capabilities?"

"Certainly. For one, the fact that she has remained in therapy this long, exploring difficult issues, is an accomplishment. It has led Lynne to realize a lot about herself, including what a valuable person she is. Another example would be, she broke out of her routine when she changed shifts at work. That was significant for Lynne. Also, getting into that family support group was big; those parents talk about very thorny problems they face with their teenagers. It must be hard for Lynne to hear what those families are going through as she prepared for Christine to come home."

Lynne looked down at her hands; it was hard, very hard.

"And, of course," Howe continued, "maintaining her total commitment and support for Christine the entire time. It was devastating for Lynne at times. It took real strength and courage to see her child in so much pain, and yet stand by her without wavering. Lynne grew into that strength and courage over time, with each of the challenges she and her family faced." Miranda nodded to Lynne.

The courtroom was hushed when Howe stopped speaking. Her last words rung in the silence. Mark, *what a bitch.* Christine, *Yeah, Miranda!* Lynne, *Thank you!*

Fitzgerald held the silence a moment longer. "In the course of your work with Lynne, has she addressed the matter of Christine moving away from home last summer?"

Directing her answer to the judge, Howe answered, "Yes. She held herself responsible for the Christine's hardships because, in her mind, they all stemmed from her decision to allow Christine to move to Burlington. Lynne had to get past that, not wallow in ineffectual guilt. She had to do what was needed to get Christine healthy and back home safely. Which she has done. Those things I've already mentioned; the shift change, therapy and the like. She also had to understand what led to her decision to allow Christine to move out, so she won't repeat that mistake."

Howe looked in Lynne's direction, but Lynne didn't notice, caught up in the memories the therapist's words had triggered.

"Did Lynne try to understand the decision she made?"

"Yes, she understands what happened. Christine is a strong willed young woman. She had shown, in various ways that she was extremely bored with her life in Branford. Remarkably, she proposed to Lynne this idea of spending the summer in Burlington, staying with a young man, who was supposedly, a college student. And I say *remarkably* because it speaks to the quality of their relationship that Christine didn't simply run off, as many rebellious teens might have done. That being said, however, Lynne saw how unhappy her daughter was and feared, if she tried to stop her, Christine would take off anyway and likely break off all communication with her. Christine promised to stay in regular contact, and I understand that she did."

Howe turned to the judge, "You have to understand that Lynne faced a horrible dilemma. She felt there was too much at stake if she said no. She felt she could lose Christine forever."

Lynne watched the judge's expression remain stolid.

Fitzgerald noted the judge's lack of response as well, yet stayed the course he had set out, "How would the work Lynne has been doing with you influence her response if Christine threatened to run away again?"

Howe nodded back to the lawyer, "Lynne is more self-confident, so I think she is better able to manage Christine's strong personality. She's also not as isolated as before. She faced that dilemma alone, with no one to help her assess the situation. Now she can talk with me or the members of the family support group, which should help her handle difficult situations more effectively."

Howe looked directly at Lynne, who held her gaze. "Finally, I think her bond with Christine has grown stronger because of all they have been through together this past year. In fact, from the information I've received, Christine has been doing very well lately, which I attribute in large part to Lynne's dedication to Christine."

Fitzgerald, speaking in the judge's direction, "Do you feel that Lynne is capable of safely parenting Christine at home now, considering the other demands of her life? Her job, parenting Christine's siblings, and whatever else?"

"I do. I say that because she has proven her commitment. She has better tools for dealing with difficult family issues. And she has the strength and confidence to use those tools and meaningfully follow through on her dedication. That being said, I would recommend that Lynne continue in individual therapy to address the underlying issues in her life, and she continue to participate in the family support group so she knows she's not the only one facing problems that teenagers like Christine can present. I'd also recommend family counseling, so that she and Christine make sure they get their issues on the table and dealt with effectively. I'm confident that Lynne will make every effort to be the parent Christine needs."

Howe smiled gently at Christine. Christine mouthed "Thank you" back. The judge noted the gesture. Lynne, in tears, beamed when Howe turned to her.

Fitzgerald concluded, "Nothing further, your Honor."

Blum had signaled the State's attorney to pass on his chance to cross examine the therapist. She was dangerous. A clod, like Derosia, could blow their case by asking this woman the wrong questions.

Blum rose from his seat, walked around the table and placed himself between the witness and Lynne's table. "Ms. Howe. You talk about 'bonds' and 'strength' and 'underlying issues' and a 'steadfast relationship' between mother and daughter. But I am hard pressed to say whether you told us what any of that means..."

Fitzgerald, "Objection, counsel is testifying."

Judge Greenleaf, "Mr. Blum would you get to the question, if there is one."

Blum smiled sardonically, "Of course there is your Honor. Ms. Howe, you testified about the remarkable relationship the mother and daughter had when the mother allowed her sixteen year old daughter to go live with an older man in a city over a hundred miles away, who just happened to be a cocaine dealer—that's your idea of remarkable?"

Calmly responding, "Your question doesn't make sense, but I'll try to answer it. What I regard as remarkable was that a teenage girl, who was determined to escape her hometown, considered it important to keep her ties with her mother."

Blum rubbed his chin, "Perhaps Christine kept in touch with her mother for other reasons, considering their background. She was living with her mother since she was fifteen, correct?"

"Since she was born, I believe."

Quickly, "Without her father in the house since she was fifteen. And she had been using illegal drugs, by her own admission since she was fifteen, correct?"

"I don't know about that."

"Did you discuss Christine's drug abuse history with your client?" Blum asked. "We had spoken somewhat about how Christine's drug use affected her life and the life of the family, if that answers your question."

"So, did your client know about her daughter's drug usage?"

"I believe so, yes." Howe unintentionally shot a quick look at Lynne. Hardening, "And what consequences did Lynne hand down when she knew that

Christine was using drugs?"

Flustering, "We hadn't spoken about... none that I recall discussing." "Did she talk about trying to get Christine into treatment?"

Recomposed, "No she didn't. Lynne wasn't in any kind of shape to take that forceful a measure at that time."

"Why not?"

"She was in terrible shape herself then..." *Screw it,* "She was recovering from her marriage to Christine's father. She was in really bad shape. She could barely handle her life after a difficult divorce. But she's much better now. Like I said, stronger and more capable."

Blum spoke at the judge, projecting incredulity, "And that would be because...?"

Howe despised the lawyer's gesture, "Because she's worked hard in therapy to realize her own worth, to realize she could get done what she needs to get done. That she could withstand Mark's emotional abuse. Huge progress. From there, she has been able to take control of the rest of her life. The things we talked about pertaining to Christine, along with other matters in her life. It's been a long, ongoing recovery."

Blum continued, as if Howe had said nothing of consequence. "Do you feel your client has opened up to you, given you her complete history in the course of therapy?"

Wary of the trap she knew was coming, "She's opened up a lot, but I don't think I've heard it all. That's pretty common with women coming out of abusive relationships. It's hard for them to tell all of what happened."

Lynne and Christine looked to each other, both worried.

Blum nodded, "Of course. Did Lynne discuss with you what affect her use of drugs at the time period in question, the period when her own daughter was using drugs, had on her ability to cope with her family responsibilities?"

Bastard! Lynne felt the trap coiling. Christine cringed.

Fitzgerald, "Objection, lack of foundation."

"I'll allow the question." To Howe, "Please answer."

Calmly, "I have no information that Lynne used drugs. So, to answer your question...no, I have never had such a discussion."

Taunting, "But Lynne has a trusting relationship with you, correct?" She hated this man, "I believe so."

Shifting to a neutral tone, "Have you counselled persons with substance abuse problems?"

Before Fitzgerald or Simmons could object, Howe answered, "Yes I have, and I have no reason to believe that Lynne has a substance abuse problem."

"Are clients with substance abuse problems secretive, duplicitous?" Fitzgerald, "Objection!"

"Sustained."

Blum didn't miss a beat, "You've never met Mark Bancroft, have you?" "No."

"And all of your information about Lynne's marriage has come from her?" "That's correct."

Blum walked back to his table, asked slowly. "If Lynne wasn't able to control, or even help Christine last summer, when she was apparently abusing cocaine and marijuana, wouldn't it make sense that Christine would want to return to her mother's, expecting to take up her former lifestyle without interference?"

Fitzgerald and Simmons both objected to the question as speculative, but the judge wanted to hear Howe's answer.

Weary and wary, "I can't answer that question, the way you've phrased it..." Quickly,

"Then let me rephrase the question Ms. Howe. Isn't it possible that Christine wanted to stay in contact with her mother because she was able to freely use drugs while living in her mother's home, expecting that she would be able to resume using drugs without interference, should she return?"

"It's hard for me to say..."

Cutting her off, "Isn't it possible that's the reason, or a reason, why Christine kept in contact with her mother after she moved out?"

"It's possible, but..."

"Thank you Ms. Howe, you've answered the question. Nothing further."

Christine stared her hatred at the lawyer. Lynne, crushed, stared blindly at the table before her.

Simmons had to get Howe back on the offensive. She rose, took a quiet breath. "Ms. Howe, do you have any knowledge that Lynne had begun family counseling last spring because of her concern about Christine's behavior, among other things?"

"That's right. Lynne had gone to Tom Hansson at Family Support Services before seeing me. In fact, Tom had referred Lynne to me because she needed individual attention."

"So, Lynne was addressing Christine's behavior problems, before she moved out?"

"Yes, I believe so."

Simmons nodded, "Turning to the present, are you aware that Lynne has offered to put Christine on a drug and alcohol screening schedule, monitored by SRS through protective supervision?"

"Yes, Lynne spoke to me about that." "Is that significant?"

Howe spoke to the judge, "Well, it indicates to me that she has her daughter's safety foremost in mind, guarding against a possible relapse. Lynne's offer doesn't surprise me. She's faced with two opinions, stating Christine does and does not have a drug problem and, on the side of caution, she has offered to have Christine closely monitored in order to take measures necessary for her daughter's health and safety."

"And Lynne spoke to you about what it would mean if Christine tested positive for drugs or alcohol in her system?"

"Yes, she's aware the State could take Christine back into custody should she test positive. She was aware of that consequence before she made the offer."

"How does Lynne regard her future with Christine?"

Miranda shifted in the witness stand, "I'd characterize her view as cautiously optimistic. She has been encouraged by Christine's growth these past few months, very encouraged. And she is aware of her own growth as well. So, she believes she and Christine have a good chance of continuing the progress both of them have made."

"Do you regard Lynne's view as realistic?"

"Yes, absolutely. I'd say she can point to specific accomplishments in her life, and in Christine's life during these past few months that would support her belief they won't return to the conditions of their past. They have moved on, in a more positive direction. It is reasonable to expect they will continue making progress if they continue the work they have begun. I see Lynne's dedication to that work, so I believe her sense of accomplishment is very realistic."

Simmons smiled, "Thank you Ms. Howe. Nothing further, your Honor."

Fitzgerald and Derosia passed on re-cross.

Blum approached, "Ms. Howe, again you regale us with generalized concepts and rhetorical flourishes, but I need to ask, and this court needs to hear, in plain language, about Christine's future. Lynne still lives in the same location as when Christine left, the same bad actors presumably still in the vicinity. She really couldn't stop Christine from turning back to drugs, could she?"

Miranda fixed Blum with a firm gaze, "No less than any other parent. But the quality of Lynne and Christine's relationship supports my opinion that there is a greatly reduced likelihood that she will take up drugs."

"Have you ever met with Christine?" "No."

"Or spoken to her about her relationship with her mother?" "No."

"Or her relationship with her father?" "No."

"So, your opinion about the mother daughter relationship is based on the information provided you by the mother?"

Reddening, "Basically, yes."

Dismissive, "Nothing further from this witness, your Honor."

Christine watched the therapist leave the witness stand—a strong, well-spoken woman who was just blown off by her father's lawyer: *Fucked, very fucked.* Lynne had to look away from Miranda. Mark grinned at her humiliation.

Fitzgerald whispered to Lynne, "We're not going to put Sally Peck on." He wasn't going to give Blum a shot at depicting the group as a bunch of suicidal teenagers and their neurotic parents. He asked, "You ready to take the stand?"

Lynne nodded yes. She wasn't ready at all. She saw nothing as she walked to the witness stand. Sweat stung her eyes, she rubbed at them with her knuckles when she was seated. She saw Christine looking at her: *Be strong.*

Fitzgerald gently walked Lynne through her testimony, finishing with her vow that she would do everything in her power to keep Christine away from drugs and that, should Christine use drugs, she would expect her to be returned to State's custody. She tried to sound as convincing as possible, tried to avoid the glares of her ex-husband and his lawyer. Fitzgerald finished his questions and sat down.

Lynne watched the State's attorney and Christine's lawyer speak to the judge about waiving examination, then Blum was up and coming at her. He stopped no more than five feet away, looked at her sourly for a full moment. *He's not going to ruin me.*

Blum cleared his throat, signaling that he was going to rip this woman apart, "Good morning, Mrs. Bancroft. Do you remember being in this court on another matter, last May?"

Lynne nodded, looking down. She knew what was coming.

"You need to answer audibly, Mrs. Bancroft." He took a step closer.

The judge craned his neck to look harder at her.

She answered, "Yes."

"And do you recall at that hearing, I believe it was a child support hearing, that you admitted you were using controlled substances then?"

Silence swallowed the courtroom. Lynne croaked, "Yes."

"And that was merely a month or so before Christine moved in with the cocaine dealer?"

"Yes."

Taking his time, letting her twist, "What drug counseling have you received since then?"

"None...it was only pot, once in a while" Lynne said.

"I see. You haven't used drugs since then, and will never use drugs again?" "No, I haven't. And I won't."

"Not since that man who was living with you moved out?" "Well, yes." Tears rose in Lynne's eyes. *Bastard.*

"A man was living with you and your children, with whom you were having sexual relations last spring?"

Through burning tears., "Yes."

"And he provided you with drugs?" "Yes, pot."

"But he no longer lives with you?" "No." Her voice was soft.

"Is there any chance that he's moving back anytime soon?" "No."

Blum looked to the judge, suggesting that the woman was not to be believed. He asked, "Is there a man living with you and your children now, with whom you're having sexual relations?"

"No."

"Is it likely that a man will be moving in with you soon, with whom you will be having sexual relations?"

Lynne screamed, "No" at the bastard. Screamed it twice.

Blum breathed contempt through his nostrils before announcing, "Nothing more from this witness."

Christine shook violently. It was all terrible. The light was shading darker.

Fitzgerald rose. He had to plunge into unknown territory, if he was going to pull out of this disaster. "Pot, once in a while. What did you mean by 'once in a while'?" He asked Lynne.

His tone helped. *Be strong.* Lynne looked to Christine stroking the red necklace.

> She answered, "Maybe once a month, when Frank brought some home."

Patiently, "Frank? He was the man you were speaking about in your earlier testimony? You no longer see him?"

Lynne rubbed at her wet eyes with her wrist before answering, "No, not since he moved out, not since last May."

"You've had no marijuana since then?" She shook her head, "No."

As Fitzgerald hesitated, wondering whether to risk any more, Lynne spoke, "Listen, Frank was a mistake. He came along shortly after the divorce, he treated me nice. I needed that after the way Mark had treated me. I let Frank into my life. I shouldn't have, but I was having a really rough time."

Blum objected that no question had been asked, and demanded that the testimony be stricken. Greenleaf concurred.

Fitzgerald nodded, and asked, "Lynne, how about now. If Frank, or someone like Frank, came along, treated you nice, would you let him move in and live with you and your family?"

Lynne found her strength, "No. Things are a lot different than they were last spring. I'm not hurting like I was then, thanks to Miranda. Mark's paying the child support now, which matters a lot. Because Mark was skipping the support then. I needed Frank to stay and help with the bills. I couldn't make ends meet. I was stuck, we all were stuck. It was terrible. Finally, I just had to kick him out." Lynne was looking at the judge, who wouldn't look back at her. She didn't care.

Fitzgerald sickened; he'd blown it, had allowed Lynne to go too far. He had to get her off the stand. "No further questions, your Honor."

Blum stood after the other lawyers passed on re-cross examination. He began speaking, harshly, "You claim you needed another man's help to make ends meet because your ex-husband wasn't paying child support?" He glared at Lynne, who withered.

Be strong. "Yes."

"But in this court, Mark, your ex-husband, was found to have been paying you everything he owed you and the children, even while this Frank person lived in your home. Do you recall that as the finding of this court?"

A scream tore through Lynne. "He was lying. He lied to the judge. It was all lies."

Blum let the shrill echo of Lynne's voice scrape the room, before he indicated to the judge that he was finished with the witness.

A scream had torn through Christine as well, continued to tear through her.

No other lawyer stood to continue the questioning. Greenleaf didn't look at Lynne when he told her to return to her seat. She did not move. Through her tears she saw Christine looking up at her. The judge announced the lunch recess. Lynne remained in the witness box.

When the black edged lawyer had finished tormenting her mother, she saw him turn to her father, also black edged. She watched them both exchange wicked smiles. They had destroyed her mother. The pain rimmed inside her skull. She heard someone say it was time for lunch. She saw her mother descend from the witness stand, returning.

Christine sat at her table, her mother stood by the table, neither speaking.

Simmons looked at the ashen faced girl, then at the shredded mother. *Christ!*

Fitzgerald said to Simmons, "Stay with them, and meet back here twenty minutes before one. I'm going to try and get Tom Hansson in here to testify about Lynne's effort back in the beginning."

In the hallway, outside the courtroom, Miranda and the Murphys were waiting when Christine and Lynne left the courtroom. Before anyone could speak, Miranda stepped forward to take Lynne's hands. Kathleen and Rosemary went to Christine and took her hands. Christine filled with light; *my angels, strong and brave.* She saw her father staring back at her, hatefully, from the exit. She drew the sisters' strength around her like a cloak.

Throughout lunch Christine said nothing, ate little, drank several glasses of water, and huddled into the Murphy sisters, who sat on either side of her in the diner booth.

Simmons kept up a meaningless banter: "...could've been worse... hung tough...made some good points... it's not over yet..."

The words came to Christine as they should, from the lawyer's mouth instead of from some vague distance. The rimming pain slowly faded to slight, a whisper but not gone altogether. She realized she'd had an episode, and she was just hanging on. She picked at her sandwich, ate small bites of bread and said nothing.

Fitzgerald and Hansson were in the conference room, when Simmons returned with the group. Lynne was glad to see Hansson. He had really tried to help her through those tough times. *Lifetimes ago.* He smiled at Lynne and asked how she was doing.

She didn't know how to answer, "Fine."

Christine smiled at the handsome man, but didn't say anything. Lynne introduced Kathleen and Rosemary to Hansson. He said hello to Miranda.

Fitzgerald joked that it was good to see everyone get along, then he explained he had talked with Hansson about Lynne's circumstances and her efforts in dealing with Frank and Christine when she had come into Family Support Services last May. He added, "I think Tom has some valuable things to say, things that will be helpful to our case." Hansson, no longer smiling, nodded at the remark.

The bailiff knocked on the door, announced that the judge would be taking the bench in a couple minutes, and all parties were to return to the courtroom. Christine's insides shifted. Lynne hugged her. Rosemary and Kathleen touched her arm. Her lawyer led her back into the courtroom.

Mark and his lawyer were already in the room, when Lynne and Christine entered. They took their seats without looking at Mark's table. Christine felt the evil thrumming from that table as loud as a hive. She sat and waited, watching the door for the executioner to enter. She felt light, like she was just outside of herself. Like a shadow blur.

Judge Greenleaf entered and took his place. He asked State Attorney Derosia if there had been any resolution reached during the recess. He was looking at Lynne when Derosia answered no. The judge then asked Fitzgerald if he had any other witnesses.

"Yes, your Honor, the mother wishes to call Thomas Hansson."

Blum bellowed, "Objection, your Honor. The mother has not provided notice of this witness."

Fitzgerald, sharply back, "Mother submits no prejudice to father given that father conducted no discovery on any of mother's noticed witnesses."

Blum, standing, "As is the father's prerogative. With no idea who this man is, I am not going to allow an insinuation that my client would not have conducted discovery in this instance."

The judge sighed, "What is the offer of proof with this witness, Mr. Fitzgerald?"

"Mr. Hansson will testify that he is a caseworker at Family Support Services and provided counseling to my client last spring around the issues she was addressing with Christine, prior to her leaving the home."

Blum snapped, "Cumulative to the testimony already given by witness, Howe, no probative value."

Before Fitzgerald could respond, Greenleaf ruled, "Objection sustained." Simmons argued to allow Hansson's testimony. Greenleaf held firm.

Lynne and Christine watched their lawyers' stark defeat. Christine's insides slid, the rimming pain increased. Lynne was sinking.

Fitzgerald had no more witnesses, he rested the mother's case.

The judge indicated it was the father's turn to present his case, and asked Blum whether the father wished to call any witnesses.

Mark's lawyer answered that he did. The first witness Blum called was the Albany social worker who prepared the evaluation of Mark's home and circumstances. She testified that he lived in a well-kept, adequate home with his new wife and infant son, that he earned enough as an engineer to provide for his current family and met his child support obligations to his former family, and that he didn't seem like the kind of person who would shirk his responsibilities to either family.

Fitzgerald's objection to her opinion testimony was denied. Neither Fitzgerald nor Simmons shook loose the caseworker's pat testimony in cross examination. Neither lawyer saw a point in pressing her hard, risking the judge's impatience, with little chance of rooting out something helpful to their case. As the woman left the witness stand, she smiled at Mark. Lynne hated the gesture, the woman, this circus. Christine only saw her blurred movement.

Blum intoned, "Your Honor, I call Mark Bancroft, the father, to the stand."

Mark rose, resolutely approached the witness stand. He took his seat—conveying confidence in his stride, his squared shoulders and his set jaw. He faced the judge briefly, with an assured, slight smile as he was sworn in. Then he turned to the parties seated at the tables below him, looked directly at Lynne a long, withering moment.

The look slashed Lynne. She had seen that look many times before. It said, *I'm going to fuck you up.*

Christine also saw the look. She knew it. His evil burned from his eye sockets. She knew the others didn't see what she saw. He sat there glowing darkly, waiting to begin.

It began. "Would you please state your name for the record?" Blum then deftly questioned Mark on his current circumstances: age, address, occupation, marital status, parental status—creating a comfortable rhythm with Mark that helped the judge perceive him as a regular guy. Blum changed the tone when he asked about the divorce; divorces were implicitly sad when children were involved, but a fact of this case. Blum had Mark testify to the basic information: date of separation, date the divorce became final. A hint of sadness. Mark was testifying well.

The lawyer paused, signaling a more serious discussion would ensue, "Mark, pursuant to the terms of the divorce decree, were you granted custody of your three children?"

Evenly, without rancor, "No, I was not." "Did you pursue custody of them?"

"No. I believed it would be in the children's best interests if they stayed in Branford with their mother. Their lives were disrupted enough as it was by the divorce. They didn't need any more upheaval by having to move to a new city, and leave behind their school and their friends."

"You agreed that the mother be granted custody of the children. Have you had any misgivings about that custody arrangement?"

Fitzgerald from his seat, "Objection!" Greenleaf, "I'll take the answer."

Mark, unruffled, "Yes, almost from the start. I know it was a very difficult time for everyone, but it just wasn't right that she kept me from seeing my children. I was missing them terribly."

Lynne's breath shallowed at the outrageous lie; there would be no stopping him.

She heard his voice: *I am going to fuck you up.* Christine heard her father's testimony through the scraping in her skull. She watched the dark light pulse from him in cadence with his speech.

Blum asked, "Visitation was provided for in the divorce settlement?" "Yes, I was to have the children every other weekend."

"And did those visitations occur?"

"Rarely. Lynne always had some excuse for not letting me see them. At first I believed her, but after a while, I began to think she was keeping the kids from me."

"Did you take legal action to enforce your visitation rights?"

"No. I was hoping things would get better, that it wouldn't be necessary to go to court. Besides, and you know this, lawyers and courts are really expensive." Mark gave a small deprecating grin that Blum and the judge shared. Returning to his sober tone, "The children and I had a really special Christmas the first year after our separation. That meant a lot to me. Maybe it made me a bit too hopeful, looking back in hindsight." Lynne wanted to scream, wanted this over with. Christine watched her father flare.

"Were there any other reasons for you to have misgivings?" Blum continued.

Sounding hurt, "Yes there were. I felt that the kids were acting strangely towards me. I couldn't say why, but they just began acting odd. Then I found out she had this boyfriend, and soon after, that he was living with them. That really upset me. Maybe it explains how the kids were behaving, why she was keeping them from me. You know, telling them to keep things hushed up."

"Did you take any legal action at that time, at the time you learned of the boyfriend moving in, concerning visitation or custody of the children?"

"No, because right about when I found out about the boyfriend, she brought me into court claiming I owed her back child support. And in court, she said he wasn't living there anymore. So, he couldn't have been there very long."

Blum asked slowly, "Was that upsetting to you?" Fitzgerald called out, "Objection, relevance." "Sustained."

Blum nodded, "In the course of the child support action brought by your former wife, did you obtain any other information that caused you concern about the custody of your children?"

Mark paused, as if he were considering the question, then nodded and answered, "Yes. I mean the very fact that she came into court and lied the way she did, saying I owed her a lot of back support, really bothered me. I had to wonder what it meant. Why was she so desperate? What was happening to the children? Then I find out, in court, out of her mouth, that she and the boyfriend had been doing drugs. So it started to make sense...keeping the kids from me, suing me for money. I was really concerned about the kids at that point."

"Mr. Bancroft, did you withhold child support from your children?" Firmly, "Not a dime. And the judge ruled that I didn't."

Raising his voice slightly, Blum asked, "Did you take any legal action upon receiving the information that your ex-wife had been using illegal drugs?"

Mark shook his head as he looked down, mimicking shame. "No, I didn't. And the reason I didn't was that after the hearing, she was like a changed person. Maybe she learned her lesson, because the judge was pretty harsh with her. But anyway, after the hearing I was getting my full visitation and we were working things out. The visits with the kids were going great and so I figured maybe we had put a bad patch behind us.

Besides, it was coming up to the end of the school year and it would have been really hard on the kids to pull them out of school and bring them to Albany. I figured I'd see how things went that summer. Last summer."

Lynne kept herself seated rigid, rather than collapse. Christine heard the flaring man's words as a drone.

Blum asked gravely, "Would you tell the judge how things went last summer, as it relates to you and Christine?"

His voice steely. "The summer began and I was having visits with the other two, Matt and Charlotte, but she, Lynne, kept saying Chris was busy, had other plans, and didn't have time to see me. I was upset. I wasn't even getting to speak with Chrissy. I knew something was wrong, after a couple weeks of it. Then..." Mark hitched his voice, "Then, you know, the arrest. And Chris is in a detention center. Then I'm told she's in the mental hospital..." Mark stopped, rubbed his eyes with his palms, causing them to redden and water. To the judge, "It happened very quickly, I had no idea. It was later that I learned Chrissy was living with a drug dealer, was doing drugs herself. That her mother allowed her to go live with this guy." Mark glared at Lynne—*I am going to fuck you up*. "I hold her responsible for Chris's hell!"

He crushed Lynne like an insect. Christine looked over at her crushed mother.

> Simmons and Fitzgerald yelled their objections, but the judge waved them off.

Christine suffered her mother's destruction. The room was full of agitated spirits, whirring bat - like among the persons present, disturbed by the violence. She pleaded to herself; *where is the Savior?* She drank a cup of water, desperately.

Blum led his client through to the conclusion: the mother should not be allowed custody of the daughter she had so grievously harmed. Lynne had failed, and she would likely fail again, causing Christine more pain and injury. The father had the right and the duty to take his daughter under his protection, and help bring her back to health. He would exercise his right through a change of custody action and he would meet his obligation to provide for all of his daughter's needs.

Mark's conviction, clear and firm, impressed the judge. Neither Christine nor Lynne heard any of it, buried beneath their own wreckage.

Under cross examination, Mark successfully held to his narrative. When pressed for details, which might undermine his testimony, he plausibly answered "I don't know" or "I can't remember specifically."

When Simmons asked him why he was only seeking custody of Christine and not his other children, Mark bolstered his esteem in the judge's eyes by explaining that, because Christine needed so much individual attention, it would be unfair to the children if he took them all in. The other two were different from Christine, and he believed were not at risk like she was. He challenged, "Besides, maybe with all of the therapy that Lynne says has helped her so much, she can do right by Matt and Charlotte. There's still time. But with Chris, it's too late."

Fitzgerald and Simmons concluded their cross examinations without damaging Mark's testimony. He stepped down from the stand triumphant, head high. He didn't look at Lynne, he didn't need to. He knew what she looked like, after he destroyed her.

Blum informed the judge that the father would call no more witnesses. Fitzgerald thrown, *damn, what happened to the wife?* He had wanted the opportunity to use her to challenge Mark's credibility. He glanced at Lynne, slumped over, wrecked... then at Christine, rocking in her chair slightly, eyes closed. *Jesus Christ!* Simmons was going to have to put on a hell of a case to convince Greenleaf to send Christine home with her mother.

The judge called the afternoon recess.

The whirling swirled wilder as Christine rose to follow the others. She had to stop it. She took her necklace off and held it tight. She didn't hear the words people spoke to her, asking if she was alright. She nodded to the sound of their concern. She tried a reassuring smile, which creased her head with pain. She was in a room with her people; her mother, and the others. Her angels. After a few minutes, she was led back into the courtroom. At her table, she nervously gulped down two cups of water.

Dr. Vrabel watched Christine's behavior, concerned that she was collapsing under the trauma of the hearing. He took Simmons aside and told her Christine might suffer extreme distress, if she continued to attend. They both watched the girl, as she stood at her table, rocking slightly, drinking another cup of water. Lynne and Fitzgerald joined them at the doorway, heard their concern.

Terrified, Lynne pleaded, "You have to protect her."

Simmons said, "I could ask the judge to continue the hearing to a later date." Vrabel, "That may be best for Christine."

Christine was facing the front of the courtroom, facing the judge's empty chair, when her mother and Dr. Vrabel came up beside her. She was breathing evenly, no longer rocking. She was back in the courtroom, with the people she knew. No hallucinations. She was trembling, told herself; *hang in there.* She had to keep it together.

Lynne asked her, "Honey, are you feeling alright?" Christine turned to her mother, softly, "I'm fine, Mom."

"This is really rough, this ..." Lynne made a small sweep with her hand, signifying what had occurred so far.

"Yeah."

"We were wondering, Dr. Vrabel and me, whether maybe ..." Christine opened a simple smile, "Mom, I'm okay."

Lynne couldn't let it rest at that, couldn't let her shrug off her pain. She said firmly,

"You don't look okay. The doctor thinks it would be best if the hearing was continued until later, when you're feeling..."

No! Christine sharply cut her mother off, "No. we have to settle this now, I can't..." She flushed red, her eyes flashed.

Uncertain, faltering, Lynne looked to Vrabel.

He asked Christine, "you're sure you're up for this?'

"Yes."

The bailiff announced that the judge was ready to return to the bench, the parties needed to take their seats.

Fitzgerald caught Simmons, before the judge took the bench. "Put Vrabel on first.

Blum's going to destroy him. We need to save the sisters for last—fourth quarter drive for the winning score." He winked at his colleague, "We can do it."

On direct examination, Vrabel's psychiatric evaluation was entered into evidence.

He testified to all of the points that Simmons needed him to make: the history of Christine's psychotic break and her depression: his conclusion that it was not drug induced psychosis, his opinion that, psychologically, she did not have a substance abuse problem, the history of the treatment she had received, including her medications history, the value of her mother's care and concern to her recovery, her conflicted feelings about her father, her ultimate decision that she wanted and needed to live with her mother, and the importance, to her long term psychological health, that her decision to return to her mother be honored. Absent were compelling reasons against her placement home.

Blum crushed him. He spiked his questions with ridicule and contempt. When Vrabel testified in terms of probabilities and likelihoods, the lawyer translated the opinions as fuzzy headed gibberish. When Vrabel described the complex diagnostics involved in Christine's case, the lawyer questioned his analysis until it was incomprehensible. This 'doctor', Blum implied, was worse than useless, he was dangerous, and his opinions should be wholly disregarded.

Blum could have stopped, but he didn't. He picked up Vrabel's evaluation, waved it slightly. The papers flapped weakly in his hand. Lynne and Christine watched helplessly. What would the lawyer do now, his mastery of the doctor, absolute?

Accusing, "You conclude in this report that Christine's health requires her return to her mother's care. Because that's what she wants. There is nothing more to it than that, is there, Doctor?"

Shifting, sweating, and parched, Vrabel rasped the answer that he knew would prolong the inquisition, "That's not correct. It's more than that. It's what I said before."

"What exactly?"

Flatly, "Her serious misgivings about her father's ability to love her. Her belief that her mother can and will love her. That's what it all comes down to."

"Doctor, Christine has endured the divorce of her parents and an extended separation from her father during the very difficult circumstances of this past year. Is it possible that her misgivings about her father's ability to love her may have, in some significant way, resulted from this separation from her father?" Blum's slower, neutral tone bathed the question in the light of eminent reasonableness.

Vrabel could not refute the assertion, "Yes, that's possible."

Sounding reasonable, "And is it not possible, doctor, that Christine could overcome her doubts about her father's love for her, if she could spend more time with him?"

"Yes that's possible." Worn down, Vrabel could have added that he thought that was not likely, but he didn't.

Calmly, "Thank you, Doctor. No further questions, your Honor."

Christine saw it, knew it; her father's lawyer controlled her. He held her life in his hands. All strings connected to him. All things did his bidding. He sat beside her father, they shared a knowing nod. *Wickedness.* The lawyer at her table , bleated at the doctor, who bleated back. They didn't matter. She watched Blum and her father, the ones who mattered, who wanted her soul and her flesh. Blackness rising. She could let the darkness swallow her. From somewhere deep within, she screamed, *No!* The room shifted—there were doors. There were voices sounding from a distance. She knew. *There will be a gathering.*

The doctor staggered down, and passed Christine.

The potter was next; sweet, innocent. Christine watched. *She doesn't know what he will do to her.* Her lawyer's questions, the pleasant answers. She heard snatches of kind words: 'wonderful', 'a great help', 'the girls love her', 'beautiful work', 'dedicated to her craft', and so on. The kind words helped ease the skull pain. The doors faded. *For how long?*

He rose, her father's lawyer, pulsing malevolence. A nail scraped inside her skull. He spared the potter. He did not sneer or ridicule. He did not twist her words or shred her meaning. She answered 'I don't know' a handful of times. Which satisfied Him. He let her go. Judy smiled at Christine. Christine smiled back, wanly.

Kathleen took the stand - warm, kind Kathleen. Christine heartened at the sight of her; soft and round in her plain dress and waved white hair. Then she feared what he would do to her. She watched her father, agitated, whispering to his lawyer. The two cocooned in darkness. Christine knew: *She threatens him, they're plotting her ruin.* She gathered her focus to listen to Kathleen's testimony, to support brave Kathleen in the witness box. She fingered her necklace, desperately. One of her angels, one of her protectors willing to sacrifice herself, *for me. She needs my prayers*, and Christine implored the Good God to bestow strength and guidance on her foster mother.

Kathleen, the Brave and Gentle, told the room how wonderful Christine was. She described the daily routines and recounted many instances of her willing assistance with the chores and with the other foster children. She testified that she believed Christine's kindness had helped the younger foster children heal from their painful pasts

Christine watched her father and Blum listen to the woman. She knew: *They are waiting to strike.*

Fitzgerald watched the judge, sensed he might be developing a picture of Christine as a decent young woman, and not some depraved addict. The tone was good, building on the positive tone the potter had set. Fitzgerald snapped out of his complacency; it was going too well.

Simmons was still questioning, "Kathleen, did Christine have visits with her parents, while she was living in your home?"

Fitzgerald cringed; *don't go there.*

Her father and Blum stirred, alerted their forces. "And were you present during any of these visits?" Christine saw. *They are assembling.*

"And could you describe how these visits went?"

Christine cried within, knowing that Kathleen, bathed in white, would soon utter words that would call down His destruction. She prayed: *Lord protect her, Lord protect her, Lord protect her.*

Kathleen smiled at the lawyer, then answered in quiet detail, "Well, as I said, most of the visits happened at the house. Both parents traveled a long ways, so they only had a few hours together at best. Christine's visits with her mother always went well, they got along very nicely. Her mother, Lynne, seemed genuinely interested in what Christine was doing; her studies, her projects. The times with her father were different. He always seemed uncomfortable with Christine. I remember times when he hardly spoke to her at all, mostly making small talk with me and my sister. When he did speak to her, it seemed like he didn't know what to say. He never showed any interest in the things she was enthusiastic about. I think that was really hard for Christine. She was always very upset, after her father's visits. She'd go off to her room, or stare out the window for hours after he left, not talking to anyone, which was unlike her. She was very depressed. I'm just glad she has her mother. These kids need their parents, no matter what's happened to them. And it's very hard if their parents can't give them the love they need. Lynne did though, thank God. She gave Christine the love she needed. I think that helped her get better."

Her father and his lawyer, dark auras crackling with agitated tension, waited for their turn, hungrily. Simmons thanked Kathleen and ended her questioning.

Blum was careful to restrain himself on cross examination. The judge wouldn't like it if he attacked an old lady. Solicitously, "Mrs. Murphy, what is your educational background?"

"I went to teacher's college, taught elementary school for many years, before taking in foster children. That was sixteen years ago."

Kindly, "I see, so you don't have a degree that would qualify you as an expert on the causes of depression, or what factors contribute to recovery from mental or psychological illness, do you?"

Kathleen steeled, "I might not have the degree, but I've been around dozens, maybe hundreds of sick children, twenty four hours a day, seven days a week, for sixteen years. I've read their reports and listened to their doctors. I think I have a lot ofmexperience behind what I say. And I don't say these things lightly. If you were me and saw what I've seen with Christine, I imagine you'd say the same thing."

Christine's heart flooded, *Kathleen, my Angel!*

Blum kept a sharp comeback in check. "You don't have many teenagers stay at your home do you?"

Warily, "No, not many."

"How many over those sixteen years?" "Oh a handful, five or six."

"Before Christine, when was the last time a troubled teenager stayed with you?"

"Umm, maybe four, five years ago."

"Would you say Christine is smart?" Kathleen smiled, nodded, "Oh, yes."

"And she has been helpful, doing what you have asked her to do?" Nodding,

"Always."

"And she wants to get home to her mother's as soon as possible, doesn't she?" "Yes, yes she does."

The lawyer smiled at Kathleen, a saccharine smile, "Thank you Mrs. Murphy. No further questions."

Christine was tearfully relieved that Kathleen had been spared.

Fitzgerald caught Blum's insinuation, stood for cross examination, "Kathleen, did you ever feel that Christine was manipulating you, by being helpful and studying hard, so that she could return home to her mother?

"No, never."

"Nothing further, your Honor."

Blum rose, still solicitous of the older woman, "You've never had occasion to believe that Christine was being untruthful or insincere?"

Kathleen answered without hesitation, "No, not that I can recall."

Slightly condescending, "Based on your experience, isn't that rare for a troubled teenager?"

"Yes, you may be right."

"Am I? Have you ever had a teenager like Christine live with you?"

"No, we haven't. I've never seen a child as co-operative and helpful as Christine." "No further questions."

Christine, bursting with love: *My wonderful angel.*

Fitzgerald saw the trap; *he's going to spring it on the sister!* He had to alert Simmons, before she began questioning Rosemary. "Your Honor, if I may take a few moments to confer with counsel before the next witness takes the stand?"

Greenleaf looked at the clock mounted on the wall: 3:45. Annoyed, "No, Mr. Fitzgerald. The hour's late and I want to conclude this matter today." Fitzgerald was powerless to prevent what was about to unfold.

Christine stared at the lawyer's swarming aura: *There's something wrong.* Her skin itched, the bottom fell out of her stomach. The rimming pain cycled up in her head.

Fitzgerald's tension charged through Lynne, sitting beside him. It unnerved her. Simmons caught his despair: *what?* Uneasy, she continued her case.

Rosemary took the stand. Her denim frock and round collared cotton blouse didn't soften her appearance, her large rough hands, muscled shoulders, square jaw. Christine saw her. *Brave, strong Rosemary!* She could match her father's power.

She also testified to Christine's helpfulness, and what a pleasure she was. As Christine's primary educator, Rosemary testified about her academic accomplishments: she had tested well above grade level in English literature, current events, and the natural sciences. She was on track for her grade level in mathematics. Her sculpting and pottery were exceptional, even marketable. Rosemary described Christine as having a genuine thirst for knowledge, a dogged persistence, and a genuine desire to excel. Concluding her testimony on direct examination, she offered that Christine should do well back in school.

Blum stood for cross examination. He had decided he could be blunt with this woman, that the judge would let him treat her coarsely. "Miss Murphy, you live off of a small dirt road, how far is the nearest town?"

"Four miles."

"And how big is the town?" "About twelve hundred."

Briskly, "Does Christine ever go into town?"

Rosemary answered at her own pace, "Sure, about once a week with us. And when she started caring for Judy's girls, a few more times a week."

"She's never gone there alone, has she?" "No."

"She couldn't just get up and go to town on her own, could she?" "Well I guess she could, if she really wanted to."

"But that would not be very convenient, four miles away, would it?" Pursing her lips, impatient with questions that had obvious answers, "No."

"So the large percentage of her time she's been home with you, your sister, and a couple younger foster children?"

"You could say that."

"You don't have a television do you?" "No."

"A radio?" "Sure we do."

Blum placed his fingertips on the table, leaned slightly forward, "You don't have too many distractions out at your cabin, do you?"

"I don't know about that. We stay entertained I think." "There's a lot of time to read and study it sounds like." "You could say that."

He straightened up, slowed his question, "Miss Murphy, are you aware of Christine's scholastic record during the previous school year, and if so, would you describe it for the court?"

Rosemary spoke to the judge. "Yes. I was given Christine's transcripts, talked to a couple of her teachers and her guidance counselor, so I had a pretty good idea. And she wasn't doing very well with her grades. She was close to failing a couple courses that spring semester. Ended up failing algebra, as I recall."

"And Christine's attendance, her participation in school while she lived with her mother, did you have any information about that?"

"Well it wasn't so good, it was a problem. Missed classes and the like."

Blum unsheathed a smile that slashed Christine, "Any attendance problems when you educated Christine?"

Christine knew: *He's going to attack*. She heard her father's voice: *I am going to ruin you for choosing your mother.* The room shifted. The doors came into focus, encircling. Murmuring voices. Christine fought to hear Rosemary's testimony.

Blum pursuing, "Were you informed of the reason for Christine's arrest in Burlington?"

Scraping pain. The darkness rising at the fringes of her vision.

"Were you prepared to house a teenager who had recently been using cocaine?"

Before Rosemary answered, the lawyer struck again, "Did Christine ever use regulated drugs or alcohol while living with you?"

Christine heard Rosemary answer, angrily. "No, never."

Sharply, "Can you be so certain? Can you be certain that she didn't when she spent afternoons with the potter?"

The lawyer spewing bile. Christine heard Rosemary's voice sound from a distance. Rosemary, resolute, battled for her, she knew.

> Attacking, "How about boys? During these past several months that Christine has been living with you, has she spent time with any boys her age? Or any young men?"

The room spun slowly, the doors attaining prominence. *There will be a gathering.*

> Blum, attacking. "None whatsoever? How can you be so certain, after all ...?" *They're in the room now.* Slowly circling.

Lynne was weeping. The lawyers yelled objections. The judge cautioned Blum, who promised to be circumspect. Christine heard her father through it all, *I'm fucking you.*

Blum, relentless, "In light of her history, that's on the record..." Rosemary battled

Him.

They're here. Closing her off, slowly circling. She called for help, *Rosemary!*

Relentless, "...unlikely, would you agree?" Words from a far distance, wrung hollow.

The circling bodies, shrouded, close in to witness. She knew. *It's happening!*

God no! No one hears her scream. *Something presses against her, flesh. She turns to see what, but she misses it. Again, clammy flesh. She turns to see what, misses it. She hears... I'm fucking you. She turns again, into it, the torso inches from her face. She tries to push it away—she has no arms. The black birds descend, clawing her shoulders, tearing bloody snatches of hair from her scalp. No one will come through those doors to save her. The penis down her throat, gagging her—that is what always comes next. No! She throws her head back, eyes blood stung, but seeing. She sees him. She knows! The torso recedes to a vanishing point. The birds, gone. The doors thrown open – nothing beyond. There is only the memory of her father's face.*

Christine returned, fully aware of the courtroom. All things were clear, as sharp as crystal. Her mother's lawyer was asking Rosemary a question. Rosemary dazed, sweaty hair plastered to her brow. Christine turned to her mother, who appeared like she'd been clubbed. She poured herself a cup of water, drank its coolness. She forced herself to look at him, her father. He was no longer haloed in malevolence, but the expression on his face broadcast his wickedness, his satisfaction, his victory.

Blum, then Fitzgerald, indicated to the judge they had no more questions for Rosemary.

Christine leaned to her lawyer and spoke more clearly than she had ever spoken in her life, "I need to testify."

CHAPTER 40

Simmons stood up. "Your Honor, I call Christine Bancroft."

Fitzgerald couldn't believe what he heard; it was suicide. Blum was going to wipe the floor with this kid, and Greenleaf was going to allow it. Simmons didn't look at Fitzgerald, she knew what he was thinking. When she had told Christine it was a bad idea, Christine insisted she would stand on her own and testify from the table if that's what she had to do.

Lynne trembled as her daughter crossed the room to the witness stand.

Judge Greenleaf watched Christine approach the stand, not pleased. The hour was late. The evidence was clear. This was crass indulgence, giving the juvenile the "opportunity" to address him. Spoiled kids. Liberal lawyers, fouling up the legal system. He'd give Simmons a short leash and get this over with.

Blum saw Greenleaf's sour expression; the judge wanted to go home. It was time to wrap this up. He probably wouldn't cross examine the girl.

Mark stared at his daughter as she walked past him. He knew she felt him burning. *How dare she!*

Christine walked directly to the stand. She did not look at her mother nor her father. She did not look at the judge. She saw only the witness chair, before her, crystal clear. She felt her father's glare burning into her, but it didn't harm her. Seated. When asked if she swore to tell the truth, she looked at the judge and said evenly, "I do."

He looked displeased – it was no concern to Christine.

Simmons began, "Would you please state your name for the record?"

Her eyes on attorney Simmons, nothing else, in clear light. "My name is Christine Bancroft. I am the daughter of Lynne Bancroft and Mark Bancroft. I want to go home to my mother. I cannot live with my father because he sexually abused me when I was a young girl."

The courtroom exploded. Mark leaped to his feet, roaring, "She's lying!" He charged from his table, at Christine. Lynne screamed.

The judge banged the gavel, shouting, "Be seated, back to your seat."

The bailiff struggled to get out of his chair. Fitzgerald, closer to the witness stand, raced to Christine.

Blum commanded Mark, "Sit down!"

He swiveled to the direction of Blum's voice, saw nothing through his rage. Fitzgerald reached Christine. The bailiff raced across the room at Mark.

Mark's fury splintered. Only a few feet from Christine, he growled at her. "You can't! You won't!"

Greenleaf pressed the alarm under the bench for more security. He demanded, "Mr.

Bancroft, you are to take your seat!"

Mark ripped his eyes away from Christine. "Go to hell." He spun, strode to the exit. Without looking back, he smashed open the doors, slammed them shut. He was gone.

The room returned around Christine. Until that moment, she had seen only her father: wounded, dangerous, charging her. She had not been afraid, she had been ready to protect herself. Now he was gone, and she was swarmed by the frenzy that surrounded her.

The judge, white faced, ordered, "Sit down. Everyone is to return to their places." Her face smeared with tears, Lynne gaped up at the judge, gulped back sobs.

Fitzgerald and the bailiff stood where they had stopped when Mark had spun away. LaValley, Simmons, Derosia and Mrs. Fromme, froze in their seats, looked to the judge.

Blum studied Christine. She stared back at him. "It's true." She touched her necklace. He looked away.

His composure returning, the judge ordered the sheriffs who had just arrived, "Secure the building. If that man is on the premises, you are to detain him. Place him in the holding cell, until I am ready to deal with him."

The two men scrambled for the exit. It didn't matter. Christine knew he was gone. He would never be back.

Everything seemed to pass in slow motion. Christine watched her mother come to her, wiping at her face with the sleeves of her blouse, smearing mascara across her temples. She watched her mother's lawyer come to her, mouthing words she couldn't hear, "Are you alright?"

Christine nodded. She slowly rose from the chair, resolute, saw Blum leave the courtroom.

She held her mother in her arms, her mother's face buried in her shoulder. Lynne murmured through her tears, "I didn't know, I didn't know..." again, and again. Before her clarity was overtaken by the usual static and distortion of living, Christine thought, *But you did. Somehow you did.*

That knowledge slipped under the waves, as Christine felt her mother holding on to her. She pressed Lynne tight and felt her own tears burn paths down her cheeks. She consoled her mother. "It's alright, it's over now." *No matter what, it's over.*

***

Christine, Lynne, Kathleen, Rosemary, Mrs. Fromme clustered together at one end of the hallway. They watched attorneys Simmons and Fitzgerald at the other end of the corridor argue with LaValley and State's Attorney Derosia that the State should allow Christine to return home. LaValley responded that she couldn't agree to anything until she spoke with her supervisor.

Fitzgerald and Simmons came back to the others and joined the nervous silence. No one spoke about what had happened in the courtroom. They didn't move. They waited. Five minutes passed. LaValley came out of the conference room and signaled Simmons and Fitzgerald.

The group watched the lawyers walk the length of the hallway, stop, and listen to the caseworker.

Fitzgerald suddenly bellowed, "You're kidding me, right?" Christine's eyes met Rosemary's; she wasn't going home.

Simmons and Fitzgerald returned to the group. Simmons explained that, although Mark was no longer involved, the State still held the position that Lynne was not a suitable placement and therefore Christine needed to remain in SRS custody.

Lynne whispered, "No. They can't."

Rosemary spoke, "How much time before we have to be back in court?"

Someone answered. "Less than five minutes."

"I'll be back."

Without more, Rosemary separated from the rest. She strode the hallway to LaValley and Derosia. The two stood motionless, watching her approach. When she arrived, she said a few words, then the three disappeared into the conference room.

Fitzgerald asked, "Anyone know what she's doing?"

No one answered.

Christine was beaming, she knew. Rosemary was going to straighten everything out.

Simmons offered, "I'll go see what's happening, maybe she could use some help..."

Kathleen put her hand on Simmons' arm, signaling it wouldn't be necessary. The lawyer remained where she was. They stood in silence, all eyes on the conference room door. A white surge filled Christine.

The bailiff appeared, announced that the judge was ready to take the bench. Fitzgerald asked for five minutes. As he spoke, the conference room door opened, sounding down the corridor. Rosemary emerged. She looked at the group, then the smallest smile creased her face. Christine knew. *Yes!*

They raced to the woman, Christine ahead of the rest. Rosemary had taken a few steps towards them by the time Christine flew into her arms, laughed into her ear, "You did it, didn't you!"

She pulled her face away for Rosemary's reply, saw the twinkling eyes and heard, "I think maybe, yes."

Over Christine's head, Rosemary addressed Simmons and Fitzgerald, "They're ready to discuss an agreement. I believe they are willing to allow Christine to return to Lynne's custody, so long as they have protective supervision. One of the conditions is that she remain placed with us for as long as she needs. Of course, I have to speak with Kathleen..." Rosemary hesitated. She saw her sister's eyes well up with tears, nodding her head passionately. She had her answer. "Kathleen agrees, Christine can stay with us, if that's alright with everyone else."

Christine exploded, "Oh my God, yes, yes Rosemary! Kathleen, oh my God!"

Lynne laughed and cried, *oh my God, yes! This is so right!*

The women threw their arms around each other, buried their faces into each other, laughed and cried together.

Simmons rested her hand on one of the women's shoulders and announced, "We should get this ironed out with the State." To the bailiff, still standing at the door, "Would you ask the judge if we can have a few minutes, I think we have an agreement."

EPILOGUE

Seated with his wife at the fund raiser for the Welcome House homeless shelter, Fitzgerald saw Lynne at the buffet line, across the hall. Seeing her triggered a rush of memory. Christine in the witness stand, her voice clear, ringing *My name is Christine Bancroft. I am the daughter of Lynne Bancroft and Mark Bancroft...* Six years ago that February.

"Emmett?" Lynne was standing beside him, holding a plate of manicotti and salad, smiling.

He hadn't spoken to her since the end of Christine's case. Strange how that can happen, even in a small town. Lynne looked good, her eyes shined.

"How have you been?" She asked.

Fitzgerald answered "Fine" and introduced his wife, Eileen.

Lynne introduced her husband, Stan Wotjiewicz, the director of the homeless shelter. Fitzgerald smiled. He knew Stan from when the played basketball together in the men's league, years ago. Somehow he already knew they were married. And somehow he knew that Lynne still worked at the hospital, and that she was now an RN.

But he knew nothing of what had happened with Christine. He asked, "How's Christine?" He immediately regretted his impulse. Had he put Lynne on the spot? Was he forcing her to gloss over any hell she and her daughter had been through since that day in court?

Lynne expected the question. "She's doing well. She got her degree from The New School, if you can believe that. Fine arts, with a minor in political science. She stayed with her pottery and sculpting. Does pretty well with it, making a living. She met a fellow from England, Thomas, when he was in New York with a film production crew. Nice fellow. They're together now, she's living in London. I got a postcard from her today, in fact. They're in France, I forget where. He's on a shoot." Lynne's eyes told Fitzgerald, *she's alright.*

He smiled. "And the Murphys? Any word from them?"

"Oh yes!" Lynne shared she kept in touch at least once a year. The sisters wrote her lovely letters. They still cared for children, which Fitzgerald knew. Lynne added Christine lived with the Murphys for a year and a half, until she went off to college. Christine had visited them at least once a year before she headed off to Europe. The last visit she brought along Thomas, so he could meet Kathleen and Rosemary.

Fitzgerald warmed with the good news. He was very glad to see that Lynne was doing well, and to hear that Christine was doing very well, also.

A shadow passed over Lynne's eyes as a cloud crossed her heart. A wisp from that brutal time. She could never forget. "Really good to see you." She touched Fitzgerald's shoulder, began to leave but stopped. "Emmett, all these years I've wanted to ask Rosemary, but haven't: Do you know what she said that made those people change their mind and give Chris back to me?"

Fitzgerald laughed. "I heard she told LaValley they would never take another foster child if they didn't let Christine remain with them under your custody. She had them over a barrel!"

Lynne smiled. She loved those women.

***

Christine woke suddenly to a sharp noise. She sat bolt upright, lost in the night. *Where?* She scoured the room, desperate for clues to her situation. She smelled and felt the man lying beside her – *Thomas, her husband.* She recognized the room, the hotel room; they were in Arles.

A wind rose and a shutter banged against the wall outside. Her focus flew to the sound, its violence; to the glass doors that opened to a narrow balcony, the window panes wet from the rain that had just ended. The near full moon threw brief, brilliant light against the glass, illuminating rain rivulets like silver veins running down the panes. Breaking clouds scudded across the sky, across the moon. Everything swiftly disappeared to shocking black, then the doors reappeared in sudden light, the wet silver veins. Then, again, the drenched darkness. The wind sounded against the building, through the streets, desolate. The moonlight full on, then gone again.

The doors. A shifting inside her. Always the beginning. The wind and the gathering storm. It had been a long time since...*No! Thomas!* He was there. She held on to that. The room lit, then plunged black. The wind scoured inside her. She could feel herself slipping.

"Thomas, wake up."

He grumbled in his sleep.

"I need you to wake up." She jolted his bare shoulder with the heel of her hand.

She saw him, in full silver light, look back at her, before he disappeared in the dark. A fierce dread seized her.

He sat up, put his thick arms around her and asked, "What is it, love?"

Staring at the glass doors, she began, "There was a night like this... when I was a kid." A long silence, then into the void spread before her, she began... *"I was little – five, maybe six. It was night, always night. And I'm in bed. I'm asleep. I wake up feeling something against me, but I don't know what. I lie there. Freeze up. I don't say a thing. Then I feel it against my face, pushing against my face, my mouth, I don't know what it is. He spoke, he told me I had been bad. My father. He said he was punishing me. I had to open my mouth and not make a sound. That was my punishment. I did what he said. I didn't know what I had done that was bad, what I was being punished for. I felt it at my mouth. I thought about all the things I had done that might have been bad. I had spilled sand on the kitchen floor that morning, from my sneakers. We were on vacation, there was a beach. I had played all day in the sand. It was everywhere. I couldn't breathe, he was pushing it into me, he was grabbing my hair... I couldn't say 'I'm sorry.' Someone had to tell him I was sorry, but no one came. I watched the door, the blowing wind was the only sound..."*

Christine broke away. "No, that can't be right. I wouldn't have been able to see the door." Quietly, "There was no wind."

Cold sweat poured from her. She felt Thomas watching her. He had been listening; he was hurting for her, she knew. He held her. She turned to see his face, inches distant, in the dawn's first weak light—she had talked through the night. About the other times. Her punishment that summer. He had threatened worse punishment if she told anyone. Anyone.

She told no one, ever, what had happened. No one ever came through the door for her. She couldn't sleep that summer, she began to cry at night. Her mother heard her crying, would come to her. She never told—he would punish them both, if her mother knew. He stopped the punishment after she had started crying. Those nights, that summer. Now spoken.

"I've never told this to anyone." She whispered.

Thomas placed his cheek against her temple. Christine felt his tears.

She finished, "That day in court, when they let me live with the Murphys, that's when I first knew. And I told them then, he had abused me." Looking out at the pale sky. "They wanted me to tell them what happened, the police and all. I couldn't. I couldn't remember. I only knew that he had. They said it wasn't enough to charge him with a crime. My shrink told me that someday, I might remember, when I was ready. Tonight... I was." Christine turned away from the doors. "I've never seen him again, since that day in court. My mother said he moved, but she didn't know where to."

She leaned into Thomas' body, felt his arms around her. The nightmare was out, released.

Author's Bio

Ea Burke lives in southern Vermont where he raised a wonderful family and has practiced law for over thirty years. He was born, raised and educated in Philadelphia, with its trenchant wisdom. From there he explored a variety of lives in Denver, Boulder, Maui, San Francisco, Seattle, Akutan and Bristol Bay, Alaska before settling down in his heartland, Vermont. Ea graduated from Vermont Law School. Since then he has represented ordinary and extraordinary people with simple and complex needs in Vermont's criminal, juvenile and civil court systems.

Ea's poetry has been published in a number of literary journals and poetry collections over the years, most recently being Ginosko Literary Journal, Vol. 20, Winter 2017-2018; PoemCity 2017, 2018 and 2019; and was honored with third place recognition in the Putney Mountain Poetry Contest, 2018. His short story Maia's Call appears in the Running Wild Short Story Anthology, Volume 3, due to be released in September, 2019

Past Titles

Running Wild Stories Anthology, Volume 1

Running Wild Anthology of Novellas, Volume 1

Jersey Diner by Lisa Diane Kastner

Magic Forgotten by Jack Hillman

The Kidnapped by Dwight L. Wilson

Running Wild Stories Anthology, Volume 2

Running Wild Novella Anthology, Volume 2, Part 1

Running Wild Novella Anthology, Volume 2, Part 2

Running Wild Stories Anthology, Volume 3

Running Wild's Best of 2017, AWP Special Edition

Running Wild's Best of 2018

Build Your Music Career From Scratch, Second Edition by Andrae Alexander

Writers Resist: Anthology 2018 with featured editors Sara Marchant and Kit-Bacon Gressitt

Magic Forbidden by Jack Hillman

Frontal Matter: Glue Gone Wild by Suzanne Samples

Mickey: The Giveaway Boy by Robert M. Shafer

Dark Corners by Reuben "Tihi" Hayslett

The Resistors by Dwight L. Wilson

Upcoming Titles

Running Wild Stories Anthology, Volume 4

Running Wild Novella Anthology, Volume 4

Open My Eyes by Tommy Hahn

Legendary by Amelia Kibbie

Christine, Released by E. Burke

Recon: The Anthology by Ben White

The Self Made Girl's Guide by Aliza Dube

Sodom & Gomorrah on a Saturday Night by Christa Miller

Turing's Graveyard by Terry Hawkins

Running Wild Press, Best of 2019

Running Wild Press publishes stories that cross genres with great stories and writing. Our team consists of:

Lisa Diane Kastner, Founder and Executive Editor

Barbara Lockwood, Editor

Cecile Sarruf, Editor

Peter Wright, Editor

Rebecca Dimyan, Editor

Benjamin White, Editor

Andrew DiPrinzio, Editor

Amrita Raman, Operations Manager

Lisa Montagne, Director of Education

Learn more about us and our stories at www.runningwildpress.com[1]

Loved this story and want more? Follow us at www.runningwildpress.com[2], www.facebook/runningwildpress, on Twitter @lisadkastner @JadeBlackwater @RunWildBooks

1. http://www.runningwildpress.com/
2. http://www.runningwildpress.com/

Running
Wild
Press

www.ingramcontent.com/pod-product-compliance
Lightning Source LLC
LaVergne TN
LVHW010049110826
845155LV00028B/266

* 9 7 8 1 9 4 7 0 4 1 2 7 1 *